BUG-JARGAL

Frontispiece from the original 1826 edition of *Bug-Jargal*

BUG–JARGAL

Victor Hugo

edited and translated by Chris Bongie

broadview editions

NATIONAL LIBRARY OF CANADA CATALOGUING IN PUBLICATION DATA

Hugo, Victor, 1802-1885
    Bug-Jargal / Victor Hugo ; edited and translated by Chris Bongie.

(Broadview editions)
Includes bibliographical references.
ISBN 1-55111-446-1

    1. Haiti—History—Revolution, 1791-1804—Fiction.
I. Bongie, Christopher Laurence   II. Title.   III. Series.

PQ2285.B813 2004   843'.7   C2004-901164-2

Broadview Press, Ltd. is an independent, international publishing house, incorporated in 1985. Broadview believes in shared ownership, both with its employees and with the general public; since the year 2000 Broadview shares have traded publicly on the Toronto Venture Exchange under the symbol BDP.

    We welcome comments and suggestions regarding any aspect of our publications—please feel free to contact us at the addresses below or at broadview@broadviewpress.com / www.broadviewpress.com

North America
Post Office Box 1243,
Peterborough, Ontario, Canada K9J 7H5
TEL (705) 743-8990; FAX (705) 743-8353

3576 California Road,
Orchard Park, New York, USA 14127

E-MAIL customerservice@broadviewpress.com

United Kingdom and Europe
NBN Plymbridge.
Estover Road, Plymouth PL6 7PY, UK
TEL 44(0) 1752 202301
FAX 44 (0) 1752 202331
FAX ORDER LINE 44 (0) 1752 202333
CUST. SERVICE cservs@nbnplymbridge.com
ORDERS orders@nbnplymbridge.com

Australia & New Zealand
UNIREPS University of New South Wales
Sydney, NSW 2052
TEL 61 2 9664099; FAX 61 2 9664520
E-MAIL infopress@unsw.edu.au

BROADVIEW PRESS, LTD. gratefully acknowledges the financial support of the Government of Canada through the Book Publishing Industry Development Program for our publishing activities.

Series Editor: Professor L.W. Conolly
Advisory Editor for this volume: Michel W. Pharand

Cover design by Lisa Brawn.
Typeset by Liz Broes, Black Eye Design.

Printed in Canada

Contents

Acknowledgments

I would like to thank the following friends and colleagues for reading over drafts of my translation of Hugo's novel: Chris Arnett, Jon Beasley-Murray, Deborah Jenson, Alex Miller, and Grace Moore. My thanks also go out to David Geggus, who answered every bit of Saint Domingue trivia I threw his way; to Michael Pacey, who produced the map of Hugo's Saint Domingue; and to the Pope of Oregon Hill, Peter DeSa Wiggins, who first got me thinking about this project.

Particular debts of gratitude are owed to Laurence Bongie, who generously responded to every translational query of mine, regardless of whether I supplied him with an adequate context for it or not, and to the editorial team of Broadview Press (especially Barbara and Leonard Conolly and Julia Gaunce) for their encouragement and for their help in getting the manuscript down to a manageable—and, fingers crossed, marketable!—size.

The timely completion of this book was made possible by a year-long National Endowment for the Humanities Research Fellowship in 2001-02. I am extremely grateful to the NEH for awarding me this grant, as I am to long-time supporters Christopher L. Miller and Richard Terdiman, who wrote the letters of recommendation for it.

The title page and frontispiece of the original edition of *Bug-Jargal* are reproduced here by permission of the Bibliothèque nationale de France.

Finally, I would like to offer a special word of acknowledgment to Leah Gordon, who provided such a brilliantly appropriate photograph for the cover of this book, and who took the time to show me the road from the Hotel Oloffson to that improbable but necessary place where the ghost trains still run and the pigs have remained the colour of the Haitian earth.

Introduction

Bug-Jargal, 1791: Language and History in Translation

Attributed simply to "the author of *Han d'Islande*," Victor Hugo's *Bug-Jargal* made its first appearance in book form at the end of January 1826, less than a month before his twenty-fourth birthday. The first readers of that novel could hardly have guessed from its title alone what the book was about. To be sure, in trying to make sense of the apparently senseless word (or should we say words?) on the title page, some readers might well have recognized its kinship with a long line of exotic-sounding names that had graced the title page of so many stories and novels in France over the past century—*Oronoko, Ziméo, Zoflora, Bythis, Atala, Ourika* ...—and deduced from this that the book would, at the very least, take them beyond the geographical and cultural confines of Europe. This deduction would have been quickly confirmed by the opening line of the preface, which identifies "the Saint Domingue slave revolt in 1791" as the source of the book's content. As French readers in 1826 would have been all too well aware, this revolt in 1791 marked the beginning of the end for their prosperous colony of Saint Domingue: the onset of twelve years of revolutionary turmoil that would lead to the ouster of the French by their former slaves and the creation of the independent Caribbean nation of Haiti on 1 January 1804. Hugo's preface thus immediately stabilizes the text's meaning by anchoring it in a recognizable historical event. And yet that initial, fleeting moment of doubt as to what the book's mysterious title might signify should not be discounted: one central theme of *Bug-Jargal* is, after all, the difficulty of communication, the anxiety about meaning that arises in a world where people are not transparent to one another, where signs are not easily readable or perhaps not readable at all, and it is precisely this opacity, this difficulty in communicating (or, worse, this inability to communicate), that the novel communicates to the reader from its very first (un)readable word(s).

In the space of just over thirty years (1833-66), *Bug-Jargal* would be translated into English no less than four times, and the ways in which its mostly anonymous translators chose to render the novel's enigmatic title reveal a deep-seated need to attenuate its opacity by adding explanatory tags to it, or quite simply erasing the uncommunicative signifier "Bug-Jargal" from view. In 1833, the first translation of *Bug-Jargal* was published as *The Slave King, from the Bug-Jargal of Victor Hugo*; this same translation would be later republished under the even more forthcoming title, *The Slave-King: A Historical Account of the Rebellion of the Negros in St. Domingo*. In 1844, the novel was translated a second time as *Bug-Jargal; or, A Tale of the Massacre in St. Domingo. 1791*, and in 1845 as *The Noble Rival; or, The Prince of Congo*. In 1866, several years after completing the first English-language translation of Hugo's *Les Misérables*, Charles Edwin Wilbour chose the opposite tack, reducing the novel's opaque, double-barrelled title to the more economical and emphatic *Jargal*.

These clarificatory English translations of the novel's title help us better understand why Hugo and his publishers might themselves have felt it necessary to supplement his original title with information that would make better sense of it. For in 1832, the fifth French edition of the novel bore a slightly different title from its predecessors, one that would be retained for the sixth edition of the novel (1839), but that would give way to the original title in all subsequent editions during Hugo's lifetime: *Bug-Jargal. 1791*. Since he wrote a new preface for the 1832 edition of the novel, it is likely that Hugo himself had a hand in choosing this new title, although I have come across no documentation that confirms this, nor any that establishes who was responsible for dropping "1791" from the title after 1839. What this alternative title makes visible, from the novel's outset, is a second central theme of the novel: not just, as with the initial title, the problem of what things mean and how we make them mean, but in addition the problem of history (the numbers "1791") and its relation to language (the word, or words, "Bug-Jargal"). What does history mean? How is its meaning conveyed through language? What is gained and what is lost in the translation of history into language, and of language back into history? These are questions that the double title of the 1832 edition ably conveys, situating history and language together and yet apart, separated by a period that marks both the point of contact between them and the acknowledgment of their difference: on the one side, history, defined in linear, numerical terms, and on the other, something altogether more indefinable and less readable, which can only be grasped through language and which is not history, at least *not* history as *we* recognize it.

The question of history is one that will never be far from my own discussion of the novel, either here in the Introduction or in the endnotes and appendix materials. For the remainder of this opening section, however, I would like to keep the focus on language and its inherent opacity by engaging in a close reading of Hugo's mysterious title.

Perhaps the first thing to strike one about Hugo's original 1826 title is its doubleness (a doubleness that, as we will see, the 1832 title itself redoubles). *Bug-Jargal* would appear, to the reader who knows it only by its title, to be one thing, but one thing made up of two parts—parts that are joined together by a hyphen relating them one to the other and yet also marking their apartness. Where the 1832 title brings history and language into a differing relation with one another, the original title situates this same ambiguous relation within language itself. To each side of the hyphen stands a word: these words are clearly different, and yet they also stand in a sort of mirror-relation to one another—an imperfect relation that we might refer to as one of (un)likeness. Language is, imperfectly, double: that is a state of affairs to which the title *Bug-Jargal* alerts Hugo's readers from the very beginning. Examples of the doubleness—and, potentially, the duplicity—of language saturate the novel, perhaps most notably in the dizzying array of foreign words that find their way into this French-language text. The thematic importance of doubling to the novel cannot be overestimated (as I have tried to signal to readers through the photograph used for the cover of this book). Doubling is vital not only to the novel's use of language but to its presentation of character: doubles proliferate in *Bug-Jargal*, nowhere more obviously than in the (un)likely pairing of its equally noble white and black protagonists, the French narrator Captain d'Auverney and the African slave-king Bug-Jargal, so different and yet in important respects so very similar, looking at one another, as it were, across the divide of the cultural hyphen that differentiates and relates them.

If the hyphenated (or, we might say, hybridized) word "Bug-Jargal" initially appears to make no sense when taken as a whole, a certain sense can be gleaned from it if we begin by reading its two parts as separate words. It is not difficult, for instance, to recognize the presence of the word "jargon" in the unrecognizable "Jargal," even if such recognition depends upon an act of translation—one that, like all translation, is not a matter of finding a word's perfect double but, rather, one of its many partial look-alikes. In any reading of the novel that is sensitized to the role played in it by (the problem of) language, translating "Jargal" into "jargon" seems more than justified (and, as I have been arguing, the self-conscious opacity of Hugo's title ensures that no reading of this novel is possible without such a sensitivity). The word "jargon," which crops up seven times in Hugo's novel, signals the doubleness of language, pointing at one and the same time toward an "improper" language and a more "proper" language that has somehow escaped the degraded condition of jargon. Nuancing Samuel Johnson's one typically straightforward definition of "jargon" as "unintelligible talk; gabble; gibberish," Littré's nineteenth-century dictionary of the French language cites four main senses of the word—"corrupted language"; "a foreign language that one doesn't understand"; "a particular language adopted by certain people"; "language with a double meaning." All four of Littré's senses seem relevant not simply to the specific ways Hugo uses this word but to the general problem of language raised throughout the novel: namely, that—whether by virtue of their corrupted state, their foreign origin, their cultural specificity, their polysemic potential, or even their sheer unintelligibility—words might fail to make themselves understood, communication might fail to take place. Jargon signals the possibility of language's corruption; in turn, "Jargal," in its distortion of the "jargon" it evokes, enacts that corruption—or at least what can only seem like corruption to those for whom such distortions can be nothing more than "improper" deviations from the norm rather than legitimate translations into another('s) as yet undecipherable language.

As we will see in the following section of this Introduction, the Hugo who wrote *Bug-Jargal* in 1825 was someone still strongly committed to linguistic norms, to a strong distinction between the corruption of jargon and the purity of language, but part of what makes this early novel of his worth reading today is his inability to enforce the norms in which he believes. Everywhere in *Bug-Jargal* linguistic order gives way to a chaotic world of words-in-translation, just as the black and white portrait of racial relations this novel attempts to uphold is repeatedly overwhelmed by what it violently rejects: namely, cultural hybridity and the symbolic embodiment of that hybridity, the mulatto (for an extended reading of *Bug-Jargal* along these lines, see my *Islands and Exiles* 231-61). Hugo's novel, then, explicitly rejects the corrupted world of jargon, but it cannot help coming to terms with (or, more pessimistically, falling within the terms of) that world, as one might guess from the muted autobiographical resonance of the other word in the title, "Bug," which shares with the name "Hugo" what Graham Robb, in his recent biography of Hugo, has referred to as "the emblematic 'ug'" (123). If the title's hyphen, as marker of difference, places *Hugo* on the side opposite to "Jargal" and the corrupted language it evokes, that hyphen also places the two opposing sides in relation with one another—a complicitous relation that renders chimerical the project of separating the author's pure language from the impurity of jargon, of distinguishing norms of any sort from so-called abnormalities. If the explicit ideology of *Bug-Jargal* will endorse this chimera, the novel's title undermines it from its very first syllable by improperly translating (or jargonizing) Hugo's proper name and placing it in relation with what the bearer of that name contests.

More obviously, of course, the presence of "the emblematic 'ug'" turns Hugo and Bug-Jargal into imperfect doubles of one another. The imperfect doubling of protagonist and author that is readable in the word "Bug" allows for Hugo's partial projection of himself onto (or translation of himself into) the black protagonist of his novel. What, if anything, are we to make of this mirroring of white author and black protagonist, which itself doubles not only that of d'Auverney and Bug-Jargal but that of d'Auverney and Hugo, who signed a number of his youthful articles with the pen name "d'Auverney"? If Flaubert's famous gender-bending phrase "Madame Bovary, c'est moi" has proved a constant source of fascination for critics, the onomastic play of Hugo's title raises the equally interesting question of what it means to cross racial lines and say, howsoever indirectly, "Bug-Jargal, c'est moi." What does it mean for a "white" author to (dis)identify with a "black" protagonist in this way, to graft a trace of his own signature onto the mysterious and apparently meaningless title of an anonymously published novel about the Saint Domingue revolution?

A question such as this takes on a new resonance if one re-situates it in the context of the 1832 edition of the novel, not simply because Hugo's name is now there for all to see on the title page, but because his (dis)identification with his black double Bug-Jargal is here doubled by a (dis)identification with the chronological forces of history represented by the date "1791." If we look for Hugo in *Bug-Jargal. 1791*, we find him situated not only on the other side of Jargal/jargon, but on the other side of history, in the realm of a language that includes both "Bug" and "Jargal"—an opaque language that is subject to incomprehension, but that might nonetheless be viewed as offering an alternative to history and its seemingly transparent dates. As the young Hugo put it in an 1823 essay on Walter Scott's *Quentin Durward*, "I would rather believe in the novel than in history, because I prefer moral truth to historical truth." The fiction of *Bug-Jargal* may, in other words, point toward a truth that the history of 1791 cannot envision, and no reader of this novel can fail to notice that Hugo has a quarrel with history—and, more specifically, the revolutionary history represented by the date "1791." I will elaborate on the specifics of that quarrel in the following section; here, though, I would simply like to point out, again, that the 1832 title does not simply cordon off the differing worlds of language and history, but also connects them. What is the relation between *Bug-Jargal* and *1791*? To what extent can the "moral truths" of the former be kept separate from the "historical truths" of the latter? To what extent must they be read together (and thereby simultaneously cross-fertilize and contaminate one another)?

Almost fifty years after the publication of what Hugo called his "first work," he would publish his last novel, *Quatre-vingt treize* (*Ninety-Three*; 1874). If *Bug-Jargal* was the conservative young Hugo's indirect way of voicing his distaste for the French Revolution by parodically representing its transatlantic double, the Haitian Revolution, Hugo's last novel directly tackles, and from a more sympathetic perspective, some of the key events in France during the year 1793. It is a critical commonplace that Hugo's attitude toward revolution changed radically over the course of that half-century, but his many ideological perambulations in later life need not concern us here. The only detail on which I would like to comment involves the evident discrepancy between the titles *Bug-Jargal. 1791* and *Quatre-vingt treize*. The first title sets up a binary opposition, in which language—in all its opacity—is differentiated from, if nonetheless connected to, history and its supposed truths: language (*Bug-Jargal*) might be thought of as having the potential for creating truths that would differ from those upon which history (*1791*) depends. The truth is not that simple, of course, and the period that not only separates but joins together *Bug-Jargal* and *1791* ensures that the opposition of language and history will produce not simply opposing but confusing truths—truths in which the one side of history cannot be disentangled from its other side, the other side of the story that language tells. Hugo offers a less oppositional, and perhaps less confusing, view of the world in the title of his last novel, where the difference between history and language is dissolved, or sublated. History as we know it, Hugo seems to be saying, is created by language: for us, there can be no such thing as "1793" until that date has been translated into the words "Quatre-vingt treize"—words that are, if one interrogates them closely enough, no less difficult to read than the enigmatic ones with which Hugo entitles his "first work" but that at least point us *toward* history, rather than, as with "Bug-Jargal," away from it and toward what might be other than it.

The linguistic turn of the title of Hugo's last novel might well be a step forward in his understanding of the obvious differences between, and the vexed relations of, language and history. At a very basic level, what we know and what things mean can only be conveyed through language. The title of Hugo's last novel conveys this fact very well. And yet there is something to be said for the title(s) of Hugo's "first work." *Quatre-vingt treize* conveys a great deal, for those familiar with the history of the French Revolution, and at least a glimmer of something for those with a basic knowledge of French. *Bug-Jargal* conveys very little of anything, at least until one begins the work of translating its unknown language into a language one knows. *Bug-Jargal. 1791* adds a nuance to Hugo's original title, positing the oppositional relation of language and history: the seemingly opaque words of language are opposed to, or doubled by, the seemingly transparent dates of history. Or, to frame this binary relation somewhat differently: in the title *Bug-Jargal. 1791* the abstract enunciations of language and the literary conventions of fiction are opposed to, or doubled by, the concrete enactments of life, the embodied presence of what really happened, that which words can never adequately convey. After all, language is not all there is to history, even if language is the only tool we have for representing that history: the absence of history in the title *Bug-Jargal* and the oppositional presence of history in *Bug-Jargal. 1791* perhaps makes this point more clearly than do the words *Quatre-vingt treize*, in which history is, as it were, simply swallowed up by language. Be that as it may, what all of these titles point toward is the problem of what it means to read language and history together (and apart), the problem of what meaning can come from the always imperfect translation of the one into the other. As flawed a novel as it may be, from a certain "aesthetic" point of view, I can think of few works of literature that confront this problem in as dramatic and as pressing a way as *Bug-Jargal*, and that, it seems to me, is justification enough for reintroducing it to anglophone audiences over a century after it was last translated into English.

The problem of *translation*—the translating of words into meaning, of meaning into words, of language into history, of history into language, of one culture into another—is a pervasive one in *Bug-Jargal*; in drawing attention to the ways in which this problem plays out in the novel's paratextual margins, the self-consciously "opaque" reading of Hugo's title that I have just presented will, I hope, spur readers to explore on their own the role of translation in the actual novel. I myself will be returning to the issue of translation in the final section of the Introduction, albeit less with an eye to mapping out its specific place in Hugo's novel than to addressing the more general question of what it means to translate a text like *Bug-Jargal* now, in a critical context informed by the insights of postcolonial theory—a context in which, by virtue of its vigorous engagement with colonial history, Hugo's novel might now be (re)read, after over a century of relative neglect, as a newly pertinent and even urgent literary intervention. At this point, however, it is time to take a step back from the text itself and say a few words about the situation of Saint Domingue in the 1790s and of Victor Hugo in the 1820s, supplying some of the background information that should, at the very least, render *Bug-Jargal* a little more readable than it might, on the sole evidence of its mysterious title (and of my playfully, but I would hope also productively, close reading of that title), at first appear.

1791, 1825: Haiti and Hugo—Historical and Biographical Contexts

This is a novel about colonial Saint Domingue that was written by a young man in Restoration France. To what extent is a knowledge of the history of either place and time, to say nothing of that young man, necessary in order to read *Bug-Jargal*? The question must seem like a very naive one in a critical climate that has benefited from the insights of New Historicist critics into the inadequacies of any and all literary criticism that sacrifices historical context for the fruitless pleasures of close readings intent merely upon unearthing a text's "aesthetic" value, or lack thereof. Always historicize, we have been told, and I have certainly tried to take that imperative to heart in my presentation of the novel: in this section, notably, I will be providing a good deal of information about both Saint Domingue in 1791 and Hugo in 1825; the reader will find many more such details in the critical apparatus of this edition. But just how useful is all this kowtowing to history? How much of it do we really require? And what motivates the apparently transparent "need" for history and its supposed truths that dominates our current approaches to reading literature?

These are the "unnatural" meta-critical questions I found myself asking when I read the first English-language translation of Hugo's novel, *The Slave King* (1833). Not only does that translation feature a wealth of footnotes authoritatively pronouncing on such things as Hugo's misrepresentations of history and geography (the sort of pronouncements that repeatedly find their way into my own footnotes), but it concludes with a forty-page appendix entitled "Santo Domingo," which provides an admirably thorough overview of the Haitian Revolution and its aftermath authored by a friend of the translator's "who has lately travelled in St. Domingo" (viii), and who is clearly sympathetic to the new Republic and its "nascent people." I draw the reader's attention to this translation because of the highly serious historical commitment to which it bears witness—a nineteenth-century commitment which disturbingly mirrors that of our own day and age. What is the relation between my own insistence on history as an explanatory tool and that of the translator of *The Slave King*? What would it be to read *The Slave King* without its lengthy appendix (an appendix that was deemed expendable when the translation was republished under a new title in 1852)? What would it be to read my own translation of *Bug-Jargal* without the information I will be providing in this section, and upon which the endnotes and appendices will greatly expand? What, for that matter, would it be to read Hugo's novel without the sixty or so "authoritative" footnotes that he himself included in his novel? What would it be to read the novel without knowing anything about Hugo's own personal history? Are such readings possible and, if so, what are we to make of this possibility? What would such a reading amount to? Sheer ignorance, an ignorance of the past that must inevitably lead to an "improper" reading of the novel? Or might there not be a liberatory force to an amnesiac reading of this sort, a reading that was not predicated upon a "knowledge" of the novel's historical object or biographical subject, or that at the very least was capable of relativizing such "knowledge," deflating its high seriousness, and putting it into relation with other ways of knowing, or unknowing, the past?

Without, for the moment, further pursuing the implications of these meta-critical questions (to which I will return in the final section of this Introduction), I would now like to provide a concise account of the novel's historical and biographical contexts, starting with some basic facts about the "immense topic" (to quote Hugo's 1832 preface) that he tackled in *Bug-Jargal*: namely, "the revolt of the Saint Domingue blacks in 1791, a struggle of giants, three worlds having a stake in the matter—Europe and Africa as the combatants, America as the field of battle."

The pivotal date in this novel is 22 August 1791. That is the day on which the novel's main protagonist and narrator, Leopold d'Auverney, marries his childhood sweetheart Marie, the daughter of his uncle, a violent-tempered man who owns a large sugar plantation near Cap Français, capital of the North Province of the prosperous French colony of Saint Domingue. That is also the date, to quote the historian Carolyn Fick, "which marked the beginning of the end of one of the greatest wealth-producing slave colonies the world had ever known—the pearl of the Antilles, as it was extravagantly called" (91). What, we might ask, led up to this double date (the 22nd, fittingly enough), in which a fictional story about two young lovers (married during the day) intersects with real history in the form of a slave revolt (begun at night) that would eventually lead to the ouster of the French from the island and the creation of the independent state of Haiti?

In 1789 when the Revolution broke out in France, the French had been in official possession of Saint Domingue for almost a century, the western third of the island of Hispaniola having been ceded to them by the Spanish in 1697 as part of the Treaty of Ryswick. Over that brief period of time Saint Domingue had been transformed into the richest colony in the New World, largely on the backs of an ever-escalating number of slaves brought over from Africa to work the plantations, most of whom died soon after arrival. By 1789, it is estimated that the slave population of the island was somewhere around 500,000, with about 30,000 Africans a year being imported on average during the 1780s (Cauna, *Haiti* 105), a decade in which "production nearly doubled" (James 44). Saint Domingue was undergoing an extraordinary boom in the years before 1789: as C.L.R. James put it in his memorable study of the Haitian Revolution, *The Black Jacobins* (1938), "never before, and perhaps never since, has the world seen anything proportionately so dazzling as the last years of pre-revolutionary Sa[int] Doming[ue]" (44). Despite the ever-escalating influx of slaves, there was little sense that the society was about to be ripped apart by a major slave rebellion. Slave resistance had, to be sure, always been a fact of life in colonial Saint Domingue (see Fick 46-75), but until the events of August 1791 the ruling classes were blindly confident that the slaves would be incapable of mounting a revolt that might seriously threaten the foundations of colonial society; indeed, in the months following the start of the insurrection, no end of conspiracy theories were produced as to who its real instigators were—counter-revolutionary royalists, pro-revolutionary abolitionists, presumptuous mulattoes, devious Jesuits, scheming Englishmen … anything but the "genius of liberty" that one liberal commentator in the late 1790s, upon reviewing these various theories, identified as the most obvious source of Saint Domingue's current troubles (Garran 2.194).

"The slaves," in James's words, "had revolted because they wanted to be free. But no ruling class ever admits such things" (77). As the variety of very different theories that circulated regarding who was truly responsible for stirring up the revolt makes clear, though, the "ruling class" in Saint Domingue was by no means a cohesive ideological bloc, apart from its commitment to slavery. Ever since word that Louis XVI was going to convene the Estates General had reached it in 1788, the colony had been the scene of increasing tensions and violence between the various factions of the free population, white and coloured, who were trying to promote, channel, or contest revolutionary change for their own benefit. August 22 was the beginning of something altogether new, but it was also a product of what Hugo's protagonist d'Auverney refers to as "the political debates that, by this time, had already been stirring up the colony for two years"(p. 70), and it cannot be understood in isolation from those debates. What, then, were the main issues in dispute and who were the main players in the years 1789-91?

The free population of the island was divided into whites and coloureds (*gens de couleur*). The main division in white society was between the *grands blancs* (big whites) and the *petits blancs* (small whites). The former were mostly plantation owners and the wealthiest merchants in the land, while the latter could be anything from respected artisans and shop owners to vagabonds and adventurers. Another important distinction within the white camp involved place of birth: those born on the island (Creoles) as opposed to those born in France. Some of the French-born whites on the island were, furthermore, not long-term inhabitants but part of the colonial bureaucracy headed by the Governor and the Intendant, the ultimate authorities in Saint Domingue and the object of great resentment on the part of both the *grands* and the *petits blancs*, but especially of the former, who saw themselves as the rightful rulers of the land. (For a good summary of these differences, see James 26-29.) By contrast, it was the *petits blancs* who were especially resentful of the free coloured population on the island (mostly but not entirely made up of mulattoes) and who did all they could to humiliate and terrorize what had become an increasingly sizable and even wealthy class. The free coloured population "had probably more than doubled, possibly quadrupled in the fifteen years prior to 1789" (Nicholls 30), and in 1789 numbered around 30,000—more or less the same size as the white population. Although statistics vary, one recent historian asserts that they "owned one-third of the plantation property, one-quarter of the slaves, and one-quarter of the real estate property in Saint Domingue" (Fick 19). As their numbers and the wealth of many of them increased, ever more repressive legislation was put into place to ensure that even the most influential among them would have fewer rights than the smallest of the *petits blancs*. As Hugo's d'Auverney notes about the period immediately preceding the August revolt, "between the whites and the free mulattoes alone there existed enough hatred for the volcano that had been bottled up so long to convulse the entire colony at the dreaded moment when it would rip open" (p. 71).

The events of 1789-91 in Saint Domingue can be loosely divided into three overlapping phases, each dominated by one of the three main groups on the island—whites, free coloureds, black slaves. The first phase actually began in 1788 when news that the Estates-General was going to be convened the next year reached the colony. Much discussion ensued in committees and in the newly created assemblies in each of the colony's three provinces (North, West, South) about how to fashion a new, fairer relationship between France and its rich colony—a relationship that would involve both greater autonomy for the latter (devolving power from the Governor and the Intendant onto local assemblies) and some access to free trade (doing away with the Exclusive, by which the maritime bourgeoisie in France kept tight economic control over the colonies, which were only permitted to trade with the *mère-patrie*). At this point in the proceedings, the impetus for reform was coming from the *grands blancs*, and it was their representatives who arrived in Paris for the convening of the Estates General. Six of these representatives were eventually seated with the Third Estate, although it soon became clear to the *grands blancs* that throwing their lot in with the National Assembly meant that the colonial *reforms* they wanted could no longer be detached from the bourgeois *revolution* that, with the fall of the Bastille, was quickly becoming a reality in France—a revolution that, in its commitment to the rights of man, might very well seek to destroy the peculiar institution of slavery they were bent on protecting and consolidating.

The rights of man were all very well on paper, of course, but the awkward colonial issue (any just resolution of which would have threatened the interests of the maritime bourgeoisie who were among the prime motors of the Revolution) was put on the back burner for many months before any specific directives from the National Assembly were sent to the colonies. It was only on 8 March 1790 that the Assembly produced its first significant decree on colonial issues, which gave the colonies strong legislative powers and broad leeway in creating their own constitution. This was exactly what the whites on Saint Domingue wanted, but the decree notably fudged the question of exactly who was eligible to be elected to the new Colonial Assembly and draft a constitution. As Carolyn Fick notes, the instructions of 28 March that accompanied this decree "remained ambiguous on the explosive question of the political rights of mulattoes and free blacks. Article 4 merely stated that the right to vote and hold office be accorded to all persons twenty-five years of age who owned property or paid the requisite amount of taxes, and who fulfilled a two-year residence requirement" (81). The National Assembly had declined explicitly to state in these instructions that all free people in the colonies meeting the other requirements were eligible. In the words of Hugo's single most important source on the events in Saint Domingue, Pamphile de Lacroix's *Mémoires pour servir à l'histoire de la Révolution de Saint-Domingue* (1819), it was clear that Article 4 "was going to open the door for a wide array of interpretations" (1.29), but the Assembly had the political will neither to side with the cause of the *gens de couleur* nor simply to stifle it. They sent the "ambiguous decree" to Saint Domingue and, in James's words, "hoped for the best" (58).

By the time this decree arrived in the colony, its white inhabitants had anticipated the decree and established a Colonial Assembly to deliberate on a new constitution. On April 14 the three provincial assemblies had formed the Assembly of St. Marc (named after the town midway between the north and the south of the colony where they met) and were already beginning to map out a new relation with France. This Assembly quickly became dominated by the *petits blancs*, who had eagerly seized on the egalitarian rhetoric of the Revolution as legitimizing their own hopes and aspirations, which included greater power for them in the island's affairs, greater power for the island in determining its own affairs, and destruction of their rivals, the free coloureds. Alarmed by the increasingly strident positions adopted by the St. Marc Assembly, the *grands blancs* began taking their distance from it, turning the Provincial Assembly of the North into an alternative power base. The proposed constitution that the St. Marc Assembly came up with on May 28 was an abrasive document that, as one colonist later put it ruefully, "proved that the Assembly of St. Marc did not look upon itself as a petitioner, and believed it had the right to negotiate as an equal with France, to draw up jointly with [France] the charter that would henceforth link them to one another" (Dalmas 1.51). These self-styled Patriots, ardent supporters of the French Revolution (as long as it did not include equal rights for the free coloureds), were also proving the most zealous advocates of political and economic independence in all but name. Under orders from the island's then-Governor, de Peynier, troops led by Colonel de Mauduit dissolved both the Provincial Assembly of the West at Port-au-Prince on July 29 and, a week later, the St. Marc Assembly, many of whose members fled aboard the *Leopard* to France, where to little avail they defended their actions and complained to the National Assembly of their treatment by Mauduit and his counterrevolutionary *pompons blancs* (so called because they wore white pompoms on their hats, as opposed to the Patriots who wore *pompons rouges*).

The struggles between the two white factions did not end with the dispersal of the St. Marc Assembly in August, but would soon be complicated by the entry of the *gens de couleur* into the fray. Ever since the first days of the National Assembly, their representatives in Paris had been working to secure the full civil rights that their status as free men logically demanded. Despite the efforts of these representatives, and of abolitionists like the Abbé Grégoire, little headway had been made. As we saw, the decree of 8 March and instructions of 28 March were ambiguous enough to be interpreted as either acknowledging or denying these rights. Frustrated at this lack of progress, one of the mulatto representatives in France, a wealthy landowner by the name of Vincent Ogé, set off for Saint Domingue in August 1790 with the express purpose of securing the full promulgation of the decree of 8 March or, failing that, leading an insurrection of his people. After a circuitous route through England and the United States (necessitated by the fact that free coloureds had been expressly forbidden to leave France for the colonies), Ogé arrived on the island in mid-October where, after the failure of his diplomatic overtures, he led an aborted revolt that was easily quashed for a variety of reasons—among them the facts that he launched it too soon, before more than a few hundred free coloureds could assemble in support of him, and that he refused to enlist the help of the slave population, despite the urgings of his second-in-command Chavannes. After fleeing to the Spanish part of the island, Ogé and Chavannes would be quickly extradited, held for several months, summarily tried, and then brutally executed in late February 1791—a response that, as Lacroix dramatically put it, "separated the mixed-blood and [white] creole classes forever" (I.64), and that across the Atlantic had the undesired effect of "mak[ing] France as a whole fully aware of the colonial question" (James 60).

Ogé's failed insurrection drew new attention on the streets of Paris and in the National Assembly to the anomalous state of the *gens de couleur*, who were free and yet second-class citizens. Renewed efforts were made to resolve the situation. After great debate, a "compromise proposal" was reached (James 62): this was the decree of 15 May 1791, which Hugo's narrator characterizes, in an ideologically charged moment early on in the novel, as "that disastrous decree of 15 May 1791, whereby the National Assembly of France granted the free men of colour the same political rights as the whites" (p. 70). Never officially promulgated on the island, this decree was, as Fick points out, "in fact a conservative measure that enfranchised only a small minority of the mulattoes and free blacks in Saint Domingue" (85), some 400 by James's count (62). That proved more than enough, though, for the whites on the island: in Lacroix's words, "lightning could not have produced a conflagration more quickly than the one that broke out when news of the decree reached Saint Domingue" (1.80). Whites from all social strata, from the timorous Governor de Blanchelande down to the most virulently racist *petits blancs*, refused to accept this measure; a second Colonial Assembly was formed, made up mostly of the same Patriots who had dominated the St. Marc Assembly, and after initial meetings at Léogane in the south of the island, it arranged to sit in Cap Français as of August 25, by which time, of course, the slave revolt had begun. (See Chapter 16 of the novel for Hugo's sarcastic account of the proceedings of this Assembly.) In the West and South provinces, where there was a greater concentration of mulattoes, battles were already being fought in support of the equality tentatively enshrined in the decree of 15 May 1791: mulatto leaders like Rigaud and Beauvais were emerging as key figures who, by force of arms, might be capable of achieving what legislation had not. By the end of October, as a result of this military pressure and as a response to the alarming events in the North, whites in the West province had agreed to a concordat that would meet all the demands of the *gens de couleur*. By early November, however, before the official ratification of this concordat, news had reached the island that the National Assembly in France had, on September 24, reversed the decree of 15 May and put the fate of the free coloureds back in the hands of the island's white population. The machinations of the *petits blancs* in Port-au-Prince, who felt threatened by any alliance between the white and mulatto landowners, did the rest: by the end of November, when three Commissioners from France arrived at Cap Français charged with overseeing the implementation of the 24 September decree, whites and mulattoes were once again at loggerheads across the country.

By that time, after four months of insurrection, the slave revolt in the North "had come to a dead end" (James 84). The initial effects of the attacks launched on the night of August 22 had been devastating: "By September, all of the plantations within fifty miles either side of le Cap had been reduced to ashes and smoke; twenty-three of the twenty-seven parishes were in ruins, and the other four would fall in a matter of days" (Fick 105). There is no point lingering here over what happened during those months: Hugo himself presents a vivid, if chronologically vague, account of the insurrection and its leaders, and the excerpts from Hugo's main historical source materials (see Appendix E) recount the events of those months in detail—from a markedly European perspective, to be sure. A word or two does, however, need to be said about the "dead end" that the slave revolt had reached by the final months of 1791, because it is also the place where Hugo leaves off his account of the Haitian Revolution.

In December 1791, the leaders of the slave revolt, Jean-François and Biassou, unable to envision a positive outcome and faced with the prospect of famine, sent a letter to the new Commissioners from France and the Colonial Assembly in which they offered peace in return for the freedom of several hundred of the main players in the revolt. It was a "betrayal" of the worst sort (James 84), but had it been accepted there is little doubt that the future of Saint Domingue would have been significantly altered. Despite the Commissioners' eagerness to accept this offer, they were overruled by the Colonial Assembly who predictably, if rashly, refused to budge an inch even when confronted with such generous concessions on the part of a hostile force that so vastly outnumbered them. In James's memorable words, "the colonists, supremely confident that they would without difficulty drive these revolted dogs back to their kennels, answered that they would grant pardon only to repentant criminals who returned to work" (86). As a consequence, the revolt continued, expanding into a war once the neighbouring Spanish lent their support to it. The colonists lost a golden opportunity to put the brakes on a series of events that would soon sweep them off the historical stage; as the historian Pierre Pluchon puts it, "this refusal, as unrealistic as it was impolitic, sounded the death-knell of the French colony of Saint Domingue" (118).

Hugo has his fictional Biassou show d'Auverney a very distorted version of Jean-François and Biassou's actual letter in Chapter 38, which thus allows us to situate the novel's concluding chapters in historical time, despite the fact that the second half of *Bug-Jargal* features virtually no chronological signposts. In large part, of course, Hugo's use of this actual document simply serves the purposes of enhancing verisimilitude, and in this respect performs the same function as the wealth of often random historical references in the novel to the events of 1789-91: de Peynier and Mauduit, Ogé and Jean-François, Colonial and Provincial Assemblies, *petits blancs* and *pompons blancs*—all are present and accounted for in *Bug-Jargal*. But this particular detail also gets us thinking about the larger issue of why Hugo tells his story about Saint Domingue in the way that he does: why, for instance, it ends when it does, at a moment that, in retrospect, might seem like the French colony's "death-knell" but that also, viewed from the perspective of December 1791, situates the insurgent slaves in a position of weakness and retreat. As Bertrand Mouralis has pointed out, "by limiting the action of *Bug-Jargal* to the year 1791, the author can give only a very inadequate image of the process that would end up leading to the independence of Saint Domingue" (59), and there can be no doubt that Hugo's "refusal to situate his novel in this broader perspective" is an ideological decision that has to be factored into any reading of the novel. We hear nothing about the National Assembly's decree of 4 April 1792, which finally granted full civil rights to the *gens de couleur*; nothing about the five-year British invasion that began in 1793 and was ardently supported by many of the whites on the island; nothing about the freeing of the slaves on 29 August 1793 by Sonthonax, leader of the Second Civil Commission, nor about the confirmation of this act by the Jacobin-led National Convention in February of the next year; nothing about the rise of Toussaint Louverture to a position of supreme power on the island, or the wars of colour fought between his forces and the mulatto leader Rigaud's; nothing about Napoleon's ill-considered attempt in 1802 to wrest the island away from Toussaint and restore slavery; and nothing about the eventual defeat of those French forces and the declaration of Haitian independence on 1 January 1804—an independence that would only be officially recognized by France in 1825. What, the reader cannot help asking, does it mean to represent the Haitian Revolution in such a truncated fashion?

As readers will discover once they have examined the excerpts from Lacroix's 1819 *Mémoires* (Appendix E.2), it is not exactly true to say that *Bug-Jargal* takes the story of the Haitian Revolution no further than December 1791. Not only is post-1791 history visible in a couple of the novel's footnotes as well as its epilogue, which makes a passing reference to the burning of Cap Français in 1793, but this history can also be read back into the novel itself: Hugo has taken a number of incidents in Lacroix from the later years of the Revolution, and even from the period immediately after Haitian independence, and "translated" them back to the year 1791. His version of Jean-François and Biassou's December 1791 letter, for instance, is actually a *pastiche* of three documents, being made up of excerpts from the original but also bits and pieces from two others that date from 1793 (see Appendix E.2c). A number of anecdotes that Hugo attributes to Biassou in 1791 in fact belong to the years 1800-02, when Toussaint held absolute power in the colony; one anecdote is even taken from the reign of Dessalines (1804-06), the first leader of independent Haiti (see Appendix E.2d). Thus, the Haitian Revolution as a *completed* process both is and is not present in this novel: it hovers in the intertextual and paratextual background, doubling the novel "proper"—doubling that incomplete fragment of history which, it would appear, is the only story about Saint Domingue the young Hugo could, or wanted to, tell. That he was unable explicitly to acknowledge the finality of revolutionary history is hardly surprising if one thinks that at this point in his career he was still very much committed to the anti-revolutionary ideals of the Restoration—to the fantasy, that is, of a return to an earlier way of life which, it was hoped, the French Revolution had not destroyed but merely interrupted.

In the years after the fall of Napoleon in 1814-15 and the restoration of the Bourbon monarchy, an erasure of revolutionary history was certainly part of many people's ideological agenda ... and not just *French* revolutionary history. If for us today January 1804, the date of Haitian independence, seems like the final conclusion to the events of 1791 that Hugo chronicles in *Bug-Jargal*, neither in France nor Haiti did it seem quite so final at the time. Just as a number of expatriate Cubans and reactionary United States politicians today might still be incapable of registering the finality of the date January 1959, the traumatic loss of the "pearl of the Antilles" was not readily accepted by many in France, and after Napoleon's fall hopes resurfaced that a "restoration" of French rule on the island might be possible, through negotiations or military force. The lengthy subtitle of Colonel Malenfant's 1814 *Des Colonies et particulièrement de celle de Saint-Domingue* exemplifies this dream of restoration: "Considerations on the importance of reattaching [Saint Domingue] to the metropolis and on the methods of how this can be gone about with success, so as to bring back a durable peace, and reestablish and augment its prosperity." In the years immediately following 1814, secret negotiations over a return to French rule were carried out between France and the leaders of the southern half of Haiti. (It should be noted that since 1807, after the assassination of Dessalines the year before, Haiti had been effectively split in two: the "black" Henry Christophe's kingdom to the north and the "mulatto" Alexandre Pétion's republic to the south; the two halves of the country were reunited in 1820 under Jean-Pierre Boyer after Christophe's suicide.) No country had yet officially recognized Haiti's independence, and the threat of military intervention was always present in Haitian minds. The "reality" of Haiti, even of the name itself, was still contested: commenting in 1819 on the alteration of the island's name from Saint Domingue to Haiti, the secretary to King Henry Christophe, Baron de Vastey, noted that "while we uniformly adopt these new names [Haiti, Haitians], the *French* pertinaciously adhere to the term Saint Domingue, both in their Acts and writings" (44). Only in 1825 would France renounce its claims over the former colony: on April 17 of that year, with eleven French warships off Port-au-Prince, the Franco-Haitian accord was signed and the country's independence acknowledged, for which privilege Haiti agreed to pay France "an indemnity of 150 million francs, and reduced customs charges on French vessels to half that paid by those of other countries" (Nicholls 65). This indemnity bankrupted the public treasury and proved impossible to pay off; indeed, because of these unpaid debts, Haitian independence would not be unconditionally recognized by France until 1838. Colonialism, the French would discover a century and a half before neo-colonialism attached such a big question mark to the apparent finality of "Third World" decolonization, did not necessarily have to be restored; it could simply be translated anew, to the continued advantage of the erstwhile colonists.

   Similar to the way that the final conclusion of Haitian independence in 1804 both is and is not present in Hugo's novel about the revolutionary events of 1791, one finds the Franco-Haitian accord of 1825 obliquely referred to in his 1826 preface to the novel. He begins this preface by noting that because it deals with Saint Domingue the novel "has a circumstantial look to it," the subject of Haiti having lately "acquired a new degree of interest." He defends himself against this charge by alerting readers to the fact that the novel is actually a much expanded version of a short story he had published years earlier, in 1820. (On Hugo's translation of the short story "Bug-Jargal" into the novel *Bug-Jargal*, see the introductory note to Appendix A.) This fact allows him to argue that "events have accommodated themselves to the book, not the book to events." Practically speaking, of course, Hugo's audience would for the most part have known that he was talking here about the 1825 Franco-Haitian accord, and yet this coy refusal to speak directly about current events seems yet another symptom of Hugo's unwillingness or inability openly to confront the final consequences of the revolutionary events that he has narrated in his novel.

   Whether we are to believe Hugo when he says there was no connection between the April accord and his decision to dust off his youthful short story and expand it into a novel, and whether his oblique reference to the accord betrays an ideological anxiety about Saint Domingue or is merely a marketing ploy in the guise of anti-marketing rhetoric, must remain a moot point, but it certainly raises the biographical question of who Hugo was and what he believed in 1825. The year France acknowledged Haitian independence was an important one for this young poet with a rapidly rising reputation, who celebrated his twenty-third birthday on February 26 of that year. At this time, Hugo was still firmly ensconced in the anti-liberal royalist ideology that had underwritten the Restoration since 1814. With an eye both to currying favours and basking in the pomp and circumstance of what would prove a rather disappointing ceremony, Hugo attended the coronation (*sacre*) of the new King, Charles X, on May 29 and wrote a "stunningly old-fashioned ode" about it, "Le sacre de Charles X" (Robb 120). The opening lines of this poem, which would earn Hugo a royal audience on June 23 (the King eventually "bought 300 copies, ordered a special luxury edition from the Imprimerie Royale and rewarded Hugo with a Sèvres dinner service" [Robb 120]), give a good idea of Hugo's political affinities at this time:

> L'orgueil depuis trente ans est l'erreur de la terre.
> C'est lui qui sous les droits étouffa le devoir;
> C'est lui qui dépouilla de son divin mystère
> Le sanctuaire du pouvoir. (OC 2.724)

> (For thirty years arrogance has been the error of the land.
> In the name of rights, the call of duty was banned,
> And power's sanctuary robbed by this arrogant hand
> Of its divine mystery.)

When reading *Bug-Jargal*, the reader will encounter a great deal of this self-righteous anti-revolutionary rhetoric, especially in the novel's epilogue (which is situated at the height of the Terror in 1794), but the novel—and this is one of its decided strengths—cannot be simply reduced to the straightforward politics of Hugo's ode or the often blunt political formulations to be found in the essays he wrote around this time. As one might guess from the fact that the greatest defenders of royalism in the novel turn out to be villainous leaders of the slave revolt like Biassou, the young Hugo's white and black division between royalty's "divine mystery" and the revolutionary "error" that arrogantly dismantled it is altogether more blurred in the novel than in his ode, although still very much in evidence.

It is a biographical commonplace in Hugo studies (one that he himself initiated) to chronicle his passage in the mid-1820s from a youthful, misguided attachment to the most nefarious brand of conservative royalist ideology (*ultraism*, as it was called) to a more adult commitment to a kinder, gentler liberalism in the last years of the decade—a liberalism more compatible with the increasingly "revolutionary" Romantic poetics that he would first fully formulate in the 1827 preface to *Cromwell*. In this vein, for instance, the Hugo specialist Jacques Seebacher has spoken of the year 1825 as marking "perhaps the real turning point in this young career" (70). While it is certainly possible to overstate the rapidity of Hugo's ideological transformation in the late 1820s, it nonetheless seems unquestionable that his politics began slowly to shift as of 1825, at the same time as his creative work confidently established a new literary direction. *Bug-Jargal* at one and the same time anticipates this shift and yet remains on the "wrong" side of it, "a transitional text" in Roger Toumson's words (23), not quite the "masterpiece" one would expect from the creator of *Notre-Dame de Paris* (1831) nor the politically "mature" statement one would hope for from the man who authored that prescient indictment of capital punishment, *Le Dernier Jour d'un condamné* (1829). It has proven exceptionally hard for critics of Hugo not to agree that "an astonishing maturation distances the pages [of *Last Day of a Condemned Man*] from *Han of Iceland* and *Bug-Jargal* and draws them near to *Les Misérables*" (Meschonnic ii). The most pressing question about *Bug-Jargal* from the perspective of Hugo studies has always been: to what extent, if at all, do the narrative strategies and ideological positions of this early novel anticipate the "real" Hugo, their undeniable "immaturity" notwithstanding?

Necessary and vital as such a question might be to those who specialize in Hugo, it is certainly not the most interesting one to be asked of *Bug-Jargal* for readers who have been schooled in colonial discourse analysis and postcolonial studies. Each generation of readers (and publishers!) chooses its texts according to certain criteria and the ways in which *Bug-Jargal* is and is not typical of Hugo's oeuvre will, I suspect, be of far less importance and interest to most readers today than the fact that it is among the more substantial nineteenth-century European novels to have dealt with issues of race in general, and certainly the most substantial to have dealt with the Haitian Revolution in particular. For those primarily interested in Hugo's greatness as a novelist there are better places to go than *Bug-Jargal*. However, if *Bug-Jargal* ostensibly lacks the "moral complexity" claimed for Hugo's "mature" novels (Porter 15), it nonetheless allows us to ask questions that his later novels do not: notably, questions about the representation of race and cultural hybridity, about the language and history of colonialism and postcolonial reworkings of that language and that history. These will be the questions of primary importance to a contemporary audience informed by several decades of postcolonial theory, and for that reason situating *Bug-Jargal* in terms of its relation to Hugo's oeuvre, or even to the occasional representations of "blackness" scattered through his later work, must remain secondary to the task of reading the novel on its own terms—the terms available to Hugo in 1825.

Reading *Bug-Jargal* on its own terms—the terms of 1825—allows us to focus on its specificity as a novel, without forcing it into the predictable patterns of understanding that seem hard to avoid when reading it within the majestic trajectory of Hugo's overall career. It allows us to take the text much more seriously than Hugo critics have in general been able to (both because of its "aesthetic" deficiencies and its dubious politics), and to read it instead as one of the preeminent nineteenth-century representations of race in European literature—a colonial text from which, perhaps, we still have something to learn in a postcolonial age. However, attention to this specificity *also* should make us wary of imposing other, equally predictable patterns of understanding on the text, transforming it simply into a timeless exemplar of, say, Africanist discourse. Useful as such general categories have been to the emergence of postcolonial theory, they are—as no end of critics have pointed out in the twenty-five years since Edward Said published the massively generalizing *Orientalism*—far too all-encompassing, far too oblivious to the specificities of the texts grouped within such seductive rubrics as "Orientalist" or "colonial" discourse. Attending to the specific terms of 1825 certainly frees up Hugo's novel for a reading more attuned to race and colonialism and less concerned with the usual obsessions of Hugo criticism (symbolism, myth, linguistic cleverness, and so on), but it also forces us to confront the fact that this novel could have been written *only* in 1825, and by someone with a point of view that was *Hugo's alone*; this point of view, to be sure, was deeply saturated in various literary traditions and ideological positions, ensuring that the novel Hugo produced about Saint Domingue would be (un)like other novels dealing with exotic locales and peoples of African descent, but to read *Bug-Jargal* as simply a representative "Western" vision of the "Other," a typical "white" representation of "blacks," would be to do as great a disservice to its specificity as Hugolians enamoured of *Les Misérables* have done it in the past.

In short, if biographical considerations about Hugo's entire career, or even his career up to and including 1825, are of necessity secondary to any postcolonial reading of *Bug-Jargal*, concerned as that reading will be with broader historical and cultural contexts, they must nonetheless be kept in mind, if only peripherally, as a way of countering the temptation to read this novel as nothing more than an exemplary colonial text (which, up to a point, it no doubt is). To give the reader some sense of Hugo's individual point of view in the years immediately preceding the publication of *Bug-Jargal*, I have included in the appendices two of his most important works of literary criticism from that time: his 1823 article on Walter Scott's *Quentin Durward* and the 1824 Preface to his *Nouvelles Odes* (see Appendix C). These two articles nicely convey the ideological outlook of the young Hugo, a writer still deeply committed to the conservative values of the Restoration and yet attempting to convince his readers (and himself) that this commitment was not incompatible with artistic innovation. We find him praising Scott for pointing the way toward a new "dramatic" form of the novel that would synthesize earlier "narrative" and "epistolary" forms; and yet at the same time that he praises the innovatory method of Scott's historical novels, we also find him commenting approvingly on the new critical climate in Restoration France, where "popularity is no longer bestowed by the populace" (as in "the years that immediately preceded and followed upon our convulsive revolution") but stems, rather, "from the only source that can impress upon it a character of immortality as well as universality—namely, the approbation of that small number of delicate minds, exalted souls, and serious individuals who represent morally civilized peoples." In the 1824 Preface, we find him arguing strenuously that "present-day literature can be in part the *result* of the revolution, without being the *expression* of it," thereby attempting to justify the innovations of writers such as himself who were already being damned with the label "Romantic" (a label that at this point in his career Hugo firmly rejected), while at the same time contending that these literary innovations in no way expressed the values of "a political revolution which affected all levels of society from top to bottom, which touched on every glory and every infamy, which disunited everything and mixed it all together."

Already in the haughty formulations of this young *ultra*, we get an incipient sense of the unresolved tensions that proliferate in *Bug-Jargal*, a novel that is undeniably anti-revolutionary in tone and yet that nonetheless seems caught up in the unsettling process about which it seems so anxious. When we imagine Hugo in 1825 reading book after book about Saint Domingue in preparation for reworking his story into a novel, it is this double-mindedness that we need to keep to the fore: we will see, time and again, that in his selection, manipulation, and distortion of these sources he was *reading with a vengeance*, on the look-out for whatever might help further a negative, parodic interpretation of the events in Saint Domingue. And yet that negative reading by no means exhausts what he has actually written: in his translation of these events onto paper an *other* reading of the material is also visible, one more open to the revolutionary energies that his primary reading is vigorously intent upon dispelling.

Before we can conclude this introductory account of Saint Domingue in 1791 and Victor Hugo in 1825, one last obvious biographical question remains to be asked: namely, what drew Hugo to the slave revolt of 1791 in the first place? To read Hugo's article on Scott's historical novels, or to examine the wealth of source materials that he consulted when writing the novel, makes a certain contextual sense of *how* Hugo dealt with the slave revolt, but in no way explains *why* he dealt with it. The simple answer, alas, is that we do not know and, barring the discovery of some new document, are unlikely ever to know exactly what led Hugo to represent this "struggle of giants."

Critics have, to be sure, attempted to provide a definitive response to this question by positing biographical links between Hugo and the former colony that would explain his interest in the events of 1791 and their aftermath. Some have seized upon a letter dated 18 December 1829 in which Hugo complained about financial difficulties related to the problem of securing his father's inheritance and cited, among other unresolved problems, "the holding back of my indemnity from Saint Domingue by Boyer [President of Haiti from 1820 to 1843]" (OC 3.1269). Although this one comment seems like irrefutable proof of some biographical link between Hugo and Saint Domingue, those readers of Bug-Jargal most familiar with the colonial archives in Haiti and France have been unable to substantiate it (see Cauna, "Sources"). Was Hugo distantly related to a Saint Domingue planter dispossessed of his property by the insurgent blacks and hence eligible for remuneration after the Franco-Haitian accord of 1825? In Chapter 28 of the novel, "Generalissimo" Biassou has his obi (sorcerer) set up an altar on a sugar-box confiscated from the Dubuisson plantation: given the fact that Hugo's mother, Sophie, was the grand-daughter of a man named René-Pierre Le Normand du Buisson (see Hovasse 1304-05), and that her father Jean-François Trébuchet (born at Auverné, near Nantes; d. 1783) "had spent most of his life sailing from Nantes to the West Indies, filling up with slaves at West African ports on the way out, and returning with sugar and molasses" (Robb 4), it certainly seems possible that Hugo might have some biographical connection with the island—either through one of the many Le Normands who lived in colonial Saint Domingue, or through stories passed on to him by his mother about her father and debts owed him by some dispossessed planter in Saint Domingue (as the historian Carolyn Fick notes, "during the final decade of the Old Regime, the period from 1783 to 1792, the slave-trading debts of colonial planters to the Nantes traders had reached some 45 million livres, much of which, with the outbreak of the Saint Domingue slave revolution, would never get paid" [24]). Any number of scenarios directly linking Hugo and Saint Domingue are remotely possible, but none of them are at present verifiable.

The reference to Hugo's Haitian indemnities tantalizes, of course; regardless of its unverifiability, it clearly signals a personal investment in the events of 1791 that leaves many a trace in Bug-Jargal, nowhere more obviously than in the name of the novel's white protagonist. I mentioned earlier that Hugo signed several of his early articles with the name d'Auverney: this establishes a link with his mother's side of the family (the Trébuchets owned property in Auverné); d'Auverney's first name being Leopold, the name of Hugo's father, it is clear enough that some sort of family romance is being played out in this novel. Speculation along these lines could be, and has been, pursued in any number of ways by Hugo critics: d'Auverney and Bug-Jargal's desire for the same woman has been, for instance, interpreted as Hugo's projection of the rivalry between himself and his brother Eugène over Adèle Foucher, the woman who became Victor's wife in October 1822, at more or less the same time that the schizophrenic Eugène was permanently confined to an asylum; Eugène as the good Bug-Jargal, then, but also the evil dwarf Habibrah, since one can see "a transposition, manifestly unconscious, of Eugène onto the character of the slave Habibrah" (Juin 484). *Bug-Jargal*, like all of Hugo's novels, lends itself to such speculations and the psychoanalytic interpretations they entail. Whatever personal debts are being reclaimed, or paid back, in this novel, however, must remain on the periphery of a contemporary reading of it: as I have stressed in the preceding paragraphs, if *Bug-Jargal* is of interest to audiences today, this will be largely on account of the fact that it is *not* a novel like all of Hugo's novels but, rather, one that—by venturing so openly and so disturbingly into colonial territory— permits us to discuss other, more world-historical and very much unpaid debts that have been incurred by centuries of Western imperialism. What is the relevance of Hugo's colonial (or what I will be calling post/colonial) novel to a new generation of readers informed by postcolonial studies? That is the question I will address in the final section of this Introduction.

(1791)/2002, 2004: Reading Hugo and the Haitian Revolution in a Post/Colonial Age

Bug-Jargal has consistently generated diametrically opposed interpretations amongst critics—both in Hugo's time and in our own. I have included in this edition a few of the more extensive reviews that greeted Hugo's novel when it first came out (see Appendix D), so readers will be able to see for themselves the contradictory responses that it initially provoked. Is *Bug-Jargal* a novel with essentially "benevolent" intentions when it comes to its portrayal of blacks and their revolution, which will provide readers with "new grounds for thanking heaven for the existence and the liberty of Haiti" (*Le Globe*), or is it a novel that inspires "hatred," reviving racial antag- onisms that ought to have been laid to rest by the 1825 Franco-Haitian accord (*Le Mercure du dix-neuvième siècle*)? Does the portrait of Bug-Jargal "grant to the African race a capacity for advanced civilization that it in no way possesses" (*Le Drapeau blanc*), or can that portrayal be justified both on aesthetic and philosophical grounds (*La Revue encyclopédique*)? Such wildly differing readings have been repeatedly reworked by critics in our own day and age: Hugo's biographer Graham Robb identified *Bug-Jargal* as "a splendid example of the creative imagination escaping the prejudices of its age" because it provides Western literature with "one of its first wholly admirable Black heroes" (123), while Léon-François Hoffmann, in the most exhaustive analysis of Hugo's representations of blackness throughout his career, cited the novel as evidence that "Hugo always lacked sympathy for Blacks (as was his right) but also objectivity and human respect (as was rather less excusable)" ("Victor Hugo" 87). Jacques Seebacher, editor of Hugo's complete works and deeply invested in Hugo's status as an artistic genius, after hearing a conference paper emphasizing the novel's colonialist and racist aspects, rejected any such argument on the grounds that *Bug-Jargal* is an "ironic text" and that its representations of race are thus not open to that sort of direct critique; in response, the first critic asserted that the "univocality of the text" far outweighs its ambiguities (for this exchange, see Gewecke 63–65). A Caribbean critic blasted the novel as "a work of sarcasm, a singularly caustic pamphlet directed against revolution in general and against its specific manifestation, the black revolution," and argued that Hugo's "nostalgia for a lost unity" produced a text that voices regret for "the time when masters and slaves lived on good terms and in harmony" (Toumson 32, 79), to which an American Hugo specialist responded that this nostalgia led him, rather, "to dream of a transcendent order that unites humankind in liberty rather than servitude" and that Bug-Jargal is the "hybrid" creation who embodies "the essence of Hugo's utopian hero" (Grossman 99, 107).

In *Islands and Exiles*, I argued the case for an interpretation of *Bug-Jargal* that would take both sides of the debate into account. By way of transition to my concluding comments, I will provide one example here of what that double-sided argument involves. We earlier noted that in Chapter 38 Hugo includes a letter supposedly written by the rebel leaders Biassou and Jean-François but actually patched together out of three separate documents that he found in Lacroix's *Mémoires*. On the one hand, Hugo's *bricolage* provides clear evidence of the novel's anti-revolutionary bias, its manifestly parodic intentions. If readers compare these documents (Appendix E.2c) with the fictional letter in Chapter 38, it should be clear that Hugo chose to supplement his heavily edited version of Biassou and Jean-François's letter of 6 December 1791 with materials from 1793 because the 1791 letter was quite simply not "ridiculous" enough to be used as a revealingly representative "specimen of negro diplomacy." The real letter, as one early commentator on the troubles in

Saint Domingue tendentiously put it, lacks "the character of coarseness and deepest ignorance" that was to be found in the rebels' other communications, and hence supplies proof that they were "directed by a foreign force" (Tarbé 12, 5); such coarseness is, by contrast, easily read into the two documents from 1793 that Hugo grafts onto his fictional version of the 1791 letter—a letter that "could have come from the pen of a man who had spent all his life in diplomacy" (James 86). That the authentic 1791 letter is itself a wretchedly evasive example of diplomatic double-talk, undoubtedly not dictated by the rebel leaders themselves, need not concern us here; the important point is simply that Hugo felt compelled, in order to further his parodic representation of the Haitian Revolution, to supplement the letter with other odds and ends found in Lacroix, and to manipulate all three items so as to construct a unified fiction that serves his ideological and artistic ends.

Interestingly, Hugo appended a footnote to his pastiched (or should we say translated?) version of the letter that impudently states, "it would appear that this ridiculously characteristic letter was indeed sent to the assembly" (153). A little historical research is all it takes to disprove this statement and to deconstruct the unified fiction of the letter, showing how it was cobbled together out of Lacroix's *Mémoires*: scholars interested in Hugo's use of historical sources long ago did this research (see, e.g., Etienne, Debien), unmasking what is, when all's said and done, one of the more troublingly racist digs in the novel. And yet, while necessary, such unmasking of Hugo's spiteful *bricolage* almost feels like an empty gesture because the episode virtually unmasks itself. Without the footnote, which ambivalently (con)fuses the realms of appearance ("it would appear") and reality ("was indeed sent"), readers would not, after all, necessarily assume that they were in the presence of a real historical document; because of the footnote's inclusion, however, readers are forced into asking questions about the relation between Hugo's fiction and the historical reality it purports to be representing. Was the letter sent or not? Was this the exact same letter that was sent or not? Questions such as these lead, albeit by no means ineluctably, back to the author who has forced them upon his readers, and who seems to be daring them to reveal him for the *bricoleur* that he is, someone who has presented as a unified whole and an historical truth that which is in fact an assemblage of disparate parts and an historical fiction.

Indeed, even without the author's provocative footnote, the appearance of the letter in d'Auverney's narrative provokes similar questions about this narrator's reliability as a storyteller. The conventions involved in reading first-person narratives permit readers to accept as "realistic" even the most incredible feats of memory (such as repeating lengthy conversations verbatim), and readers would thus have little reason to blink when d'Auverney informs his audience of the exact contents of Biassou's letter ... except that Hugo forces them to blink by having d'Auverney assure his audience that the memory of this letter "has stuck in my head, word for word." At that point the conventions are broken and the reader cannot help but be struck by the unlikeliness of this feat of memory. How, readers may well ask when prodded in this way, could d'Auverney not be misrepresenting the letter to some degree? Explicitly drawing our attention to the "word for word" status of this memory forces us to consider the possibility that this authoritative memory is simply a (re)construction, an imitation of the original or, if you will, its imperfect translation. Hugo thus draws attention in two complementary ways to the letter's problematic status: the narrative provokes us into registering the obvious probability that d'Auverney has not remembered every last word of Biassou's letter and must thus be manipulating his own story; while the footnote attached to the narrative compels us to question whether Hugo has represented the historical letter as it really was or whether he has manipulated history in order to patch his own story together.

Hugo's treatment of the 1791 letter is but one of many incipiently *meta-fictional* moments in the novel where he tentatively reveals himself as a *bricoleur* and thereby *implicates himself in the very thing he is criticizing*—for throughout the novel it has been Hugo's parodic strategy to identify the rebellious blacks in general, and the villainous mulattoes Biassou and Habibrah in particular, as abject *bricoleurs* who put together whatever odds and ends they might have on hand regardless of whether the mixing together of these objects is appropriate or not, and regardless of established protocols for the use of these objects. (For instance, in Chapter 28 when we first meet "Generalissimo" Biassou, his patently ridiculous uniform is described at length and we learn that for one of his epaulettes he has made do with the rowels from a set of spurs, and that this makeshift epaulette is, moreover, not secured in its "natural place.") It is at such moments that *Bug-Jargal* tentatively moves beyond its indubitably reactionary foundations, forcing us to question their seeming authority. If, as I believe it does, "great" literature consistently presents us with such de-authorizing moments of self-revelation and the undoing of whatever "official" position the author is attempting to ground him- or herself in, then it must be admitted that *Bug-Jargal* is at best only intermittently great. The ideological biases that motivate Hugo's scathing critique of a mulatto *bricoleur* like Biassou and the hybrid modernity he embodies dominate this novel from start to finish, and one has to work hard to get beyond them. But I would argue that this duplicitous text *does*, in its more self-conscious moments, create a limited amount of space in which that sort of work can be done, not just against the ideological grain of its overtly colonial assumptions but in accord with what I would like to call its post/colonial premonitions; Hugo's novel is not (simply) an exemplary instance of colonial discourse but one that makes room, obliquely, for a postcolonial vision—of subaltern resistance and cultural hybridity, for instance—to which it is ostensibly opposed.

Pursuing a double reading of *Bug-Jargal* along such lines allows us to take seriously both those critics who stress the reactionary, and even racist, dimensions of the novel and those who privilege its carnivalesque "multi-vocality," rather than write off one or the other camp as simply mistaken in their interpretation. After completing Hugo's novel, it should be clear to contemporary readers of *Bug-Jargal* that, ideologically speaking, Hugo's representation of the Haitian Revolution is deeply problematic by virtue of its refusal to take seriously the history of that revolution—or, at least, the history of the Haitian Revolution *as we know it today*. For the young man who wrote *Bug-Jargal*, this history was something to be contested, dismissed, parodied—as were the men and women who made it possible. We, of course, see things very differently today, and can only be disheartened at the extent to which Hugo's novel reduces one of the most momentous events in the history of anti-colonial resistance to a reactionary tale about villainous mulattoes, frenzied negresses, and one rather docile noble savage. But if this colonial tale no longer rings true to our postcolonial ears, if its ideological distortion of a world-historical event strikes us as misguided and even repugnant, there is still something of value to be learnt from Hugo's refusal to take this history as seriously as we do, and as we must. For Hugo's refusal to treat revolutionary history with the respect that it clearly (to us) requires does not simply signal his disagreement with that particular history but, more radically, self-consciously points to the ways in which language itself is always, in a very basic sense, in disagreement with history. What the incipiently meta-fictional moments in the novel suggest is that language inevitably betrays history, reducing it to a story constructed out of words that can never truly re-*present* what actually happened—words that can only, with inexorable bias, re-present the past, translating it into something that is, for better or worse, (un)like the original. In a duplicitous process of *(un)knowing the past*, Hugo's meta-fictional *play* with history in *Bug-Jargal* puts into question the colonial "knowledge" that so evidently frames his account of the Haitian Revolution, yet without simply invalidating that authoritative "knowledge." Our own postcolonial "knowledge" of the Haitian Revolution departs radically from what Hugo knew, to the point where we can barely recognize the (that is, our) history of that Revolution amidst the distortions to which Hugo subjected it; nevertheless, I would suggest, the (un)knowing of the past that can be discerned in *Bug-Jargal* remains relevant to us today as a model for relativizing our own distorted—if ethically imperative—historical insights, our self-righteous translations of colonial history into postcolonial language.

In the remainder of this concluding section I would like to pursue the question of what (un)knowing the past might involve; in order to do so, I will have to take a bit of a detour away from *Bug-Jargal* and draw the reader's attention to one of the more dramatic controversies in the historiography of the Haitian Revolution—a controversy that has much to tell us about the troublingly close relation between the colonial and postcolonial that, in my *Islands and Exiles*, I have referred to as the post/colonial condition. In the preceding section of this Introduction, I remarked upon the way that Hugo concludes his (hi)story of the Haitian Revolution at the end of 1791: he refuses to tell—except obliquely in the occasional footnote—what happened beyond that date, and thereby frames the world's "only successful slave revolt" (in James's words) as an unfinished and potentially reversible event. If the "end" of the Haitian Revolution is, for obvious ideological reasons, not present in *Bug-Jargal*, neither for that matter is what has come to be seen as its symbolic point of "beginning," "the famous and awesomely impressive voodoo ceremony in Bois-Caïman" (Fick 263). Although Hugo provides a vivid chronicle of the first days of the revolt, he makes no mention of this ceremony, which was supposedly presided over by Boukmann and an anonymous priestess just before the outbreak of the slave revolt in August 1791 so as to secure divine approval for the insurrection, and which is traditionally identified by both historians and the Haitian people as the founding moment of the Haitian Revolution.

None of Hugo's known sources mentions this ceremony, so there are good, practical reasons for its absence from *Bug-Jargal*. We do, however, find a lengthy description of it in one of the more prominent accounts of the Saint Domingue revolution published between 1791 and 1826, Antoine Dalmas's two-volume *Histoire de la Révolution de Saint-Domingue*, which was purportedly written right after Dalmas had fled to the United States when Cap Français was burned to the ground in 1793, but which was only published in 1814. As a close comparison of it with *Bug-Jargal* confirms, Hugo never read Dalmas's *Histoire*, although given his own lurid portrayal of the goings-on at Biassou's camp, there can be little doubt that Hugo's eye would have been caught by the former colonist's vivid account of the ceremony, had he ever come across it:

> Arrangements for the uprising had been drawn up by its principal leaders a few days before, on the Le Normand plantation at Morne Rouge. Before putting it into action, they held a feast or sacrifice in the middle of a wooded plot of land called *Caïman*, a part of the Choiseul plantation that was not under cultivation; the negroes gathered there in great numbers. A completely black pig—circled round with *fetishes* and weighed down with offerings, each one more bizarre than the last—was the holocaust offered up to the all-powerful spirit of the black race. The religious ceremonies that the negroes performed while slitting [the pig's] throat, the avidity with which they drank its blood, the great value they placed on possessing a few of its hairs—as a sort of talisman that, so they thought, would render them invulnerable: all of these things serve to characterize the African. For a caste so ignorant and so degraded, it was natural that the superstitious rites of an absurd and bloodthirsty religion would act as prelude to the most horrendous outrages. (1.117-18)

In its authoritative appeal to "race" and "caste," its dismissive portrait of "ignorant," "degraded" Africans who "naturally" engage in "characteristically" superstitious and absurdly "bloodthirsty" rituals, and its metonymic identification of negroes with the black pig they slaughter, Dalmas's account of what went on in the Bois Caïman is firmly entrenched in the colonial discourse that a revisionist history like C.L.R. James's *Black Jacobins* acerbically contests.

Here is James's seminal representation of the same ceremony, which occupies more or less the same amount of space in his text as it does in Dalmas's:

> On the night of the 22nd a tropical storm raged, with lightning and gusts of wind and heavy showers of rain. Carrying torches to light their way, the leaders of the revolt met in an open space in the thick forests of the Morne Rouge, a mountain overlooking Le Cap. There Boukman gave the last instructions and, after Voodoo incantations and the sucking

of the blood of a stuck pig, he stimulated his followers by a prayer spoken in creole, which, like so much spoken on such occasions, has remained. 'The god who created the sun which gives us light, who rouses the waves and rules the storm, though hidden in the clouds, he watches us. He sees all that the white man does. The god of the white man inspires him with crime, but our god calls upon us to do good works. Our god who is good to us orders us to revenge our wrongs. He will direct our arms and aid us. Throw away the symbol of the god of the whites who has so often caused us to weep, and listen to the voice of liberty, which speaks in the hearts of us all.'

The symbol of the god of the whites was the cross which, as Catholics, they wore round their necks.

That very night they began ... (70-71)

It is obvious that the Haitian past is *known* in an entirely different way here than in the colonial text. James does not provide a static tableau of the ceremony as does Dalmas but, rather, offers a dynamic narrative, in which the insurgent slaves become actors in their own destiny rather than the passive objects of an outsider's gaze. James's representation of the event is dominated not by his own words but by the words of Boukmann; the subaltern slaves are given a voice and a language of their own (as opposed to the creole "jargon" Hugo would have given them), and with this language they speak to us across the centuries—albeit in English translation—from the thick forests of the Morne Rouge, the place where it all began.

It is tempting, of course, to draw a firm boundary line between these two representations, the one so clearly colonial, the other so obviously postcolonial. The following randomly chosen comment about the impor- tance of James's *Black Jacobins* exemplifies this understandable urge to detach a "good" writer like James from his "bad" colonial predecessors: "The Haitian political lineage, which stretched from Toussaint and Dessalines to the Duvaliers, was unknown before the Trinidadian jour- neyed to Paris to research this momentous event in postcolonial history. James's work attempted to counteract the silences about Toussaint and Dessalines and the (thousands of) slaves who became soldiers, military leaders, and statesmen" (Farred 227-28). James is here represented as working *ab ovo*, breaking a "silence," finally making known what had hitherto been "unknown." This euphoric and completely erroneous por- trait of James's contribution to the historiography of Haiti wilfully overlooks the extent to which his enterprise is caught up in an intertextual relation of dependence upon writers like Dalmas whose colonial vision of the world James is attempting to contest (Hugo's main source, Lacroix's *Mémoires*, for instance, is translated more or less verbatim for pages on end in *Black Jacobins*). The colonial and the postcolonial cannot be as easily disentangled as the passage I have just quoted, with its naive belief in an original and originating postcolonial history of the Haitian Revolution, would have it: James has *translated* his colonial sources into something that is (un)like them, producing not an entirely new, *post*colonial vision of the world but, rather, one that is entangled in the post/colonial condition— a discursive and existential condition in which the colonial and the post-colonial cannot be separated from one another but have to be read and lived together, as part of one contradictory whole, somewhere in between the two extremes of "colonial" and "postcolonial" representation into which James's and Dalmas's very different accounts of the Bois Caïman ceremony can be so easily, far too easily, made to fall.

One sign of the post/colonial complicity of Dalmas's and James's representations of the Haitian Revolution, notwithstanding their very different ways of knowing what took place in the Bois Caïman, is the simple fact that they both share the assumption that the founding moment of the Haitian Revolution really happened. However, in a conference paper delivered in 1991 as part of the bicentenary commemorations of the 1791 slave revolt, the respected Haitian scholar Léon-François Hoffmann put this apparently unquestionable assumption into serious doubt. Taking as the starting point of his argument the striking fact that not a single one of the multitude of books, pamphlets, and manuscripts written about the slave revolt by French writers between 1791 and 1814 makes any mention of this ceremony, Hoffmann cogently maintains—on the basis of a great deal of documentary evidence—that it is "very probable that [the ceremony] was not an historical event but rather a myth, the origin of which, paradoxically, can be credited to the ill intentions of a Frenchman from Saint-Domingue," namely Antoine Dalmas, whose dismissive account of the Bois Caïman ceremony is not, I should now reveal, just a typically colonial representation of this founding event but in fact "the earliest mention" of it ("Histoire" 267). Since, according to Hoffmann, "not a single eye-witness account corroborates directly or indirectly Dalmas's, it is difficult not to conclude that the ceremony is an invention, pure and simple, or at least that Dalmas might have confused and merged, with the passage of time, unrelated memories or rumours" (270-71).

Pursuing his argument that the ceremony "belongs to the world of the imagination rather than that of historical objectivity" (272), Hoffmann goes on to provide a somewhat baroque hypothesis regarding how Dalmas's "invention," or confused rendering of "unrelated memories or rumours," might have made its way back across the Atlantic from France to independent Haiti in the early 1820s, via a French abolitionist and Haitianophile, Civique de Gastine, whose representation of the event in his *Histoire de la République d'Haïti ou Saint-Domingue* (1819), obviously indebted to Dalmas, would in turn be taken up in 1824 by the Haitian writer Hérard Dumesle, who introduced a rousing anti-colonial speech (in alexandrines, no less!) into his account of the ceremony, which would in turn several decades later be attributed to Boukmann by the French abolitionist Victor Schoelcher and then eventually find its way, in translated form, into James's rendering of the event. As Hoffmann shows, over the course of the nineteenth century several symbolically satisfying details were added to Dalmas's initial narrative, such as having the ceremony take place on a stormy night (a detail that James picks up on). In the twentieth century, Hoffmann adds, the Bois Caïman ceremony was given a new prominence, not just by anti-colonial writers like James who were laying the foundations for a resistant, postcolonial vision of the world, but in Haiti itself by the dictator Duvalier as part of his pro-negritude, anti-mulatto politics: "Just as the fascist regime of Philippe Pétain appealed to Joan of Arc, burned by the perfidious English, François Duvalier's regime appealed to Boukmann, disdained by the haughty Mulattoes" (298). Other elements of the story as it developed over the course of the nineteenth century have, since that time, gained new emphasis, in line with our revised "knowledge" of history and increasing awareness of the ways in which subaltern voices have been silenced in and by the past: for instance, it is now a commonplace in Haitian historiography to place great emphasis on the "fact" (first asserted in 1818) that the ceremony was presided over not just by Boukmann but by a (presumably vodou) priestess (e.g., Renda 43). The absence of this (invented?) priestess in both Dalmas's and James's accounts is thus yet another sign of their unexpected post/colonial complicity, their indebtedness to a decidedly masculinist vision of the world.

Although Hoffmann himself seems serenely unconcerned about the possibility that the inaugural moment of the Haitian Revolution might be nothing more than a "myth," one that has been "manipulated by a people intent on founding their identity" (301), as well as by postcolonial critics intent on helping us "know" how colonialism was defeated in the past and how, in its modern but equally vicious neo-colonial avatars it might be defeated in the future, his claims have been—predictably enough—greeted with outrage in many quarters. When Hoffmann first presented his argument, he was, for instance, roundly taken to task by a preeminent Haitian novelist, Jean Métellus, who accused him of the historical equivalent of blasphemy. But blasphemous or not, is his argument correct?

No doubt the most considered and historically responsible attempt at providing an answer to this question was made very soon after Hoffmann launched his argument by one of the foremost historians of the Haitian Revolution, David Geggus. In an article published in 1991 (and recently included, with slight—but, as we will see, significant—revisions, in his *Haitian Revolutionary Studies* [2002]), weighing up all the documentary evidence, Geggus confirmed that the ceremony "is not mentioned in any surviving contemporary manuscript source," and that Dalmas's 1814 text is "by far the earliest" of the handful of published accounts that "*apparently* derive from eyewitness testimony" ("Bois Caïman" 42; my italics). While very aware that "much of what has been written about [the ceremony] is unreliable" (42), Geggus cautiously concluded—basing his claim on the same handful of "credible sources" as Hoffmann (though backed up by a stunning array of contextualizing references to archival and published material from the revolutionary era)—that "taken together, I think these sources prove that a voodoo ceremony involving the sacrifice of a pig did take place in the Bois Caïman shortly before the insurrection" (43). At the same time as he argued for the reality of what Hoffmann claimed was simply "invented," though, Geggus also made a point of noting that "the details of what happened at Bois Caïman ... remain elusive, beyond the fact that a pig was sacrificed by a priestess in some sort of religious ceremony in preparation for war" (50). Beyond that "fact," any other details about the ceremony should, Geggus asserted, be greeted with scepticism. As he noted,

> the significance of the Bois Caïman has been overstated because it is usually confused with the earlier meeting on the Lenormand de Mézy plantation [on 14 August, for which there is much better documentary evidence]. All the evidence suggests that, as regards the organization of the 1791 insurrection, the Lenormand meeting was the more important. Even the prayer of Boukman, if authentic, was evidently spoken there and not at Bois Caïman [on 21 August, the day Geggus believes the vodou ceremony happened, if it indeed happened]. (52)

As the republication of the article in *Haitian Revolutionary Studies* testifies, Geggus stands by his well-documented conclusions and I, for one, am firmly convinced by his argument, just as I am by Joan Dayan's assertion that, even if the ceremony never took place, "what matters is how necessary the story remains to Haitians who continue to construct their identity not only by turning to the revolution of 1791 but by seeking its origins in a service quite possibly imagined by those [i.e., Dalmas] who disdain it" (29).

It is worth noting, however, that Geggus's argument has, over the course of the last decade, changed in at least a couple of minor respects. On the basis of further research, notably, he has come to the conclusion that the ceremony almost certainly did not take place in "the thick forests of the Morne Rouge" (as most historians, like James, have argued) but, rather, precisely where Dalmas said it took place, on the Choiseul plantation in the plains near a swamp called the Lagon à Cayman. "It does not seem that a place called Bois Caïman has ever existed" (*Haitian* 86), Geggus states in the revised version of the article; for this reason he has had to translate his original claim—"I think these sources prove that a voodoo ceremony involving the sacrifice of a pig did take place in the Bois Caïman shortly before the insurrection"—into something distinctly (un)like it—"I think these sources prove that a vodou ceremony involving the sacrifice of a pig did take place shortly before the great insurrection" (*Haitian* 82). Furthermore, notwithstanding the growing insistence on the part of certain scholars as to the important role of a vodou priestess in the ceremony, Geggus has elided her presence in his own revised representation of the "facts": his earlier assertion regarding "the fact that a pig was sacrificed by a priestess in some sort of religious ceremony" has been translated into the far less assertive claim that all details remain elusive "beyond the fact that a pig was sacrificed in some sort of ceremony in preparation for war" (*Haitian* 90).

What Hoffmann's argument and Geggus's extremely cautious counterargument force us to consider in very dramatic terms, then, is the dilemma that confronts each and every one of us who attempts to know the past: the massive uncertainty surrounding the Bois Caïman ceremony suggests that our "knowledge" of the past is always in one way or another *questionable*. The "facts" come to us filtered through language, through memories that have been transcribed into words that can only represent what may or may not ever have been present. To emphasize this banal, but also radically disruptive, point is not to write the past off as simply invented, but to assert that this past—as an object of study, to be analyzed, deplored, or celebrated—must always be approached with caution, with a recognition of the extent to which the "facts" are subject to error, inseparable from the fictions through which we cannot help telling them. To return to our point of departure in this section, it is this inseparability of fact and fiction to which the incipiently meta-fictional moments in Hugo's novel alert us, in a necessarily duplicitous manner (as when its seemingly authoritative footnotes are seemingly de-authorized); what we can learn from such moments is that we must be cautious with regard to a history about which we cannot help speaking authoritatively. The manifestly (to us) false colonial memory of the Haitian Revolution to which *Bug-Jargal* gives expression and the ways in which this memory is itself falsified by the meta-fictional play of Hugo's novel vividly alert us to our own distorted relation to a past that we (il)legitimately seek to remember, be it for purposes of condemnation or celebration.

To retain a sense of the extent to which myth and fiction imaginatively and inventively shape and make sense of an (un)knowable past is the imperative that can be drawn from the contemporary debates about the Bois Caïman ceremony. Hugo's *Bug-Jargal* forces this imperative upon us: both because it is so visibly entrenched in colonial myths and fictions that bear no relation to *our* postcolonial understanding of reality, and because it has (or at the very least, in my reading appears to have) the self-conscious strength—the strength that underpins all works of what we call "great literature"—to stretch the boundaries of the myth upon which it is erroneously founded. It is this strength that is especially required at those points in history when the will to commemorate a fixed, consecrated past threatens to prevail. Correct or not, Hoffmann's "blasphemous" argument provided a useful counter-balance to the bicentenary celebrations of the 1791 slave revolt. My own double-edged argument here in this Introduction about the differing relations of language and history, about the need to (un)know the past, has been in great part motivated by the hope that it will provide an equally useful counter-balance to the commemorative logic that makes possible such events as the bicentenary celebrations of the birth of Hugo in 1802 and of the black republic of Haiti in 1804.

Two years ago the Hugo bicentenary was celebrated in grandiose fashion in France, with the publication of a slough of books by and about this "man-ocean" (to cite the title of the 2002 exhibition that was devoted to him at the new Bibliothèque nationale)—so named because, in the inflated words of the exhibition catalogue, "only the ocean measures up to the amplitude, the polymorphism, the permanence of Hugo's oeuvre." Needless to say, *Bug-Jargal*, that embarrassing colonial novel produced in Hugo's Jacobite youth, had little part to play during a bicentenary year devoted to celebrating his "genius": its all too apparent lack of ethical amplitude, stylistic polymorphism, and ideological permanence rendered it of little use to the Hugo industry in France, intent on diving into the ocean of this great French genius rather than wandering through the desert of an "immature" novel that puts this "genius" into question on both ideological and stylistic grounds. Not surprisingly, unlike so much of Hugo's oeuvre, *Bug-Jargal* was not deemed worthy of a bicentenary edition.

And in this year of 2004, the independence of Haiti will have been celebrated, no doubt with the same commemorative fervour as the bicentenary of Hugo's birth, though doubtless with less governmental sponsorship and fewer marketing opportunities. But while celebrating what is unquestionably one of the most important events in human history, we must nonetheless ask the same difficult questions I have been posing here as to what we know, and what we are commemorating, when we speak of the "independence" of a country that has suffered through two centuries of neo-colonial domination and self-inflicted authoritarian regimes that have sucked it dry and left it one of the poorest nations in what used to be known as the Third World—a world that can be seductively represented and translated anew as "postcolonial," but only if one brackets out the all too likely possibility that we are, in Aijaz Ahmad's words, living "in the moment of imperialism's greatest triumph in its history" (65). To commemorate the past, in our twenty-first century post/colonial circumstances, is inevitably to smooth over and commodify that past, to betray its dizzying complexity through an official memorialization that makes sense of and consecrates it, binding the past to the certainty of historical dates and "facts" that become the pedagogic tools enabling us, compelling us, to value the artistic genius of "Victor Hugo" or the ethico-political significance of the independence of "Haiti." The lesson of *Bug-Jargal*, as I have attempted to represent it in the theoretical portions of this Introduction, may well be that there is something besides these official histories and these predictable lessons that remains to be (un)known about Hugo and about Haiti: something that can only be (un)known through ambiguous words that can never simply accredit but also must disavow the linear vision of time upon which the transparent sense made by bicentenary commemorations depends, contesting the historical clarity such commemorations assume and that alone allows us to (believe that we) know the past. That we can and must (un)know this past is the unsettling lesson that can be gleaned from Hugo's reactionary novel about revolutionary Saint Domingue—a novel that still stands, despite and because of its failure to correspond to what we "know" about Victor Hugo's "genius" and the Haitian Revolution's foundational significance to the doubtfully post-colonial world in which we all live, as an essential contribution to our (mis)understanding of both.

Victor Hugo: A Brief Chronology

1797   15 November: Marriage of Léopold Hugo (b. 1773) and
        Sophie Trébuchet (b. 1772); divorced in 1818
1802   26 February: Victor Hugo born in Besançon, the youngest of
        three brothers (Abel: b. 1798; Eugène: b. 1800)
1804   1 January: Declaration of Haitian Independence
1815   June: Final defeat of Napoleon; restoration of the Bourbon
        monarchy under Louis XVIII
1819   April: "Bug-Jargal" completed (according to date on manuscript)
1820   March: Receives first royal stipend for his poetry
        May-June: Publishes "Bug-Jargal" in *Le Conservateur littéraire*
        (journal edited by Hugo and his brothers from December 1819
        to March 1821)
1821   27 June: Death of his mother Sophie
1822   June: Publishes his first collection of poetry, *Odes et Poésies
        diverses*
        12 October: Marries Adèle Foucher (b. 1803)
1823   January: *Odes* (2nd edition)
        February: Publishes his first novel, *Han d'Islande* (*Han of Iceland*)
        June: Hugo's brother Eugène interned in Charenton asylum
        July: Birth of first child, Léopold (d. 1823); contributes article
        on Walter Scott to *La Muse française* (Appendix C1)
1824   March: Publishes *Nouvelles Odes* (with Preface: Appendix C2)
        August: Birth of second child, Léopoldine (d. 1843)
1825   17 April: Franco-Haitian Accord confirms Haiti's indepen-
        dence from France
        July: Attends coronation of Charles X
1826   30 January: Publishes *Bug-Jargal*
        November: Birth of third child, Charles (d. 1871); publishes
        Odes et Ballades
1827   December: Publishes the play *Cromwell* (its influential preface
        would serve as a manifesto for French Romanticism)
1828   29 January: Death of his father Léopold
        August: Publishes definitive version of *Odes et Ballades*
        October: Birth of fourth child, François-Victor (d. 1873)
1829   January: Publishes *Les Orientales* (poetry)
        February: Publishes *Le Dernier Jour d'un condamné* (novel; *Last
        Day of a Condemned Man*)

July: Royal censor prevents his play *Marion de Lorme* (publ. 1831) from being staged at the Comédie-Française

1830 25 February: His play *Hernani* is staged (the "battle of *Hernani*" at the Comédie-Française becomes a landmark in the struggle between classicism and romanticism)

27-29 July: The July Revolution; France becomes constitutional monarchy under Louis-Philippe

August: Birth of last child, Adèle (interned in asylum 1872; d. 1915)

1831 March: Publishes *Notre-Dame de Paris* (novel)

November: Publishes *Les Feuilles d'automne* (poetry)

1832 December: Publishes *Le Roi s'amuse* (play)

1833 January: Meets actress and life-long companion Juliette Drouet (b. 1806)

February: Publishes *Lucrèce Borgia* (play)

November: Publishes *Marie Tudor* (play)

1834 March: Publishes *Littérature et philosophie mêlées* (collected essays)

September: Publishes *Claude Gueux* (anti-capital punishment narrative)

1835 May: Publishes *Angelo, tyran de Padoue* (play)

October: Publishes *Les Chants du crépuscule* (poetry)

1837 20 February: Death of brother Eugène in Charenton asylum

June: Publishes *Les Voix intérieures* (poetry)

1838 November: Publishes *Ruy Blas* (play)

1840 May: Publishes *Les Rayons et les Ombres* (poetry)

1841 7 January: Elected to the Académie française

1842 January: Publishes *Le Rhin* (travelogue)

1843 March: Publishes *Les Burgraves* (its lack of success causes Hugo to stop writing plays)

1845 13 April: Named *Pair de France* (House of Lords)

1848 22-24 February: 1848 Revolution (creation of the Second Republic)

4 June: Elected to the Constituent Assembly (sits with conservatives)

1849 13 May: Elected to the Legislative Assembly (gradually moves toward left)

1851 2–11 December: Organizes resistance against Louis-Napoléon's *coup d'état*

11 December: Leaves France for Brussels (will spend next nineteen years in exile)

1852   August: Publishes *Napoléon-le-Petit* (political essay); moves to the Channel Island of Jersey

1853   November: Publishes *Les Châtiments* (poetry)

1855   8 February: Death of brother Abel
31 October: Expelled from Jersey; settles in neighbouring Guernsey

1856   April: Publishes *Les Contemplations* (poetry)

1859   September: Publishes first series of *La Légende des siècles* (poetry); subsequent series published in 1877, 1883
2 December: Publishes anti-slavery letter deploring the execution of John Brown ("There is something more terrifying than Cain killing Abel: namely, Washington killing Spartacus")

1862   March-June: Publishes *Les Misérables* (novel)

1864   April: Publishes *William Shakespeare* (literary criticism)

1865   October: Publishes *Chansons des rues et des bois* (poetry)

1866   March: Publishes *Les Travailleurs de la mer* (novel; *Toilers of the Sea*)

1868   27 August: Death of his wife Adèle

1869   April-May: Publishes *L'Homme qui rit* (novel; *The Man Who Laughs*)

1870   5 September: Returns to France after Napoleon III deposed and the Third Republic proclaimed

1871   8 February: Elected deputy to Constituent Assembly for Paris (sits on the left; resigns 8 March)

1872   April: Publishes *L'Année terrible* (poetry)

1874   February: Publishes *Quatre-vingt treize* (last novel; *Ninety-Three*)

1876   30 January: Elected Senator

1877   May: Publishes *L'Art d'être grand-père* (poetry)

1878   27 June: Suffers cerebral congestion; after this date, publishes little new material, although many books of unpublished writings come out in the years immediately preceding and following upon his death
October-March: Publishes *Histoire d'un crime* (account of Louis-Napoléon's *coup d'état* written in 1852)

1883   11 May: Death of Juliette Drouet

1885   22 May: Dies
1 June: State funeral; is buried in Pantheon

A Note on the Text

Published anonymously, the first edition of *Bug-Jargal* came out in one volume with Urbain Canel on 30 January 1826. The 1826 edition differs in one important respect from later editions of the novel: it lacks any chapter divisions, progressing from beginning to end with only two breaks (between what would later become Chapters 3 and 4 and between Chapter 58 and the concluding Note). The 1826 edition also features an epigraph by an "unknown author" (Hugo himself), which would eventually be dropped in the 1830s: "C'est le bonheur de vivre / Qui fait la gloire de mourir!" ("In the joy of living / Resides the glory of dying!") In 1829 the novel was republished in three volumes by Charles Gosselin as part of the twenty-seven-year-old Hugo's precociously entitled *Oeuvres complètes*: no changes were made to the actual text, but chapter divisions were introduced so as to make the novel seem longer and thereby justify the multi-volume approach; the chapters of each volume were separately numbered (1-19, 1-18 [equivalent to chapters 20-37], and 1-21 [equivalent to chapters 38-58]). The continuous numbering of chapters from 1 to 58 was introduced in the next edition (the fifth edition in name, but in reality the third), which was published by Eugène Renduel in 1832 as Volume 2 of Hugo's collected novels, with the slightly revised title *Bug-Jargal. 1791.* (For a close reading of this title change, see the opening section of the Introduction.) Aside from the insertion of chapter breaks between 1826 and 1832, there are no substantive differences between the first edition of 1826 and other editions of the novel published during Hugo's lifetime.

The short story "Bug-Jargal" (Appendix A) on which Hugo based his novel was most probably written in April 1819. The story came out in 1820 in the *Conservateur littéraire*, a journal published by Hugo and his two brothers from December 1819 to March 1821; it was published in five instalments (May 6, 20; June 3, 10, 17). The manuscript of the novel, which is held at the Bibliothèque nationale de France, consists of the original 21-page short story manuscript, with revisions from 1825 written in the margins, as well as 68 pages of new intercalated material. The most recent edition of Hugo's complete works in France, edited by Jacques Seebacher and Guy Rosa (1985-90; republished 2002), features a version of both Hugo's novel and the short story that, in terms of such minutiae as paragraph breaks and punctuation, occasionally differs from the standard versions reproduced in twentieth-century paperback editions of the text and in Jean Massin's eighteen-volume edition of the *Oeuvres complètes* (cited as

OC). Since Seebacher and Rosa provide no explanation for these changes, I have chosen to use the standard version as the basis for my translations here (OC 2.573-704 for the novel; 1.349-79 for the short story).

I have provided editorial notes for Hugo's novel as well as for the two articles of his included in Appendix C; these have been numbered and endnoted in the usual way, and are to be distinguished from Hugo's own footnotes, which are marked by asterisks and daggers. (On the role played by the sixty-plus authorial notes in *Bug-Jargal*, see the final section of the Introduction.) In the few cases where it was necessary to gloss material in Hugo's footnotes, my own note can be found, in square brackets, immediately following his. For the other appendix materials in this edition, although I have retained many of the authors' own footnotes, I did not deem it necessary to include editorial notes of my own, limiting myself where necessary to inserting a brief gloss, in square brackets, in the body of the text.

BUG-JARGAL,

PAR L'AUTEUR

DE

HAN D'ISLANDE.

——

.... C'est le bonheur de vivre
Qui fait la gloire de mourir !
AUTEUR INCONNU.

Paris,

URBAIN CANEL, LIBRAIRE,
RUE SAINT-GERMAIN-DES-PRÈS, N. 9.
1826.

Title-page of the original 1826 edition of *Bug-Jargal*

Preface (1826)

The episode you are about to read, the content of which was taken from the Saint Domingue slave revolt in 1791, has a circumstantial look to it that would in itself have been enough to prevent the author from publishing it. However, a preliminary sketch of this opuscule having already been printed and distributed in a limited number of copies in 1820, at a time when the politics of the day were but little occupied with Haiti, it stands to reason that if the subject matter treated therein has acquired a new degree of interest since that time this is in no way the author's fault. Events have accommodated themselves to the book, not the book to events.

Be that as it may, the author had no plans for rescuing this work from the half-light, so to speak, in which it was buried; however, informed that a bookseller in the capital intended to reprint his anonymous sketch, he thought it best to forestall this reprint by bringing his story out in a revised, and one might even say reworked, form—a precaution that saves the author and his self-respect a spot of bother, and the aforementioned bookseller a bad speculation.

Having learned of the upcoming publication of this episode, several distinguished people who either as colonists or as functionaries found themselves mixed up in Saint Domingue's troubles have, on their own initiative, been good enough to pass along to the author materials that are all the more precious because scarcely any of them have ever been published. The author wishes to express here his warmest gratitude to them for these documents, which have been uncommonly useful to him in correcting those details in the tale of Captain d'Auverney that were incomplete with regard to local colour and questionable in relation to historical truth.

Finally, he must also inform readers that the story of *Bug-Jargal* is only a fragment of a more extensive piece of work, which was to have been entitled *Tales under the Tent*. The author's idea was to have several French officers during the revolutionary wars agree to pass the long hours of their bivouac by telling, each in turn, the tale of one of their adventures. The episode being published here was part of that series of narratives; it can be detached from it without any inconvenience to the reader and, besides, the larger work of which it was to have been a part is not finished, will never be finished, and is not worth the trouble of finishing.

Preface (1832)

In 1818, the author of this book was sixteen years old; he made a wager that he would write an entire volume in fifteen days. He produced *Bug-Jargal*. Sixteen ... the age when one wagers on anything and improvises on whatever is at hand.

This book was thus written two years before *Han of Iceland*. And even though, seven years later, in 1825, the author in large part reshaped and rewrote it, that does not make it any less, by virtue both of its content and many of its details, the author's first work.

He begs his readers' pardon for occupying them with details of such little importance, but he thought that the small number of people who enjoy classing the writings of a poet—no matter how obscure he might be—according to their stature and their order of birth would not take it amiss of him for having provided them with the age of *Bug-Jargal*. As for himself, what he set out to do here, like those travellers who turn round in the middle of their journey to see if they can still discern in the misty folds of the horizon the place from which they set out, was cast a reminiscent look back at that time of serenity, boldness, and confidence when he grappled face to face with such an immense topic: the revolt of the Saint Domingue blacks in 1791, a struggle of giants, three worlds having a stake in the matter—Europe and Africa as the combatants, America as the field of battle.

24 March 1832

WHEN CAPTAIN Leopold d'Auverney's turn came up, he looked surprised and admitted to the assembled gentlemen that he really knew of no event in his life which would merit their attention.

"And yet, Captain," Lieutenant Henry said to him, "they say you've travelled, seen the world. Haven't you been to the Antilles, Africa and Italy, Spain?... Captain, look, it's your lame dog!"

Startled, d'Auverney dropped his cigar and turned abruptly toward the entrance of the tent where an enormous dog was limping toward him as quickly as it could.

On its way over, the dog trampled on the cigar, not that the captain took any notice of this.

Licking the captain's feet and rubbing against him with its tail, the dog yelped and gambolled about to the best of its ability, then came and settled down in front of him. Overcome with emotion, the captain mechanically stroked it with his left hand, while with the other he undid the strap of his helmet, repeating from time to time "It's you Rask![1] You're here!" At length, he exclaimed: "But who was it that brought you back?"

"By your leave, my Captain ..."

It had been several minutes now since Sergeant Thaddeus had lifted up the flap of the tent. He had been standing there all that time—his right arm wrapped in his overcoat, tears in his eyes, gazing in silence at the concluding act of this odyssey. Finally, he ventured those words: "By your leave, my Captain ..." D'Auverney looked up.

"Thad, it's you. How the devil were you able to...? Poor dog! I thought he was in the English camp. Where did you end up finding him?"

"God be thanked! As you can see, my Captain, I'm as overjoyed by it as your nephew gets when you make him do his declensions: *cornu*, the horn; *cornu*, of the horn ..."[2]

"But go on, tell me, where did you end up finding him?"

"I did not find him, my Captain. I went out in search of him."

The captain stood up and held out his hand to the sergeant. Although the captain failed to notice it, the sergeant's hand stayed wrapped in his overcoat.

"You see, my Captain, ever since this poor Rask got lost, it was very clear to me—by your leave, if I may be so bold—that you were missing something. Truth to tell, I believe it wouldn't have taken much for old Thad to start crying like a child that evening when he didn't show up as usual to share my ration of bread. But no, God be thanked, I've only cried twice in my life. The first time, when ... The day that ..." And the sergeant gave his master an anxious look. "The second time, when that rascal Balthazar, corporal in the seventh demi-brigade, got it into his head that he'd make me peel a bunch of onions."

Henry burst out laughing. "It seems to me, Thaddeus, that you haven't said what made you cry for the first time."

"No doubt, old friend, it was when you received the accolade from La Tour d'Auvergne, First Grenadier of France?"[3] the captain asked affectionately, while continuing to stroke the dog.

"No, my Captain. If Sergeant Thaddeus cried, it could only have been, you will have to admit, on the day when he gave the order to open fire on Bug-Jargal, otherwise known as Pierrot."

D'Auverney's entire face clouded over. He rushed over to the sergeant and made to squeeze his hand, but despite such an excess of honour old Thaddeus kept it hidden under his greatcoat.

"Yes, my Captain," Thaddeus continued, stepping back a few paces, while d'Auverney's distraught eyes tracked his every move. "Yes, that time I cried. He was well and truly worth it, that's for certain! He was black, it's true, but gunpowder is also black, and ... and ..."

The worthy sergeant would have liked to bring his bizarre comparison to an honourable close. Perhaps there was something about the comparison that attracted him but it was in vain that he tried to express it. After several times attacking his idea from all sides, like the general of an army who fails to take possession of a fortified town he abruptly lifted the siege and, not noticing the smiles of the young officers who were listening to him, carried on.

"Say now, my Captain, do you remember that poor negro? When he got there all out of breath, at the very same time as his ten comrades? There was no getting around it, we'd had to tie them up. I was the one giving the orders. And then, when he himself went and untied them and took their place even though they didn't want him to? But there was no stopping him. Oh, he was a man, he was! A real rock of Gibraltar. And then, my Captain, when he was standing there, as stiff-backed as if he were about to take his turn at a dance, and his dog, the very same Rask who's here, who understood what they were going to do to him, and who leapt at my throat ..."

"As a rule, Thad," the captain interrupted, "you wouldn't let this part of your tale go by without giving Rask a stroke or two. See the way he's looking at you."

"Right you are," said Thaddeus, embarrassed. "He's looking at me, poor Rask, but ... Old Malagrida once told me that if you stroke anything with the left hand it brings misfortune."

"And why not the right hand?" d'Auverney asked with surprise, noticing for the first time that Thad's hand was wrapped in the overcoat and that his face was all pale.

The sergeant seemed to grow even more uneasy.

"By your leave, my Captain, the fact is ... You already have a lame dog. I fear you will end up with a one-armed sergeant as well."

The captain sprang out of his seat.

"What? How in the...? Thad, old man, what are you saying? One-armed? Let's see your arm ... One-armed, good God!"

D'Auverney was trembling. The sergeant slowly peeled off his coat, revealing to his chief officer an arm wrapped in a bloodied handkerchief.

"My God!" the captain murmured, as he cautiously lifted up the cloth. "But, my friend, what's the meaning of this...?"

"Oh, it is a simple enough matter. I told you I had seen how distressed you were since those confounded Englishmen robbed us of that fine dog of yours, poor Rask, the mastiff of Bug ... That was all it took. Today I resolved to get him back, even if it cost me my life, so that at least I could eat with a hearty appetite this evening. That's why, after telling your man Mathelet to give your full-dress uniform a good brushing for tomorrow's battle, I slipped away from the camp, without a peep, armed with only my sabre. I cut through the hedges so as to get to the English camp sooner. I hadn't even reached the first line of trenches when, by your leave, my Captain, in a little wood to the left I saw a great mob of redcoats. I edged forward to get a sense of what was going on. They didn't notice me, and that gave me a chance to locate Rask. There he was in their midst, leashed to a tree, while two fine gentlemen, naked as heathens down to here, were going at one another with their fists, cracking blows that made as much noise as the big drum of a demi-brigade. It was two English chaps, if you will, who were fighting a duel for your dog. But now Rask sees me, and he gives such a tug on the rope that it breaks, and in the blink of an eye the rascal's at my heels. As you can imagine, the rest of the pack aren't slow to follow. I shoot into the woods. Rask follows me. Several bullets go whistling by my ears. Rask was barking, but luckily they couldn't hear him because they kept shouting 'French dog! French dog!'[4]—as if your dog weren't a Saint Domingue dog born and bred. No matter. I'm making my way through the thicket, and I was almost clear of it when two redcoats pop up in front of me. My sabre got rid of one of them, and it would have rid me of the other, no doubt, if his pistol hadn't been loaded. You see my right arm ... But no matter! '*French dog*' grabbed hold of his neck, as if they were old acquaintances, and I can assure you they had a hearty embrace ... The Englishman fell, strangled. That devil of a fellow, why did he have to go chasing after me, like some pauper dogging a seminarian! In any case, Thad is back at the camp, and Rask as well. My only regret is that the good Lord did not choose to send this my way at tomorrow's battle instead. Anyway, there you have it!"

The old sergeant's features had turned gloomy at the thought of not having received his wound in battle.

"Thaddeus!..." the captain burst out in an irritated tone. Then he added, more gently: "How can you have been so mad as to risk yourself like that—and for a dog?"

"It was not for a dog, my Captain, it was for Rask."

D'Auverney's expression softened completely. The sergeant continued: "For Rask, the mastiff of Bug ..."

"Enough, Thad! Enough of that, my friend," the captain appealed, placing his hand over his eyes. "Let's go," he added after a brief silence. "Lean on me, and come along to the ambulance wagon."

After putting up a respectful resistance, Thaddeus obeyed. The dog, who during this scene had joyfully gnawed its way through a good half of its master's fine bearskin, got up and followed the two of them out.

2

THIS EPISODE had caught the attention of the high-spirited story-tellers, keenly arousing their curiosity.

Captain Leopold d'Auverney was one of those men who, no matter on what rung they might have been placed by the vagaries of nature or the shifting course of society, always inspire a certain respect mingled with interest. Granted, at first sight there was perhaps nothing striking about him: he was cold-mannered, and had a look of complete indifference. The sun of the tropics might have darkened his face, but it had not given him that animation of gesture and speech which, in creoles,[5] is accompanied by an often graceful nonchalance. D'Auverney spoke little, rarely listened, and was always ready for action. Ever the first on his horse and the last under the tent, he seemed to be trying to exhaust his body as a way of distracting himself from his thoughts. These thoughts, the bleak severity of which was carved in the premature lines on his brow, were not the kind that one disposes of by communicating them to someone else, and nor were they the kind that, in a casual conversation, mix readily with other people's ideas. Leopold d'Auverney, whose exertions in the war could not break his body, appeared to experience an intolerable weariness when it came to what we call the struggles of the spirit. He avoided discussions in the same way that he sought out battles. If he sometimes let himself get dragged into debate, he would utter three or four remarks full of good sense and solid reasoning—but then, on the point of convincing his adversary, he would pull up. "What's the use?" he would say, and go off in search of his commanding officer to see whether there was anything that needed doing in the lull before the charge or the assault.

His comrades excused his cold, reserved, and taciturn habits, because whenever he was called upon they found him to be brave, good, and of a kindly disposition. At the risk of his own life, he had saved the lives of several among them, and everybody knew that, if he rarely opened his mouth, his purse at any rate was never closed. He was well liked in the army, and he was even forgiven for having become almost an object of veneration.

And yet he was young. You would have said he was thirty, but he still had a long way to go before reaching that age. Although he had been fighting in the republican ranks for some time now, nothing was known about his adventures. The only one who, besides Rask, could extract any strong show of affection from him—old Sergeant Thaddeus, who had entered the corps with him and never left his side—sometimes provided vague accounts of a few incidents from his life. It was known that d'Auverney had experienced great adversity in America: that, having gotten married in Saint Domingue, he had lost his wife and his entire family during the massacres which marked the revolution's invasive arrival in that magnificent colony. At that time in our history, calamities of this type were so common that there had formed a sort of general fund of pity concerning them, which everybody drew on or contributed to. People thus felt sorry for Captain d'Auverney, less for the losses he had suffered than for the way in which they made him suffer. For the fact is that, underneath his glacial indifference, you could see the incurable wound inside him and the tremors it provoked.

As soon as a battle began, his face would again take on a calm appearance. In his actions, he displayed as much fearlessness as if he had wanted to become a general, and as much modesty after the victory as if he had wanted nothing more than to be a private. His comrades, seeing his disdain for honours and promotions, could not understand why, before every battle, he had the look of someone who was hoping for something; they had no clue that d'Auverney, among all the chance circumstances of war, desired only death.

At one point, the people's representatives assigned to the army named him to the post of battlefield brigade commander. He refused it, on the grounds that separating from the company would have meant having to leave Sergeant Thaddeus behind. Several days after that, he volunteered to lead a risky expedition and, against all expectation and contrary to his own hopes, he returned from it alive. At the time, he was heard expressing his regret at not having accepted the promotion: "Since the enemy's cannon always spares me," he would say, "perhaps the guillotine, which strikes down all those who rise to the top, might have favoured me with its attention."

3

SUCH WAS the man concerning whom, once he had left the tent, the following conversation started up.

"I'd wager ..." Lieutenant Henry exclaimed, as he wiped away a large patch of mud that the dog, on its way over, had deposited on his red boot, "I'd wager that the captain wouldn't exchange his dog's broken paw for those ten hampers of Madeira we laid eyes on in the general's wagon the other day."

"Hush, now! That would be a bad transaction," Paschal the aide-de-camp said merrily. "The hampers are empty at present, and I should know. Moreover," he added with a serious look, "you have to admit, Lieutenant, that thirty opened bottles are most certainly not worth that poor dog's paw. After all, that paw has its uses: you could turn it into a bell-handle."

At the solemn tone with which the aide-de-camp uttered these last words, the assembled company broke out in laughter. Alfred, the young officer of the Basque hussars, was the only one not to have laughed. He had a peeved look on his face:

"I fail to see, gentlemen, any reason for mockery with regard to what has just taken place. If anything, this dog and this sergeant, whom I have always seen by d'Auverney's side for as long as I have known him, seem to me capable of eliciting a certain interest. This scene, when all is said and done ..."

Paschal, nettled both by Alfred's peevishness and the other soldiers' good spirits, interrupted him:

"This scene is very sentimental. Come now! A rescued dog and a broken arm!"

"Captain Paschal, you're mistaken," said Henry, throwing the bottle that he had just emptied out of the tent. "This Bug, otherwise known as Pierrot, piques my curiosity in a singular fashion."

Paschal, on the point of getting angry, calmed down when he saw that his glass, rather than being empty as he had thought, was full. D'Auverney returned. He went back to his place and sat down without uttering a word, lost in thought but with a calmer look on his face. So preoccupied did he appear that he heard nothing of what was being said around him. Rask, who had followed him, lay down at his feet and watched him anxiously.

"Your glass, Captain d'Auverney. Have a try of this."

"Oh! Thank God," said the captain, thinking that he was answering Paschal's question, "the wound isn't dangerous, the arm isn't broken."

The involuntary respect that the captain inspired in all his comrades-in-arms was the only thing that kept Henry from bursting out in laughter.

"Since you're no longer as worried about Thaddeus," he said, "and since we've each agreed to recount one of our adventures so as to make the time go by during this night's bivouac, I hope, my dear friend, that you'll be so good as to fulfil your part of the bargain by telling us the story of your lame dog and of Bug ... whatever, otherwise known as Pierrot, that real rock of Gibraltar!"

To this question, offered in a tone that was half-serious and half-joking, d'Auverney would have made no reply had everybody else not joined in with the same request as the lieutenant.

Finally, he yielded to their appeals.

"I'll grant your wish, gentlemen, but don't expect anything more than the recital of an extremely simple anecdote, in which I play only a very secondary role. If the affection that exists between Thaddeus, Rask, and myself has made you hope for something extraordinary, I must warn you that you'll be disappointed. So, to begin ..."

Everyone fell silent. Paschal emptied his brandy flask with one swig, and Henry wrapped himself in the half-gnawed bearskin to keep away the chill of the night, while Alfred left off humming the Galician tune "*Mata-perros*."[6]

D'Auverney remained lost in thought for a moment, as if conjuring up in his memory events long since displaced by others. At length, he began to speak, slowly, almost in a whisper and with frequent pauses.

4

"ALTHOUGH BORN in France, I was sent at an early age to Saint Domingue to stay with one of my uncles, a very rich colonist whose daughter I was intended to marry.

My uncle's settlements were near Fort Galifet,[7] and his plantations occupied the greater part of the Acul plains.

This ill-fated location, the details of which will no doubt seem of little interest to you, was one of the primary causes of the disasters and total ruin that befell my family.

Eight hundred negroes worked the immense domains of my uncle. I will admit to you that the sad condition of these slaves was made even worse by the insensitiveness of their master. My uncle was one of those planters, fortunately rather limited in number, whose heart had been hardened by a longstanding habit of absolute despotism. Accustomed to seeing himself obeyed at the first blink of an eye, he would punish the slightest hesitation on a slave's part with the greatest severity, and often the intercession of his children served only to heighten his anger. So, most of the time we could do no more than relieve in secret the ill-usage we could not prevent."

"What? There's some high-sounding talk for you!" said Henry under his breath, leaning over to the person beside him. "I do hope the captain won't let the misfortunes of the *ci-devant* 'blacks'[8] pass by without contributing some nice little speech on the duties of humanity, *et cetera*. That's the very least we'd have been in for at the Massiac Club."*

---

* Our readers have no doubt forgotten that the *Massiac* Club of which Lieutenant Henry speaks was an association of *negrophiles*. This club, formed in Paris at the beginning of the revolution, had instigated most of the insurrections that broke out in the colonies around that time.

One might also be astonished at the rather daringly flippant manner in which the young lieutenant pokes fun at the *philanthropists*, who still held the reins of power during this period thanks to the executioner's good offices. But it must be kept in mind that before, during, and after the Terror, freedom of thought and of speech had taken refuge in the military camps. From time to time this noble privilege cost some general his head, but it is what absolves from all reproach the splendid glory of these soldiers, whom the Convention's inquisitors used to refer to as "the 'lordly gentlemen' of the Rhine army." [Editor's note: Far from being an association of negrophiles along the lines of the Amis des Noirs (formed in 1788), the Massiac Club (named after the Paris residence of the Marquis de Massiac, where its meetings were held) was made up of pro-slavery Saint Domingue planters. Founded on 20 August 1789 it played an influential role in retarding colonial reforms over the next several years. Jean-Philippe Garran, one of Hugo's probable sources on Saint Domingue, noted the "counter-revolutionary principles of this Club" (2.204), identifying it as "one of the principal causes of the disasters that befell the colonies by virtue of its opposition to everything that had the stamp of liberty" (1.54). The role of the Massiac Club would still have been common knowledge in the 1820s, so one cannot help thinking that Hugo is here challenging the reader to recognize the erroneousness of his apparently authoritative footnote.]

"I thank you, Henry, for saving me from ridicule," said d'Auverney icily, having overheard him.

He resumed:

"Among all these slaves, only one had found favour with my uncle: a Spanish dwarf, a griffe* in colour, given to him as a toy monkey of sorts by Lord Effingham, Governor of Jamaica.[9] Having resided for a long time in Brazil, my uncle had acquired the habits of Portuguese ostentation and liked to surround himself with trappings that befitted his wealth. Numerous slaves, trained for service like European domestics, gave his household a

---

* A precise explanation will perhaps be necessary for understanding this word. Monsieur Moreau de Saint-Méry, building on Franklin's system, has classified into generic types the different hues displayed by the mixtures of the coloured population. [Editor's note: Médéric-Louis-Elie Moreau de Saint-Méry (1750-1819). Born in Martinique, he trained as a lawyer in Paris, then settled in Saint Domingue. As deputy for Martinique, he served in the Constituent Assembly but was forced to leave France in 1793 for the United States. During his five years in Philadelphia, he published the work for which he is now best remembered, *Description ... de la partie française de l'isle Saint-Domingue* (1797). An encyclopedic font of information on colonial Saint Domingue, the book also contains the systematic account of "the different hues displayed by the mixtures of the coloured population" referred to in Hugo's footnote (for Hugo's plagiarism of Lacroix's synopsis of Moreau, see Appendix E.2a). Moreau would return to France to serve under Napoleon; after the deterioration of his relations with the Emperor, he lived out the last decade of his life in relative obscurity. As for Benjamin Franklin's role in the development of racial taxonomies, none of the Franklin scholars I consulted have been able to trace this reference; Franklin was, however, a correspondent with the Cercle des Philadelphes, a learned society in Saint Domingue that Moreau co-founded.]

He posits that men are made up of a total of one hundred and twenty-eight parts, the parts being white in the case of the whites and black in the case of the blacks.

Starting from this principle, he establishes that how close to or far away from one or the other colour you are depends on your proximity to or distance from the sixty-fourth term, which serves as their proportional mean.

According to this system, any man not in possession of eight full parts white is said to be black.

Moving from this colour toward the white, nine principal stocks can be identified, which have even more varieties between them according to how many or how few parts they retain of one or the other colour. These nine species are the *sacatra*, the *griffe*, the *marabou*, the *mulatto*, the *quadroon*, the *metiff*, the *mameluco*, the *quarteronné*, the *sang-mêlé*.

The *sang-mêlé*, if he keeps on uniting with the white, ends up in a way becoming confused with this colour. However, it is claimed that he always retains on a certain part of the body the ineffaceable trace of his origin.

The *griffe* is the result of five combinations, and can have between twenty-four and thirty-two parts white and ninety-six or one hundred and four parts black. [Editor's note: Although it is by no means certain that Hugo consulted Moreau de Saint-Méry's *Description*, Moreau's portrait of griffes is worth noting here, if only because it highlights an erotic (and olfactory!) dimension that is tellingly absent from Hugo's representation of Habibrah: "The Griffe is so favoured by nature that it is very rare to see one who does not have an agreeable countenance and pleasing features as a whole. He has all the advantages of the mulatto; none of the other combinations generated by colonial mixtures, though, results in progeny so given over to amorous impulses (and this holds equally true of both sexes). Continency in an individual of this shade is a very rare thing indeed—perhaps even unheard of—and, doubtless as a consequence of this irrepressible disposition, the regrets that accompany pleasure are even more bitter when they are procured by this class. It can also be noted that in general Griffes are often liable to offend one's nostrils" (1.94).]

certain seigniorial splendour. So as not to be lacking in any particular, he had transformed Lord Effingham's slave into his *fool*, imitating the feudal princes of old who kept jesters at their courts. It has to be said that the choice was singularly felicitous. The griffe Habibrah (for that was his name) was one of those creatures whose physical configuration is so strange that they would seem like monsters, if it weren't that they made one laugh. This hideous dwarf was thick-set, short, paunchy, and moved about with exceptional rapidity on two thin, spindly legs which, when he sat down, folded up under him like the limbs of a spider. His enormous head, awkwardly squashed between his shoulders and bristling with crinkly reddish wool, was accompanied by two ears so large that his fellow slaves liked to say Habibrah used them to dry his eyes whenever he cried. His face was one long grimace, and it never stayed the same; this bizarre mobility of his features at least gave his ugliness the benefit of variety. My uncle was fond of him on account of his unusual deformity and his unfailing gaiety. Habibrah was his favourite. While the other slaves were brutally overburdened with work, Habibrah had no care other than to trail behind his master carrying a large fan made of bird-of-paradise feathers to drive away gnats and mosquitoes. During meals, he was made to sit on a rush mat at the feet of my uncle, who would always be sure to give him, off his very own plate, some scrap from one of his favourite dishes. Habibrah, in turn, made sure that his gratitude for so many kind acts did not go unnoticed: if he availed himself of his privileges as a jester—his right to do or say anything—it was only in order to entertain his master with a barrage of crazy words and physical contortions, and at the slightest sign from my uncle he'd come running, as agile as a monkey and as submissive as a dog.

I didn't like this slave. There was something too grovelling about his servility, and while there is nothing dishonourable about being a slave, there is something thoroughly degrading about being domesticated. I had a feeling of benevolent pity for those poor negroes I saw working all day with scarcely any clothing to hide their chains, but this deformed clown, this idle slave with his ridiculous outfits—gaudily strewn with ribbons and sprinkled with little bells—inspired in me nothing but contempt. And besides, the dwarf made no use, as a good brother should, of the credit that all his grovelling had built up for him with the owner they had in common. Never once had he begged a pardon from his master, who was so given to handing out punishments. Indeed, he was overheard one day, when he believed himself alone with my uncle, encouraging him to show even more severity toward his unfortunate fellow slaves. And yet these slaves, who ought to have viewed him with distrust and jealousy, did not appear to hate him. He inspired in them a sort of respectful fear which in no way resembled friendship: when they saw him going past their huts with his big pointed bonnet all decorated with bells, on which he had drawn bizarre figures in red ink, they would whisper amongst themselves: 'He's an obi!'[*10]

These details, gentlemen, to which I've just now been drawing your attention, took up very little of my time back then. Entirely wrapped up in the pure emotions of a love that nothing seemed likely to thwart, a love felt and shared since childhood by the woman who was destined for me, I paid only the slightest attention to anything that didn't involve Marie. Accustomed from a most tender age to consider as my future wife she who was already in some ways my sister, there had formed between us a bond of tenderness that you would not even come close to understanding if I were to say that our love was a mixture of fraternal devotion, passionate exaltation, and conjugal trust. Few men have spent their early years more happily than I; few men have felt their souls opening out to life under a lovelier sky, their present happiness and future hope so deliciously harmonized. Surrounded almost from birth with all the gratifications of wealth, with all the privileges of rank in a country where one's colour was enough to confer it; passing my days next to the being who possessed all my love; seeing this love looked upon favourably by our relatives, the only ones who could have blocked it; experiencing all this at an age when the blood is boiling over, in a country where the summer is eternal and nature reveals itself in all its glory: surely that was reason enough to give me a blind faith in my lucky star? Surely that is reason enough to give me the right to say that few men have spent their early years more happily than I?"

The captain paused for a moment, as if he were at a loss for the words with which to describe those memories of happiness. Then he continued, in a tone of deep sadness:

"To be sure, I now also have the right to add that no one will spend his last days more pitiably."

As if he had gained new strength from the sentiment of his own unhappiness, he resumed his story in a steady voice.

---

* A sorcerer.

5

"IN THE MIDST of these illusions and these blind hopes, my twentieth birthday drew near. It was to take place in the month of August 1791, and my uncle had settled upon this as the date for my union with Marie. You can readily understand how the thought of imminent happiness absorbed all my faculties, and how vague my memory must be of the political debates that, by this time, had already been stirring up the colony for two years. So I won't be treating you to stories about the likes of Count de Peynier,[11] or Monsieur de Blanchelande,[12] or that unlucky Colonel de Mauduit, who came to such a tragic end.[13] I won't be portraying the rivalry between the *provincial* assembly of the north[14] and the *colonial* assembly, which took the title of *general* assembly on the grounds that the word *colonial* smacked of slavery.[15] All of these wretched trifles, which at the time threw everyone into convulsions, are of interest now only because of the disasters they produced. For me, if I had any opinions when it came to this mutual jealousy that divided the Cape and Port-au-Prince, they would necessarily have favoured the Cape, it being the district in which we lived, and the provincial assembly, of which my uncle was a member.

Only once did I happen to get caught up in a debate concerning the affairs of the day. It was on the occasion of that disastrous decree of 15 May 1791, whereby the national assembly of France granted the free men of colour the same political rights as the whites.[16] At a ball given by the Governor at the city of the Cape, several young colonists were vehemently arguing over this law which so cruelly wounded the self-esteem—perhaps justified—of the whites. I had yet to intervene in the conversation when I saw a rich planter approaching the group, a person whom the whites only grudgingly admitted into their company and whose equivocal colour raised doubts about his origins. I went directly up to this man, saying to him in a loud voice: 'Move along, monsieur. Things are being said here that would not be to the taste of someone like you, who have *mixed blood* in your veins.' This imputation angered him so much that he challenged me to a duel in which both of us were wounded. It was wrong of me to provoke him, I admit. It is likely, though, that what people refer to as *the prejudice of colour* would not in itself have been enough to drive me to it: for some time now this man had had the audacity to set his sights on my cousin, and when I humiliated him in such an unexpected manner he had just left off dancing with her.

Whatever the case might be, it was in a veritable state of intoxication that I watched the moment draw near when I would possess Marie, and I remained oblivious to the escalating tumult that was bringing everyone else around me to the boiling point. Eyes fixed on my approaching happiness, I didn't notice the grim cloud that was already covering over almost every point of our political horizon—a cloud that, when it burst, would uproot everybody's lives. It's not that anyone at the time, even those quickest to sound the alarm, seriously expected a slave revolt—this class was too greatly despised for it to be feared; but between the whites and the free mulattoes alone there existed enough hatred for the volcano that had been bottled up so long to convulse the entire colony at the dreaded moment when it would rip open.

In the first days of that month of August so eagerly summoned by all my vows a strange incident occurred that tinged my calm hopes with an unexpected anxiety.

6

ON THE BANKS of a lovely river that watered his plantations, my uncle had put up a little pavilion made out of branches. Surrounded by a thick clump of trees, this was where Marie would go every day to drink in those gentle sea breezes that blow steadily over Saint Domingue from morning to evening during the most sweltering months of the year, their coolness rising or falling depending on whether the day is more or less hot.

I made it a point every morning to decorate this retreat with the most beautiful flowers I could find.

One day Marie rushed up to me in a great state of alarm. She had entered her leafy arbour as usual only to find, her surprise mingling with terror, that all the flowers I had scattered there that morning had been torn apart and trampled underfoot. A bouquet of freshly gathered wild marigolds had been placed on the spot where she usually sat. She had not yet recovered from her shock when she heard the sounds of a guitar coming from the thicket that surrounded the pavilion. Then a voice, which wasn't mine, had begun softly to sing to her in what she thought was Spanish. Because of her agitated state, and doubtless also due to a certain virginal modesty, she had understood not a word of it except her name, which was frequently repeated. Then she had made a run for it—

fortunately enough encountering no obstacles along the way during her headlong flight.

On hearing this story, I was beside myself with indignation and jealousy. My first conjectures fell on the free *sang-mêlé* with whom I'd recently had an altercation but, given the state of perplexity in which I found myself, I resolved to do nothing rashly. I reassured my poor Marie, and promised myself I would watch over her constantly until the moment, now near at hand, when I would be entitled to offer her even closer protection.

Presuming rightly that the boldfaced individual whose insolence had so terrified Marie would not limit himself to this first attempt at familiarizing her with what I surmised to be his love, that very evening—after everyone on the plantation had gone to sleep—I lay in wait for him near the main building where my betrothed was resting. Hidden in a thicket of tall sugar cane, armed with my dagger, I waited. I did not wait in vain. Toward the middle of the night, my attention was abruptly roused by a melancholy, solemn prelude which rose up out of the silence, only a few steps away from me. That sound struck me like a blow. It was a guitar, right under Marie's very own window! Furious, brandishing my dagger, I leapt out toward the place where the sounds were coming from, crushing the brittle stalks of the sugar canes in my path. All of a sudden, I felt myself being grabbed and knocked down with a brute force that seemed altogether extraordinary to me. First my dagger was violently torn away from me, and then I saw it glinting above my head. At the same time two fiery eyes sparkled in the darkness, close up against mine. In the shadows, I glimpsed a double row of white teeth, opened wide, spilling out in a rage the words: '*Te tengo! Te tengo!*'*

Even more astonished than alarmed, I struggled in vain against my formidable adversary; the tip of the steel had already dug its way through my clothes when Marie, who had been awakened by the guitar and all the trampling and shouting, suddenly appeared at her window. She recognized my voice, saw the glint of the dagger, and let out a scream of anguish and terror. This harrowing scream seemed to paralyze the hand of my triumphant antagonist. He held back, as if petrified; he let the dagger run indecisively over my chest for a few seconds longer and then, suddenly casting it away, he said, this time in French: 'No! No! She would weep too much!' After these bizarre words, he disappeared into a clump of rushes, and by the time I got back on my feet, bruised by this strange

---

* I've got you! I've got you!

and unequal struggle, not a sound nor a trace was left attesting to his presence or his passing.

It would be extremely difficult for me to put into words what was going through my mind when, having recovered from my initial state of shock, I found myself in the arms of my sweet Marie, for whose sake I had been so unexpectedly spared by the very man who seemed bent on winning her from me. I was more indignant than ever at this unexpected rival, and ashamed that I owed him my life. 'When all is said and done,' my self-esteem told me, 'I owe it to Marie, since it was only the sound of her voice that caused the dagger to drop.' However, I couldn't overlook the fact that there was indeed some generosity in the sentiment that had persuaded my unknown rival to spare me. But who could this rival be? I was awash with suspicions, all of which cancelled one another out. It couldn't be the *sang-mêlé* planter, whom my jealousy had at first singled out. He was far from possessing such extraordinary strength, and in any case that was not his voice. It seemed to me the individual with whom I'd been fighting had been naked from the waist up. Slaves were the only ones in the colony who went around half-dressed like that. But it couldn't be a slave: feelings such as the one that had made him cast away the dagger did not strike me as the sort that a slave could possess and, besides, every bone in my body rejected the revolting supposition that I had a slave for a rival. Who, then, could he be? I resolved to wait and keep an eye out.

7

MARIE HAD woken up the old nurse, who had been like a mother to her ever since she lost her own when but an infant. I spent the rest of the night close by her and, as soon as day broke, we apprised my uncle of these inexplicable events. He was extremely surprised by it all, but his overweening pride, like mine, could not entertain the idea that his daughter's secret admirer might be a slave. The nurse was given orders to stay with Marie at all times. My uncle did not have a moment to spare—what with the sessions of the provincial assembly, the duties imposed on the principal colonists by the ever more menacing disposition of colonial affairs, and the work that needed doing on the plantation—so he authorized me to accompany his daughter on all her walks right up to the day of my wedding, which was fixed for the 22nd of August.[17] At the same time, assuming that the new suitor could have come only from outside his domains, he ordered that henceforth their borders be guarded day and night more strictly than ever.

These precautions taken in concert with my uncle, I decided to try an experiment. I went to the pavilion by the river and, clearing up the disorder from the day before, I decorated it for Marie as usual, lining it again with garlands of flowers.

When the hour of day she normally went there came round, I armed myself with a fully loaded carbine and suggested to my cousin that I accompany her to the pavilion. The old nurse followed us.

Marie was the first to enter the leafy arbour; I had said nothing to her about having got rid of all trace of what had alarmed her the day before.

'You see, Leopold,' she alerted me, 'my bower is in exactly the same state of disorder I left it in yesterday. All your work spoiled, your flowers torn to pieces and sullied. What astonishes me,' she added, while picking up a bouquet of wild marigolds that had been placed on the grassy bench, 'is that this nasty bouquet has not wilted since yesterday. See, my dear friend, it looks for all the world as if it has just been freshly picked.'

Astonishment and anger left me frozen to the spot. The work I'd done that very morning had indeed already been destroyed and those wretched flowers, whose freshness astonished my poor Marie, had once again insolently taken the place of the roses I had scattered there.

'Calm yourself,' Marie said to me, seeing how agitated I was. 'Calm yourself. It's over and done with. That insolent fellow will doubtless never be coming back. Let's put it all behind us, like this odious bouquet.'

I was careful not to disabuse her, out of fear of alarming her, and without telling her that the man who, according to her, was 'never coming back' had already come back, I let her trample the marigolds underfoot in a bout of innocent indignation. Then, hoping that the time had come when I would find out who my mysterious rival was, I had her sit down in silence between her nurse and myself.

Scarcely had we taken our seats than Marie put her finger to my lips: some sounds, muffled by the wind and by the murmuring of the water, had just reached her ears. I listened. It was the same sad, slow prelude that had roused my fury the previous night. I wanted to leap out of my seat, but Marie motioned me back.

'Leopold,' she whispered to me, 'keep a hold of yourself. Perhaps he's going to sing, and no doubt what he says will inform us who he is.'

And, indeed, a moment later there rose up from the depths of the wood a voice, the harmony of which had something both manly and plaintive about it. The low-pitched notes of the guitar blended in with the words of a Spanish romance—each of which reverberated so deeply in my ears that even today my memory can still conjure them up almost word for word.

'Why do you flee from me, Maria.* Why do you flee from me, young girl? Why this terror that freezes your soul whenever you hear me? I am indeed formidable! To love, to suffer, and to sing is all I know!

When, through the slender trunks of the coconut trees by the river, I see your lithe, pure form gliding along, a bedazzlement clouds my vision, O Maria, and it is as if a spirit has passed me by!

And, O Maria, whenever I hear the enchanted strains that like a melody steal from your lips, it seems to me as if my heart has just been throbbing in my ear, and its plaintive droning mingles with your harmonious voice.

Alas! Your voice for me is even sweeter than the song of young birds beating their wings in the sky, birds that have come from the land of my fathers—

The land of my fathers where I was king, the land where I was free!

Free and a king, young girl! I would forget all that for you. I would forget them all: kingdom, family, duties, vengeance, yes, even vengeance—though the moment will soon come to pluck this bitter and delicious fruit, which ripens so late!'

The preceding stanzas had been sung with frequent and sorrowful pauses, but these last words were delivered in a terrifying voice.

'O Maria! You resemble the lovely palm tree, svelte and gently swaying upon its trunk, and you are mirrored in the eyes of your young lover, like the palm tree in the transparent waters of a spring.

But could it be you have no inkling? In the depths of the desert there is betimes a hurricane jealous of the happiness of that beloved spring: onward it rushes, and the air and the sand mix together under the flapping of its heavy wings. It envelops the tree and the water in a whirlwind of fire; the spring goes dry and the palm tree feels the green circle of its leaves shrivel up at death's exhaling—those leaves which once possessed the majesty of a crown and the grace of a mane of hair.

Tremble, O white daughter of Hispaniola!† Tremble, lest soon everything round you be nothing more than a hurricane and a desert! Then you will regret the love that could have led you toward me, just as the joyful

---

* It has been deemed unnecessary to reproduce here in their entirety the words of the Spanish song: '*Porque me huyes, Maria?*' etc.

† Our readers will doubtless not be unaware that this was the first name given to Saint Domingue, by Christopher Columbus, at the time of the discovery in December 1492.

kata, the bird of salvation, guides the traveller across the sands of Africa to the cistern.

And why would you shun my love, Maria? I am a king, and my brow rises above those of all other men. You are white, and I am black, but the day needs to join with the night in order to bring forth the dawn and the sunset, which are more beautiful than it!'

8

DRAWN OUT on the trembling chords of the guitar, a long sigh accompanied these last words. I was beside myself with rage. 'King! Black! Slave!' A mass of incoherent ideas, brought on by the inexplicable song I had just heard, whirled round in my head. A violent need took hold of me to have done with the unknown individual who dared in this manner to associate the name of Marie with love songs and threats. Convulsively, I grabbed hold of my carbine and rushed headlong from the pavilion. Marie, in alarm, reached out her arms to hold me back but by that time I had already disappeared into the part of the thicket from which the voice had been coming. I scoured the woods in all directions. I thrust the barrel of my musket into every part of the dense underbrush. I circled every tree of any size. I poked around in every patch of tall grass. Nothing, nothing, and still nothing! This useless search, along with some equally useless reflections on the romance I had just heard, made me as confused as I was angry. Would this insolent rival always prove as evasive in the flesh as he was to my mind? Could I neither guess who he was nor meet him face to face?... At that moment, a jingling of bells snapped me out of my revery. I turned round. The dwarf Habibrah was at my side.

'Good day, master,' he said to me. He gave a deferent bow, but the shifty look on his face, obliquely directed up at me, seemed—with an indefinable expression of malice and triumph—to register the anxiety etched on my brow.

'Speak!' I yelled at him. 'Have you seen someone in these woods?'

'No one other than you, *señor mio*,' he answered calmly.

'Did you not hear a voice?' I shot back.

The slave paused for a moment, as if trying to think what answer he could give me. I was boiling over.

'Quick,' I snapped at him. 'Quick, you wretch, answer! Did you hear a voice?'

His two eyes, round like a tiger-cat's, brazenly fastened upon mine.

'*Que quiere decir usted** by a voice, master? There are voices everywhere and for everything: there is the voice of the birds, there is the voice of the water, there is the voice of the wind in the leaves.'

Giving him a rough shake, I cut this short.

'Wretched buffoon! No more playing around with me, or I'll make sure you hear, up close, the voice that comes from the barrel of a carbine. Answer me straight. Did you hear in these woods a man singing a Spanish air?'

'Yes, *señor*,' he retorted, without seeming at all flustered, 'and words in the air ... Hold on, master, I am going to tell you all about it. I was strolling along the edge of this grove, listening to what the little silver bells of my *gorra*† were whispering in my ears. All of a sudden, the wind bolstered this concert with some words from a language that you call Spanish, the first that ever I lisped—when my age was counted by months and not by years, when my mother used to carry me on her back in a sling made of red and yellow strips of wool. I love that language. To me it recalls the time when I was merely small and not yet a dwarf, just a child and not yet someone's fool. I moved closer to the voice and I heard the end of the song.'

'So, is that all?' I shot back impatiently.

'Yes, *hermoso* master, but if you wish I will tell you who the man is who was singing.'

I could have hugged the poor jester.

'Oh, speak!' I exclaimed. 'Speak. Here's my purse, Habibrah! And ten purses, fuller than this one, are yours if you tell me who the man is.'

He took the purse, opened it, and smiled.

'*Diez bolsas* fuller than this one! *Demonio!* That would make a whole *fanega*'s[18] worth of real écus with the image *del rey Luis quince*, as many as would have been needed to sow the field of the magician Altornino from Grenada, who knew the art of making *buenos doblones* grow there. But do not anger yourself, young master, I am coming to the point. Do you recall, *señor*, the last words of the song: "You are white, and I am black, but the day needs to join with the night in order to bring forth the dawn and the sunset, which are more beautiful than it!" Now, if this song speaks the truth, the griffe Habibrah, your humble slave, born of a negress and a

---

* What do you mean?

† By this name, the little Spanish griffe designates his bonnet.

white man, is more beautiful than you, *señorito de amor*. I am the issue of the joining of day and night. I am the dawn or the sunset referred to in the Spanish song, and you are only the day. So I am more beautiful than you, *si usted quiere,** more beautiful than a white man.'

The dwarf mixed long bursts of laughter in with these bizarre meanderings. I cut him short again.

'What are you getting at with all this foolishness? Will any of it tell me who the man is who was singing in these woods?'

'Precisely, master,' replied the jester with a malicious look. 'It is evident that *el hombre* who could have sung such "foolishness," as you call it, can only be and is none other than a fool just like me! I have earned *las diez bolsas!*'

I was raising my hand to punish the emancipated slave's insolent pleasantry when an awful scream suddenly rang through the grove; it came from the direction of the pavilion by the river. It was Marie's voice. I'm off like a shot, I'm running, flying, wondering in terror what new calamity might lie ahead of me. Out of breath, I arrive at the arbour. A frightful sight awaited me there. A monstrous crocodile, whose body was half-hidden under the reeds and mangroves in the river, had shoved its enormous head through one of the leafy vaults that held up the roof of the pavilion. Its gaping, hideous maw was turned menacingly on a young black man of colossal stature who with one arm was holding up the terrified girl and with the other was boldly thrusting a mortising axe between the monster's sharp jaws. The crocodile struggled furiously against this bold, powerful hand that was keeping it at bay. The moment I showed up at the entrance to the arbour Marie let out a cry of joy, tore herself from the arms of the negro, and sank into mine, exclaiming:

'I'm saved!'

At these actions and these words of Marie's, the negro abruptly turns round, folds his arms on his heaving chest and, fastening a pained look on my betrothed, stands motionless—without seeming to notice that the crocodile is there next to him, that it has shaken off the axe, and that it's on the point of devouring him. The courageous black man would have been done for if—hurriedly setting Marie down on the knees of her nurse, who all this time had been riveted to a bench, more dead than alive—I hadn't run up to the monster and discharged my carbine into his maw at point-blank range. The mangled animal opened and shut its bloody jaws and its listless eyes two or three more times, but these were nothing more

---

* If you will.

than convulsions. All of a sudden it crashed over on its back and its two fat scaly legs went stiff. It was dead.

The negro I had so luckily managed to save turned his head and saw the monster's last tremors. Then, after staring at the ground and slowly raising his eyes toward Marie, who had returned to make sure I was all right, he said to me, in a tone of voice that expressed something well beyond despair:

'*Porque le has matado?*'*

Then he strode away without awaiting my response, returning into the grove where he disappeared from sight.

9

THIS TERRIFYING scene, this peculiar dénouement, all the varied emotions that had preceded, accompanied, and followed upon my futile searches in the woods, threw my mind into a state of chaos. Marie was still absorbed in her terror, and a rather long time went by before we could communicate our incoherent thoughts to one another except by exchanging looks and squeezing hands. Finally, I broke the silence.

'Come,' I said to Marie, 'let's get out of here! This place has something deathly about it!'

She got up eagerly, as if she had only been awaiting my permission, and leaned her arm on mine; we set off.

I asked her then how it had all happened. The miraculous assistance of that black man, at the moment she found herself in such horrible danger, how had that come about? Did she know who this slave was (for the pair of coarse breeches that barely veiled his nakedness was proof enough that he belonged to the lowest class of inhabitants on the island)?

'That man,' Marie said to me, 'is doubtless one of my father's negroes who was busy working near the river when the appearance of the crocodile made me scream, which alerted you to the danger I was in. All I can tell you is that he leapt out of the wood, at that very instant, and flew to my aid.'

'From which direction did he come?' I asked her.

'The other direction from where the voice had come just the moment before, directly opposite from where you ran into the grove.'

---

* Why did you kill it?

This circumstance unsettled the connection I couldn't help making between the Spanish words the negro had addressed to me in parting and the romance my unknown rival had sung in that same language. Other links had, in any case, already occurred to me. This negro, of an almost gigantic height and prodigiously strong, could very well be the rugged adversary with whom I had struggled the previous night. The fact that he was naked was another striking clue. The singer in the grove had stated: 'I am black.' Yet another similarity. He had declared himself to be a king and this fellow was only a slave, but I recalled, not without astonishment, the air of ruggedness and majesty stamped on his face in the midst of the characteristic signs of the African race; the gleam in his eyes; the whiteness of his teeth against the gleaming blackness of his skin; the width of his brow, especially surprising in a negro; the disdainful swelling that imparted something so lordly and so powerful to the thickness of his lips and nostrils; the nobleness of his bearing; the beauty of his form, still possessed of what one might call Herculean proportions, for all that it had been worn away and damaged by the strain of daily toil. I pictured to myself in its totality the imposing appearance of this slave and I saw that it could very well have suited a king. Then, weighing up a host of other circumstances, my conjectures broke off in a shudder of anger at this insolent negro; I wanted him to be tracked down and punished ... And then all my uncertainties came back to me. In reality, where was the foundation for so many suspicions? Since a good deal of the island of Saint Domingue belonged to Spain, many negroes—whether they had originally belonged to colonists in Santo Domingo or were born there—mixed the Spanish language in with their own jargon.[19] Just because this slave had addressed a few words to me in Spanish, was that a reason to suppose he was the author of a romance in this language, something that necessarily bespoke a degree of mental culture which, as far as I was concerned, was altogether beyond the ken of negroes? As for that peculiar way in which he reproached me for having killed the crocodile, it bespoke in the slave a disgust with life that needed no further explanation than his own condition, without it being necessary to drag in the hypothesis of an impossible love for the master's daughter. His presence in the grove by the pavilion might well have been only fortuitous; his strength and his size were far from enough to establish his identity with my nocturnal antagonist. On the basis of such flimsy clues, could I make such a dreadful accusation in the presence of my uncle, handing over to the implacable vengeance of his overweaning pride a poor slave who had shown so much courage in coming to Marie's aid?

Just when these ideas were beginning to parry my anger, Marie dispelled it entirely by saying to me in her sweet voice:

'Leopold, my dear, we owe a debt of gratitude to this brave negro. Without him, I was done for! You would have arrived too late.'

These few words had a decisive effect. They did not change my intention of having the slave who had saved Marie tracked down, but they changed the reason behind this search: it was no longer a question of his being punished but of how he would be rewarded.

I informed my uncle that he owed his daughter's life to one of his slaves and he promised me the man's freedom if I could find him in that crowd of unfortunate souls.

10

UNTIL THAT DAY, the natural disposition of my mind had kept me away from the plantations where the blacks worked. It was too painful for me to see people suffering without being able to offer them any relief. But on the very next day, when my uncle suggested that I accompany him on his round of surveillance, I eagerly accepted, hoping to meet among the workers the man who had rescued my beloved Marie.

As we walked along I had a chance to see just how much power a master's look has over his slaves, but also at what high cost this power is bought. The negroes, trembling in my uncle's presence, doubled their efforts and their activity when he passed by, yet how much hatred there was in this terror!

Irascible by force of habit, my uncle was on the point of getting angry at not having anything to get angry about when his jester Habibrah, trailing behind him as always, suddenly pointed out to him a black man who had fallen asleep under a clump of date-palms, overcome with weariness. My uncle rushes over to this poor wretch, wakes him up with a shove, and orders him back to work. In a fright, the negro gets up and, as he does so, reveals the presence of a fledgling Bengal rose he had lain down on by accident. The shrub, which my uncle took particular pleasure in growing, was ruined. At this sight the master, already irate at what he called the slave's laziness, became furious. Beside himself with rage, he reaches for his belt and unhooks the whip that he carried on his rounds. He raises his arm, ready to inflict its steel-tipped lashes on the negro, who by this point is on bended knees. The whip did not come down. I shall never forget that moment. In a flash, a powerful hand stayed the colonist's hand. A black man (he was the very one I was looking for!) cried out to him in French:

'Punish me, for I have just trespassed against thee,[20] but leave my brother be, who has only laid hands on your rosebush.'

This unexpected intervention of the man to whom I owed Marie's safety, his deed, his look, the commanding tone of his voice, all left me dumbfounded. But, far from shaming my uncle, his generous imprudence only doubled the master's rage, diverting it from the kneeling man to his defender. In exasperation, my uncle wrenched himself away from the arms of the big negro; showering him with threats, he once again raised the whip to strike him with it in turn. This time the whip was ripped out of his hand. The black man broke its nail-studded handle as if it were a piece of straw and trampled the shameful instrument of vengeance underfoot. I couldn't move for surprise, my uncle for fury. This sort of affront to his authority was something he had never encountered before. His eyes were bouncing around as if they were about to leave their sockets; his lips were trembling, livid. The slave calmly looked him over for a moment and then, with great dignity, suddenly offered him a hatchet that he was holding in his hand.

'White man,' he said, 'if you wish to strike me, at least use this axe.'

My uncle, who had completely lost control of himself, would certainly have granted this wish, and he was lunging for the axe when I intervened in turn. Briskly taking hold of the hatchet, I threw it into the shaft of a near-by *noria*.[21]

'What are you doing?' my uncle said to me heatedly.

'I am saving you,' I responded, 'from the calamitous act of striking down your daughter's defender. It is to this slave that you owe Marie's life. He is the negro whose liberty you have promised me.'

It was a poorly chosen moment to mention that promise. My words barely registered on the colonist's envenomed mind.

'His liberty!' he answered me with a dark look. 'Yes, he has earned an end to his slavery. His liberty! We'll see what sort of liberty the judges give him at the court-martial.'

These sinister words made my blood run cold. Marie and I implored him, but to no avail. The negro whose negligence had been the cause of this scene was punished with a flogging and his defender was thrown into the dungeons of Fort Galifet for having raised his hand against a white man. Slave against master, it was a capital crime.

YOU CAN imagine, gentlemen, to what extent all these circumstances must have aroused my interest and my curiosity. I made inquiries about the prisoner. Some odd details emerged. I was informed that his companions appeared to have the deepest respect for this young negro. A mere sign from him was enough for them to obey him, even though he was a slave like them. He wasn't born in the slave huts. Whether he had a father or a mother was not known; indeed, it was said that only a few years had passed since a slave ship had landed him on Saint Domingue. This circumstance made it even more remarkable that he exercised such dominion over all of his companions, including even the *creole* blacks who, as you're no doubt aware, gentlemen, normally profess the deepest contempt for the *congo* negroes—an improper and too general term used in the colony to designate all slaves brought from Africa.[22]

Although he seemed buried in a dark melancholy, his extraordinary strength combined with his marvellous dexterity made him an object of the greatest value when it came to working the plantations. The best horse could not have turned the wheels of the *norias* more quickly or for longer than he did. It often happened that he would end up doing in one day the work of ten of his comrades so as to shield them from the punishment specified for negligence or fatigue. He was adored by the slaves, yes, but the veneration in which they held him—entirely different from the superstitious terror which surrounded the fool Habibrah—also appeared to have some hidden cause: it was a type of worship.

I was further informed that what was really strange was to see him being as gentle and as modest with his equals, who considered it an honour to obey him, as he was proud and haughty in his relations with our drivers. It is fair to say that these privileged slaves—intermediary links binding the chains of servitude and despotism, their lowly condition coupled to the insolence of their authority—took a malignant pleasure in overburdening him with work and badgering him in all sorts of ways. It seemed, nonetheless, that they couldn't help but respect the feeling of righteous pride that had led him to affront my uncle. Not one of them had ever dared inflict any humiliating punishments on him. If it so happened that any were imposed on him, twenty negroes would offer to undergo them in his place, and he, standing still as could be, would solemnly watch the punishments being carried out as if these men were doing nothing more than fulfilling a duty. This bizarre man was known in the slave huts by the name of *Pierrot*.[23]

12

ALL THESE details inflamed my youthful imagination. Full of gratitude and compassion, Marie commended my enthusiasm and Pierrot became a matter of such keen interest to us that I resolved to visit him and be of what service I could. I mulled over the best means of approaching him.

Although very young, as the nephew of one of the richest colonists in the Cape I was captain of the Acul parish militias. Fort Galifet was entrusted to their care, as well as to that of a detachment of yellow dragoons whose leader—normally a non-commissioned officer in that company—had command of the fort. It so happened that at precisely this time the officer in command was the brother of a poor colonist for whom I had been lucky enough to perform some by no means negligible services; he was entirely devoted to me ..."

Here everybody interrupted d'Auverney, calling out the name of Thaddeus.

"You've guessed it, gentlemen," resumed the captain. "You can easily understand that I had no difficulty in getting him to admit me into the negro's cell. As captain of the militias, I had every right to visit the fort. However, in order not to arouse any suspicions in my uncle, who was still conspicuously angry, I took care to go there only when he was taking his siesta. All the soldiers, except those on guard, were asleep. Guided by Thaddeus, I arrived at the cell door; Thaddeus opened it and withdrew. I entered.

The black man was sitting down, for his great height prevented him from standing. He was not alone: an enormous mastiff reared up, growling, and came toward me. 'Rask,' the black man called out. The young mastiff fell silent and returned to lie down at its master's feet, where it finished off devouring some miserable scraps of food.

I was in uniform; what little light there was coming through the venthole of this narrow cell was so dim that Pierrot couldn't make out who I was.

'I am ready,' he said to me calmly.

As he spoke these words, he got up in a crouch.

'I am ready,' he repeated.

'I thought,' I said to him, surprised by the freedom of his movements, 'that you were in chains.'

Emotion made my voice tremble, but the prisoner did not seem to realize this.

With his foot he pushed bits and pieces of something that made a clinking noise.

'Chains! I have broken them.'

There was something about the way in which he uttered these last words that seemed to say: 'I am not made to bear chains.' I proceeded:

'They did not tell me they had let you keep a dog.'

'I am the one who let him in.'

I was ever more astonished. The cell door was shut from outside with a triple bolt. The vent-hole was scarcely six inches wide and had two iron bars across it. He seemed to understand where my thoughts were tending. He stood up, at least as much as the very low vault allowed him to, and effortlessly detached an enormous stone from beneath the vent-hole; taking away the two bars fastened above this stone, he thereby made an aperture through which two men could easily have passed. This aperture opened out on a level with the stand of banana and coconut trees that covers the morne directly behind the fort.

The dog, seeing the breach opened, thought its master wanted it to go out. It sat up, ready to leave; the black man motioned it back to its place.

Surprise rendered me speechless. Suddenly, a ray of sunlight illumined my face. The prisoner bolted up as if he had accidentally stepped on a snake, hitting his forehead against the stones of the vault. An indefinable mixture of a great many conflicting feelings flashed through his eyes: a strange expression of hatred, benevolence, and pained astonishment. But, quickly regaining a hold over his thoughts, his facial expression immediately turned calm and cold again and he stared at me with indifference. He was looking straight at me as if he didn't know me.

'I can live two more days without eating,' he said.

I made a horrified gesture. It was then I noticed how thin the poor fellow was. He added:

'My dog can eat only from out of my hand. Had I not been able to enlarge the vent-hole, poor Rask would have died of hunger. Better it be me than him, since I have to die anyway.'

'No,' I exclaimed. 'No, you will not die of hunger!'

He misunderstood me.

'No doubt,' he responded, smiling bitterly, 'I could have gone two more days without eating, but I am ready, officer. Better today than tomorrow. Do no harm to Rask.'

I realized then what his 'I am ready' meant. Accused of a crime which was punishable by death, he thought I had come to lead him to the place of execution. Just think, a man endowed with such colossal strength, with all means of escape available to him, gently and calmly repeating to a child, 'I am ready'!

'Do no harm to Rask,' he repeated yet again.

I could not contain myself.

'What!' I protested. 'Not only do you take me for your executioner, but you even harbour doubts regarding my humanity toward this poor dog who has done me no wrong!'

He was moved; his voice faltered.

'White man,' he said, holding his hand out to me, 'white man, pardon me. I love my dog. And,' he added after a brief silence, 'your people have done me much harm.'

I embraced him, squeezed his hand, set him straight.

'Don't you recognize me?' I asked him.

'I knew you were a white man, and as far as the whites are concerned, no matter how good they might be a black man counts for so very little! Besides, I also have a grievance against you.'

'About what?' I responded in astonishment.

'Have you not twice preserved my life?'

This strange indictment made me smile. He noticed it, and continued bitterly:

'Yes, I ought to bear you a grudge. You saved me from the crocodile and from the colonist. Worse yet, you deprived me of the right to hate you. I am indeed unlucky!'

His odd way of talking and his odd ideas hardly surprised me any longer. It was all in keeping with the man.

'I owe you much more than you owe me,' I said to him. 'I owe you the life of my betrothed, of Marie.'

It was as if an electric shock had just run through him.

'*Maria!*' he cried out in a choked voice. His hands violently clutched at his head as it sank down; he sighed heavily, his broad chest heaving up and down.

I admit that my slumbering suspicions were reawakened, but I felt no anger, no jealousy. I was too close to happiness, and he too close to death, for such a rival—if indeed he was one—to excite in me any feelings other than those of benevolence and pity.

He finally raised his head.

'Go!' he said to me. 'Do not thank me!'

After a pause, he added:

'Even so, I am not of a rank inferior to yours!'

This remark seemed to hint at an order of ideas that keenly piqued my curiosity. I urged him to tell me who he was and what he had suffered. He maintained a gloomy silence.

My conduct had touched him; my offers of assistance, my appeals, appeared to overcome his disgust for life. He went out and brought back some bananas and an enormous coconut. Then he closed up the aperture and set about eating. Chatting with him, I noticed that he spoke French and Spanish fluently, and that his mind did not appear devoid of culture. He knew some Spanish romances, which he sang with feeling. This man was so inexplicable in so many other respects that up until then the purity of his speech had not struck me. I tried yet again to find out the cause of this, but he remained silent. At length, I took my leave, ordering my faithful Thaddeus to show him every possible attention.

13

I SAW HIM every day at the same hour. His case worried me: despite my appeals, my uncle insisted on prosecuting him. I did not hide my fears from Pierrot. He listened to me with indifference.

Often while we were together Rask would show up carrying a large palm leaf around his neck. The black man would untie it, read the unfamiliar characters which were traced on it, and then rip it up.[24] I made it a point not to ask him any questions about this.

One day I entered without his seeming to take any notice of me. He had his back turned to the door of his cell and was singing in a melancholy tone the Spanish tune 'Yo que soy contrabandista.'[*][25] When he had finished, he turned abruptly toward me and exclaimed:

'Brother, promise, if ever you find yourself doubting me, put aside all your suspicions when you hear me singing that tune.'

He cut an imposing figure. I promised what he asked, without having much idea what he meant by those words 'if ever you find yourself doubting me ...' He took the deep shell of the coconut that he had culled on the day of my first visit, and which he had kept ever since; filling it with palm wine, he bade me put it to my lips, and then emptied it at one go. From that day on, he only ever referred to me as his 'brother.'

---

* A smuggler am I.

Meanwhile, I began to have some reason for hope. My uncle's anger had started to abate. The festivities surrounding my upcoming wedding with his daughter had turned his mind in more pleasant directions. Marie joined her entreaties to mine. Every day I pointed out to him that Pierrot had not wanted to affront him, but merely wished to prevent him from committing an act of perhaps excessive severity; that this black man had, through his daring struggle with the crocodile, saved Marie from certain death; that we were both in his debt, he for his daughter, and I for my betrothed; that, besides, Pierrot was the most vigorous of his slaves (for I no longer dreamt of obtaining his liberty, it was now only a question of saving his life); that, single-handedly, he did the work of ten men; and that with just one arm he could get the rollers of a sugar mill turning. He listened, and gave me to understand that perhaps he would not be following up on the charge. I said nothing to the black man about my uncle's shift in attitude, wishing to have the pleasure of announcing his outright liberty to him, if I obtained it. What astonished me was that, believing himself condemned to die, he did not take advantage of any of the means of escape that were in his power. I asked him about this.

'I must stay,' he answered icily. 'They would think I was afraid.'

14

ONE MORNING, Marie approached me. She was beaming, and on her sweet face there was something even more angelic than the joy of a pure love—namely, the thought of a good deed.

'Listen,' she said to me, 'in three days it will be the 22nd of August, the day of our nuptials. We are soon going to …'

I interrupted her.

'Marie, "soon" is hardly the word, since there are still three days to go!'

She smiled and blushed.

'Now don't interrupt me, Leopold,' she said. 'An idea has occurred to me that will surely please you. You know that I went into town yesterday with my father to buy the trousseau and ornaments for our wedding. It's not that I set a high value on these jewels and diamonds, which won't make me any more beautiful in your eyes. I would give all the pearls in the world for just one of those flowers that the nasty man with the bouquet of marigolds spoiled—but no matter. My father wants to shower me with all those sorts of things, and I pretend to fancy them in order to please him. Yesterday, I spent a lot of time looking at a dress that was on display in a sandalwood box: a Chinese satin *basquina*,[26] embroidered with large flowers. It's very expensive, but very distinctive. My father noticed it had caught my attention. On the way back, I asked him to promise he would bestow a gift upon me, the way the knights of old used to do. You know he likes it when people compare him to the knights of old. He swore to me on his honour that he would grant me the thing I asked for, whatever it was. He thinks it's the Chinese satin basquina. Not at all, it's Pierrot's life. That will be my wedding gift.'

I could not help but clasp this angel in my arms. My uncle's word was sacred, and while Marie went off to find him and make sure he kept it, I ran off to Fort Galifet to inform Pierrot of what was now his certain deliverance.

'Brother!' I shouted out to him upon entering. 'Brother, rejoice! Your life is saved. Marie has asked her father to spare it, as her wedding present!'

The slave gave a start.

'Marie! Wedding! My life! How can all those things go together?'

'That's very simple,' I went on. 'Marie, whose life you saved, is getting married.'

'To whom?' the slave cried out, a wild and terrible look on his face.

'Don't you know?' I answered gently. 'To me.'

His formidable countenance once again turned benevolent and resigned.

'Ah, yes! That is true,' he assented. 'To you! And when is the day?'

'It's the 22nd of August.'

'The 22nd of August! Are you mad?' he shot back, a look of anguish and alarm on his face.

He stopped. I was staring at him in astonishment. After a brief silence, he squeezed my hand warmly.

'Brother, I am so much in your debt that I must give you a word of advice. Trust me, go to the Cape and get married before the 22nd of August.'

I tried in vain to find out the meaning of these enigmatic words.

'Adieu,' he said to me solemnly. 'Perhaps I have already said too much about it, but I hate ingratitude even more than the violation of an oath.'

I took leave of him, full of uncertainties and anxieties, though these were soon effaced by my thoughts of the happiness to come.

My uncle withdrew his complaint that very day. I returned to the fort to secure Pierrot's release. Knowing that he was free, Thaddeus entered the prison cell along with me. He had vanished. Rask, who was there alone, came up to me wagging his tail. A palm leaf was attached to his neck. I removed it, and read these words: 'Thank you, you have saved my life a third time. Brother, do not forget your promise.' Below this, by way of signature, were written the words '*Yo que soy contrabandista.*'

Thaddeus, unaware of the secret of the vent-hole, was even more astonished than I; he imagined that the negro had changed into a dog. I let him believe what he wanted, merely insisting that he keep silent about what he had seen.

I wanted to take Rask along with me, but no sooner were we out of the fort than he dashed into the near-by hedges and disappeared.

15

MY UNCLE was incensed at the slave's escape and ordered that he be tracked down. He wrote to the Governor placing Pierrot at his entire disposition if he was found.

The 22nd of August arrived. My union with Marie was celebrated with pomp at the Acul parish church. How happy a day that was—the day that marked the beginning of all my troubles! I was intoxicated with a joy that cannot be conveyed to those who have never felt it. I had completely forgotten Pierrot and his ominous warnings. Night, so impatiently anticipated, finally came. My young bride withdrew to the nuptial chamber, but I was unable to follow her there as quickly as I would have liked. A tedious but indispensable duty still awaited me. As captain of the militias I was required that evening to do a round of the Acul posts. This precaution was rendered all the more imperative at this time because of the disturbances in the colony, the partial revolts of the blacks (which, although promptly suppressed, had taken place on the Thibaud and Lagoscette plantations during the preceding months of June and July, continuing on even into the first days of August), and especially the surly mood of the free mulattoes, which had only been aggravated by the recent torture and execution of the rebel Ogé.[27] My uncle was the first to remind me of my duty; I had to resign myself to it. I put on my uniform and set out. I looked in on the first stations without encountering any cause for worry but, toward midnight, as I was taking a turn near the batteries on the bay, lost in my thoughts, I noticed a reddish light on the horizon flaring up and spreading out from the direction of Limonade and Saint-Louis du Morin. The soldiers and I at first attributed it to some accidental fire, but moments later the flames became so conspicuous and the smoke, driven by the wind, began to mass and thicken to such an extent that I promptly set off back to the fort to sound the alarm and have a relief force sent out. Passing by the huts of our blacks, I was surprised by the extraordinary commotion that was going on there. Most of them were still up, and they were talking in an extremely animated manner. Uttered with reverence, a bizarre name—*Bug-Jargal*—cropped up time and again in the midst of their unintelligible jargon. I nonetheless managed to catch a few words, the gist of which seemed to me to be that the blacks of the Northern Plain were in full revolt and were setting fire to the settlements and the plantations situated on the other side of the Cape. As I was crossing a marshy tract of land, my foot stumbled against a pile of axes and picks hidden in the rushes and mangroves. Justifiably worried, I there and then put the Acul militias on armed alert and ordered that an eye be kept on the slaves. Calm was restored.

Meanwhile, with every passing minute the havoc appeared to be growing and drawing nearer to Limbé. You could even, it seemed, make out the distant sound of artillery and rifle fire. I had woken up my uncle and, around two in the morning, unable to contain his anxiety he ordered me to leave a portion of the militias in Acul under the lieutenant's orders. While my poor Marie slept or waited for me, I obeyed my uncle—who was, as I've already said, a member of the provincial assembly—and I set off with the rest of the soldiers on the road to the Cape.

I shall never forget the sight of that city as I approached. The flames, devouring the surrounding plantations, were casting over it a sombre light darkened by the torrents of smoke that were being driven through the streets by the wind. Like a thick snowfall, a whirlwind of sparks formed by little bits of blazing sugar cane was furiously piling onto the roofs of the houses and the rigging of the ships anchored in the harbour.[28] Any minute now it was threatening the city of the Cape with a conflagration no less heart-rending than the one that was devouring the surrounding areas. It was an awful, imposing spectacle to behold: on land, pale settlers still risking their lives in order to save their houses, all that remained to them of so many riches, from the terrible scourge; in the harbour, ships—fearing the same fate, but at least favoured by the wind that was proving so deadly to the luckless colonists—bearing off under full sail on a sea coloured with the blood-red fires of the conflagration.

DEAFENED BY the gunfire coming from the forts, the panic-stricken cries of those fleeing, and the distant crash of buildings caving in, I was at a loss where to take my soldiers. On the parade-ground, though, I ran across the captain of the yellow dragoons, and he served as our guide. I will not linger, gentlemen, over descriptions of the fire-ravaged plain we saw before us; many another person has depicted the first disasters that befell the Cape, and I need to pass quickly over those memories of blood and fire. I will simply inform you that the rebel slaves were said to be already masters of Dondon, Terrier-Rouge, the town of Ouanaminthe, even of Limbé and its ill-fated plantations—this last detail fuelling my anxiety on account of their proximity to Acul.

I went post-haste to the residence of the Governor, Monsieur de Blanchelande. Confusion reigned there, even over the mind of its master. I asked him for orders, at the same time urging him to attend as quickly as possible to the safety of Acul, which was thought to be already under threat. He was in the company of Monsieur de Rouvray, a brigadier-general and one of the principal landowners on the island;[29] Monsieur de Touzard, lieutenant-colonel of the Cape regiment;[30] a few members of the colonial and provincial assemblies; and several of the leading colonists. When I made my appearance, this informal council was engaged in tumultuous deliberations.

'My lord Governor,' a member of the provincial assembly was saying, 'it is only too true. The slaves, that's who it is, not the free sang-mêlés. We said it would happen, we have been predicting it for a long time now.'

'You said it without believing a word of it,' a member of the colonial assembly—the so-called *general* assembly—sourly retorted. 'You said it to gain credit for yourselves at our expense, and you were so far from expecting a real slave rebellion that it was the scheming of your assembly, back in 1789, which simulated that notorious, that ludicrous revolt of three thousand blacks on the morne behind the Cape. A revolt in which only one national volunteer died, and even then he was killed by his own side!'[31]

'I repeat to you,' the *provincial* carried on, 'that we see things more clearly than you do. It's simple. We stayed here to keep watch on the colony's affairs, while your assembly went off to France, en masse, and was awarded that risible ovation which concluded with your being reprimanded by the representatives of the nation. *Ridiculus mus!*'[32]

With bitter disdain, the member of the colonial assembly answered:

'Our fellow citizens reelected us unanimously.'

'It's because of you,' the other man replied, 'it's because of your excesses that the head of that poor wretch who showed up in a coffee-house without a tricolour cockade was paraded around town. It's because of you that the mulatto Lacombe was hanged for having written a petition that began with the *outdated* words: "In the name of the Father, the Son, and the Holy Ghost!"'[33]

'That is false,' exclaimed the member of the general assembly. 'The struggle between principles and privileges, between the *Bossus* and the *Crochus*: that's what this is all about.'[34]

'I always thought it was the case, monsieur: you are an *indépendant!*'

At this reproach from the member of the provincial assembly, his adversary answered with an air of triumph:

'A statement like that proves you're a *pompon blanc*.[35] I leave you with the burden of such an avowal.'

The quarrel would probably have dragged on even longer had the Governor not intervened.

'Gentlemen, please! What does this have to do with the imminent danger threatening us? Here are the reports that have reached me. The revolt began at ten this evening among the negroes of the Turpin settlements. The slaves, commanded by an English negro named Boukmann,[36] convinced the gangs working for the Clément, Trémès, Flaville, and Noé plantations to join in with them. They set fire to all the settlements and slaughtered the colonists, engaging in unheard-of acts of cruelty. One single detail should give you a sense of the horror of it all: their standard is the body of a child set on the end of a pike.'

A collective shudder interrupted Monsieur de Blanchelande.

'So much,' he continued, 'for what is happening outside the city. Inside, everything has been thrown into confusion. Several of the Cape's settlers have killed their slaves; fear has made them cruel. The more mild-mannered or braver ones have limited themselves to shutting their slaves up under lock and key. The *petits blancs*[*37] blame these disasters on the free sang-mêlés. Several mulattoes very nearly fell victim to the popular fury. I have given them asylum in a church where they are guarded by a battalion. Now, to prove that they are not in collusion with the rebel blacks, the sang-mêlés are asking me for a post to defend, and for arms.'

'Do nothing of the kind!' shouted a voice that I recognized. It belonged to the planter suspected of being a sang-mêlé, the one with

---

* Non-propertied whites in the colony plying a trade of any sort.

whom I had fought a duel. 'Do nothing of the kind, my lord Governor. Do not give any arms to the mulattoes.'

'So you do not wish to fight?' a colonist interrupted brusquely.

Seeming not to have heard, the other man continued:

'The sang-mêlés are our worst enemies. They alone are the ones we should be worried about. I admit, one could only have expected a revolt originating with them and not with the slaves. Do the slaves amount to anything?'

The poor man hoped with these invectives against the mulattoes to separate himself completely from them, to eradicate from the minds of his white audience the verdict that relegated him to this despised caste. It was too low a ploy to succeed. A murmur of disapproval drew this to his attention.

'Yes, monsieur,' said old Brigadier-General de Rouvray. 'Yes, the slaves do amount to something: they amount to forty against three, and we'd be in a sorry state if whites like you were all we had to set against the negroes and mulattoes.'

The colonist bit his lips.

'General,' the Governor resumed, 'what are your thoughts on the mulattoes' petition?'

'Give them arms, my lord Governor,' answered Monsieur de Rouvray. 'When making a sail any material will do!' Then he turned toward the suspect colonist: 'Do you hear that, monsieur? Go and arm yourself.'

The humiliated colonist departed, displaying all the signs of intensified rage.

All this while, the cries of distress that were bursting out all over the city kept filtering into the Governor's residence, reminding the participants of their reason for being at this gathering. Monsieur de Blanchelande dashed off an order in pencil, handed it to an aide-de-camp, and then broke the gloomy silence in which the assembly sat listening to that frightful uproar.

'The sang-mêlés will be armed, gentlemen, but there are still many other measures to take.'

'The provincial assembly must be convened,' said the member of this assembly who had been speaking when I entered.

'The provincial assembly!' retorted his antagonist from the colonial assembly. 'And just what is this provincial assembly anyway?'

'Exactly what one would expect from a member of the colonial assembly!' shot back the *pompon blanc*.

The *indépendant* interrupted him.

'I no more recognize the *colonial* assembly than I do the *provincial*. The general assembly is all there is, do you understand, monsieur?'

'Well, now,' the *pompon blanc* responded, 'let me be the one to inform you that the national assembly of Paris is the only one that matters.'

'Convene the provincial assembly!' the *indépendant* repeated, laughing. 'As if it hadn't been dissolved from the moment the general assembly decided it would hold its sessions here.'

Having had their fill of this pointless discussion, the rest of the room broke out in protest.

'Gentlemen,' shouted a crop merchant, 'while you, our deputies, busy yourselves with these trifles, what's happening to my cotton plants and my cochineal?'

'And my four hundred thousand indigo shrubs at Limbé!' added a planter.

'And my negroes, who cost thirty dollars a head on average!' said the captain of a slaver.

'Every minute you waste,' another colonist chimed in, 'is costing me— watch and tariff rates in hand—ten quintals of sugar, which, at seventeen hard piastres the quintal, makes one hundred seventy piastres, or nine hundred three livres ten sous in good French money!'

'The colonial assembly, your so-called general assembly, is overstepping itself!' broke in the other disputant, dominating the fray with his loud voice. 'By all means, stay in Port-au-Prince manufacturing decrees for a territory of two leagues and a duration of two days, but stay out of our affairs here. The Cape belongs to the provincial congress of the north, and to it alone!'

'I maintain,' retorted the *indépendant*, 'that his excellency the Governor is authorized to convene no other assembly than the general assembly of the colony's representatives, presided over by Monsieur de Cadusch!'

'But where is he, your president, de Cadusch?'[38] asked the *pompon blanc*. 'Where is your assembly? No more than four members have arrived so far, whereas the provincial is all present and accounted for. You wouldn't be wanting, by any chance, to represent an entire assembly, an entire colony, all by yourself?'

This rivalry of the two deputies, faithful echoes of their respective assemblies, once again required the Governor's intervention.

'Gentlemen, what exactly are you driving at with your never-ending assemblies—*provincial, general, colonial, national*? Will invoking three or four other assemblies be of any help in the decisions that this one has to make?'

'Zounds!' General de Rouvray thundered, slamming the council table. 'Confounded prattlers! I'd rather have a shouting match with a twenty-four pounder. What do we care about these two assemblies. It's like two companies of grenadiers arguing over who should go first when they're about to launch a charge! Well, then! Convene both of them, my lord Governor. I'll turn them into two regiments, march them against the blacks, and we'll see if their rifles make as much noise as their tongues.'

After this vigorous outburst, he leaned over to the person next to him (it was I) and said under his breath: 'Between the two assemblies of Saint Domingue, both of which claim to be sovereign, what do you expect someone who is Governor merely by order of the king of France to do? It's the fine talkers and the lawyers who are ruining everything, here's no different than France. If I had the honour of being the king's lieutenant-general, I'd throw all this riff-raff out the door. I'd say, "The king rules, and I govern." I'd send the so-called representatives and their precious "responsibility" to the devil, and with twelve Saint-Louis Crosses,[39] promised in his majesty's name, I'd make a clean sweep of all those rebels—off with them to the island of Tortuga, where the buccaneers, brigands of their ilk, used to quarter. Remember what I'm telling you, young man. The *philosophes* gave birth to the *philanthropists*, who engendered the *negrophiles*, who begat the white-eaters, which will do as a name until something in Greek or Latin can be found for them.[40] These supposedly liberal ideas that people in France find so intoxicating are poison in the tropics. What the negroes required was kind treatment, not all this talk about their immediate enfranchisement. All the horrors you're now witnessing in Saint Domingue were hatched in the Massiac Club; the slave insurrection is nothing more than an upshot of the fall of the Bastille.'

While the old soldier expounded his political views—narrow ones, to be sure, but brimming with frankness and conviction—the discussion raged on. A colonist, one of the few who shared in the revolutionary frenzy, and who styled himself Citizen-General C*** because he had presided over several bloody executions,[41] was in the middle of clamouring:

'What's called for is torture and execution, not battles. Horrendous examples are what nations require. Let us terrify the blacks! I am the one who put down the revolts in June and July by planting fifty slaves' heads on either side of the avenue of my settlement as if they were palm trees. Let everyone contribute his share for the proposal that I am going to make. Let us defend every approach to the Cape with our remaining negroes.'

'What! Sheer imprudence!' was the answer from all sides.

'You misunderstand me, gentlemen,' the *citizen-general* continued. 'Let us make a cordon of negro heads, surround the city with it from Fort Picolet to Point Caracol.[42] Their rebel comrades won't dare approach. At moments such as this, sacrifices have to be made for the common cause. So let me be the first to do so. I've got five hundred slaves who have not revolted; I offer them to you.'

This loathsome proposal was greeted with a stir of horror.

'That's abominable! Horrible!' every voice rang out.

'It's measures of this sort that have ruined everything,' said one colonist. 'If people hadn't been in such a hurry to execute the ones who revolted in June, July, and August, it might have been possible to grasp the thread of their conspiracy. The axe of the executioner severed it.'

Chagrined, Citizen C*** kept silent for a moment, then muttered:

'I would hardly have thought myself suspect. I am on good terms with the negrophiles. I correspond with Brissot and Pruneau de Pomme-Gouge in France, Hans Sloane in England, Magaw in America, Pezzl in Germany, Olivarius in Denmark, Wadstrom in Sweden, Peter Paulus in Holland, Avendaño in Spain, and the Abbé Pierre Tamburini in Italy!'[43]

His voice grew louder the further he progressed through his catalogue of negrophiles. When he finally got to the end of it, he shrugged:

'But there are no philosophers here!'

Monsieur de Blanchelande, for the third time, asked everybody for their ideas about what ought to be done.

'My lord Governor,' said a voice, 'here's my advice. We should all of us board the *Leopard*, which is anchored in the roadstead.'[44]

'We should put a price on Boukmann's head,' said another man.

'We should notify the Governor of Jamaica about what's going on,' said a third.

'Yes,' retorted a deputy of the provincial assembly, 'so that he can once again bestow upon us the inconsequential assistance of five hundred rifles.[45] My lord Governor, send a dispatch-boat to France, and then let us wait and see.'

'Wait and see!' Monsieur de Rouvray interrupted forcefully. 'And will the blacks wait? And the flames that are already encircling this city, will they wait? Monsieur de Touzard, sound the call to arms, get your guns, take your grenadiers and your chasseurs, and go at the main body of the rebels. My lord Governor, have camps set up in the eastern parishes; establish posts at Trou and Vallière. As for me, I shall take charge of the Fort Dauphin plains and oversee the work that needs doing there. My grandfather, who was a colonel in the Normandy regiment, served under

Marshal de Vauban; I've studied Folard and Bezout,[46] and I've got some practical experience when it comes to defending a country. In any case, the Fort Dauphin plains, practically enclosed by the sea and the Spanish frontier, are shaped like a peninsula, and will thus pretty much protect themselves; the Môle peninsula offers a similar advantage.[47] Let us put all that to good use. Let us take action!'

The veteran's energetic and practical language abruptly silenced all discordant voices and opinions. The general was right. The awareness all men possess regarding where their true interest lies brought them all round to Monsieur de Rouvray's plan of action. While the Governor showed, by a grateful squeeze of the hand, how much he valued the brave general officer's advice—even if it had the appearance of an order—and the importance of his assistance, the colonists all called for the prompt execution of the suggested measures.

The two deputies from the rival assemblies were the only ones who seemed to diverge from the general consensus. In their corner, they were muttering words like 'encroachment on the executive power,' 'hasty decision' and 'responsibility.'

I grabbed this opportunity to get from Monsieur de Blanchelande the orders I had been impatiently awaiting, and then took my leave. It was my intention to gather up the troop and set right back off on the road to Acul despite how exhausted everyone felt, with the exception of me.

17

DAY WAS beginning to break. I was on the parade-ground, waking up the members of the militia. They were lying about on their coats, scattered pell-mell amidst yellow and red dragoons, people who had taken refuge from the plain, farm animals that were bleating and bellowing, and baggage of all sorts that had been hauled into the city by planters from the surrounding areas. I had begun to gather my little troop together out of this disorder when I saw a yellow dragoon covered with sweat and dust riding toward me at full speed. I approached him and, from the few broken words that escaped his lips, I learned with dismay that my fears had been realized: the revolt had reached the Acul plains, and the blacks were laying siege to Fort Galifet, where the militias and the colonists were holed up. This Fort Galifet, I should add, was really nothing to speak of: in Saint Domingue, they used to call any earthen structure a 'fort.'

There wasn't a minute to lose. Those of my soldiers for whom I could find horses saddled up; guided by the dragoon, I arrived at my uncle's domains around ten in the morning.

I hardly even glanced at these immense plantations which were now nothing more than a sea of flames cascading along the plain, making thick waves of smoke through which every so often you could see large tree trunks blanketed with fire being swept along like sparks in the wind. Creaking, whispering sounds mixed in with a frightful crackling that seemed as if it were echoing the distant howls of the blacks, whom we could already hear but not yet see. As for me, I had only one thought on my mind— Marie's safety—and the disappearance of so many riches that were to have been mine could not distract me from it. If Marie were safe, what did everything else matter to me! I knew she was shut up in the fort, and all I asked of God was that I might arrive in time. This hope was all that sustained me in my distress; it gave me the courage and strength of a lion.

Finally a bend in the road brought Fort Galifet into view. The tricolour flag was still fluttering over the ramparts, and a well stoked fire crowned the perimeter of its walls. I shouted for joy. 'Full gallop! Dig in with both spurs! Slacken the reins!' I cried out to my comrades. With redoubled speed, we headed across the fields toward the fort, at the foot of which you could see my uncle's house; its doors and windows were broken, but it was still standing—all red in the reflected blaze of the fire, which hadn't reached it because the wind was blowing from the sea and it was a good distance from the plantations.

Lying concealed in this house, a throng of negroes suddenly sprang into view at each of the casements and even on the roof; their torches, pikes, and axes glinted amid the constant stream of gunfire they directed at the fort, while another mob of their comrades relentlessly scurried up the besieged walls, which they had covered with ladders, only to fall off and then scurry up again. From a distance, this flood of blacks, continually being pushed back and then resurfacing on those grey walls, resembled a swarm of ants trying to scale the shell of a big tortoise and being shaken off at intervals by that plodding animal.

We were finally closing in on the first entrenchments around the fort, our every gaze fixed on the flag that towered above it. I urged my soldiers on in the name of their families, trapped like mine within those walls and waiting for us to help rescue them. A collective cheer answered me and, lining my little squadron up in a column, I prepared to give the signal to charge that herd of men laying siege to the fort.

Just then, a great shout rose up from within the fort. A whirlwind of smoke enveloped the entire building. The walls, through which you could hear a rumbling sound like the roar of a great furnace, were enfolded in smoke. When it eventually cleared, we could see a red flag flying atop Fort Galifet. The game was up.

18

I CANNOT begin to tell you what went on inside me at the sight of this horrible spectacle. The fort captured, the throats of its defenders slit, twenty families massacred: I must admit, to my shame, that the wider ramifications of the disaster didn't cause me a moment's thought. Marie, lost to me! Lost to me only a few hours after she had been given to me forever! Lost to me through my own fault, since if I hadn't left her the night before and gone to the Cape on my uncle's orders, I could at least have defended her, or died next to her and with her—which, you might say, would have been one way of not losing her! These devastating thoughts drove my grief to the point of madness. My despair was born of remorse.

In the meantime, my companions had been yelling out in exasperation: 'Vengeance!' Sabres between our teeth, a pistol in each hand, we swooped down into the midst of the victorious insurgents. Although far greater in number, the blacks fled at our approach, but we had a clear view of them— to our right and our left, in front of us and behind us—massacring whites and racing to burn down the fort. Their cowardice exacerbated our fury.

At one of the fort's posterns, Thaddeus came up to me, all covered in wounds.

'My Captain,' he said, 'your Pierrot is a sorcerer, an *obi*, as those damnable negroes say, or at the very least a devil. We were holding firm, you had almost arrived, the situation was saved, when he found his way into the fort, I don't know how, and look! As for your uncle, his family, Madame …'

'Marie!' I broke in. 'Where is Marie?'

Just then, a huge black man emerged from behind a burning pallisade; he was carrying off a young woman who was screaming and struggling in his arms. The young woman was Marie; the black man was Pierrot.

'Traitor,' I screamed back at him.

I levelled a pistol at him. One of the rebel slaves threw himself in the bullet's path and fell dead. Pierrot turned round and seemed to call out some words to me; then he disappeared with his prey into the midst of the blazing canebrakes. Seconds later, an enormous dog followed in his wake, its jaws holding a cradle with my uncle's youngest child inside it. I recognized the dog as well: it was Rask. Beside myself with rage, I fired my second pistol at him but missed.

I set off running like a madman on his trail but my double night journey, so many hours passed without resting or eating, my fears for Marie, the sudden passage from the height of happiness to the very depths of adversity—all these violent emotions of the soul had exhausted me even more than the body's exertions. After a few steps, I began to stagger; my eyes clouded over, and I fell in a faint.

19

WHEN I AWOKE, I was in my uncle's gutted house and in Thaddeus's arms. Thaddeus, that excellent fellow, was staring at me anxiously.

'Victory!' he cried, as soon as he felt my pulse revive under his hand. 'Victory! The negroes have been put to flight, and the captain is restored to life!'

I interrupted his cry of joy with my eternal question:

'Where is Marie?'

I had not yet gathered my thoughts; I had an awareness of what had befallen me but no recollection of it. Thaddeus hung his head. And then it all came back to me: my horrendous wedding night; the big negro carrying Marie off in his arms through the flames. He loomed up at me like an infernal vision. Everything in the colony appeared in a different light: in the eyes of every white person, their slaves were now enemies; in my eyes, Pierrot—so good, so generous, so devoted, and who owed me his life three times over—was now an ingrate, a monster, a rival! The abduction of my wife, on the very night of our union, proved to me what I had initially suspected; I finally came to a clear recognition that the singer by the pavilion was none other than the loathsome ravisher of Marie. In so few hours, how very many changes!

Thaddeus told me he had pursued Pierrot and his dog but to no avail. The negroes had withdrawn, even though the sheer weight of their numbers could easily have crushed my small troop; my family's properties were still being put to the torch and nothing could be done to stop it.

I asked him if anyone knew what had become of my uncle, into whose bedroom I had been brought. He silently took my hand and, leading me toward the alcove, drew aside the curtains.

There was my ill-starred uncle lying on his blood-soaked bed, a dagger driven deep into his heart. From his calm expression, it was evident he had been struck down in his sleep. Also spotted with blood was the cot belonging to the dwarf Habibrah, who usually slept at his feet; similar stains could be seen on the poor fool's spangled waistcoat, which lay on the floor a few steps from the bed.

There was no doubt in my mind that the jester had died a victim of his well-known attachment to my uncle, that he had been slaughtered by his fellow slaves, perhaps while defending his master. I bitterly reproached myself for the biases that had led me to make such false judgments regarding Habibrah and Pierrot; the tears wrung from me by my uncle's premature end were mingled with a sense of regret for his fool. On my orders, his body was searched for but in vain. The negroes, I assumed, had carried the dwarf off and thrown him into the flames. I gave orders that, during the funeral service for my father-in-law, prayers be said for the repose of the faithful Habibrah's soul.

20

FORT GALIFET was destroyed. Our settlements had disappeared off the face of the earth. It was both pointless and impossible to remain among these ruins any longer. That very evening, we returned to the Cape.

There, I was seized by a raging fever. The effort I had made to overcome my despair had been too violent. The spring, too tightly wound, snapped. I fell into a delirium. My disappointed hopes, my profaned love, my betrayed friendship, my lost future, and, above all, my implacable jealousy drove my reason astray. It was as if flames were coursing through my veins. My head was bursting; the Furies had a hold of my heart. I pictured Marie in the power of another lover, in the power of a master, of a slave, of Pierrot! I've since been told that I would then spring out of my bed in a frenzy, and that it took six men to keep me from cracking my skull against the wall. Would that I had died then!

The crisis passed. The doctors, Thaddeus's care and attention, and youth's unaccountable grip on life conspired to overcome my ills, ills that could have done me such good. I recovered after ten days, and didn't grieve over the fact. I was happy enough to keep on living for a while, for the sake of vengeance.

Barely convalescent, I went to Monsieur de Blanchelande's and asked to see service. He wanted to give me a post to defend, but I pleaded with him to enlist me as a volunteer in one of the flying columns that were being sent out from time to time to drive off the blacks.

The Cape had been hurriedly fortified. The insurrection was making alarming progress. The negroes of Port-au-Prince were beginning to stir; Biassou was in command of those from Limbé, Dondon, and Acul;[48] Jean-François had had himself proclaimed generalissimo of the insurgents from the Maribarou plain;[49] Boukmann, since made famous by his tragic end, was patrolling the banks of the Limonade with his brigands; and, lastly, the bands of Morne Rouge had recognized as their leader a negro named Bug-Jargal.

The latter's character, if one were to believe the reports about him, was in singular contrast with the ferocity of the others. While Boukmann and Biassou devised any number of ways to kill the prisoners who fell into their hands, Bug-Jargal made every effort to furnish them with the means to get off the island. Those two leaders negotiated with the Spanish vessels that cruised up and down the coasts, selling to them in advance whatever they had managed to plunder from the poor souls they were forcing to flee; Bug-Jargal scuttled several of these corsairs. Monsieur Colas de Maigné and eight other prominent colonists were, by his orders, released from the wheel on which Boukmann had them bound.[50] Countless other acts of generosity were reported of him—too many to tell you about here.

My hopes of vengeance seemed no closer to being realized. I heard nothing more about Pierrot. The rebels commanded by Biassou continued to harass the Cape. On one occasion they even dared to occupy the morne overlooking the city, and the guns of the citadel had a difficult time of it driving them away. The Governor resolved to push them back into the interior of the island. Our army in the field was made up of the militias of Acul, Limbé, Ouanaminthe, and Maribarou, along with the Cape regiment and the redoubtable yellow and red companies. The militias of Dondon and Quartier-Dauphin, reinforced by a volunteer corps under the command of the merchant Poncignon,[51] formed the city's garrison.

The Governor wanted first to eliminate Bug-Jargal, whose diversionary tactics alarmed him. He sent out the Ouanaminthe militia and a battalion from the Cape against him. The detachment returned two days later, utterly defeated. Intent on trying to subdue Bug-Jargal, the Governor had the same detachment set out again, this time with a reinforcement of fifty yellow dragoons and four hundred militiamen from Maribarou. The second army fared even worse than the first. Thaddeus, who took part in that expedition, came back from it bearing a real grudge; he swore to me upon his return that he'd have his revenge on Bug-Jargal."

There was a tear in d'Auverney's eyes. He folded his arms on his chest and for several minutes seemed immersed in a painful revery. At length, he resumed his tale.

21

"NEWS ARRIVED that Bug-Jargal had left Morne Rouge and was leading his troop through the mountains to join up with Biassou. The Governor could not have been more elated: 'We've got him!' he said, rubbing his hands. The next day the colonial army was a league's distance from the Cape. At our approach, the rebels hastily abandoned Port Margot and Fort Galifet, where they had established a post defended by heavy siege artillery plundered from batteries on the coast. All the bands fell back toward the mountains. The Governor was triumphant. We kept moving forward. As we passed through those barren and devastated plains, each of us sadly cast a look around for the place where his fields, his settlements, and his riches had been; often you couldn't even tell where they were any more.

Sometimes our advance was halted by fires that had spread from the fields under cultivation to the forests and the savannahs. In those climates, where the land is still virgin and where the vegetation is superabundant, a forest fire is accompanied by some odd phenomena. Even before it comes into view, you can often hear it in the distance welling up and gurgling like the rumble of a torrential cataract. The splintering of tree trunks, the crackling of branches, the creaking of roots in the ground, the whispering of the tall grass, the bubbling of lakes and marshes shut away in the forest, the whistling of the flame as it swallows up the air—all these produce a sound that alternately dies down or intensifies with the progress of the fire.

You will sometimes see, encircling the blaze, a green fringe of trees that remains unscathed for quite some time. Suddenly a tongue of fire catches hold of one end of this ring of trees, a serpent of bluish flame slithers rapidly from trunk to trunk, and in the blink of an eye the exterior of the forest disappears beneath a veil of moving gold; everything starts burning all at once. Now and then, driven by the wind, a canopy of smoke descends, enveloping the flames. It coils and uncoils, rises and falls, clears and thickens, suddenly turns black. Then a band of fire cuts through on all sides, and you hear a great roar; the band vanishes, the smoke rises up again, and as it drifts away pours out a flood of red ash which rains down onto the ground for a long time.

22

ON THE evening of the third day, we entered the gorges of the Grande Rivière. It was estimated that the blacks were some twenty leagues away in the mountains.

We pitched our camp on a small morne, which—to judge by the way it was stripped bare—seemed to have served the same purpose for the blacks. This position was by no means ideal, but it was certainly peaceful enough. Sheer cliffs, covered with dense forests, towered over the morne on all sides. The place had been given the name of *Dompte-Mulâtre* on account of the ruggedness of these escarpments.[52] Behind the camp flowed the Grande Rivière. Boxed in by the cliffs, it was narrow and deep in this spot. Sloping down abruptly, its banks were blanketed with clumps of bushes that were impenetrable to the eye. Even its waters were often hidden by garlands of liana. Clinging to the branches of red-flowering maples scattered amongst the bushes, these vines worked their way across the river, joining their shoots with those on the other side; crisscrossing one another in a myriad of ways, they formed large tents of foliage over the water. Anyone contemplating them from the top of the neighbouring rocks would think he was looking at meadows still wet with dew. A muffled noise or the occasional wild teal suddenly piercing through this flowery curtain provided the only evidence of the flowing river beneath.

The sun's golden hues soon disappeared from the jagged peak of the distant mountains of Dondon. Little by little darkness spread over the camp and silence fell, broken only by the cries of a crane and the measured steps of the sentinels.

Then all at once, directly above our heads, were heard the fearsome strains of '*Wa-Nassé*' and '*Camp du Grand-Pré.*'[53] The palm trees, acomas, and cedars atop the rocks blazed up, and the livid glow of the conflagration revealed to us numerous bands of negroes and mulattoes on the neighbouring summits, their copper complexion appearing red in the gleam of the flames. These were Biassou's men.

Danger was imminent. Startled out of their sleep, the commanding officers hurriedly rounded up their soldiers. The drum beat out the call to arms and the trumpet sounded the alarm. In a jumble, our lines were formed. The insurgents, instead of taking advantage of our disorderly state, just stood there watching us and singing '*Wa-Nassé.*'

A gigantic black man appeared, alone, on the highest of the secondary peaks that enclose the Grande Rivière. A feather the colour of fire fluttered over his brow; an axe was in his right hand, and a red flag in his left. I recognized Pierrot! If there had been a carbine within my reach, sheer rage might perhaps have made me commit a cowardly act. The black man repeated the chorus of '*Wa-Nassé,*' planted his flag on the peak, threw his axe into our midst, and was then swallowed up by the current. A sense of regret came over me at the thought that now he would no longer die by my hand.

The blacks then began to roll enormous blocks of stone onto our columns; bullets and arrows showered down on the morne. Furious at not being able to get at their attackers, our soldiers were drawing their last desperate breath: they were being crushed by boulders, riddled with bullets, pierced by arrows. A horrible confusion held sway over the army. All of a sudden, a frightful noise seemed to issue from the middle of the Grande Rivière. An extraordinary scene was taking place there. The yellow dragoons, faring poorly against the mass of stones that the rebels were launching from the mountain tops, had hit upon an idea for how to avoid them: by taking refuge under the pliant liana arches covering the river. Thaddeus was the first to suggest this plan of action—which was, by the way, an ingenious one ..."

At this point the narrator was suddenly interrupted.

23

MORE THAN a quarter of an hour had passed since Sergeant Thaddeus, his right arm in a sling, had slipped back unnoticed into a corner of the tent. Until that moment, only his bodily gestures testified to his involvement in the captain's tales but now, believing it would be disrespectful to let such direct praise go by without thanking d'Auverney for it, he began to stammer confusedly:

"You are too kind, my Captain."

A general outbreak of laughter ensued. D'Auverney turned round and burst out at him in a stern tone:

"What! *Vous!* Thaddeus, you're here! And your arm?"

Hearing himself addressed in this unaccustomed way, the old soldier staggered, his features darkening; he tilted his head back, as if to stop the tears that were welling up in his eyes.

"I did not believe," he said finally, in a whisper, "I would never have believed, that my captain could be so inconsiderate to his old sergeant as to address him as '*vous*.'"

The captain hastily rose to his feet.

"Forgive me, my old friend. I didn't realize what I was saying. Thad, come now, won't you forgive me?"

Tears gushed from the sergeant's eyes, despite himself.

"So this is the third time," he stammered. "But this time it is for joy."

Peace was made. A short silence followed.

"But, tell me, Thad," the captain asked gently, "why did you leave the ambulance wagon to come back here?"

"It's that, by your leave, I had come to ask you, my Captain, if the horse-cloth, with galloons, should be placed on your charger tomorrow."

Henry started laughing.

"You'd have done better, Thaddeus, to ask the army surgeon if two ounces of lint, in shreds, should be put on your game arm tomorrow."

"Or," Paschal followed up, "to inquire if you could drink a little wine to refresh yourself. Until you find that out, here's some brandy, which can only do you good. Have a try, my brave sergeant."

Thaddeus came forward, made a respectful bow, excused himself for taking the glass with his left hand, and emptied it after toasting their health. He grew animated.

"You had arrived at the moment, my Captain, at the moment when … Well then, yes, I was the one who suggested going under the lianas so that we good Christians wouldn't be crushed to death by the stones. Our officer, he didn't know how to swim and so he was afraid of drowning—a natural enough reaction. He fought the idea as hard as he could until—by your leave, gentlemen—he saw a huge slab of rock, which just missed smashing into him, get stopped by the vines as it hurtled toward the river. 'Better to die like the Pharaoh of Egypt than like Saint Stephen,' he said.[54] 'We're not saints, and the Pharaoh was a military man like us.' My officer, a learned fellow as you can see, was thus happy enough to follow my suggestion, on condition that I be the first to try it out. I'm on my way. I go down the bank. I leap under the trellis, holding on to the branches above, and then, my Captain? Well, I feel my leg being grabbed. I fight back, I shout for help, a sabre cuts into me several times, and now here come the dragoons, real devils they were, hurling themselves under the lianas, one on top of the other. The blacks of Morne Rouge had been lying in wait there, without anyone suspecting it, probably in order to fall upon us, like a sack full to bursting, when they had a chance. It certainly wouldn't have been a good time to go fishing!... There was fighting, swearing, shouting. Since they were completely naked, they moved around more easily than we did, but our blows hit home more than theirs. We were swimming with one arm and fighting with the other, as one does in those cases. And those who didn't know how to swim, my Captain? Well, they were hanging from the lianas with one arm, and the blacks were grabbing them by the feet. Right in the thick of this brawl, I saw a big negro defending himself against eight or ten of my comrades, like Beelzebub himself he was. I swam over and recognized Pierrot, otherwise called Bug ... But we don't find that out yet, right, my Captain? I recognized Pierrot. Ever since the capture of the fort, we hadn't been on the best of terms. I seized him by the throat. He was about to dispose of me with one thrust of his dagger when he saw who I was and, instead of killing me, surrendered. Which was a great misfortune, my Captain, for had he not surrendered ... But that's for later. As soon as the negroes saw he was captured, they leapt on us and tried to free him. So much so that the militias were also going to jump in the water when Pierrot, no doubt seeing that the negroes were all going to be slaughtered, said a few words. It must have been a real hocus pocus since it put them all to flight. They dived down and disappeared in the blink of an eye ... This underwater battle would have been really quite agreeable, it would have amused me no end, had I not lost a finger in it and drenched ten cartridges, and if ... poor man! But the writing was on the wall, my Captain."

After respectfully placing the back of his left hand over the ornament on his forage cap, the sergeant raised it upward with an inspired look.

D'Auverney seemed violently agitated.

"Yes," he said. "Yes, you're right, my old Thaddeus, that night was a fateful night indeed."

He would have fallen into that state of deep reflection to which he was prone had not his listeners eagerly urged him to continue. He took up his tale again.

24

"WHILE THE scene Thaddeus has just described …" (Thaddeus went and sat down in triumph behind the captain.) "While the scene Thaddeus has just described was taking place behind the morne, I had managed, with a few of my men, to scramble up from one bush to another onto the *Pic du Paon*,[55] so-called because of the iridescent hues it would throw off when the sun's rays hit against the mica on its surface. This peak was on a level with the positions held by the blacks. Now that a path had been cleared, the summit was soon rife with militia, and we opened fire with a vengeance. The negroes, less well armed, couldn't return our fire as briskly. They began to lose heart; we responded even more fiercely. Soon the nearest rocks were evacuated by the rebels. They nonetheless made sure before leaving to roll the bodies of their dead comrades down onto the rest of our army, which was still marshalled for battle on the morne. We then felled several trunks of those enormous wild cotton-trees that the first inhabitants of the island used to make into pirogues big enough for a hundred oarsmen, and we tied them together with palm leaves and ropes. With the help of this improvised bridge, we crossed over onto the abandoned peaks and a part of our army thus found itself in an advantageous position. The sight of this unnerved the insurgents. We kept up our fire. Plaintive howls, mixed in with the name of Bug-Jargal, suddenly rang through Biassou's army. They sounded terror-stricken. A number of the Morne Rouge blacks appeared on the rock where the scarlet flag was flying; they prostrated themselves, removed the standard, and hurled themselves along with it into the chasms of the Grande Rivière. This seemed to signify that their leader was dead or captured.

We grew so bold on seeing this that I resolved to attack the rebels at close quarters and drive them from the cliff-tops they still occupied. I had my men fell some trees to form a bridge between our peak and the nearest rock, and I was the first to dash across it into the negroes' midst. My men were about to follow when one of the rebels, with the stroke of an axe, smashed the bridge to pieces. The debris fell into the abyss, striking against the rocks with a dreadful noise.

I turned my head. At that moment I was grabbed hold of by six or seven blacks who disarmed me. I fought back like a lion. They tied me up with strips of bark, heedless of the bullets raining down on them from my side.

Only one thing alleviated my despair: the shouts of victory that I heard all around me an instant later. It wasn't long before I saw the blacks and mulattoes scrambling pell-mell up the steepest summits, letting out howls of distress as they went. Those guarding me imitated them. The most vigorous one among them loaded me onto his shoulders and carried me off toward the forests, leaping from rock to rock with the agility of a chamois. The gleam of the flames soon ceased to guide him; the faint light of the moon was all he needed. He kept on walking, but at a slower pace.

25

AFTER TRAVELLING through various thickets and crossing over a number of torrents, we came to a highland valley. Strikingly wild in appearance, it was a place absolutely unknown to me.

The valley was situated in the very heart of the mornes—in what people in Saint Domingue call 'the double mountains.' It was a large green savannah, enclosed by bare rock walls and dotted with clusters of pine, guaiacum, and palm. The biting cold that almost always prevails over that region of the island, even though it never freezes there, was reinforced by the cool of the night, which was only just drawing to a close. The highest tops of the surrounding mountains were beginning to whiten with the dawn, while the valley—still entirely steeped in darkness—was illuminated only by a great many fires lit by the negroes whose rallying point it was. The routed members of their army were assembling there in disarray. One after another, flustered gangs of blacks and mulattoes arrived, letting off cries of distress or howls of anger; new fires, glinting like the eyes of a tiger in the dark savannah, signalled that with every passing minute the circle of the camp was expanding.

The negro whose prisoner I was had set me down at the foot of an oak; from there, I dispassionately observed this bizarre spectacle. The black man tied me by my belt to the trunk of the tree I was leaning against, tightened the double knots that constrained my every movement, placed his red woolen cap on my head—doubtless to indicate that I was his property—and, after thus making sure that I wouldn't be able to escape and that nobody could steal me away from him, he got ready to move off. I resolved to speak to him, and asked him in creole patois if he was part of the Dondon band or that of Morne Rouge. He stopped and answered me with a proud look: '*Morne Rouge!*' A thought struck me. I had heard tell of the generosity of that band's leader, Bug-Jargal, and though I was thoroughly reconciled to a death that would put an end to all my troubles, I could not help feeling a certain horror at the thought of what lay in store for me were I to receive it at the hands of Biassou. I would have been only too happy to die, but to be tortured was another matter. Perhaps this was weak of me, but I believe at such moments it is only human nature for us to protest against our fate. I reasoned that, if I could stay out of Biassou's clutches, I might perhaps receive from Bug-Jargal a death without torture, a soldier's death. I asked this Morne Rouge negro to take me to his leader, Bug-Jargal. He gave a start. 'Bug-Jargal!' he wailed, striking his forehead in despair. Then his expression rapidly turned to one of fury. He gnashed his teeth and, shaking his fist at me, yelled out a name that rang with menace: 'Biassou! Biassou!' After which, he took his leave of me.

The negro's anger and his grief made me think back to that point in the battle when we had been led to conclude that the leader of the Morne Rouge bands had been captured or killed. I no longer had any doubts on the matter, and I resigned myself to what the black man seemed to be threatening me with: Biassou's vengeance.

26

MEANWHILE, the valley was still covered in darkness. The mobs of blacks and the number of fires kept on growing. A group of negresses came and lit a fire close by me. Everything about them—the numerous bracelets of blue, red, and purple glass glittering at intervals on their arms and legs; the rings weighing down their ears, and those adorning every one of their fingers and toes; the amulets affixed to their breast; the string of 'charms' hanging down from their neck; the apron of gaudy feathers, the only piece of clothing veiling their nakedness; above all, their rhythmic clamouring and the shadowy, frantic look on their faces—led me to conclude that they were *griotes*.[56] Perhaps you are not aware that among the blacks of various regions in Africa there exist negroes gifted with a sort of crude talent for poetry and improvisation that is akin to madness. These negroes, wandering from kingdom to kingdom, fill the same role in those barbarous lands as did the ancient rhapsodists and, during the Middle Ages, the *minstrels* of England, the *minnesingers* of Germany, and the *trouvères* of France. They are called *griots*. Their wives, the griotes, likewise possessed by a crazed demon, accompany their husbands' barbarous songs with lewd dances, offering a grotesque parody of the bayadères of Hindustan and the Egyptian almahs. Well then, it was several of these women who had just sat themselves down only a few steps away from me. Their legs folded under them in the African manner, they were seated in a circle around a large pile of seared branches; as it burned, the red light of its flames flickered over their hideous faces.

As soon as their circle was formed, they all took each other by the hand and the oldest woman, who had a heron feather stuck in her hair, began shouting '*Wanga!*' It dawned on me that they were going to carry out one of the magic spells they designate by this name. '*Wanga!*,' they all repeated. After a contemplative silence, the oldest tore out a handful of her hair and threw it into the fire, speaking those ritual words, '*Malé o guiab!*,' which in the jargon of the creole negroes signifies: 'I will go to the devil.' Imitating their elder, all the griotes surrendered a lock of their hair to the flames and again solemnly intoned: '*Malé o guiab!*'

This strange invocation, and the outlandish grimaces that accompanied it, provoked in me what is called a laughing-fit, a sort of involuntary convulsion that often, despite themselves, grabs hold of the most serious of men or even those most overwhelmed with grief. I tried to suppress it but in vain. Out it burst. This laughter, let slip from a heart full of sadness, gave rise to a strangely dark and frightful scene.

The negresses, disturbed in their mysteries, all jumped up as if they had woken with a start. Until that point, they had been unaware of my presence. In an uproar, they ran toward me, howling '*Blanco! Blanco!*' I've never seen a collection of more diversely horrible faces than all those infuriated black mugs with their white teeth and the whites of their eyes streaked with large bloodshot veins.

They were set on tearing me to pieces. The old one with the heron feather made a sign and yelled several times: '*Zoté cordé! Zoté cordé!*'* The frenzied women suddenly came to a stop, and with no small amazement I saw each and every one of them take off their feather aprons and throw them onto the grass; then they surrounded me and launched into that lascivious dance the blacks call *la chica*.[57]

The grotesque poses and lively motions of this dance express only pleasure and gaiety, but here various added features gave it a sinister character. It was all too evident—from the withering looks that the griotes flashed at me in the midst of their sprightly turns; from the dirge-like note that they gave to the joyful strain of *la chica*; from the piercing and prolonged groan that the venerable president of this black sanhedrim[58] every so often extracted from her *balafo*, a sort of spinet that murmurs like a small organ and is composed of about twenty pipes of hard wood, of gradually diminishing thickness and length; above all, from the horrible laughter that each naked sorceress in turn, during certain breaks in the dance, would come and direct at me, almost pressing her face into mine— what ghastly punishments lay in wait for the *blanco* who had profaned their Wanga. I recalled the custom of those savage tribes who dance around their prisoners before slaughtering them, and I patiently stood by as these women performed the ballet portion of a play that was to end with me soaked in blood. However, I couldn't help shuddering at that point in the dance, underscored by the balafo, when I saw each griote stick into the blazing fire the tip of a sabre blade, the head of an axe, the tip of a long sail-needle, the jaws of a pair of pincers, or the teeth of a saw.

The dance was drawing to a close; the instruments of torture were red-hot. At a signal from the old woman, the negresses went in procession, one after the other, to look for some horrible weapon in the fire.

Those who couldn't arm themselves with a glowing piece of iron took up a blazing firebrand. It was then that I clearly understood what form of torture was in store for me, and that every dancer would also be my executioner. At another command from the chorus leader, they began one last round of dancing, wailing all the while in an alarming fashion. I closed my eyes so that at least I would no longer have to witness the revels of these she-demons who, panting from exhaustion and rage, had lifted their glowing scraps of iron above their heads and were rhythmically banging them together, producing a piercing noise and myriads of sparks. Growing tense, I awaited the moment when I would endure the tortures of the

---

* Get in step! Get in step!

flesh, feel my bones turning to cinders, my nerves buckling under the searing bite of the pincers and the saws; a shiver ran through my every limb. It was a ghastly moment.

Fortunately enough, it didn't last long. The griotes' chica was approaching its climax, when I heard from a distance the voice of the negro who had taken me prisoner. He was racing forward and shouting, '*Que haceis, mujeres de demonio? Que haceis alli? Dexaïs mi prisionero!*'* I opened my eyes. It was already broad daylight. The negro rushed up, making no end of angry gestures. The griotes had stopped, but they seemed less moved by his threats than taken aback by the presence of a rather bizarre looking character who accompanied the black man.

It was a very thick-set, very short man, a sort of dwarf whose face was hidden by a white veil with three holes pierced in it for the mouth and eyes, in the fashion of penitents. The veil hung down over his neck and shoulders. His hairy chest, though, was left exposed; its colour seemed to me that of a griffe's and on it, suspended from a gold chain, glittered a mangled silver monstrance. You could see the handle of a crude dagger, shaped like a cross, protruding from his scarlet belt; it was holding up a green, yellow, and black-striped skirt, the fringes of which reached all the way down to his large, misshapen feet. His arms, bare like his chest, brandished a white rod. A rosary, its beads made of azedarac, hung from his belt next to the dagger. His head was topped with a pointed bonnet decorated with bells; once he drew near I was more than a little surprised to discover that it was the *gorra* of Habibrah, except now, alongside the hieroglyphs that covered this makeshift mitre, you could see blood stains. No doubt this blood was that of the faithful jester. To me, these traces of murder seemed a new proof of his death, and they kindled in my heart one last regret.

The minute the griotes noticed this inheritor of Habibrah's bonnet, they all cried out together, 'the *obi*!' and prostrated themselves. I guessed that he was the sorcerer of Biassou's army. '*Basta! Basta!*' he said in a low, muffled voice when he got close to them. '*Dexaïs el prisionero de Biassu.*'† Picking themselves up in a jumble, the negresses disposed of their instruments of death, took back their feathery aprons and, at a signal from the obi, scattered like a cloud of locusts.

Just then, the obi's gaze seemed to fasten on me; he gave a start, drew back a pace, and lifted up his rod in the direction of the griotes, as if want-

---

* What are you doing, demon women? What are you doing there? Leave my prisoner alone!

† That's enough! That's enough! Leave the prisoner of Biassou alone!

ing to call them back. However, after grumbling the word *maldicho*** under his breath and whispering a few more words in the negro's ear, he slowly withdrew with his arms folded and in a pose of deepest meditation.

27

MY KEEPER then informed me that Biassou wished to see me and that I should prepare myself for an interview with this leader one hour hence.

It was, to be sure, one additional hour of life. While waiting for it to elapse, my eyes roamed over the rebel camp, the unusual features of which I could make out down to the last detail now that it was daylight. In another frame of mind, I wouldn't have been able to stop myself from laughing at the fatuous vanity of the blacks, almost all of whom were wearing some form or other of military or ecclesiastical clothing which they had stripped from their victims. Most of this finery was now little more than shredded, blood-soaked rags. It wasn't rare to see the glint of a gorget underneath a priest's collar, or an epaulette on top of a chasuble. No doubt seeking relaxation from the labours to which they had all their lives been condemned, the negroes were in a state of inactivity that you do not find among our soldiers, even when they are back under their tents. Some were sleeping out in the sun, their heads next to a scorching fire; others, with a look in their eyes that was by turns lacklustre and full of fury, were singing a monotonous tune as they squatted down on the threshold of their *ajoupas*—a sort of hut covered with banana or palm leaves and having a conical form similar to that of our bell-tents.[59] Their black or copper-coloured women, with the help of their pickaninnies, were preparing food for the combatants. I watched them using pitchforks to stir yams, bananas, sweet potatoes, peas, coconut, maize, the Caribbean cabbage they call taro, and a host of other indigenous fruits that were bubbling away alongside slabs of pork, tortoise, and dog in large sugar boilers stolen from the planters' factories. In the distance, at the limits of the camp, the griots and the griotes formed large circles around the fires; snatches of their barbarous songs, mingled with the sound of guitars and balafos, wafted over to me on the wind. A few watchmen, positioned on the summits of near-by crags, were keeping an eye on the area surrounding Biassou's headquarters, which

---

* Accursed.

had as its only line of defence in case of attack a circular cordon of ox-carts loaded with booty and munitions. These black sentinels, standing on the sharp tip of the granite pyramids that blanket the mornes, frequently spun round on themselves, like weather vanes on gothic spires, shouting back and forth to one another at the top of their lungs, '*Nada! Nada!*'*—thereby confirming that the camp was secure from danger.

From time to time, crowds of inquisitive negroes would gather round me. Every last one of them cast a menacing look my way.

2 8

EVENTUALLY a platoon, composed of soldiers of colour and passably well-armed, made its way to me. The black man to whom, apparently, I belonged untied me from the oak to which I was fastened and handed me over to the squad leader, from whose hands he received in exchange a largish sack which he opened on the spot. It was filled with piastres. While the negro, kneeling down on the grass, greedily counted them, the soldiers took me away. I examined their get-up with curiosity. They wore a brown, red, and yellow uniform of coarse cloth, cut in the Spanish fashion. A kind of Castilian *montera*,[60] decorated with a big red cockade,† hid their wooly hair. Instead of a cartridge-box, they had a gamebag of sorts attached to their sides. As for weapons, they had a heavy rifle, a sabre, and a dagger. I afterward found out that this was the uniform of Biassou's own special guard.

After weaving through the crooked rows of ajoupas that cluttered up the camp, we arrived at the entrance of a cave carved out by nature's hand at the foot of one of those immense rock faces that walled in the savannah. A large curtain made out of a Tibetan material called cashmere, distinguished less by the vividness of its colours than by its soft folds and its varied patterns, sealed off the interior of this cavern from view. It was surrounded by several double lines of soldiers, fitted out like the ones who had escorted me there.

After an exchange of watchwords with the two sentinels who were pacing up and down the threshold of the cave, the squad leader raised

---

* Nothing! Nothing!

† This colour being, of course, that of the Spanish cockade.

the cashmere curtain and ushered me in, letting it drop back down behind him.

A copper lamp with five wicks dangled from chains that were attached to the vault; it cast an unsteady light on the dank walls of the cavern, which was sealed off from the light of day. Between two lines of mulatto soldiers, I caught sight of a man of colour seated on an enormous mahogany trunk that was half covered by a carpet of parrot feathers. This man was a *sacatra*, which as a species is distinguishable from the negro only by virtue of an often imperceptible nuance.[61] His outfit was ridiculous. A magnificent silk-plaited belt, from which dangled a Saint-Louis Cross, was keeping a pair of blue breeches made out of coarse fabric up around the level of his navel; a jacket of white dimity, too small to reach down to his belt, completed his costume. He was wearing grey boots, a round hat topped with a red cockade, and a pair of epaulettes, one of which was made of gold, with the two silver stars for brigadier-generals, and the other of yellow wool. Fastened onto the latter, no doubt in order to make it worthy of figuring next to its sparkling companion, were two copper stars that seemed to have been the rowels from a set of spurs. These two epaulettes, not being secured in their natural place with crosswise braids, were dangling down both sides of his chest. A sabre and several impressively inlaid pistols were to be found on the feather carpet next to him.

Behind where he was seated stood, silent and motionless, two children dressed in slaves' breeches, each carrying a broad fan made of peacock feathers. These two slave children were white.

Two crimson velvet cushions, apparently belonging to the prayer-stool of some presbytery, marked out two seats to the right and left of the mahogany block. Occupying one of these seats, on the right, was the obi who had rescued me from the fury of the griotes. He was seated with his legs folded under him, holding his wand upright, as motionless as a porcelain idol in a Chinese pagoda. Through the holes in his veil, though, I could see the glint of his fiery eyes, which tracked me unremittingly.

At either side of the chief were bundles of flags, banners, and pennants of all sorts, among which I noticed the white fleur-de-lis, the tricolour, and the flag of Spain. The others were fanciful ensigns. Among them, you could see a large black standard.

At the back of the room, above the chief's head, yet another object caught my attention. It was a portrait of the mulatto Ogé, who the previous year had been broken on the wheel at the Cape for the crime of rebellion along with his lieutenant, Jean-Baptiste Chavannes,[62] and twenty other blacks or sang-mêlés. It represented him in his customary attire: as in other portraits of him, Ogé, the son of a butcher from the Cape, was wearing the uniform of a lieutenant-colonel, decorated with a Saint-Louis Cross and the Order of Merit of the Lion which he had purchased in Europe from the Prince of Limburg.[63]

The sacatra chief into whose presence I had been ushered was of middling height. His ignoble features presented a rare mixture of shrewdness and cruelty. He bade me approach, and studied me for some time in silence; at length, he began sniggering in the manner of a hyena.

'I am Biassou,' he said to me.

I was expecting this name, but I was unable to hear it from that mouth, amid that ferocious laughter, without shuddering inwardly. However, I retained a calm, proud demeanour. I made no reply.

'So,' he carried on in rather bad French, 'is it, perchance, that you've just had a good impaling? Is that why you can't bend your back bone in the presence of Jean Biassou, Generalissimo of the Conquered Territories and Brigadier of *su magestad catolica*?' (The tactic of the principal rebel leaders was to make it seem as if they were acting at times on behalf of the king of France, at other times on behalf of the revolution, and at yet others on behalf of the king of Spain.)

I folded my arms on my chest, and looked at him intently. He started sniggering again. This 'tic' was habitual with him.

'Ho! Ho! *Me pareces hombre de buen corazon.** Well then, listen to what I'm going to tell you. Are you creole?'

'No,' I answered, 'I am French.'

My self-assurance made him frown. Sniggering, he went on:

'All the better! I see from your uniform that you're an officer. How old are you?'

'Twenty.'

'When did you turn twenty?'

At this question, which revived some deeply distressing memories for me, I remained for a moment lost in my thoughts. He put it to me again, testily. I answered him:

'On the day your companion Leogri was hanged.'[64]

His features contorted with anger, and his snigger was unrelenting. He kept control of himself, however.

'It's been twenty-three days since Leogri was hanged,' he said to me. 'Frenchman, this evening you'll have a chance to tell him from me that

---

* You seem like an upstanding fellow.

you outlived him by twenty-four days. I want to keep you around for the rest of the day. That way you'll be able to tell him about the liberty of his brothers and how matters are faring, what you've seen in the headquarters of Brigadier Jean Biassou, and exactly what authority this generalissimo has over the *gens du roi*.'[65]

It was with this name that Jean-François, who went by the title of *Grand Admiral of France*, and his comrade Biassou designated their hordes of rebel negroes and mulattoes.

After ordering that I be sat down between two guards in a corner of the cave, he made a sign with his hand to some negroes who were decked out in aide-de-camp uniforms:

'Let the call to arms be sounded. Rally the entire army to our head-quarters, that we might pass it in review. And you, my good chaplain,' he said turning toward the obi, 'put on your church robes and celebrate for us and our soldiers the holy sacrifice of the mass.'

The obi got up, bowed low before Biassou, and whispered a few words to him. Abruptly and in a loud voice, the chief interrupted:

'You have no altar, you say, *señor cura!* Is that any surprise in these mountains? What does it matter! Since when does the *bon Giu** need to be worshipped in a magnificent temple or with an altar adorned in gold and lace? Gideon and Joshua glorified him in front of a pile of stones.[66] Let's do as they did, *bon per.*† The *bon Giu* wants nothing more than ardent hearts. You have no altar! Well then, what about that big sugar-box, which the *gens du roi* seized from the Dubuisson settlement a couple of days ago? Couldn't you make one out of that?'

Biassou's proposal was promptly carried out. In the blink of an eye the interior of the grotto was readied for this parody of the divine mystery. A tabernacle was brought in, as well as a ciborium, both of which had been pilfered from the Acul parish church—the very place of worship where my union with Marie had received a heavenly benediction so promptly followed by disaster. The stolen sugar-box was promoted into an altar and covered with a white sheet in lieu of an altar cloth; even with the sheet, you could still read on the sides of this altar the words *'Dubuisson and Co., Nantes.'*

When the sacred vessels were placed on the cloth, the obi noticed that a cross was lacking; he pulled out his dagger, which had a cross-shaped hilt, and drove it upright between the chalice and the monstrance in front

---

* Creole patois. The good Lord.

† Creole patois. Good father.

of the tabernacle. Then, without taking off his sorcerer's bonnet and his penitent's veil, he promptly threw over his naked back and chest a cope stolen from the prior at Acul, opened the silver-clasped missal-book next to the tabernacle—from which the prayers at my fateful marriage had been read—and, turning toward Biassou, whose seat was a few steps from the altar, made it known through a low bow that he was ready.

There and then, at a sign from the chief, the cashmere curtains were pulled aside, disclosing to us the entire black army drawn up in close-packed square formations in front of the grotto's opening. Biassou took off his round hat and kneeled before the altar. 'On your knees,' he cried, in a loud voice. 'On your knees!' repeated the leaders of each batallion. A drum roll was heard. All the hordes were on their knees.

I, alone, had not moved from my seat, revolted as I was by the horrible profanation about to be enacted before my very eyes. But the two robust mulattoes who were guarding me stole my seat from under me, gave my shoulders an unceremonious push, and I fell to my knees like the others, forced into conferring a simulacrum of respect on this simulacrum of worship.

The obi celebrated the mass solemnly. Biassou's two little white page boys acted as deacon and sub-deacon.

Still prostrate, the crowd of rebels followed the ceremony in a contemplative spirit, emulating their *generalissimo*. At the moment of the elevation, the obi raised the consecrated host in his hands and, turning toward the army, cried out in creole jargon: '*Zoté coné bon Giu; ce li mo fe zoté voer. Blan touyé li, touyé blan yo toute.*'* At these words, delivered in a powerful voice—but one that I seemed already to have heard in another place and at other times—the entire horde let out a roar; they banged their weapons together for a long time, and were it not for Biassou's bodyguards this ominous din would have tolled my last hour on earth. I understood what excesses of courage and atrocity could be committed by men for whom a dagger was a cross, and for whom every impression is immediate and deep.

---

* "You know the good Lord; he it is whom I display to you. The whites have killed him, kill all the whites." Subsequently, Toussaint Louverture was in the habit of addressing this same little speech to the negroes after receiving communion. [Editor's note: The story of Toussaint's rise and fall—the rapid emergence of this freed slave from under the shadow of Jean-François and Biassou as a leader of the revolt; his shift of allegiances from the Spanish to the French in 1794, and his subsequent rise to a position of ultimate authority in the colony; his betrayal by a Napoleon bent on the restoration of slavery; and his exile in 1802 to a French prison, where he would die the next year—is gloriously told in C.L.R. James's *The Black Jacobins*. Hugo's novel repeatedly transposes onto his fictional Biassou anecdotes about the historical Toussaint that he found in Lacroix's *Mémoires* (see Appendix E.2d).]

29

THE CEREMONY at an end, the obi turned toward Biassou and bowed respectfully. The chief then stood up and addressed me in French: 'They accuse us of having no religion. You see that it's a slander, and that we're good Catholics.'

I don't know if he was speaking ironically or in good faith. A moment later, he had someone bring him a glass vase full of grains of black maize. He threw in some grains of white maize and then, lifting the vase over his head so that his entire army could get a better view of it, he declared:

'Brothers, you are the black maize; the whites, your enemies, are the white maize!'

At these words, he shook the vase and, when almost all the white grains had disappeared under the black ones, he cried out with an air of inspiration and triumph: '*Guetté blan si la la.*'*[67]

The chief's parable was greeted by a new round of cheers, which echoed from one mountain to the next. Biassou continued, frequently mixing creole and Spanish phrases in with his bad French:

'*El tiempo de la mansuetud es pasado.*† We have for a long time now been as patient as the sheep whose wool the whites liken to our hair. Let us now be as implacable as the panthers and jaguars of the lands from which we were torn away. Rights can be obtained only through force; everything belongs to those who show themselves to be strong and without pity. Saint Lupus has two feast days in the Gregorian calendar;[68] the paschal lamb has only one! Is that not right, my good chaplain?'

The obi bowed by way of signifying his agreement.

' ... They came,' Biassou carried on, 'they came, the enemies of humanity's regeneration, those whites, those colonists, those planters, those traffickers, *verdaderos demonios* vomited forth from the mouth of Alecto![69] *Son venidos con insolencia.*‡ They were covered, these vainglorious men, with weapons, plumes, and outfits that were magnificent to the eye, and they held us in contempt because we are black and naked. They thought, in their arrogance, they could drive us off as easily as these peacock feathers chase away the black swarms of mosquitoes and midges!'

---

* See what the whites are in relation to you!

† The time for being meek of heart is over.

‡ They came insolently.

As he was finishing this comparison, he snatched from the hands of a white slave one of the fans that was being carried behind him and waved it over his head with a great many vehement gestures. He started up again: ' ... But, O my brothers, our army descended on theirs like swarms of gnats upon a corpse. They and their lovely uniforms fell under the blows of those naked arms—arms they thought lacking in power. But what they did not know is that good wood is all the harder when the bark has been stripped from it. They are trembling now, those loathsome tyrants! *Yo gagné peur!*'*

Their chief's battle cry was met with a howl of joy and triumph, and all the hordes kept on repeating: '*Yo gagné peur!*'

' ... You creole and congo blacks,' Biassou continued, 'vengeance and liberty! You sang-mêlés, do not let yourselves be lulled by the seductions *de los diabolos blancos.* Your fathers are in their ranks, but your mothers are in ours. And besides, *o hermanos de mi alma,*† they have never treated you like fathers, only like masters: you were slaves like the blacks. Back then when a miserable bit of cloth was all that shielded your scorched body from the sun, your barbarous fathers strutted around under *buenos sombreros,* wearing nankeen jackets on work days and dressing up in camlet or velvet on holidays, *a diez-y-siete quartos la vara.*‡ A curse on these unnatural beings! However, as the holy commandments of the *bon Giu* forbid it, do not be the one to strike down your own father. If you come upon him in the enemy ranks, who is to stop you, *amigos,* from saying to one another: *"Touyé papa moé, ma touyé quena toué!"*§ Vengeance, you *gens du roi*! Liberty for all men! This cry echoes across all the islands. Launched from *Quisqueya,*** it can be heard from Tobago to Cuba. It is a black man from

---

* Creole jargon. They are afraid.

† O brothers of my soul.

‡ At seventeen *quartos* the *vara* (Spanish measurement that is more or less equivalent to an ell).

§ "You kill my father, I'll kill yours." Striking a bargain, so to speak, with parricide, mulattoes were indeed heard uttering these loathsome words. [Editor's Note: Hugo's seemingly authoritative footnote significantly distorts a passage from Lacroix's *Mémoires*: "The laws of morality and of nature were all violated in the war between the Whites and the men of colour; it was a case of fathers destroying their own sons, or of sons thrusting their bloody arms into their fathers' breasts. In their mutual delirium, they goaded one another on by saying: 'You kill mine, I'll kill yours'" (1.195-96). Lacroix condemns the "criminality" of both parties, white and coloured, whereas Hugo's white fathers have become blameless victims of parricidal mulatto aggression, their own role in the internecine bloodbath having been totally whitewashed, as it were, from Hugo's fiction.]

** Former name of Saint Domingue which signifies "Great-Earth." The indigenous peoples also called it *Aity.*

Jamaica, Boukmann, leader of one hundred and twenty-five maroons from the Blue Mountains, who has raised the banner of revolt amongst us. A victory was his first act of fraternity with the blacks of Saint Domingue. Let us follow his glorious example, torch in one hand, axe in the other! No mercy for the whites, no mercy for the planters! Let us slaughter their families, let us lay waste their plantations, let us not leave one tree on their domains that has not been upended. Let us turn the earth upside down so that it swallows up the whites! Take heart then, friends and brothers! Soon we will go into battle and exterminate. We will triumph or we will die. Victorious, it will be our turn to delight in all the joys of life. Dead, we will go to heaven, where the saints await us in paradise, where each brave warrior will receive a double measure of *aguardiente** and one piastre-gourde a day!'

This soldierly sermon of sorts, which to you, gentlemen, must appear quite ridiculous, had a tremendous effect on the rebels. It has to be said that Biassou's extraordinary pantomime, the inspired tone of his voice, the strange sniggering that punctuated his words, all gave his harangue an indescribable power to impress and entrance. The artful way he sprinkled his speech with details likely to flatter the passions or the self-interest of the insurgents only strengthened his powers of persuasion, which were well suited to that audience.

I won't make any attempt to describe for you the disquieting enthusiasm that took hold of the insurgent army after Biassou's exhortation. It was a discordant chorus of shouts, groans, and howls. Some beat their chests, others banged their cudgels and sabres. Several, on their knees or prostrate, were riveted to the ground in an ecstatic pose. Negresses lacerated their breasts and arms with the fishbones they use in lieu of combs to untangle their hair. The sound of guitars, tomtoms, drums, and balafos mingled with volleys of musket fire. It was as if all hell had broken loose.

Biassou made a sign with his hand, and as if by a miracle the uproar ceased. Each negro silently got back into line. The discipline Biassou had enforced on his equals through simple ascendancy of mind and will struck me, you might say, with admiration. All the soldiers of this rebel army seemed to speak and move at a wave of the chief's hand, like the keys of a harpsichord at the touch of a musician's fingers.

---

* Brandy.

30

ANOTHER spectacle, another type of charlatanism and entrancement, next drew my attention: the dressing of the wounded. The obi, who performed double duty in the army as doctor of the soul and doctor of the body, had begun inspecting his patients. He had stripped off his ecclesiastical robes, and a large box with compartments in which he kept his drugs and his instruments had been brought to him as directed. He made sparing use of his surgical tools; apart from a very deft bleeding that he performed with a fishbone lancet, he seemed to me rather clumsy when it came to handling the pair of pincers that served him as forceps or the knife that took the place of a scalpel. Most of the time he limited himself to prescribing infusions of sour orange, draughts of china-root and sarsaparilla, and a few mouthfuls of old cheap rum. His favourite remedy, and one that he claimed to be most efficacious, consisted of three glasses of red wine in which he mixed ground nutmeg and the hard yolk of an egg cooked in the ashes. This was the specified cure for every type of wound or illness. You can readily imagine that this medical treatment was as laughable as the worship that went on under his ministry, and it's more than likely that the small number of cures it chanced to bring about would not have been enough to retain the blacks' trust in the obi had his drugs not been accompanied by all sorts of trickery, and had he not sought to act all the more on the imagination of the negroes the less he acted on their afflictions. Thus, he would sometimes do no more than touch their wounds while making a few mystical signs with his hand; at other times, skilfully exploiting that remnant of old superstitions they mixed in with their recently acquired Catholicism, he would place in their wounds a little fetish stone wrapped in lint and the patient would attribute to the stone the beneficial effects of the lint. If he happened to be informed that a certain wounded man he'd treated had died from the wound, and perhaps from the remedy he'd applied, he would respond in a solemn voice: 'I had foreseen it; he was a traitor. When a certain settlement was put to the torch he saved a white man's life. Death is his punishment!' The crowd of astounded rebels would applaud, their feelings of hatred and desire for vengeance growing ever more bitter. Among the charlatan's healing methods, there was one that particularly struck me: he applied it to one of the black leaders, who had been quite severely wounded in the latest fighting. After examining the wound for a long time, he dressed it as best he could and then, climbing up onto the altar, he announced: 'All that's of no account.' Then he tore out three or four pages from the missal, set them alight with burning tapers that had been stolen from the church at Acul and, mixing the ash of this consecrated paper with a few drops of wine poured into the chalice, said to the wounded man:

'Drink. This is the cure.'*

The man drank it down in a daze, his trusting eyes fixed on the trickster who had his hands raised over him as if to call down heaven's blessings. Who knows? Maybe the conviction that he was cured played a part in curing him.

31

ANOTHER scene in which the veiled obi was once again the principal actor followed this one: the doctor had taken over from the priest, and now the sorcerer took over from the doctor.

'*Hombres, escuchate!*'† exclaimed the obi, leaping with incredible agility onto the improvised altar, where he sat himself down with his legs folded under his gaudy skirt. '*Escuchate, hombres!* Let those who wish to read in the book of destiny the solution to their life's riddle draw nigh, I will tell it to them. *Hé estudiado la ciencia de los gitanos.*'‡

A crowd of blacks and mulattoes rushed forward.

'One at a time,' said the obi, whose muffled, contained voice sometimes took on a strident tone that dashed against me like a memory. 'If you all arrive together, you will all enter the grave together.'

They stopped short. At that moment, a man of colour came up to Biassou; he was dressed in a white jacket and trousers, his head bound in a madras handkerchief in the fashion of rich colonists. Dismay was etched on his face.

---

* This remedy is still rather frequently practiced in Africa, notably by the Moors of Tripoli, who often sprinkle the ashes of a page from the book of Mohammed into their drinks, making up a potion to which they attribute sovereign virtues.

    An English traveller—I no longer remember which one—calls this drink "an infusion of Al-Koran."

† "Men, listen!" The meaning that the Spanish attach to the word "hombre," in this case, cannot be translated. It means more than "man" and less than "friend."

‡ I have studied the teachings of the gypsies.

'So!' said the *generalissimo* in a whisper. 'What is it? What's the matter, Rigaud?'

This Rigaud was the mulatto who headed the forces from Les Cayes, subsequently known under the name of *General Rigaud*, a sly man beneath his candid exterior, a cruel man beneath an appearance of gentleness.[70] I examined him closely.

'General,' answered Rigaud (and he spoke in a very low voice, but being situated close to Biassou I could hear what was being said), 'over on the outskirts of the camp an emissary from Jean-François has arrived. Boukmann has just been killed in an engagement with Monsieur de Touzard and it is rumoured that the whites are displaying his head as a trophy in their city.'

'Oh, is that all?' replied Biassou. His eyes sparkled with joy at seeing the number of leaders diminish and, as a consequence, his own importance grow.

'Jean-François's emissary also has a message to deliver to you.'

'That's fine,' Biassou said. 'Stop looking so deathly glum, my dear Rigaud.'

'But, General,' Rigaud objected, 'are you not afraid of the effect that Boukmann's death will have on your army?'

'You're not as simple as you let on, Rigaud,' retorted the chief. 'You'll soon see what stuff Biassou is made of. Just be sure to delay the messenger's arrival for a quarter of an hour.'

Then he went up to the obi, who during this dialogue heard by me alone had begun performing his duties as soothsayer: examining the reverent negroes, interrogating the signs on their foreheads and hands, and meting out to them a greater or lesser measure of future happiness—depending on the sound, the colour, and the size of the coin each negro pitched at his feet into a gilded silver paten. Biassou whispered a few words to him. Without breaking off, the sorcerer continued his metoposcopic operations.[71]

'"Whoever,"' he intoned, '"bears in the middle of his forehead, on the sun wrinkle, a little square figure or a triangle will make a great fortune without effort and without toil.

The figure of three close-set *S*'s, on whatever part of the forehead they are to be found, is an extremely ill-fated sign; whoever bears this sign will drown without fail, unless he is very careful to stay away from water.

Four lines beginning at the nose, and curving over in pairs on the forehead above the eyes, portends that some day this person will be a prisoner of war, and that he will groan in captivity at the hands of the foreigner."'

Here the obi paused.

'Companions,' he added solemnly, 'I had observed this sign on the forehead of Bug-Jargal, leader of the brave warriors of Morne Rouge.'

These words, which again confirmed for me that Bug-Jargal had been captured, were followed by the wailing of a horde composed only of blacks, and whose leaders wore scarlet breeches. It was the band from Morne Rouge.

Meanwhile the obi started up again:

'"If on the right half of your forehead, on the moon wrinkle, you have some figure that resembles a pitchfork, then dread a life of idleness or the heated pursuit of debauchery.

A little sign, but a very important one, the Arabic numeral 3, on the sun wrinkle, is the presage that you will receive a good thrashing."'

An old negro from the Spanish part of the island interrupted the sorcerer. He dragged himself up to the obi and implored that he be given treatment. He had been wounded on the forehead, and one of his eyes, ripped out from its socket, was hanging down in a bloody mess. The obi had overlooked him during his medical inspection. No sooner did he notice the fellow than he exclaimed:

'"Round figures on the right half of the forehead, on the moon wrinkle, portend disorders of the eye." *Hombre*,' he said to the wounded man, 'this sign is conspicuous on your forehead. Let us see your hand.'

'*Alas! exelentisimo señor*,' the other replied, '*mir'usted mi ojo!*'*

'*Fatras*,'†72 the obi retorted ill-humouredly, 'as if I needed to see your eye! Your hand, I tell you.'

The poor fellow extended his hand, muttering all the while: '*Mi ojo!*'

'Good!' said the sorcerer. '"If on the line of life there is found a dot surrounded by a little circle, that person will be blind in one eye, because this figure portends the loss of an eye." And so it is. Here is the dot and the little circle, you will be blind in one eye.'

'*Ya le soy*,'‡ answered the old man, groaning pitifully.

But the obi, having left off being a surgeon, shoved him away and carried on without paying any heed to the groans of the one-eyed wretch:

'*Escuchate, hombres!* "If the seven wrinkles on the forehead are small, twisting, inconspicuous, they portend that a man's life will be short.

Whoever has the figure of two crossed arrows on the moon wrinkle between the eyebrows will die in a battle.

---

* Alas, most excellent lord! Take a look at my eye.

† Name designating an old negro no longer fit for work.

‡ I already am.

If the line of life that traverses the hand exhibits a cross at its tip, near the joint, it is the presage that this person will go to the scaffold ..."

And here,' the obi proceeded, 'I must tell you, *hermanos*, one of the bravest supporters of independence, Boukmann, bore these three signs of ill omen.'

At these words all the negroes perked up their heads and held their breath; fastened on the trickster, their motionless eyes expressed that sort of attentiveness which resembles stupefaction.

'Except,' the obi added, 'I cannot reconcile this double sign that threatens Boukmann at one and the same time with a battle and a scaffold. And yet my art is infallible.'

He stopped, and exchanged a look with Biassou. Biassou whispered a few words to one of his aides-de-camp, who forthwith left the grotto.

'"... A gaping mouth, all adroop,"' the obi proceeded in a malicious and mocking tone, turning back toward his audience, '"a slumped posture, arms dangling down, and the left hand turned up for no apparent reason, portend natural stupidity, inanity, emptiness, vacant curiosity."'

Biassou sniggered. At that very moment the aide-de-camp reappeared, accompanied by a negro who was covered in mud and dust and whose feet, badly gashed by brambles and stones, were living proof that he had made a long journey. It was the messenger announced by Rigaud. In one hand he held a sealed packet, in the other an unscrolled parchment bearing a seal imprinted with the figure of a heart in flames. In the middle was a monogram formed out of the characteristic letters *M* and *N*, no doubt intertwined to designate the union of free mulattoes and enslaved negroes. To the side of this monogram I read the following inscription: 'Prejudice vanquished, the rod of iron destroyed. *Long live the king!*' This parchment was a safe-conduct provided by Jean-François.

The emissary presented it to Biassou and, after bowing low to the ground, handed over the sealed packet to him. The generalissimo opened it eagerly, skimmed through the dispatches it contained, put one of them in his jacket pocket and, crumpling the other in his hands, exclaimed with an air of distress:

'*Gens du roi!...*'

The negroes made a deep bow.

'*Gens du roi!* Here is what has been conveyed to Jean Biassou, Generalissimo of the Conquered Territories and Brigadier of his Catholic majesty, by Jean-François, Grand Admiral of France and Lieutenant-General of the armies of said majesty, King of Spain and the Indies:

"Boukmann—leader of one hundred and twenty blacks from the Blue Mountains in Jamaica, who have been recognized as independent by Governor-General Bellecombe[73]—has just met his death in the glorious struggle of liberty and humanity against despotism and barbarity. This generous leader was killed in an engagement with the white brigands of the contemptible Touzard. The monsters have cut off his head and have announced they are going to display it ignominiously on a scaffold in the parade ground of their city, the Cape. Vengeance!'"

After the dispatch was read, a gloomy, dejected silence momentarily descended upon the army. But on the altar the obi had risen to his feet and was brandishing his white wand and gesturing triumphantly. He shouted out:

'Solomon, Zorobabel, Eleazar Thaleb, Cardan, Judas Bowtharicht, Averroes, Albertus Magnus, Boabdil, Jean de Hagen, Anna Baratro, Daniel Ogrumof, Rachel Flintz, Altornino![74] I give you my thanks. The *ciencia* of the seers has not deceived me. *Hijos, amigos, hermanos, muchachos, mozos, madres, y vosotros todos que me escuchais aqui,** what had I predicted? *Que habia dicho?* The signs on Boukmann's forehead were a portent to me that he would not live long and that he would die in combat; the lines on his hand, that he would go to the scaffold. The revelations of my art have been faithfully realized and events have unfolded in such a way that even those circumstances we were unable to reconcile—death on both the battlefield and the scaffold—have been fulfilled! Brothers, admire!'

During this speech, the dejection of the blacks had changed into a sort of dread and wonder. They listened to the obi, their trust mingled with terror. Intoxicated with himself, he paraded back and forth atop the sugarbox, the surface of which offered more than enough room for his little feet to move around as they liked. Biassou sniggered.

Then he addressed the obi.

'My good chaplain, since you know the things that are to come, it would please us if you were willing to read what will become of our fortune and of us, Jean Biassou, *mariscal de campo.*'

The obi, proudly coming to a stop on the grotesque altar where he was being practically deified by the gullibility of the blacks, replied to the *mariscal de campo*: '*Venga vuestra merced!*'† At that moment the obi was the most

---

* Sons, friends, brothers, young men, children, mothers, and all of you who are listening to me here.

† Approach, your grace!

important man in the army. Military power yielded before sacerdotal power. Biassou drew near. In his eyes one could read a certain resentment.

'Your hand, General,' said the obi, while he stooped down to grab hold of it. 'Empezo.* The *line of the joint*, equally conspicuous for its entire length, promises you riches and happiness. The *line of life*, long and conspicuous, is the presage that you will have a life free of troubles, a hale hearty old age; its narrowness designates your wisdom, your ingenious mind, the *generosidad* of your heart. Lastly, I see there what the *chiromancos* call the luckiest of all the signs, a mass of little wrinkles that give it the form of a tree laden with branches, rising up toward the top of the hand: this is the unfailing omen of opulence and glory. The *line of health*, very long, confirms the indications of the line of life; it also indicates courage. Curved toward the little finger, it forms a sort of hook. General, this is the sign of a useful severity.'

At these words, the sparkling eyes of the little obi fastened on me through the openings of his veil and I once again detected a familiar tone hidden under the customary solemnity of his voice. He continued with the same purposive gestures and intonation:

'... Laden with little circles, the *line of health* portends a great many necessary executions that you will have to order. It breaks off around the middle to form a half-circle, a sign that you will be exposed to great perils involving ferocious beasts, which is to say the whites, if you do not exterminate them. The *line of fortune*, which like the line of life is surrounded by little branches rising up toward the top of the hand, confirms the future power and supremacy that is destined to you; its upper part is straight and slender, which portends a talent for governing. The fifth line, that of the *triangle*, extending all the way up to the base of the middle finger, promises you the most successful of results in every undertaking. Let us now take a look at the fingers. The thumb, streaked with little lines running lengthwise from the nail to the joint, promises you a great inheritance. Doubtless that of Boukmann's glory!' the obi added in a loud voice. 'The small protuberance that forms the base of the index finger is laden with little, mildly conspicuous wrinkles: honours and a high rank! The middle finger portends nothing. Your ring finger is furrowed with criss-crossing lines: you will overcome all of your enemies, you will surpass all of your rivals! These lines form Saint Andrew's crosses, signs of genius and foresight! On the joint that unites the little finger to the hand there are twisting wrinkles: fortune will shower down favours upon you. I also see there the

---

* I begin.

figure of a circle: yet another presage, this one portending power and a high rank for you!

"Happy is he," says Eleazar Thaleb, "who bears all these signs! His prosperity is in the care of destiny, and his star will provide him with the genius that gives rise to glory." Now, General, let me examine your forehead. "Whoever," says the gypsy Rachel Flintz, "in the middle of the forehead, on the sun wrinkle, bears a little square figure or a triangle will make a great fortune ..." And here it is, very pronounced. "If this sign is on the right, it promises an important legacy ..." Again, that of Boukmann! "The sign of a horseshoe between the two eyebrows, below the moon wrinkle, is the portent of one who knows how to avenge himself for insult and tyranny." I bear this sign; you bear it as well.'

The way in which the obi uttered the words, 'I bear this sign,' once again struck me.

'You find it,' he added in the same tone of voice, 'on the brave souls who know how to plot a courageous revolt and break the chains of bondage through combat. The griff of the lion imprinted above your eyebrows is proof of your fiery courage. Finally, General Jean Biassou, your forehead exhibits the most striking of all the signs of prosperity: namely, a combination of lines that form the letter M, first letter of the Virgin's name. On whatever part of the forehead, and whichever of its wrinkles, this figure appears, it portends genius, glory, and power. Whoever bears it will always guide the cause that he embraces to victory; those whose leader he is will never have any defeat to regret. His worth equals that of all his supporters combined. You are this man chosen by destiny!'

'Gratias, my good chaplain,' Biassou replied, preparing to return to his mahogany throne.

'Wait, General,' the obi continued, 'I forgot one last sign. The sun wrinkle, very conspicuous on your forehead, is proof that you know the proper way of doing things, that you desire to make other people happy, that you are exceedingly liberal and inclined to munificence.'

Biassou seemed to understand that the forgetfulness was all on his part rather than the obi's. He pulled a weighty purse from his pocket and threw it onto the silver plate, so that the sun wrinkle would not be proved wrong.

All this while, their leader's dazzling horoscope had made its impression on the members of his army. Since the news of Boukmann's death, the obi's words had gained an even stronger hold over all the rebels and they had gone from dejection to enthusiasm. Trusting blindly in their infallible sorcerer and their predestined general, they began to vie with each other in howling: 'Long live the obi! Long live Biassou!' The obi and Biassou looked at one another and I thought I could hear the obi's stifled laughter echoing the generalissimo's snigger.

I don't know why the thought of this obi so preoccupied my mind. It seemed to me as if, somewhere else, I had already seen or heard something that resembled this peculiar creature. I wanted to force him to speak.

'My good obi, *señor cura, doctor medico*, my good chaplain, *bon per!*' I called out to him.

He abruptly turned toward me.

'There is still someone here whose horoscope you have not drawn, and that is me.'

He folded his arms over the silver monstrance that covered his hairy chest, without answering me.

I kept on at him:

'I would very much like to know your augury as concerns my future, but your honest companions have relieved me of my watch and my purse, and you are not a sorcerer who prophesies *gratis.*'

He rushed forward, coming right up beside me, and whispered in his muffled voice:

'You are wrong! Let us see your hand.'

I presented it to him, looking him straight in the face. His eyes sparkled. He went through the motions of interrogating my hand.

'"If the line of life,"' he said to me, '"is cut crosswise in the middle by two small and clearly visible lines, it is the sign of an imminent death." Your death is imminent!

"If, in the middle of the hand, the line of health is not to be found but only the line of life and the line of fortune joined at their source in such a way as to form an angle, one should have no expectation, bearing this sign, of a natural death." Do not expect a natural death!

"If a line runs across the entire length of the bottom of the index finger, one will die a violent death!" Do you hear that? Prepare yourself for a violent death!'

There was something joyful in this sepulchral voice as it passed along these portents of death; I listened to it with indifference and contempt.

'Sorcerer,' I said to him with a disdainful smile, 'you're a clever fellow, you prognosticate what is certain.'

He nudged up even closer to me.

'You doubt my science! Well then, keep listening! The breach in the sun wrinkle on your forehead tells me that you take an enemy for a friend, and a friend for an enemy.'

The meaning of these words appeared to concern the treacherous Pierrot whom I loved yet who had betrayed me, and the faithful Habibrah whom I hated yet whose bloodied clothing testified to his courageous and devoted death.

'What do you mean?' I exclaimed.

'Hear me out to the end,' the obi continued. 'I have told you the future, here is the past. The moon wrinkle on your forehead has a slight curve; this signifies that your wife has been taken from you.'

I gave a start; I wanted to leap from my seat. My keepers held me back.

'You lack patience,' the sorcerer rejoined. 'Why not hear it out to the end? The little cross that cuts across the tip of this curve provides a final point of clarification. Your wife was taken from you the very night of your wedding.'

'Miserable creature!' I exclaimed, 'you know where she is! Who are you?'

I tried again to free myself and tear his veil from him, but had to yield to the sheer force of numbers. In a rage, I watched him moving away from me.

'Do you believe me now?' the mysterious obi taunted. 'Prepare yourself for your imminent death!'

32

THE STATE of perplexity that this strange scene had thrown me into was broken, if only temporarily, by the start of the next act, which followed closely upon the ridiculous comedy that Biassou and the obi had just played out in front of me and their astounded band of followers.

Biassou had settled back into his mahogany seat; the obi and Rigaud were to his right and left, seated on the two cushions that went with the chief's throne. The obi, his arms folded over his chest, seemed buried in deep contemplation, Biassou and Rigaud were chewing tobacco, and an aide-de-camp had just asked the *mariscal de campo* if the army should be passed in review, when three groups of unruly blacks arrived together at the entrance of the grotto, making a furious clamour. Each of these mobs had a prisoner in tow whom they were hoping to place at Biassou's disposal, not so much because they wanted to find out if he felt like granting a pardon but because they wanted to know his wishes regarding the sort of death these poor wretches ought to endure. '*Mort! Mort!...*' '*Muerte! Muerte!...*' '*Death! Death!*' yelled some English negroes, no doubt part of Boukmann's horde, who had already come to join forces with Biassou's Spanish and French blacks.

With a sign of the hand, the *mariscal de campo* imposed silence on them; he had the three captives brought forward to the threshold of the grotto. I was surprised to recognize two of them. One was *Citizen-General* C***, the philanthropist who corresponded with all of the world's negrophiles and who had put forward such a cruel proposal respecting the slaves during the council meeting at the Governor's residence. The other was the equivocal planter who felt such great repugnance for the mulattoes in whose ranks the whites numbered him. The third man seemed to belong to the class of the *petits blancs*; he was wearing a leather apron and had his sleeves rolled up above the elbows. All three had been captured separately while attempting to hide in the mountains.

The *petit blanc* was the first to be interrogated.

'So who are you?' Biassou asked him.

'I am Jacques Belin, carpenter at the hospital of the Fathers of Charity at the Cape.'[75]

The eyes of the *Generalissimo of the Conquered Territories* took on a look of surprise mingled with shame.

'Jacques Belin!' he said, biting his lips.

'Yes,' the carpenter affirmed. 'You don't recognize me, then?'

'You could start,' said the *mariscal de campo*, 'by acknowledging me and bowing down to me.'

'I don't bow down to my slave!' the carpenter answered back.

'Your slave, you miserable creature!' exclaimed the generalissimo.

'Yes,' the carpenter retorted, 'yes, I am your first master. You pretend not to know me, but remember, Jean Biassou: it was I who sold you to a dealer from Santo Domingo for thirteen piastre-gourdes.'

Biassou's face went into violent contortions of shame and anger.

'What's that!' the *petit blanc* continued. 'You seem ashamed of having served me! Shouldn't Jean Biassou pride himself on having belonged to Jacques Belin? Your very own mother, that half-witted old crone, has swept my workshop many a time, but I've just now sold her to the major-domo at the Fathers of Charity. She's so decrepit he wanted to give me only thirty-two francs, and six sous odd money, for her. So that's your story, and hers. But it seems you lot have become proud, you negroes and mulattoes, and that you, Jean Biassou, have forgotten the time when you served, on your knees, Master Jacques Belin, carpenter at the Cape.'

As he listened to him, Biassou had been making that ferocious snigger which gave him the air of a tiger.

'Fine!' he said.

Then he turned toward the negroes who had brought in Master Belin:

'Go and get two sawhorses, two boards, and a saw, and take this man away. Jacques Belin, carpenter at the Cape, you should thank me, for I'm furnishing you with a carpenter's death.'

His laughter settled the question as to what horrible form of torture was going to punish his old master's haughty pride. I shivered, but Jacques Belin did not blink an eyelid; he turned proudly toward Biassou.

'Yes,' he said, 'I must thank you, because I sold you for thirteen piastres, and you certainly yielded me more than you are worth.'

They dragged him away.

33

THE OTHER two prisoners had watched this frightful prologue to their own tragedy half-dead with terror. Their submissive, panic-stricken attitude contrasted with the carpenter's somewhat boastful self-assurance; they were trembling from head to foot.

With the eyes of a fox, Biassou studied one and then the other. Taking obvious pleasure in prolonging their agony, he started up a conversation with Rigaud about the different types of tobacco: the tobacco from Havana, he affirmed, was only good for smoking in cigars, and when it came to the best Spanish tobacco for snuff, well, he knew of none better than what the late Boukmann had sent him in two barrels seized from Monsieur Lebattu, proprietor of the island of Tortuga.[76] Then, abruptly turning to Citizen-General C***, he asked:

'What's your view on the matter?'

This unexpected apostrophe left the citizen reeling. He stammered back:

'I rely, General, on the opinion of your Excellency.'

'The words of a flatterer!' retorted Biassou. 'I'm asking you for your opinion, not mine. When it comes to a pinch of snuff, do you know a better tobacco than that of Monsieur Lebattu?'

'No, really, your Eminence,' said C***, whose confusion greatly amused Biassou.

'*General! Excellency! Eminence!*' the chief answered back in seeming irritation. 'Why, you're an aristocrat!'

'Oh! honestly, not at all!' the citizen-general exclaimed. 'I am a good patriot of '91 and an ardent negrophile ...'

'*Negrophile,*' interrupted the generalissimo. 'And what might that be, a negrophile?'

'He is a friend to black people,' stammered the citizen.

'It is not enough to be a friend to black people,' Biassou sternly rejoined. 'You must also be a friend to the men of colour.'

I believe I mentioned that Biassou was a sacatra.

'Men of colour, that is what I wanted to say,' the negrophile answered humbly. 'I am on close terms with all of the most famous partisans of the negroes and mulattoes ...'

More than happy to humiliate a white man, Biassou interrupted him again: '"Negroes and mulattoes!" What do you mean by that? Have you come here to insult us with those odious names invented by the contempt of the whites? There are only men of colour and blacks here, do you understand that, my fine colonist?'

'It is a bad habit picked up during childhood,' C*** resumed. 'Forgive me, it was by no means my intention to offend you, your Eminence.'

'Enough of your "Eminence." Let me repeat, I don't like those aristocratic turns of phrase.'

C*** wanted to apologize again; he started stuttering out a new explanation.

'If you only knew me, Citizen ...'

'Citizen! For whom do you take me?' exclaimed Biassou angrily. 'I detest that Jacobin jargon. You wouldn't be a Jacobin, by any chance? Keep in mind you're talking to the generalissimo of the *gens du roi*! *Citizen*!... Such insolence!'

The poor negrophile no longer had any idea which tone to adopt with this man who rejected equally the titles of *Eminence* and of *Citizen*—the language of the aristocrats and that of the patriots. He was in a state of utter consternation. Biassou, whose anger was only simulated, took cruel delight in his predicament.

'Alas!' the citizen-general said finally, 'you are mistaken in your judgement of me, noble defender of the imprescriptible rights of one half of mankind.'

In the predicament of having to give some label or other to this chief who seemed to refuse them all, he had resorted to one of those high-sounding circumlocutions that the revolutionaries so readily substitute for the name or the title of the person they are haranguing.

Biassou stared intently at him and asked:

'So, you love the blacks and the sang-mêlés?'

'Do I love them!' exclaimed Citizen C***. 'I correspond with Brissot and …'

Biassou interrupted him, sniggering.

'Ha! Ha! I am delighted to see that you are a friend of our cause. In that case, you must detest those wretched colonists who have punished our just insurrection with the cruellest forms of torture. Like us, you must think that it is not the blacks but the whites who are the true rebels, since they are revolting against nature and humanity. You must loathe those monsters!'

'I loathe them!' answered C***.

'Well!' Biassou carried on. 'What would you think of a man who, in order to suppress the latest undertakings of the slaves, planted the heads of fifty black men on either side of the avenue of his settlement?'

The paleness of C***'s countenance became truly alarming.

'What would you think of a white man who proposed that the city of the Cape be encircled by a cordon of slaves' heads?'

'Mercy! Mercy!' the terrified citizen-general whimpered.

'Am I threatening you?' Biassou rejoined icily. 'Let me finish … With a cordon of heads that would surround the city from Fort Picolet to Cape Caracol? What would you think of that, eh? Answer!'

Biassou's remark—'Am I threatening you?'—had given C*** renewed hope. Imagining that perhaps the chief had found out about these horrors without knowing who had authored them, he answered with some self-assurance in order to forestall any presumptions that might be prejudicial to him:

'I think that those are atrocious crimes.'

Biassou sniggered.

'Good! And what punishment would you inflict on the guilty party?' Here the luckless C*** hesitated.

'Well!' Biassou kept at him. 'Are you the black man's friend or not?'

Of the two alternatives, the negrophile chose the least threatening. Detecting in Biassou's eyes no hostility toward him, he replied in a faint voice:

'The guilty party deserves to die.'

'Very well answered,' Biassou said calmly, while throwing away the tobacco he'd been chewing.

His apparent lack of concern had in the meantime restored some self-assurance to the poor negrophile, who made an effort to remove any and all suspicions that might be hanging over him.

'No one,' he stressed, 'has longed more ardently than I for your cause to triumph. I correspond with Brissot and Pruneau de Pomme-Gouge in France, Magaw in America, Peter Paulus in Holland, the Abbé Tamburini in Italy …'

He was still complacently airing this philanthropic litany—which he was always more than happy to recite, and which he had parroted under other circumstances and with another purpose at Blanchelande's residence—when Biassou stopped him short.

'Eh! What good are all those correspondents of yours to me! Just tell me where your magazines and your depots are. My army needs ammunition. Your plantations no doubt bring in a lot. Your business must be doing very well, seeing as you correspond with all the merchants in the world.'

Citizen C*** ventured a timid observation:

'Hero of humanity, they are not merchants; they are philosophers, philanthropists, negrophiles.'

'Oh my, there he goes again,' said Biassou shaking his head. 'More of those devilishly unintelligible words of his. Well then, if you have neither depots nor magazines to pillage, then what good are you?'

This question offered C*** a glimmer of hope and he grabbed on to it.

'Illustrious warrior,' he answered, 'do you have an economist in your army?'

'And what might that be?' inquired the chief.

'An economist,' the prisoner said with as much gusto as his fear permitted him, 'is the most indispensable of men. He is the only one who can assess the material resources of an empire according to their respective worth, who disposes them in the order of their importance, classifies them according to their value, improves and ameliorates them by putting the raw material and the end product together, and distributes them appropriately, like so many fecundating streams in the great river of general utility which in turn will swell the sea of public prosperity into which it flows.'

'*Caramba!*' said Biassou leaning over toward the obi. 'What the devil is he trying to say with these words, all strung together like the beads of your rosary?'

The obi shrugged his shoulders as a sign that he neither knew nor cared. Meanwhile, Citizen C*** was still talking:

'I have studied, if you will be so good as to hear me out, valiant leader of the brave regenerators of Saint Domingue, I have studied the great economists: Turgot, Raynal, and Mirabeau, the friend of mankind![77] I have put their theory into practice. I am thoroughly conversant with the science that is essential for governing whichsoever kingdoms and states ...'

'The economist is not economical with words!' interjected Rigaud, with his gently mocking smile.

Biassou meanwhile had exclaimed:

'What are you prattling on about! Do I look as if I have kingdoms and states to govern?'

'Not yet, great as you are,' C*** persisted, 'but such may well become the case. Besides, my science is of an equal validity when it comes to the details of how to administer an army.'

The generalissimo curtly interrupted him again.

'My dear planter, I don't administer my army, I command it.'

'All to the good,' observed the citizen. 'You will be the General, I will be the Intendant. I possess special knowledge concerning how to breed more livestock ...'

'Do you think we raise livestock?' Biassou sniggered. 'We eat them. When there are no more cattle in the French colony for me, I'll cross over the mornes on the frontier, and I'll get myself some of those Spanish oxen and sheep that are bred on the farms of the great plains of Cotui, La Vega, Santiago, and on the banks of the Yuna.[78] If needs be, I'll also go and find myself some of those that graze on the Samaná peninsula and behind the mountain of Cibao, from the mouth of the Neiba to beyond Santo Domingo. In any case, I'd be delighted to punish those damnable Spanish planters; they're the ones who handed over Ogé. So you see that a short-age of provisions is no worry of mine and that I have no need of your "most indispensable" science!'

This vigorous declaration disconcerted the poor economist. Nevertheless, he made one last attempt at salvaging his idea.

'My studies have not been limited to the breeding of cattle. I possess other special knowledge that could be very useful to you. I will show you the methods for extracting pitch from tar and coal from mines.'

'And what do I care about that!' said Biassou. 'When I need coal, I burn down three leagues of forest.'

'I will teach you the proper use for each type of wood,' the prisoner persevered. 'Chicarrón and sabicú for the keels of boats; yaba for their bends; tecoma* for their ribs; yacca, guaiacum, cedar, acoma ...'[79]

---

* Medlar trees.

'*Que te lleven todos los demonios de los diez-y-siete infiernos!*'* exclaimed Biassou impatiently.

'I beg your pardon, my gracious patron?' The economist was trembling all over and did not understand Spanish.

'Listen,' Biassou replied, 'I don't need any ships. There's only one vacant post in my retinue, and it's not the position of *mayor-domo*, it's the position of valet-de-chambre. See if it suits you, *señor filosofo*. You'll serve me on your knees; you'll bring me my pipe, my callaloo[†] and my turtle soup. You'll carry a fan of peacock or parrot feathers behind me, as those two pages are doing right now. Humph! Answer, do you want to be my valet-de-chambre?'

Citizen C***—who had only one thing on his mind, namely, saving his life—bent low to the ground, displaying no end of joy and gratitude.

'Then you accept?' asked Biassou.

'Can you doubt, my generous master, that I should hesitate even one moment when faced with such a remarkable favour as that of serving your person?'

At this response, Biassou's diabolical sniggering became positively shrill. He folded his arms, rose with an air of triumph and, pushing away with his foot the head of the white man prostrated in front of him, exclaimed in a loud voice:

'It pleased me no end to find out just how far the whites can take their cowardice, after having seen how far they can go with their cruelty! Citizen C***, you are the man to whom I owe this double example. I know you! How could you have been so stupid as not to have noticed it? You're the one who was in charge of the executions in June, July, and August; you're the one who had fifty black heads planted on either side of your avenue as if they were palm trees; you're the one who wanted to slit the throats of your five hundred shackled negroes after the revolt, and to encircle the city of the Cape with a cordon of slaves' heads from Fort Picolet to Point Caracol. If you could have done it, you would have made a trophy of my head, but now you'd consider yourself lucky if I wanted you as a valet-de-chambre. No! No! I take better care of your honour than you yourself do; I won't make you suffer that indignity. Prepare to die.'

He gesticulated, and the blacks set the wretched negrophile down next to me. Unable to utter a word, he had fallen to his feet as if struck by lightning.

---

* May all the demons of the seventeen infernos carry you away!

† Creole stew.

34

'YOUR TURN now!' said the chief, as he turned toward the last of the prisoners, the colonist suspected by the whites of being a sang-mêlé and who had sent me a challenge for that very insult.

A collective roar from the rebels stifled the colonist's response. '*Muerte! Muerte! Death! Mort! Touyé! Touyé!*' they cried out, gnashing their teeth and shaking their fists at the wretched captive.

'General,' said a mulatto who expressed himself more clearly than the others, 'he is a white man. He must die!'

The poor planter, by dint of gestures and shouts, succeeded in making a few words heard.

'No! No, General, sir! No, my brothers! I am not a white man! It is an abominable slander! I am a mulatto, a sang-mêlé just like you, son of a negress just like your mothers and your sisters!'

'He's lying!' said the furious negroes. 'He's a white man. He's always detested blacks and men of colour.'

'Never!' the prisoner replied. 'It is the whites I detest. I am one of your brothers. I have always said along with you: "*Nègre cé blan, blan cé nègre!*"'*

'Not so! Not so!' the mob shouted. '*Touyé blan! Touyé blan!*'†

Wailing miserably, the wretch repeated:

'I am a mulatto! I am one of yours.'

'The proof?' Biassou said icily.

'The proof,' the other man answered, completely distraught, 'is that the whites have always had contempt for me.'

'That could be true,' retorted Biassou, 'but you're an insolent fellow.'

A young sang-mêlé tartly addressed the colonist.

'The whites had contempt for you, that is correct. But in return you affected contempt for the sang-mêlés, in whose ranks they placed you. I have even been told that you challenged a white man to a duel for having one day taunted you with belonging to our caste.'

Rage and indignation rumbled through the entire crowd; the calls for death, more violent than ever, drowned out the colonist's attempts to

---

* A saying popular with the rebel negroes. Its literal translation is as follows: "The negroes are the whites, the whites are the negroes." The meaning would be better conveyed by translating thus: *The negroes are the masters, the whites are the slaves.*

† Kill the white man! Kill the white man!

justify himself. Casting a sidelong glance of astonishment and entreaty at me, and weeping all the while, he kept on repeating:

'It is a slander! I have no other glory and no other happiness than to belong to the blacks. I am a mulatto!'

'If you were actually a mulatto,' observed Rigaud placidly, 'you would not use that word.'*

'Alas! Do I even know what I am saying?' the miserable wretch replied. 'General-in-chief, sir, the proof that I am sang-mêlé is this black circle that you can see around my fingernails.'†

Biassou pushed away the imploring hand.

'I don't possess the art of my good chaplain, who can tell who a person is by inspecting his hands. Now listen to me: our soldiers accuse you, some of being white, others of being a false brother. If that's the case, then you must die. You maintain that you belong to our caste, and that you've never disowned it. There remains only one way for you to prove your claim and to save yourself.'

'What is that, my general, what?' the colonist asked eagerly. 'I am ready.'

'Here it is,' replied Biassou icily. 'Take this stiletto and be so good as to stab these two white prisoners to death.'

As he said this, he designated us with a look of his eyes and a wave of his hand. The colonist shrank back in horror at the sight of the stiletto that Biassou was offering to him with a diabolical smile.

'So,' said the chief, 'you're wavering! And yet this is the only way of proving to me, as well as to my army, that you're not a white man, that you're one of us. Come, make up your mind, you're wasting my time.'

The prisoner was wild-eyed. He took a step toward the dagger, then lowered his arms and held back, turning his head away. He was shuddering from head to foot.

'Come now!' exclaimed Biassou in a tone of impatience and anger. 'I'm pressed for time. Make your choice: either be the one to kill them, or the one who dies with them.'

The colonist remained motionless, as if petrified.

'Very well!' said Biassou as he turned toward the negroes. 'He doesn't want to be the executioner, let him be the executed. I can see that he's a white man. Take him away, you lot ...'

---

* It must be remembered that the men of colour angrily rejected this label, which they said was an invention attributable to the white man's contempt.

† This sign does indeed show up at the base of the fingernails of a number of sang-mêlés; it disappears as they grow older, but crops up again in their children.

The blacks stepped forward to seize hold of the colonist. This movement determined his choice as to killing or being killed. Excessive cowardice also has its own sort of courage. He grabbed at the dagger Biassou was offering him and then, without giving himself any time to dwell on what he was about to do, the miserable creature threw himself like a tiger at Citizen C***, who was lying next to me.

A horrible struggle ensued. The negrophile had been left in a gloomy, despairing daze by the way in which the inquisition Biassou put him through had ended. He had watched blankly as the scene between the chief and the sang-mêlé planter played itself out; he hadn't seemed to understand what was going on, so absorbed was he in his terror at the thought of the torture and execution awaiting him. But when he saw the colonist swooping down on him and the steel glinting over his head, the immediacy of the danger woke him with a start. He rose to his feet and stayed the murderer's arm, crying out in a plaintive voice:

'Mercy! Mercy! What do you want from me? What have I done to you?'

'You must die, monsieur,' the sang-mêlé answered, trying to free his hand, his eyes wild with fright and fixed on his victim. 'Let me do it, I will not hurt you.'

'Die by your hand?' the economist bawled out. 'But what for? Be merciful. Perhaps you hold a grudge against me for having said in the past that you were a sang-mêlé? Only spare my life, and I assure you that as far as I'm concerned you are a white man. Yes, you are a white man, I will tell it to the world. Only show mercy!'

The negrophile had done a poor job of choosing his method of defence.

'Shut up! Shut up!' the furious sang-mêlé shouted, fearful lest the negroes hear this declaration.

But, not listening to him, the other man bellowed that he knew him to be white and of good stock. The sang-mêlé made one final effort to silence him: he violently pushed aside the two hands that were holding him back and burrowed into Citizen C***'s garments with his dagger. The unfortunate wretch felt the tip of the blade and in a rage bit the arm that was thrusting it in.

'Monster! Blackguard! You're murdering me!'

He cast a look at Biassou.

'Defend me, avenger of humanity!'

But the murderer pressed down hard on the dagger; a stream of blood gushed out around his hand, reaching all the way to his face. The knees of the poor negrophile all of a sudden buckled; his arms crumpled; his eyes dimmed; his mouth gave out a muffled groan. He fell dead to the ground.

35

I WAS FROZEN with horror at this scene in which I myself soon expected to play a part. The 'avenger of humanity' had watched the struggle of his two victims with an impassive eye. When it was over, he turned toward his terrified pages.

'Bring me some more tobacco,' he said, and serenely began chewing again.

The obi and Rigaud were frozen to their seats, and the negroes themselves seemed frightened by the horrible spectacle their chief had just bestowed on them.

However, there was still one white man left in whom to bury the dagger, and that was me. My turn had come. I looked him over, this assassin who was going to be my executioner. He inspired pity in me. His lips had gone purple; his teeth were chattering; he was trembling from head to foot, and the convulsions were making him stagger. Almost mechanically, his hand kept returning to his forehead to wipe away the splotches of blood from it. With a crazed look, he was staring down at the bloody corpse stretched out at his feet; his frantic eyes wouldn't let go of his victim.

I awaited the moment when he would finish off his task by disposing of me. I was in a queer situation with regard to this man: he had already come close to killing me in order to prove that he was a white man; now he was going to murder me in order to show he was a mulatto.

'All right,' Biassou said to him, 'that's fine. I'm pleased with you, my friend.' He cast a glance at me and added, 'You needn't bother with the other one. Clear off. We declare you a good brother, and we appoint you our army executioner.'

At these words from the chief, a negro stepped out of the ranks, bowed three times before Biassou, and exclaimed in his jargon, which I'll translate into French so as to facilitate your understanding of it:

'And me, General?'

'Well then, you! What do you have to say?' asked Biassou.

'Will you not do something for me, my General?' queried the negro. 'Here you have given a promotion to this white dog, who commits murder so as to get himself recognized as one of us. Will you not also give one to me, a good black man like me?'

This unexpected petition seemed to put Biassou in a predicament. He leaned over toward Rigaud and the head of the forces from Les Cayes said to him in French:

'We cannot grant his wish. Try to evade his request.'

Biassou then turned to the 'good black man.' 'Give you a promotion? Nothing would please me more. What rank do you fancy?'

'I would like to be *official*.'*

'Officer!' the generalissimo rejoined. 'Well now! What are your qualifications for wearing the epaulette?'

'It is I,' the black man answered with gusto, 'who set fire to the Lagoscette settlement near the beginning of August. It is I who slaughtered Monsieur Clément, the planter, and carried the head of his refiner on the end of a pike.[80] I slit the throats of ten white women and seven little children; one of those children even served as the ensign for Boukmann and his valiant band of blacks. Later, I burned down four families of colonists at Fort Galifet: they were in a room that I had doublelocked before setting fire to it. My father was broken on the wheel at the Cape, my brother was hanged at Roucou, and I myself almost fell before a firing squad. I have burned down three coffee plantations, six indigo plantations, two hundred and fifty acres of sugar cane.[81] I have killed my master Monsieur Noé, and his mother ...'

'Spare us your record of services rendered,' broke in Rigaud, whose feigned soft-heartedness concealed real cruelty, but who was ferocious with decency and had no truck with unprincipled brigandage.

'I could name you many more such deeds,' the negro answered back with pride, 'but no doubt you feel that what I have told you is enough for me to have earned the rank of *official* and to wear a gold epaulette on my waistcoat like our comrades over there.'

He pointed to Biassou's aides-de-camp and staff officers. The generalissimo seemed to weigh the matter over for a moment, then he solemnly addressed the negro:

'I'd be delighted to promote you. I'm satisfied with your services rendered, but there's one more thing that's required. Do you know Latin?'

Eyes bulging, the astounded brigand replied:

'I beg your pardon, my General?'

'That's right,' Biassou responded testily. 'Do you know Latin?'

'La ... tin...?' the dumbfounded black man repeated.

---

* Officer.

'Yes, yes, yes. Latin! Do you know Latin?' the sly chief rejoined. Then, unfurling a standard on which was written the verse of the psalm '*In exitu Israël de Ægypto*,'[82] he added: 'Explain to us what these words mean.'

The black man couldn't have been more surprised. Frozen to the spot, at a loss for words, he mechanically crumpled the flap of his breeches while his flustered gaze went from the general to the flag and from the flag back to the general.

'Go on, then, aren't you going to answer?' Biassou barked impatiently.

After scratching his head, the black man opened and closed his mouth several times. Finally, with great embarrassment, he blurted out:

'I do not know what the general means.'

Biassou's face took on a sudden expression of anger and indignation.

'What! You miserable scoundrel!' he burst out. 'How's that? You want to be an officer and you don't know Latin!'

'But, General!…' stammered the negro, confused and trembling.

'Shut up!' Biassou snapped back, his fit of anger appearing to grow. 'I don't know what's keeping me from putting you in front of the firing squad right now for your presumption. Rigaud, can you make head or tail of this ridiculous officer who doesn't even know Latin? Well then, scoundrel, since you don't understand what's written on this flag, I'm going to explain it to you. *In exitu*, any soldier, *Israël*, who doesn't know Latin, *de Ægypto*, can't be appointed officer. Is that not how it goes, my good chaplain?'

The little obi made a sign in the affirmative. Biassou continued:

'This brother, the one I've just appointed army executioner, the one you're jealous of, he knows Latin.'

He turned toward the new 'executioner.'

'Is it not true, my friend? Prove to this lout that you know more about the subject than he does. What does *Dominus vobiscum* mean?'

The poor sang-mêlé colonist, roused out of his gloomy revery by this fearsome voice, lifted his head up; even though he was still completely out of his wits at the thought of the cowardly murder he'd just committed, terror induced him to obey. The look on this man's face as he tried to recover a schoolboy memory from the midst of his terror-stricken, remorseful thoughts had something altogether strange about it, as did the doleful way he uttered the childhood definition:

'*Dominus vobiscum* … that means: may the Lord be with you!'

'*Et cum spiritu tuo!*' the mysterious obi added solemnly.

'*Amen*,' said Biassou. Then he resumed his irate tone and started shouting at the ambitious negro, interlarding his simulated wrath with a few phrases of bad Latin—of the sort that might have come out of Sganarelle's mouth[83]—so as to convince the blacks of their chief's learnedness:

'Go to the back of your row! *Sursum corda!* In future, don't get any more clever ideas about rising to the rank of your leaders who know Latin, *orate fratres*, or I'll have you hanged! *Bonus, bona, bonum!*'

The negro, simultaneously amazed and terrified, returned to his row, lowering his head in shame amidst the collective jeers of his comrades, who were indignant at such ill-founded pretensions. All eyes were fixed in admiration on their learned generalissimo.

There was an outlandish aspect to this scene which nevertheless really did inspire in me a high opinion of Biassou's adroitness. The ridiculous method he'd just used with such success[*] to thwart the ambitions that always come to the fore in a rebel band gave me the measure both of the negroes' stupidity and their chief's shrewdness.

36

MEANWHILE, the time had come for Biassou's *almuerzo*.[†][84] A large turtle shell was brought before the *mariscal de campo de su magestad catolica*: steaming inside it was a sort of *olla podrida*, abundantly seasoned with slabs of lard, turtle flesh substituting for the *carnero*[‡] and sweet potatoes for the *garganzas*.[§] An enormous Caribbean cabbage floated on the surface of this *puchero*. On each side of the shell, which served as both a stewing pot and a serving dish, were two cups made out of coconut husks and filled with raisins, *sandias*,[**] yams, and figs; this was the *postre*.[††] A loaf of maize-bread and a goatskin filled with pitch-wine completed the trappings of the feast. Biassou pulled a few cloves of garlic from his pocket and rubbed the bread with it himself. Then, without even bothering to have the twitching corpse that was lying there in full view dragged off, he started to eat, inviting Rigaud to do likewise. There was something frightful about Biassou's appetite.

---

[*] Toussaint Louverture later used the same expedient to equal advantage.

[†] Lunch.

[‡] Lamb.

[§] Chickpeas.

[**] Watermelon.

[††] Dessert.

The obi didn't share in their meal. I realized that, like all others of his kind, he never ate in public so that the negroes would believe he was a supernatural being, someone who lived without food.

While he was still lunching, Biassou ordered an aide-de-camp to get the inspection started, and the bands began an orderly march past the grotto. The Morne Rouge blacks were the first to pass in review. There were around four thousand of them, divided into small, tightly knit platoons led by chiefs who, as I've already noted, were sporting scarlet breeches or belts. These blacks, almost all of them tall and strong, were carrying guns, axes, and sabres. Many among them had bows, arrows, and spears which they themselves had fashioned for want of other weapons. They had no flag, and were marching in silence, visibly dismayed.

Seeing this horde march past, Biassou leaned over to Rigaud and, in French, whispered in his ear:

'When will Blanchelande and Rouvray's grapeshot rid me of these bandits from Morne Rouge? I hate them: they're almost all *congos*! And, besides, the only way they know how to kill people is during combat. They've followed the example of that imbecilic leader of theirs, Bug-Jargal—their idol, that young fool who wanted to act all generous and magnanimous. You haven't met him, Rigaud? I hope you never will. The whites have taken him prisoner, and they'll get rid of him for me the same way they got rid of Boukmann.'

'Speaking of Boukmann,' Rigaud responded, 'here come Macaya's black maroons.[85] I see that the negro Jean-François sent to inform you of Boukmann's death is in their ranks. Are you aware this man could destroy the entire effect of the obi's prophecies were he to tell anyone that he had been detained at the outposts for half an hour and that he had entrusted me with news of the chief's fate before you sent for him?'

'*Diabolo!*' said Biassou. 'You're right, my friend. Those lips of his need to be sealed. Hold on!'

Then, raising his voice, he shouted:

'Macaya!'

The chief of the negro maroons came forward, offering his blunderbuss as a sign of respect.

'That black man I see over there,' Biassou proceeded, 'the one who doesn't belong in your ranks: have him fall out.'

It was Jean-François's messenger. Macaya brought him to the generalissimo, whose face suddenly took on that expression of anger which he could simulate so well.

'Who are you?' he asked the disconcerted negro.

'General, sir, I am a black man.'

'*Caramba!* I can see that all too well! But what's your name?'

'My *nom de guerre* is Vavelan. My patron saint among the blessed ones is Saint Sabas, deacon and martyr, whose feast-day is celebrated on the twentieth day before the nativity of Our Lord.'[86]

Biassou interrupted him:

'How can you be so impudent as to dare show up here on parade amidst all these gleaming musketoons and white sword-belts? Look at your sabre, it lacks a scabbard; your breeches, they're ripped; your feet, they're covered in mud!'

'General, sir' answered the black man, 'it is not my fault. I was charged by Grand Admiral Jean-François with bringing you news of the death of Boukmann, chief of the English maroons, and if my clothes are ripped and my feet are dirty it is because I ran without stopping so as to bring that news to you as soon as possible. But at the camp they held me back, and ...'

Biassou frowned.

'That's not the issue here, *gavacho!*[87] The audacity of your showing up for inspection in such a mess is the issue. Commend your soul to Saint Sabas, deacon and martyr, your patron saint. Go and take a gun to your head, immediately!'

Here I had yet another proof of the moral power Biassou exercised over the rebels. The unfortunate fellow, charged with shooting his own brains out, ventured not even one murmur of complaint. He lowered his head, folded his arms over his chest, bowed three times in the direction of his ruthless judge and—after kneeling down before the obi, who solemnly gave him a brief absolution—left the grotto. A few minutes later, a burst of musket fire informed Biassou that the negro had obeyed and gone to his death.

All cause for anxiety over, the chief then turned toward Rigaud. His eyes sparkled with pleasure, and his triumphant snigger seemed to be saying: 'Admire!'*

---

* Toussaint Louverture would later exhibit this same power over the fanaticized negroes. He was formed in the school of Biassou and if he was not superior to the latter in adroitness he was at least a long way from equalling him when it came to treachery and cruelty. Like Biassou, this chief—descended, it is said, from royal African stock—had received some rudimentary education, to which he added genius. He erected for himself a republican throne of sorts in Saint Domingue at the same time as Bonaparte in France was founding a monarchy upon victory. Toussaint naively admired the First Consul but the First Consul—seeing in Toussaint nothing more than a bothersome parodist of his own fortunes—always rejected with disdain any correspondence with the enfranchised slave who dared to write to him: "From the first among blacks to the first among whites."

IN THE meantime, the inspection continued. The army that had offered me such an extraordinary picture of disorder only a few hours before was no less bizarre when mustered. First came gangs of negroes, absolutely naked, armed with cudgels, tomahawks, clubs, marching like savages to the sound of a goat's horn. Then it was batallions of mulattoes, fitted out in the Spanish or English fashion, well armed and well disciplined, keeping step to the roll of a drum. And then there were crowds of negresses and pickaninnies, wielding pitchforks and spits; old black men bent down under the weight of antiquated rifles that had neither hammer nor barrel; griotes in all their gaudy finery; griots making horrendous grimaces and contortions, singing incoherent tunes on their guitars, tomtoms, and balafos. This strange procession was from time to time laced with heterogeneous detachments of griffes, marabous, sacatras, mamelucos, quadroons, free sang-mêlés, or with nomadic hordes of black maroons—their bearing proud, their carbines glistening—who were bellowing the battle hymns of 'Grand-Pré' and 'Wa-Nassé' at the top of their lungs and dragging their loaded ox-carts or the occasional cannon seized from the whites, which served them less as a weapon than as a trophy. Fluttering above all these heads were flags of every colour, displaying every slogan imaginable: white ones, red ones, tricoloured ones, flags with the fleur-de-lis or topped with the bonnet of liberty, and bearing such inscriptions as 'Death to priests and to aristocrats!' ... 'Long live religion!' ... 'Liberty!' ... 'Equality!' ... 'Long live the king!' ... 'Down with France!' ... '*Viva España!*' ... 'No more tyrants!' etc. This striking confusion was indicative of the fact that all these rebel forces were nothing more than an agglomeration of means without an end: it was an army whose aims were just as muddled as its men.

As the bands passed in turn by the grotto, they would lower their banner, and Biassou would return the salute. He addressed some word of reprimand or praise to each troop, and whatever he said, whether it was stern or flattering, was soaked up by his men with a fanatical respect and a kind of superstitious fear.

The stream of barbarians and savages finally abated. I admit that the sight of so many brigands, which had at first served as a distraction, ended up leaving me with an uneasy feeling. In the meantime, day was drawing to a close and, by the time the last rows marched past, all that could be seen of the sun was a coppery red tinge on the granite face of the mountains to the east.

BIASSOU SEEMED lost in thought. When the inspection concluded and his last orders had been given, and once all the rebels had returned to their ajoupas, he turned to address me.

'Young man,' he said, 'you've had a chance, and a leisurely one at that, to gauge my genius and my power. Now the time has come for you to go and give an account of it to Leogri.'

'That it did not come any sooner was no fault of mine,' I answered him icily.

'Quite right,' Biassou responded. As if anticipating the effect that what he was about to tell me would have, he paused for a moment, and then added: 'But if it does come, the fault will be entirely yours.'

'What!' I exclaimed in astonishment. 'What do you mean?'

'Yes,' continued Biassou, 'your life depends on you. You can save it if you so desire.'

This fit of clemency, in all likelihood the first and the last that Biassou ever suffered from, seemed a veritable marvel to me. The obi, as surprised as I was, had leapt from the seat where, like a Hindu fakir, he'd been holding the same ecstatic pose for quite some time now. He positioned himself in front of the generalissimo, his voice raised in anger:

'*Que dice el exelentisimò señor mariscal de campo?**' Does he not remember what he promised me? Neither he nor the *bon Giu* can dispose of this life any longer: it belongs to me.'

Once again, on hearing that angry voice, I had the impression of having encountered this accursed little man somewhere, but the memory proved elusive and I was left none the wiser.

Unruffled, Biassou got up and, in a low voice, said a few words to the obi and pointed at the black flag I had noticed earlier; after a brief exchange, the sorcerer lowered his head and then raised it back up again, as a sign of assent. Both of them returned to their seats and their poses.

'Listen,' the generalissimo said to me, as he pulled the other dispatch from Jean-François out of the waistcoat pocket where he had deposited it. 'Our affairs are going badly. Boukmann has recently fallen in combat. The whites have exterminated two thousand blacks in the district of Cul-de-Sac. The colonists are continuing to entrench themselves and to blan-ket the plain with military posts. Through our own fault, we have lost the

---

* What is the most excellent lord brigadier-general saying?

opportunity of capturing the Cape, and it will be a long time before such an opportunity presents itself again. To the east, a river cuts across the main road; the whites, for the defence of this passage, have raised a battery of cannon on pontoons and have formed two small camps, one on each bank of the river. To the south, there's a major road passing through that mountainous district called the Haut-du-Cap; they've covered it with troops and artillery. The position is no less fortified on the ground: the settlers have worked to erect a sturdy palisade and have covered it with chevaux-de-frise.[88] So there's no way for us to take the Cape. Our ambush in the gorges of Dompte-Mulâtre miscarried. Along with all our setbacks, there's the yellow fever which is decimating the camp of Jean-François. Consequently, the Grand Admiral of France* thinks, and we share his opinion, that it would be advisable to negotiate with Governor Blanchelande and the colonial assembly. Here's the letter we're addressing to the assembly on this matter. Listen!

"Honourable deputies,

Great misfortunes have afflicted this rich and important colony; we have been caught up in them, and that is all that can be said by way of our justification. One day you will do us all the justice that our position merits. We ought to be included in the general amnesty that King Louis XVI has declared for one and all.

If not, since the king of Spain is a good king who treats us very well and *gives proof of his rewards* to us, we will continue to serve him with zeal and devotion.

We see by the law of 28 September 1791[89] that the national assembly and the king grant you the power to rule definitively on the status of those persons who are not free and on the political status of the men of colour. We will defend the decrees of the national assembly to the last drop of our blood as we will defend yours, presuming they bear the requisite formalities. It would indeed be a point of interest were you to *declare*, by way of a decree ratified by the governor-general, that you intend to turn your attention to the condition of the slaves. Knowing by way of their leaders, to whom you will send this decree, that they are the object of your solicitude, they would be satisfied, and the broken equilibrium would be restored in short order.

However, do not count, honourable representatives, on our agreeing to take up arms at the whim of the revolutionary assemblies. We are the sub-

---

* We have already noted that Jean-François adopted this title.

jects of three kings: the king of Congo, born-master of all the blacks; the king of France, who represents our fathers; and the king of Spain, who represents our mothers. These three kings are the descendants of those who, guided by a star, went to worship the Man-God. If we were to serve the assemblies, we would perhaps be led into making war on our brothers, the subjects of these three kings to whom we have promised fidelity.

And furthermore, we do not know what is meant by the will of the nation, in view of the fact that *ever since the world began* we have only carried out the will of a king. The prince of France loves us, and that of Spain is constantly coming to our aid. We help them, they help us; it is the cause of humanity. Moreover, if these majesties were ever to let us down, we would very soon have *throned a king.*

Such are our intentions, in consideration of which we will consent to make peace.

Signed JEAN-FRANÇOIS, General; BIASSOU, Brigadier-General; DESPREZ, MANZEAU, TOUSSAINT, AUBERT, *Ad hoc* Commissioners."*[90]

'You see,' added Biassou after reading out this specimen of negro diplomacy—the memory of which has stuck in my head, word for word—'you see that we're peace-loving people. Now, here's what I want from you. Neither Jean-François nor I were raised in the schools of the whites where one learns fine-sounding language. We know how to fight, but we don't know how to write. And yet we don't want there to be anything in our letter to the assembly that could provoke the arrogant *burlerias* of our former masters. You seem to have acquired this frivolous knowledge that we lack. Correct any mistakes in our dispatch that the whites might find laughable. At this price, I grant you your life.'

My pride found the idea of assuming the role of Biassou's diplomatic orthographer simply too distasteful for me to waver even one moment. And besides, what did life matter to me? I refused his offer.

---

* It would appear that this ridiculously characteristic letter was indeed sent to the assembly. [Editor's Note: As Mouralis, among others, points out, "this letter never really existed in the form that Hugo gives it in his novel" (56). As discussed in "(1791)/2002, 2004: Reading Hugo and the Haitian Revolution in a Post/Colonial Age" of the Introduction, it is a pastiche of three documents—one from 1791, the other two from 1793—that Hugo came across in Lacroix's *Mémoires* (see Appendix E.2c). For the events surrounding the composition of the 1791 letter, see the *Récit historique* (1793) of the colonist Gros. Gros was a white prisoner of the rebel leaders Jean-François and Biassou who eventually established a good relationship with them; forced to serve as Jean-François's "appointed secretary" (16), he was chiefly responsible for drafting this letter. It is highly probable that Hugo read or at least knew of Gros's gripping narrative, although there are no specific passages in *Bug-Jargal*—with the possible exception of a reference to "the double mountains" in Chapter 25 (compare Gros 1)— that have been directly lifted from the *Récit*.]

He seemed surprised.

'What?' he exclaimed. 'You'd rather die than fix up a few strokes of the pen on a scrap of parchment?'

'Yes,' I answered him.

My resolve appeared to place him in a predicament. After a moment of reflection, he said to me:

'Listen here, young fool. I'm not as obstinate as you. I'm giving you until tomorrow evening to make up your mind to obey me. Tomorrow, at the setting of the sun, you'll be brought before me once again. Be so good as to grant my wish then. Adieu, night brings counsel. And keep in mind that with us death is not simply a matter of dying.'

There was nothing equivocal about those last words or the ghastly laughter that accompanied them; their meaning could not have been more clear, especially if one took into account the atrocities Biassou was in the habit of dreaming up for his victims.

'Candy,[91] send back the prisoner,' Biassou went on. 'Entrust the keeping of him to the Morne Rouge blacks. I want him to see the sun set one more time, and my other soldiers perhaps wouldn't have the patience to wait for those twenty-four hours to pass.'

The mulatto Candy, chief of Biassou's bodyguard, ordered that my arms be tied behind my back. A soldier took the end of the rope, and we exited the grotto.

39

WHEN extraordinary events, times of anguish and catastrophe, suddenly come hurling down into the midst of a happy and delightfully uniform life, those unexpected emotions, those blasts of fate, rudely interrupt the slumber of a soul at rest in the monotonous condition that accompanies prosperity. And yet when misfortune arrives in this manner it does not seem like an awakening, but only a dream. For the man who has always been happy, despair begins with stupefaction. Unexpected adversity resembles the torpedo-fish: it strikes, but what it strikes it numbs, casting a sudden, dire light before our eyes which is not the light of day. People, things, actions: they all pass before us, moving as if part of a dream, with something uncanny in their features. Everything about our life's horizon, its atmosphere and prospects, has changed—but a long time goes by before our eyes outstrip the sort of luminous image of past happiness that trails behind them and that continually blocks the shadowy present from view, changing its colour and lending an indefinable falseness to reality. Everything that exists then seems impossible and absurd to us; we scarcely believe in our own existence because, finding nothing around us of what once comprised our being, we do not understand how it could all have disappeared without sweeping us away along with it, nor why we should be all that is left of our life. If this violent condition of the soul persists, it unravels the mind's equilibrium and turns into madness—a happy state, perhaps, where life, for that wretched man, is no longer anything more than a vision, and he himself its ghost.

40

IT IS NOT clear to me, gentlemen, why I am telling you all this. These are not the sort of ideas that lend themselves to being understood, by oneself or by others. They are something one needs to have felt. I have lived them. That was the state of my soul at the moment when Biassou's guards handed me over to the Morne Rouge negroes. Spectres, delivering me over to other spectres: that was how it seemed to me, and without putting up any resistance I let myself be tied by the waist to a tree trunk. They brought me some boiled sweet potatoes and I ate them out of that mechanical instinct God's goodness affords a burdened man's mind when it is preoccupied.

Meanwhile, night had come. My keepers withdrew into their ajoupas; only six remained with me, sitting or lying in front of a large fire they had lit so as to protect themselves from the night chill. It wasn't long before they all fell into a deep sleep.

The state of physical collapse I was in at the time contributed not a little to the shadowy thoughts that were wrenching me apart. I recalled those days only a few weeks before when Marie was still at my side: serene never-changing days, days passed without even an inkling of any other possibility in the future than that of an eternal happiness. I compared them to the day that had just elapsed: a day on which so many strange things had come to pass, unfolding before my eyes as if to make me doubt their very existence; a day on which I had been sentenced to die three times, without having been saved. I pondered what the future held for me at present:

one day more, that was all, and no remaining certainty other than adversity and a death that was mercifully imminent. It seemed to me as if I was struggling against a ghastly nightmare. I wondered if everything that had happened had indeed really happened; I wondered if what surrounded me was indeed really the camp of the bloodthirsty Biassou, if Marie was indeed really lost to me forever, and if this prisoner guarded by six barbarians—this prisoner made visible to me by the light glimmering from a brigands' fire, tethered fast, condemned to certain death—was indeed really me. And despite all my efforts to avoid the intrusion of a far more agonizing thought my heart kept coming back to Marie. I was filled with anguished speculations regarding her fate; I strained against my fetters as if I were going to fly to her rescue, still hoping that the horrible dream would melt away and that God had not seen fit to merge the destiny of the angel he had given me for a wife with all the horrors that I dared not contemplate. One painful thought led to another, and I found myself face to face with Pierrot. Rage almost drove me out of my senses; I felt as though the arteries on my forehead were about to burst. I hated myself, I cursed myself, I despised myself for having momentarily linked my friendship for Pierrot to my love for Marie, and without trying to fathom what motive could have driven him to hurl himself into the waters of the Grande Rivière, I wept at not having been the one to kill him. He was dead, I was going to die, and the only thing I mourned in his life or in mine was the loss of my vengeance.

All these emotions were stirring me up even as I sunk into a half-sleep caused by exhaustion. I don't know how long it lasted, but I was suddenly roused from it by the reverberations of a manly voice singing, clearly but at a distance, '*Yo que soy contrabandista.*' With a start, I opened my eyes; everything was dark, the negroes were sleeping, the fire was dying out. I heard nothing more; this voice, I thought, was an illusion, conjured up in my sleep. Once more my heavy eyelids closed. They flashed open a second time. The voice had started up again. Much closer now, it was plaintively singing this verse from a Spanish romance:

> En los campos de Ocaña,
> Prisionero caì;
> Me llevan à Cotadilla;
> Desdichado fuì!*[92]

---

*   In the fields of Ocaña, / I was taken prisoner. / They took me to Cotadilla; / Wretched was I!

This time, there was no question of it being a dream. It was Pierrot's voice! A moment later, it rose up yet again out of the shadowy silence, close as could be now. For the second time, the familiar refrain sounded: '*Yo que soy contrabandista.*' A mastiff bounded up to me, joyously rolling about at my feet. It was Rask. I looked up. A black man was in front of me, and alongside the dog stood his colossal shadow, cast by the fire's glimmering light. It was Pierrot. The desire for vengeance overwhelmed me; surprise left me frozen to the spot, at a loss for words. I was not asleep. So the dead came back! This was no longer a dream, it was an apparition. I turned away in horror. At the sight of this, his head sank to his chest.

'Brother,' he complained in a whisper, 'you promised you would never doubt me if you heard me singing that tune. Brother, have you forgotten your promise?'

Anger restored my voice.

'You monster!' I exclaimed. 'So I finally meet up with you again! Butcher! You murder my uncle, you ravish Marie, and you dare to call me your brother? Don't you come any closer!'

I forgot that I was strapped up in such a way that it was virtually impossible for me to move. Almost involuntarily I looked down at my side for my sword. This visible intention of mine struck him. An emotional, but gentle, look came over him.

'No,' he said. 'No, I will not come any closer. You are unhappy, and I have pity for you. You, you do not have pity for me, even though I am more unhappy than you.'

I shrugged my shoulders. He understood this silent reproach. He gave me a faraway look.

'Yes, you have lost a lot. But, believe me, I have lost more than you.'

In the meantime, the sound of our voices had awakened the six negroes who were guarding me. Catching sight of a stranger, they got up in a rush, grabbing hold of their weapons. However, as soon as their eyes lit upon Pierrot they let out cries of surprise and joy; prostrating themselves, they beat their foreheads against the ground.

And yet the way these negroes paid their respects to Pierrot, the way Rask ran back and forth between his master and myself, rubbing up against us while looking anxiously at me as if astonished by my chilly welcome—none of this made any impression on me at the time. I was entirely given over to my feelings of rage, which were rendered powerless by the fetters weighing me down.

'Oh!' I burst out finally, infuriated to the point of tears by the shackles that held me back. 'Oh! Wretched am I! There I was mourning the fact that this miserable creature had taken his own life, believing him to be dead, grieving for the loss of my vengeance. Now here he is, come to jeer at me himself: here, before my very eyes, alive! And I'm denied the pleasure of burying my dagger in him! Oh, who will deliver me from these loathsome bonds?'

Pierrot turned toward the negroes, who were still in the act of worshipping him.

'Comrades,' he said, 'release the prisoner!'

41

HE WAS promptly obeyed. My six guards eagerly cut the ropes that were wrapped round me. I got up, a free man, but was still unable to move; astonishment enchained me in its turn.

'And that is not all,' Pierrot added. Snatching a dagger from one of his negroes, he held it out to me and said: 'Take your satisfaction, by all means. God forbid that I should contest your right to dispose of my life! You have saved it three times; it is now well and truly yours. Strike, if you wish to strike.'

His voice held neither reproach nor bitterness, only sadness and resignation.

There was something both too strange and too easy about this unexpected opportunity to gratify my desire for vengeance—an opportunity handed to me by the very man I longed to revenge myself against. It was clear to me that all my hatred for Pierrot and all my love for Marie were not enough to make a murderer of me. Besides, appearances notwithstanding, a voice cried out to me deep down in my heart that someone who's an enemy, someone who's guilty, does not court vengeance and punishment in this manner. Truth be told, there was something about the commanding authority that emanated from this extraordinary being which subjugated me at that moment, despite myself. I pushed the dagger away.

'Wretch!' I said to him. 'I want to kill you in combat, not murder you. Defend yourself!'

'Defend myself!' he answered in astonishment. 'And against whom?'

'Against me!'

He was dumbfounded and showed it.

'Against you! That is the only particular in which I cannot obey you. Do you see Rask? I would have no problem slitting his throat; he would offer no resistance. But I could never force him to fight against me; he would not understand me. I do not understand you; I am Rask for you.'

After a pause, he added:

'I see the hatred in your eyes, as one day you had the chance to see it in mine. I know that you have suffered many calamities: your uncle butchered, your fields burned down, the throats of your friends slit. Your houses have been ransacked, your inheritance laid waste, but it is not I, it is my people, who did it. Look, one day I told you that your people had done me great harm, and you answered me that it was not you who had done it. So what is it that I have done?'

His countenance brightened; he expected to see me fall into his arms. I shot him a brutal look.

'You disown everything that your people have done to me,' I replied in a fury, 'but you say nothing about what you yourself have done to me!'

'And what is that?' he asked.

Violently, I came right up to him and thundered:

'Where is Marie? What have you done with Marie?'

At this name, a cloud spread over his brow; he appeared briefly ill-at-ease. Finally, breaking the silence, he answered:

'*Maria!* Yes, you are right ... But too many ears are listening to us.'

His uneasiness, the words 'you are right,' rekindled a hellish fire in my heart. It seemed all too evident to me that he was evading my question. At that moment, he looked at me with his candid expression, and with a voice full of emotion said:

'Do not suspect me, I beg of you. I will tell you all about it somewhere else. Come, love me as I love you, trustingly.'

He paused a moment to observe the effect of his words, and added fondly:

'May I call you brother?'

But my jealous anger had regained all of its violence, and it was only exacerbated by those tender words which appeared hypocritical to me.

'You dare to remind me of that time?' I exclaimed. 'Miserable ingrate!'

He interrupted me. His glistening eyes were swollen with tears.

'It is not I who am the ungrateful one!'

'Well then, speak!' I answered back heatedly. 'What have you done with Marie?'

'Somewhere else, not here!' he answered me. 'What we say here is not heard by our ears alone. In any case, you would doubtless not take my word for it. And besides, time is short. See, day is breaking. I must get you out of here. Look, you doubt me: that means the game is up. You might as well finish me off with a dagger. But wait just a little longer before carrying out what you call your vengeance; first of all, I must free you. Come with me and let us find Biassou.'

Such words and deeds hid a mystery that I could not fathom. Despite all my biases against this man, his voice still touched a chord in my heart. As I listened to him, some indefinable power held sway over me. I caught myself wavering between vengeance and pity, distrust and blind abandon. I followed him.

42

WE LEFT the quarters of the Morne Rouge negroes. I was amazed to be walking free in this barbarian camp where only the day before every brigand had seemed to be thirsting for my blood. Far from trying to stop us, the blacks and mulattoes prostrated themselves as we went by, uttering exclamations of surprise, joy, and respect. I had no idea what rank Pierrot held in the rebel army but I recalled the dominion he exercised over his fellow slaves and so had no difficulty accounting for the importance he seemed to possess amongst his comrades in rebellion.

When we arrived at the line of guards on watch in front of Biassou's grotto, their leader—the mulatto Candy—stepped forward. Menacing us from a distance, he asked how it was that we dared approach so close to the general. But when he got near enough to see Pierrot's features distinctly, he suddenly removed his gold-embroidered montera and, as if terrified by his own audacity, bowed low to the ground and ushered us in to see Biassou, stammering a thousand excuses which Pierrot answered with nothing more than a disdainful gesture.

The respect of the common negro soldiers for Pierrot hadn't astonished me, but upon seeing Candy, one of their principal officers, humble himself in this way before my uncle's slave, I began to ask myself who this man with such seemingly great authority could be. It was quite another matter when I saw the generalissimo, who at the moment we entered was alone and quietly eating a callaloo, get up hastily at the sight of Pierrot and, dissimulating anxious surprise and violent resentment beneath an appearance of deep respect, bow down humbly before my companion and offer him his own mahogany throne. Pierrot refused it.

'Jean Biassou,' he said, 'I have not come to take your place, but simply to beg a favour of you.'

'*Alteza*,' Biassou answered, redoubling his salutations, 'you know that you have at your disposal all that depends on Jean Biassou, all that belongs to Jean Biassou, and Jean Biassou himself.'

That Biassou accorded Pierrot this title of *alteza*, which is equivalent to that of *royal highness* or *sultanic majesty*, increased my astonishment even more.

'I do not wish for so much,' Pierrot carried on curtly. 'I am asking you only for the life and liberty of this prisoner.'

He designated me with his hand. For a moment Biassou seemed taken aback, but his discomposure was short-lived.

'Your servant is desolated, *alteza*. You request of him much more than he can grant you, to his great regret. This prisoner is not Jean Biassou, does not belong to Jean Biassou, and does not depend on Jean Biassou.'

'What do you mean?' Pierrot asked sternly. 'On whom, then, does he depend? Is there any other authority here than you?'

'Alas yes, *alteza!*'

'And who might that be?'

'My army.'

The caressing, sly manner in which Biassou was evading Pierrot's haughty, forthright questions indicated that he was determined to grant the other man nothing more than an apparently obligatory show of respect.

'What!' exclaimed Pierrot. 'Your army! And do you not command it?'

Maintaining his advantage, and yet without abandoning his pose of inferiority, Biassou answered with apparent sincerity:

'*Su alteza*, do you think that one can truly command men who have decided to revolt because they quite simply no longer wish to obey?'

I set too little store on life to break the silence, but what I had seen the previous day of Biassou's unlimited authority over his gangs could have furnished me with the opportunity to refute him and lay bare his duplicity. Pierrot answered him back:

'Well then! If you do not know how to command your army, and if your soldiers are your leaders, what motives for hatred can they have against this prisoner?'

'Boukmann has just been killed by government troops,' replied Biassou, affecting a sad look for his ferocious, mocking face. 'My people have resolved to avenge themselves on this white man for the death of the leader of the negro maroons from Jamaica. They want to set trophy up against trophy: they want the head of this young officer to serve as a counterweight to the head of Boukmann on those scales in which the *bon Giu* is weighing the two parties.'

'How could you have condoned such a horrible act of retaliation?' Pierrot rejoined.[93] Listen to me, Jean Biassou: it is cruelties such as these that will be the downfall of our just cause. Prisoner in the white camp, from which I managed to escape, I was unaware of Boukmann's death until you informed me of it. It is heaven's just punishment for his crimes. I shall inform you of another piece of news: Jeannot, the very same black chief who served as a guide for the whites in order to lure them into the ambush at Dompte-Mulâtre, Jeannot has also just met his death.[94] You know—do not interrupt me, Biassou—that he vied with Boukmann and yourself when it came to atrocities. Now, pay attention to this, it is not lightning from heaven, it is not the whites who struck him down: it is Jean-François himself who committed this act of justice.'

Biassou, who had been listening with grim respect, let out an exclamation of surprise. At this moment Rigaud entered, made a deep bow to Pierrot, and whispered something to the generalissimo. A great commotion could be heard outside in the camp. Pierrot continued:

' ... Yes, Jean-François—whose only shortcomings are an unfortunate taste for luxury and the ridiculous display he makes of himself every day in that six-horse carriage which takes him from his camp to the mass celebrated by the curé of Grande Rivière—Jean-François has punished Jeannot's acts of frenzy. That monster went before the firing squad yesterday, despite his cowardly appeals and despite the fact that, at the very last, the brigand clung with so much terror to the curé of Marmelade, who had been assigned the task of exhorting him, that he had to be forcibly dragged off him. He was brought before the firing squad yesterday, at the foot of the very tree from which he used to hang his living victims on iron hooks. Biassou, ponder this example! Why all these massacres that oblige the whites to respond with such ferocity? And why resort to trickery for the purpose of whipping our poor comrades into a frenzy when they are already past the boiling point? At Trou-Coffy there is a mulatto charlatan by the name of Romaine the Prophetess who is goading a band of blacks to the point of fanaticism: he profanes the sacred mass; he persuades his followers that he is in contact with the Virgin Mary, whose supposed oracles he listens to by placing his head in the tabernacle; he incites his comrades to murder and pillage, all in the name of *Maria!*'[95]

There was perhaps something even more tender than religious devotion in the way Pierrot uttered this name. I don't know why, but it offended and provoked me.

' ... Well then!' the slave carried on. 'In your camp you have some obi or other, some trickster like this Romaine the Prophetess! I am not unaware that you need a common bond when leading an army made up of men from so many different regions, of such diverse parentage and colour, but could you not create it through other means than a ferocious fanaticism and ridiculous superstitions? Believe me, Biassou, the whites are less cruel than we. I have seen many planters defend the lives of their slaves. I am not unaware that for a number of them it was a matter of saving a sum of money rather than a man's life, but at least their self-interest lent them a certain virtue. Let us not be any less lenient than they; for us, it is also a matter of self-interest. Will our cause be more holy and more just once we have exterminated women, slit the throats of children, tortured old men, burned colonists in their houses? And yet this is what we are doing on a daily basis. Answer me, Biassou, must the only trace we leave of our passing always be a trail of blood, a trail of fire?'

He fell silent. The gleam in his eyes, the tone of his voice, gave to his words a power of conviction and an authority impossible to reproduce. Biassou, like a fox captured by a lion, his gaze obliquely lowered, seemed to be looking around for a stratagem that might enable him to escape from such a mighty force. As he pondered, the leader of the band from Les Cayes—that same Rigaud who the previous day had observed with a calm countenance all the horrors committed in his presence—appeared to get indignant at the enormities Pierrot had depicted, and exclaimed with a hypocritical dismay:

'Ah, dear God! How terrible the fury of a people can be!'[96]

43

DURING THIS time, it was getting noisier outside, and this appeared to be worrying Biassou. Later on, I found out that the Morne Rouge negroes were the ones responsible for all that commotion: they were going from one end of the camp to the other, announcing the return of my liberator and letting it be known that, whatever motive had led him to call on Biassou, they would back him up. Rigaud had just informed the generalissimo of this situation, and it was the fear of a disastrous division in the ranks that determined the sly chief to make a concession of sorts to Pierrot's wishes.

'*Alteza*,' he said with a chagrined look, 'if we are harsh with the whites, you are harsh with us. You are wrong to blame me for the violence of the torrent: it sweeps me along with it. But in short *que podria hacer ahora** that would be agreeable to you?'

'I have already told you, *señor* Biassou,' Pierrot answered. 'Let me take this prisoner away with me.'

Biassou remained thoughtful for a moment and then, assuming as frank an expression as he could, exclaimed:

'All right then, *alteza*. I want to prove to you just how great is my desire to please you. Only permit me to have a word in private with the prisoner; he will then be free to follow you.'

'Certainly! By all means,' Pierrot answered.

His look of righteous pride and displeasure vanished, and his face lit up with joy. He moved back a few steps.

Biassou led me to a corner of the grotto and whispered to me:

'I can only grant you your life on one condition. You know what it is. Do you assent to it?'

He showed me the dispatch from Jean-François. To consent would have seemed contemptible to me.

'No!' I shot back at him.

'Ah!' he sniggered. 'As determined as ever! So, you're counting a great deal on your protector? Do you know who he is?'

'Yes,' I replied curtly. 'A monster like you, only even more hypocritical!'

He reared back in astonishment, trying to gauge from my eyes whether I was speaking seriously:

'What's that! So you don't know him?'

I answered disdainfully:

'I recognize in him only a slave of my uncle's, Pierrot by name.'

Biassou began to snigger again.

'Ha! Ha! Here's an odd state of affairs. He begs for your life and liberty, and you call him "a monster like me!"'

'What does it matter to me?' I answered. 'If I were to secure a moment's liberty, I would not be begging for my life, but demanding his!'

'How's that?' Biassou queried. 'Yet you seem to be speaking your mind, and I don't imagine you feel like trifling with your life. There's something behind all this that I don't understand. You're protected by a

---

*   What might I do now?

man you hate; he pleads for your life, and you want him dead! In any case, it's all the same to me. You desire a moment's liberty, and it's all I can grant you. I shall let you go, you're free to follow him. But first give me your word of honour that you will return and hand yourself back over to me two hours before sunset. You're a Frenchman, right?'

Truth be told, gentlemen, life was a burden to me. Besides, I was repelled by the idea of owing that life to Pierrot, whom so many appearances singled out as the object of my hatred. Indeed, I'm not sure whether my resolve might not have been strengthened by the certainty that Biassou, who wasn't one to let go of his prey readily, would never consent to my release. A few hours of freedom were all I really wanted—just enough time, before dying, to clarify my beloved Marie's fate and my own. The promise that Biassou asked of me, trusting to French honour, was a sure and easy way of securing one more day of life; I gave it to him.

After binding me in this manner, the chief went up to Pierrot.

'*Alteza*,' he said in an obsequious tone, 'the white prisoner is at your disposal. You can take him away. He is free to accompany you.'

I had never seen so much happiness in Pierrot's eyes.

'Thank you, Biassou!' he exclaimed, holding his hand out to him. 'Thank you! You have just done me a favour that entitles you to ask anything of me from now on! Remain in charge of my Morne Rouge brothers until my return.'

He turned toward me.

'Now that you are free,' he said, 'come!'

And, in a singularly energetic fashion, he led me away.

Biassou watched us leave, a look of astonishment on his face that even the many demonstrations of respect with which he graced Pierrot's departure could not mask.

44

I WAS EAGER to be alone with Pierrot. His uneasiness when I had questioned him as to Marie's fate and the insolent tenderness with which he dared to utter her name had once again instilled in me those feelings of loathing and jealousy that had first sprung up in my heart when, through the flames devouring Fort Galifet, I saw him abduct the woman whom I could scarcely even call my wife. In the face of that, what did they matter to me, all those generous reproaches he had directed in my presence at the bloodthirsty Biassou, all the pains he had taken to save my life, and even that extraordinary quality which marked his every word and action? What did it matter to me, this mystery that seemed to enshroud him—that caused him to appear before my very eyes, alive, when I thought I had witnessed his death; that revealed him to be a captive of the whites when I had seen him swallowed up in the Grande Rivière; that transformed the slave into a royal highness, the prisoner into a liberator? Of all these incomprehensible matters, the only one that was clear to me was the odious abduction of Marie: an outrage to avenge, a crime to punish. All the strange things which I had witnessed were barely enough to make me suspend my judgment, and I awaited impatiently the time when I would be able to force my rival to explain himself. That moment finally came.

We had made our way through the triple file of blacks who were prostrating themselves as we passed by and exclaiming with surprise: '*Miraculo! ya no esta prisionero!*'* I'm not sure if it was me or Pierrot they meant. We had crossed the camp's outer limits and the last of Biassou's sentinels had disappeared from sight behind trees and rocks. Rask, in high spirits, was running ahead and then doubling back on us. Pierrot was walking at a rapid pace; I stopped him brusquely.

'Listen,' I said to him, 'it's useless to go any further. The ears you were afraid of can no longer hear us. Speak, what have you done with Marie?'

Intense emotion made me gasp out my words. He looked at me kindly.

'Still that!' he replied.

'Yes, still that!' I exclaimed furiously. 'Still that! I shall put this question to you until the two of us have drawn our last breath. Where is Marie?'

'So nothing can dispel your doubts about my loyalty! You will find out soon enough.'

'Soon enough? Monster!' I retorted. 'I want to know it now. Where is Marie? Where is Marie? Do you hear me? Answer, or prepare to stake your life against mine! Defend yourself!'

'I have already told you,' he went on sadly, 'that such a thing is not possible. The torrent does not struggle against its source; my life, which you have saved three times, cannot enter into combat with yours. In any case, even if I wanted to, it would be impossible. Between the two of us, we have only one dagger.'

As he spoke these words, he pulled a dagger from his belt and offered it to me.

---

* A miracle! He is no longer a prisoner!

'Here, take it,' he said.

I was beside myself with rage. I grabbed hold of it and ran the glistening dagger up and down his chest. He made no effort to back away.

'Miserable wretch,' I stormed at him. 'Don't make me commit murder. I'll thrust this blade into your heart if you don't tell me this very instant where my wife is.'

He answered me without anger:

'You are the master. But, I pray of you, let me have one more hour of life. Follow me. You doubt the man who owes you three lives, the man you called your brother. Listen, if in an hour you still have doubts, you are free to kill me. There will be plenty of time for that. It should be clear that I have no desire to resist you. I entreat you in the very name of *Maria* ...' With great effort, he added: ' ... of your wife. One more hour, and if I beg you in this manner, well, it is not for my sake, it is for yours!'

An inexpressible mixture of conviction and distress was in his voice. Something seemed to warn me that he might well be telling the truth—that mere concern for preserving his life would not be enough to give his voice this penetrating tenderness, this imploring sweetness, and that he was pleading for more than just himself. I yielded once again to the secret ascendancy he exercised over me and which at that moment I blushed to acknowledge.

'Let's go,' I said. 'I grant you an hour's reprieve; I will follow you.'

I tried to give him back the dagger.

'No,' he answered. 'Keep it, you do not trust me. But come, let us not lose any time.'

45

HE SET OFF, once more leading the way. During our exchange, Rask had made repeated attempts at starting up again, each time eventually coming back toward us and casting a look of inquiry in my direction to see why we had stopped. Now he joyfully bounded off ahead. We disappeared into the virgin forest. After about half an hour we came out onto a lovely, verdant savannah traversed by a mountain spring and bordered by the deep shade of the forest's enormous, centuries-old trees. Opening out onto the savannah was a cavern, its greyish exterior covered with a profusion of climbing plants, a green veil of clematis, liana, jasmine. Rask was on the point of barking but Pierrot made a sign for him to keep quiet. Without saying a word, he led me by the hand into the cavern.

In this grotto, seated on an esparto mat with her back turned to the light, was a woman. At the sound of our steps, she turned ... My friends, it was Marie!

Just as on the day of our wedding, she was wearing a white dress and she still had the wreath of orange blossoms in her hair—the young wife's last virginal adornment—which my hands had not removed from her brow. She noticed me, saw who I was, let out a cry, and fell into my arms, overcome with joy and surprise. I was thunderstruck.

At this cry, an old woman carrying a child in her arms rushed out of a second room that was set up near the back of the cavern. It was Marie's nurse and the youngest child of my poor uncle. Pierrot had gone to fetch some water from the near-by spring. He threw a few drops of it onto Marie's face. The coolness of the water revived her; she, opened her eyes.

'Leopold!' she said. 'My Leopold!'

'Marie!...' I answered, and the remainder of our words was swallowed up in a kiss.

'Not in front of me, for pity's sake!' wailed a harrowing voice.

We looked up; it was Pierrot. He was there, witnessing our acts of endearment as if they were acts of torture. His heaving breast was gasping for air; an ice-cold sweat was streaming from his forehead. His every limb was trembling. All at once he covered his face with his two hands and ran out of the grotto, repeating in a terrible tone: 'Not in front of me!'

Marie half raised herself out of my arms and, as she followed him with her eyes, exclaimed:

'Good heavens, my dear Leopold! Our love appears to cause him pain. Is it possible that he loves me?'

The slave's cry had proven to me that he was my rival; Marie's exclamation proved to me that he was also my friend.

'Marie!' I answered, and a bliss I had never felt before entered my heart at the same time as a terrible pang of regret. 'Marie! Did you know nothing about it?'

'But I still know nothing about it,' she replied with a chaste blush. 'What! He loves me! I never even noticed.'

Rapturously, I clasped her tight.

'I regain my wife and my friend!' I exclaimed. 'How happy I am and how guilty! I doubted him.'

'What!' Marie responded in astonishment. 'Him! Pierrot! Oh yes, you are guilty indeed. He saved my life twice: you owe him that, and perhaps even more,' she added, lowering her eyes. 'Without him the crocodile in the river would have devoured me; without him the negroes ... Pierrot is the one who snatched me from their hands at the very moment they were doubtless going to reunite me with my poor father!'

She broke off and started weeping.

'And why,' I asked her, 'did Pierrot not return you to the Cape, to your husband?'

'He tried to,' she answered, 'but he could not manage it. Obliged as he was to hide from both the blacks and the whites, it was very difficult for him. Moreover, no one knew what had become of you. Some people said they had seen you fall dead, but Pierrot assured me this wasn't the case, and I was very sure it wasn't, for something would have warned me of it—and if you had died, I too would have died, at the very same time.'

'So,' I questioned her, 'Pierrot brought you here?'

'Yes, Leopold. This secluded grotto is known to him alone. He rescued not just me but all that remained of the family: my dear old nurse and my little brother. He hid us here. I assure you it's all very comfortable, and if it were not for the war that's stirring up the whole country, now that we're ruined I would like to live here with you. Pierrot saw to our every need. He would stop in often. He'd be wearing a red feather on his head. He consoled me, spoke to me about you, assured me that you would be restored to me. Not having seen him in three days, though, I was beginning to worry—and then he returned with you! So he went off in search of you, this poor friend of yours?'

'Yes,' I answered her.

'But if that's the case,' she went on, 'then how can it be that he's in love with me? Are you sure of it?'

'Now I'm sure!' I declared to her. 'He's the one who, on the point of stabbing me, let himself be swayed by the fear of causing you distress; he's the one who sang those love-songs to you in the pavilion by the river.'

'Really!' Marie said with naive surprise. 'He's your rival! The wicked man with the marigolds is one and the same as this good Pierrot! I can't believe it. He was so humble in my presence, so respectful—more so than when he was our slave! It's true that every so often he looked at me in a peculiar way, but it was only out of sadness and I attributed it to my misfortunes. If you knew with what passionate devotion he would talk to me about my Leopold! His friendship spoke of you almost as my love did.'

Enchantment and at the same time desolation: this was the effect of Marie's explanations on me. I remembered with what cruelty I had treated the generous Pierrot, and I felt all the force of his tender and resigned reproach: 'It is not I who am the ungrateful one.'

At that moment Pierrot returned. He had a dark, pained look on his face, like a condemned man who has come back from being tortured and yet who has successfully withstood it. He moved slowly toward me. Pointing to the dagger I had placed in my belt, he said to me in a solemn voice:

'The hour has elapsed.'

'The hour! What hour?' I asked him.

'The one you granted me; I needed it in order to lead you here. Then, I begged you to spare my life; now, I am begging you to deliver me from it.'

The sweetest feelings of the heart—love, friendship, gratitude—all came together at this moment and tore me apart. I fell at the slave's feet, incapable of saying a word, sobbing bitterly. He hurriedly lifted me up.

'What are you doing?' he said to me.

'I am paying you the tribute I owe you. I am no longer worthy of a friendship like yours. Any goodwill you have for me cannot extend so far as to pardon my ingratitude.'

For a while the look on his face remained forbidding. He appeared to be undergoing a violent struggle within himself: he took a step toward me and then drew back; he opened his mouth but then shut it again. This moment of hesitation did not last long. He opened wide his arms to me:

'Can I call you brother now?' he asked.

My only answer to him was to throw myself upon his breast.

After a slight pause, he added:

'You are a good man, but your unhappiness made you unjust.'

'I have regained my brother,' I said to him. 'I am no longer unhappy, but I am most certainly guilty.'

'Guilty, brother! I too have been so, and more than you. You are no longer unhappy. I, on the contrary, will always be so!'

46

THE FIRST transports of friendship had made his face sparkle with a joy that soon vanished; his features took on an odd, intensely sad expression. 'Listen,' he said to me in an icy tone of voice. 'My father was king in the land of Kakongo.[97] Outside his door he would dispense justice to his subjects and for each judgement that he passed he would drink—following the custom of kings—a full cup of palm wine. We were happy, we were powerful. The Europeans came; they gave me all that useless knowledge that so impressed you. Their leader was a Spanish captain; he promised my father lands more vast than his own and white women. My father followed him with his family ... Brother, they sold us!'

The black man's chest heaved; his eyes sparkled with anger. Heedlessly, he snapped in two a young medlar tree that happened to be next to him. He continued, seemingly oblivious to me:

'The master of the land of Kakongo had acquired a master, and his son became a slave stooped low over the fields of Santo Domingo. The young lion was separated from his old father so that the two of them might be more easily tamed; the young wife was taken from her husband with an eye to the profit that would come from coupling them with others; the little children looked for the mother who had nourished them, for the father who used to bathe them in the torrents, but they found only barbarous tyrants and were made to sleep with the dogs!'

He fell silent. Even though he was no longer speaking, his lips kept moving. His expression was blank, his eyes wild. At length, he grabbed me roughly by the arm.

'Brother, do you understand? I was sold to different masters as one sells a head of cattle ... You remember when Ogé was tortured to death? On that day I saw my father again. I saw him broken on the wheel! Do you hear me?'

I shuddered. He added:

'My wife was prostituted to the whites. Do you hear me, brother? She died, begging that I avenge her. Truth be told,' he continued hesitantly, lowering his eyes, 'I have been guilty. I have loved another woman ... But the less said the better!

All my people were urging me to free them and take my revenge. Rask would bring me their messages.

I was unable to do what they wanted. I was myself in your uncle's prisons. The day when you obtained my pardon, I left to rescue my children from the hands of a ferocious master. I arrived at the place ... Brother, the last of the king of Kakongo's grandsons had just expired under the blows of a white man! The others had preceded him.'

He broke off and asked me icily:

'Brother, what would you have done?'

This heart-rending account had left me frozen with horror. I answered his question with a menacing gesture. He understood me, and started smiling bitterly. He continued his account:

'The slaves rose up against their master and punished him for the murder of my children. They elected me their leader. You know the calamities that came about as a result of this rebellion. I learned that your uncle's slaves were preparing to follow the same example. I arrived in Acul the very night of the insurrection. You were away. Your uncle had just been stabbed to death in his bed. The blacks were already setting fire to the plantations. I was unable to calm their fury, for they believed that by burning down your uncle's properties they were avenging me. I had to save what was left of your family. I found my way into the fort through the breach I had created there during my imprisonment. I entrusted your wife's nurse to a faithful black man. Saving your *Maria* proved more difficult. She had run toward the part of the fort that was on fire to rescue the youngest of her brothers, the only one who had escaped the massacre. Some blacks had her encircled; they were going to kill her. I stepped forward and ordered them to let me take my own revenge. They withdrew. I took your wife in my arms, I entrusted the child to Rask, and I lodged them both in this cavern. I am the only one who knows about its existence and how to get to it ... So there you have my crime, brother.'

Increasingly overwhelmed by remorse and gratitude, I would once again have thrown myself at Pierrot's feet but, with an offended look, he stopped me.

'Come, let us go,' he urged a moment later, taking me by the hand. 'Bring your wife and the others. It is time for us to leave.'

Surprised, I asked him where he wanted to take us.

'To the camp of the whites,' he answered me. 'This hiding place is no longer safe. Tomorrow, at the break of day, the whites are set to attack Biassou's camp; the forest will certainly be set on fire. Besides, we do not have a moment to lose: ten heads are answering for mine. We can hurry, because you are free; we must hurry, because I am not.'

These words increased my surprise; I asked him to explain what he meant.

'Have you not heard that Bug-Jargal was being held prisoner?' he said impatiently.

'Yes, but what does this Bug-Jargal have to do with you?'

He seemed astonished in turn, and answered solemnly:

'I am Bug-Jargal.'

47

YOU MIGHT say that when it came to this man I was accustomed to being surprised. Not without astonishment had I seen the slave Pierrot transformed just moments earlier into an African king. I was all the more struck with admiration now that I recognized in him the redoubtable and magnanimous Bug-Jargal, leader of the insurgents from Morne Rouge. I finally understood why all the rebels, and even Biassou, paid such respect to the chieftain Bug-Jargal, the king of Kakongo.

He did not appear to notice the impression made on me by these last words of his.

'I had been told,' he carried on, 'that you were a prisoner in Biassou's camp. I came to deliver you.'

'Why then did you say to me just now that you were not free?'

He looked at me as if trying to guess what had brought about this entirely natural question.

'Look,' he said to me. 'This morning I was a prisoner amongst your people. I heard it announced in the camp that Biassou had declared his intention to have a young captive by the name of Leopold d'Auverney killed before sunset. They put more guards around me. I found out that my execution would follow yours, and that were I to escape ten of my comrades would answer for me ... You see that I am pressed for time.'

Still I kept at him.

'So you escaped?' I asked him.

'And how else would I be here? Did I not have to save you? Do I not owe you my life? Come, follow me now. It is an hour's march from here to the white camp, the same distance as to Biassou's camp. See, the shadow of those coconut trees is getting longer and its round top lies on the grass like an enormous condor egg. In three hours the sun will have set. Come, brother, time is short.'

'In three hours the sun will have set.' Such simple words, but they made my blood run cold as if I had seen a ghost. They recalled to me the fatal promise I had made to Biassou. Alas! Seeing Marie again had caused me to lose sight of the fact that we would soon be separated forever. I had felt nothing but delight and intoxication; all those emotions had deprived me of my memory, and in my happiness I had forgotten my impending death. My friend's words were a violent reminder of the fate that awaited me. 'In three hours the sun will have set.' It would take an hour to get back to Biassou's camp. My bounden duty was clear. The brigand had my word, and it was a far better thing to die than to give this barbarian the right to be contemptuous of the only thing he still seemed to trust: a Frenchman's honour. It was a harrowing dilemma. I chose what I had to choose but, gentlemen, I will admit it, I hesitated a moment. Could you blame me?

48

FINALLY, heaving a sigh, I took hold of Bug-Jargal's hand with one hand and my poor Marie's with the other. An ominous cloud had spread over my features, and she was watching it anxiously.

'Bug-Jargal,' I said haltingly, 'I entrust to you the only being in the world I love more than you, Marie. Return to the camp without me for I am unable to follow you.'

'My God,' Marie gasped. 'What new calamity is this?'

Bug-Jargal had given a start. A look of pained astonishment was in his eyes.

'Brother, what are you saying?'

Marie was so overwhelmed with terror by the mere thought of some approaching calamity, seemingly glimpsed by her overly prescient affection, that I felt compelled to conceal its reality from her and spare her any agonizing farewells. I leaned over to Bug-Jargal and whispered in his ear:

'I am a captive. I swore to Biassou that I would return and place myself in his power two hours before the end of the day. I have promised to die.'

Flying into a rage, he thundered:

'The monster! So that is why he wanted to speak to you in secret: to extract this promise from you. I should have been on my guard against that wretched Biassou. How could I not have foreseen some act of treachery? He is not a black man, he is a mulatto.'

'What is happening? What act of treachery? What promise?' Marie asked, terrified. 'Who is this Biassou?'

'Be quiet, be quiet,' I repeated in an undertone to Bug-Jargal. 'Let us not alarm Marie.'

'So be it,' he said to me grimly. 'But how could you have consented to this promise? Why did you give it?'

'I believed you to be an ingrate, I believed Marie lost to me. What did I care about life?'

'But surely a spoken promise cannot bind you to this brigand?'

'I have given my word of honour.'

He seemed to be trying to understand what I meant.

'Your word of honour! What is that? Have the two of you drunk from the same cup? Have the two of you broken a ring together or a branch of red-flowering maple?'

'No.'

'Well then! So what are you telling us? What could possibly bind you?'

'My honour,' I answered.

'I do not know what that signifies. Nothing binds you to Biassou. Come with us.'

'Brother, I cannot. I have promised.'

'No! You have not promised!' he exclaimed heatedly. Then he raised his voice: 'Sister, join with me and help prevent your husband from leaving us. He wishes to return to the negro camp from which I rescued him, under the pretext that he has pledged his death to their chief Biassou.'

'What have you done?' I exclaimed in turn.

It was too late to forestall the effect of this generous impulse which had made him call upon the woman he loved to help save his rival's life. With a cry of despair, Marie had thrown herself into my arms. With her hands clasped round my neck, she hung upon my breast, drained of strength and almost breathless.

'Oh!' she groaned in pain. 'What is he saying, dear Leopold? He is deceiving me, isn't that so? At the very moment when we have been reunited, surely you would not wish to go and leave me, and to leave me to go to your death? Answer me quickly or I shall die. You do not have the right to give up your life, because you must not give up mine. You could not possibly wish to part from me, never to see me again.'

'Marie,' I answered back, 'don't believe him. I am, indeed, going to leave you; it has to be done. But we will meet again, in another place.'

'Another place,' she replied in alarm. 'What place? Where...?'

'In heaven!' I answered, unable to lie to this angel.

Once again she fainted, only this time it was from grief. Time was getting short; my decision had been taken. I set her down in the arms of Bug-Jargal, whose eyes were full of tears.

'So nothing can keep you from doing this?' he said to me. 'There is nothing I can add to what you see before you. How can you resist Maria? For just one of the words she said to you I would have sacrificed a world for her—and you, you will not sacrifice your death for her?'

'Honour!' I answered. 'Farewell, Bug-Jargal. Farewell, brother. I bequeath her to you.'

He took my hand. Lost in thought, he scarcely seemed to hear me.

'Brother, one of your relatives is at the white camp; I shall hand Maria over to him. As for me, I cannot accept your bequest.'

He pointed out a peak to me, the summit of which towered above the surrounding countryside.

'Do you see that crag? When the sign of your death appears there, it will not be long before people hear word of my own. Farewell.'

Without stopping to consider the cryptic meaning of these last words, I embraced him. I planted a kiss on the pale forehead of Marie, who was beginning to revive thanks to the attentions of her nurse, and I slipped away hastily for fear that her first glance, her first moan, would rob me of all my determination.

49

I SLIPPED away. I plunged into the depths of the forest, following our earlier tracks without even daring to cast a glance behind me. As if to numb the thoughts that overwhelmed me, I ran without stopping through the thickets, the savannahs, and the hills until finally, from the crest of a rock, Biassou's camp—with its lines of ox-carts, its rows of ajoupas, and its seething mass of blacks—came into view. There, I halted. I was nearing the end of my journey and of my existence. Physically and emotionally exhausted, my strength was spent; I leaned against a tree so as not to fall and I let my eyes wander over the scene that stretched out beneath me in the fateful savannah.

I thought that by this point I had drunk from every cup full of bitterness and gall. But I was as yet unacquainted with the cruellest of all misfortunes, which is for a happy, living man to be compelled by a moral force—more powerful than the force of events—to renounce happiness and life of his own free will. A few hours before, what did it matter to me whether I remained in the world or not? I was not alive, and extreme despair is a type of death that makes one long for the genuine article. But I had been rescued from this despair. Marie had been restored to me; bliss—dead and buried for me—had been, so to speak, resurrected; my past had turned back into my future; and all my eclipsed dreams had reappeared more dazzling than ever. In short, life—a life of youth, love, and enchantment—had once again unfurled its radiance before me on an horizon without bounds. That life, I could begin it again. Everything—within me and without—was beckoning me to do so. There was no material obstacle, no visible hindrance. I was free, I was happy, and yet I had to die. I had taken only one step in this garden of paradise, and some vague sense of duty, which did not even have anything glorious about it, was forcing me to return to my doom. For a soul blighted by the frost of adversity, death is nothing; but how poignant is its touch, how cold it seems, when its hand falls on a heart in full bloom which is soaking up the warmth of existence and its joys! This was what I was experiencing. For one brief moment I had left behind the sepulchre, I had been intoxicated by all that is most heavenly upon earth—love, devotion, liberty—and now I had to return headlong into the tomb.

50

WHEN THIS state of dejection caused by regret had passed, a sort of rage took hold of me; I strode into the valley at a furious pace. I felt the need to get it all over and done with. I reported to the negro outposts. They looked surprised and refused to admit me. A bizarre state of affairs! I practically had to beg them. Two among them finally seized hold of me and took it upon themselves to lead me to Biassou.

I entered his grotto. He was surrounded by various instruments of torture and was busy testing out their springs. At the sound of his guards ushering me in, he turned his head; my presence did not appear to astonish him.

'Do you see?' he said, displaying the horrible apparatus around him.

I remained calm; I was familiar with the cruelty of this 'hero of humanity,' and I was determined to endure everything without blanching.

'Is it not the case,' he sniggered, 'that Leogri was very lucky to have suffered nothing more than a hanging?'

Without answering, I looked at him with cold disdain.

'Go and inform my good chaplain,' he then said to an aide-de-camp.

Both of us remained silent for a moment, looking one another in the eye. I observed him; he watched me closely.

At that moment Rigaud entered; with an agitated look on his face, he whispered something to the generalissimo.

'Rally all the leaders of my army,' Biassou calmly ordered.

A quarter of an hour later all the leaders in their diversely bizarre costumes were gathered in front of the grotto. Biassou rose to his feet.

'Listen, *amigos!* The whites plan to attack us here, tomorrow at the break of day. Our position is a bad one; we need to vacate it. Let us set off at sunset and head for the Spanish frontier. Macaya, you will form the vanguard with your black maroons. Padrejean,[98] you will spike the guns seized from Praloto's artillery;[99] we can't take them with us into the mornes. Brave warriors of Croix-des-Bouquets, you will set off after Macaya. Toussaint will follow with the blacks from Léogane and Trou. If the griots and the griotes make even the slightest clamour, let the army executioner take charge of them. Lieutenant-Colonel Cloud[100] will distribute the English rifles that were disembarked at Cape Cabron, and will lead the ci-devant "free sang-mêlés" along the trails of La Vista. If there are any prisoners left, let their throats be slit. Ready the bullets, poison the arrows. Pour three tuns of arsenic into the spring where we drew water for the camp; the colonists will think it's sugar and drink it without suspecting a thing. The troops from Limbé, Dondon, and Acul will set out after Cloud and Toussaint. Block every pathway through the savannah with boulders, block all the roads, set fire to the forests. Rigaud, you will remain with us. Candy, you will rally my bodyguard around me. The Morne Rouge blacks will form the rearguard, and they will not evacuate the savannah until sunrise.'

He leaned over toward Rigaud and whispered:

'Those are Bug-Jargal's blacks. Would that they were crushed here! *Muerta la tropa, muerto el gefe!*'* Straightening back up, he raised his voice again: 'Get going, *hermanos.* Candy will bring you the watchword.'

The leaders withdrew.

'General,' said Rigaud, 'it would be advisable to send Jean-François's dispatch. Things are going badly for us; it might stall the whites.'

---

* Gang dead, chief dead!

Biassou hastily drew it out of his pocket.

'Now that you remind me ... But they will laugh at it: there are so many grammatical errors.' He presented me with the document. 'Listen, do you want to save your life? Once again, my goodness asks it of your stubbornness. Help me to rework this letter. I'll dictate my ideas to you; you'll write it up in the *white style.*'

With a shake of my head, I signalled 'no.' He looked irritated.

'So it's no?' he asked me.

'No!' I answered.

He was insistent.

'Think it over well.'

His gaze seemed to draw my own to the torture apparatus which he was idly fingering.

'It is because I've thought it over,' I shot back, 'that I refuse. You appear to me to fear for yourself and for your people; you count on this letter delaying the advance and the vengeance of the whites. I have no desire for a life that might perhaps help save your own. Let my torture begin.'

'Ah! Ah! *Muchacho!*' Biassou retorted, nudging the instruments of torture with his foot. 'It seems to me that you're starting to feel right at home with these. It annoys me no end, but I don't have the time to try them out on you. This position is a dangerous one; I have to get clear of it as quickly as possible. Ah! You refuse to serve as my secretary! It's just as well, you're right, for in any case I would have had you killed afterwards. No one can be allowed to live with a secret of Biassou's. And besides, my friend, I promised our good chaplain the pleasure of your death.'

He turned toward the obi, who had just entered.

'*Bon per,* is your squad ready?'

With a nod, the latter signalled in the affirmative.

'Did you pick some of the Morne Rouge blacks for the job? They're the only ones in the army who don't yet have any preparations to make for the departure.'

The obi signalled 'yes' a second time.

Biassou then pointed to the large black flag that I had previously noticed in a corner of the grotto.

'That is what will let your people know when it's time to give your epaulette over to your lieutenant. By then, you understand, I'll already be on the move ... By the way, you've just gone for a little stroll. What did you think of the surroundings?'

'It struck me,' I answered icily, 'that there were enough trees around to hang you and your entire band.'

'Well now,' he retorted with a forced snigger, 'there is one place that you have doubtless not seen, and the *bon per* will make you acquainted with it. Farewell, young captain. Give my regards to Leogri.'

He saluted me with that laugh of his which reminded me of the sound of a rattlesnake, gesticulated, and then turned his back to me. The negroes dragged me away. The veiled obi accompanied us, rosary in hand.

51

I WALKED in their midst without putting up any resistance; true, to have done so would have been useless. We climbed to the brow of a mountain that was situated to the west of the savannah and there we stopped to rest for a while. I cast one last look at the setting sun—a sun that would never again rise for me. My guides got up; I followed them. We descended into a small valley that at any other time would have enchanted me. A torrent ran through it from one end to the other, imparting a fertile moistness to the soil; at the end of the valley the torrent streamed into one of those blue lakes that are so plentiful in the interior of the Saint Domingue mornes. How many times in happier days, at the twilight hour, had I sat down on the shore of those beautiful lakes to dream, watching their azure surface change into a silvery expanse on which, like golden spangles, the reflections of the first stars of evening are sown! That hour would soon come, but I had to pass it by! How beautiful this valley seemed to me! It was dotted with mighty sycamore maples of a prodigious height; dense clumps of *mauritias*—a variety of palm that prevents any other vegetation from growing under its cover; date trees; magnolias with their broad calyces; large catalpas showing off their glossy, jagged leaves against the golden blossoms of the laburnum trees. You could see the blue-azure haloes found on that species of wild honeysuckle the negroes call *coali* mixed in with the pale yellow flowers of the Canadian osier. Green curtains of liana vines hid from sight the brownish slopes of the neighbouring crags. From every corner of this virgin soil there arose a primitive perfume like the one that the first man must have breathed as he smelled the first roses of Eden.

All this time we were walking on a trail that ran along the edge of the torrent. To my surprise, the trail ended abruptly at the foot of a sheer rock face, at the bottom of which I noticed an opening in the form of an arch from which the torrent streamed forth. A muffled noise and a raging wind rose up from this natural arch. The negroes bore left, and we scaled the rock face, following a winding and uneven path which seemed to have been hollowed out of the rock by the waters of a torrent that had long since dried up. Then a vault appeared, half blocked by the brambles, holly, and wild thorns that grew there. From under this vault you could hear a noise similar to the one coming from the arch in the valley. The blacks hauled me into it. The moment I took my first step into this subterranean passage, the obi came up and said to me in a strange voice: 'Now as for predictions, here is one that I have for you. Only one of us will leave this vault and return along this path.' It wasn't worthy of a response. We advanced further into the darkness. The noise was getting louder and louder; we could no longer hear our own footsteps. I concluded that it had to be coming from a waterfall and I was not mistaken.

After ten minutes of walking in the gloom, we arrived at an internal platform of sorts formed by nature in the heart of the mountain. Most of this semicircular platform was washed over by the torrent, which made a dreadful noise as it gushed out of the mountain's veins. Above this subterranean chamber, the vault formed a sort of dome clad with yellowish ivy. Running almost all the way across the vault was a crevice through which daylight penetrated; its edge was crowned with green shrubs, which at that moment were tinged gold by the rays of the sun. At the north end of the platform, the torrent disappeared with a roar into a chasm; the shadowy glimmer of light descending from the crevice seemed to be floating at the bottom of the chasm without being able to penetrate it. An old tree leaned over the abyss, its topmost branches sprayed by the spume from the falls, its gnarled trunk piercing through the rock one or two feet below the edge. With both its top and bottom thus awash in the waters of the torrent, the tree—which jutted out over the chasm like a fleshless arm—was so stripped of foliage that its species was unrecognizable. It was an altogether singular phenomenon: the moisture soaking its roots was all that kept it from dying, while the violence of the cataract kept tearing off its new limbs, forcing it to retain the same branches for all eternity.

52

HERE, IN this awe-inspiring place, the blacks came to a halt, and I saw that the time had come for me to die.

Then, at the edge of this chasm into which I—of my own free will, as it were—was going to hurl myself, I was once again assailed by the image of happiness I had renounced only a few hours before; it came upon me like a sense of regret, almost like a pang of remorse. Any pleading would have been unworthy of me; nevertheless, I could not hold back a word of lament.

'Friends,' I said to the blacks surrounding me, 'do you know that it is a sad thing to perish at twenty, when you are full of strength and life, when you are loved by those you love, and when you are leaving behind someone whose eyes will weep until the day they close forever?'

A horrible laugh greeted my lament. It came from the little obi. This veritable demon, this impenetrable being, scurried up to me.

'Ha! Ha! Ha! You regret life. *Labado sea Dios!* My only fear was that you would not be afraid of death!'

It was that same voice, that same laugh, which had already thwarted all my conjectures.

'Miserable creature,' I said to him, 'who are you?'

'You are about to find out!' he answered me. Then, pushing aside the silver monstrance that adorned his dusky chest, he snarled: 'Look!'

I bent down over him. Two names were burnt into the obi's hairy breast in whitish letters—the hideous and ineffaceable traces left on the chests of slaves by the imprint of a burning iron. One of these names was *Effingham*, the other was that of my uncle, my own name, *d'Auverney*! I was struck dumb with surprise.

'Well then, Leopold d'Auverney!' the obi asked me. 'Does your name tell you mine?'

Astonished to hear this man call me by name, I answered, 'no,' trying hard to rally my memory. 'These two names were never joined together except on the fool's chest ... But he is dead, that poor dwarf, and in any case he was devoted to us. You can't be Habibrah!'

'None other!' he bellowed and, lifting up the blood-stained *gorra*, he removed his veil. There, in plain sight, was the deformed face of the house-dwarf, but the air of mad gaiety by which I knew him had been replaced with a threatening and sinister expression.

'Good God!' I exclaimed, dumbfounded. 'So all the dead come back to life? Habibrah, my uncle's jester!'

The dwarf placed a hand on his dagger and said in his muffled voice:

'His jester ... and his murderer.'

I drew back in horror.

'His murderer! Blackguard, is that how you showed your gratitude for his acts of kindness?'

'His kindness! You mean his insults!'

'What!' I snapped back. 'So it's you who struck him down, miserable creature!'

'I'm the one!' he responded, with a horrible look on his face. 'I drove the knife so deep into his heart that he barely had time to open his eyes before he was dead. He let out a feeble scream: "Help me, Habibrah!" I helped him all right!'

This atrocious tale, and his atrocious cold-bloodedness, revolted me.

'Villain! Cowardly assassin! Had you forgotten all the favours he granted you, and you alone? You ate next to his table, you slept next to his bed ...'

' ... Like a dog!' Habibrah curtly interrupted. '*Como un perro!* Go on! I remembered only too well those privileges that are nothing more than indignities. I avenged myself for them on him, and I'm going to avenge myself for them on you! Listen here. Do you think that just because I am a mulatto, a misshapen dwarf, that I am not a man? Ah! I've got a soul, and a soul far grander and stronger than the one I'm going to deliver your girlish little body from! I was passed on to your uncle as if I were a toy monkey. I was the servant of his pleasures, the plaything of his scorn. You say that he loved me, that I had a place in his heart. And so I did, somewhere between his real monkey and his parrot. But I carved out another place for myself there with my dagger!'

I shuddered.

'Yes,' continued the dwarf, 'it's me! It's really me! Look me straight in the face, Leopold d'Auverney! You have laughed at me often enough, now you can shudder. Ah! You want to remind me of your uncle's shameful predilection for the man he called his jester! Quite the predilection, *bon Giu!* When I entered your drawing-rooms, I would be greeted by waves of disdainful laughter: my size, my deformities, my features, my laughable costume, even the pitiable infirmities of my nature, everything about me lent itself to the mockery of your loathsome uncle and his loathsome friends. And as for me, I couldn't even remain silent: I had to join in, *o rabia*, and laugh at the laughter I provoked! Answer me. Do you believe that such humiliations entitle one to a human being's gratitude? Do you believe they are not the equal of what the other slaves have to endure—work that never ends, the beating heat of the sun, the iron collars, and the drivers' whip? Do you believe they are not reason enough for a burning hatred to take hold of a man's heart—an implacable hatred, eternal, like the infamous wound branded onto my chest? Oh! For the length of time I suffered, my vengeance was so very short! Why couldn't I have made my odious tyrant endure all the torments that afflicted me, over and over, at every moment of every day! Why couldn't he have known the bitterness of wounded pride before he died? And have felt the searing traces left by tears of shame and rage on a face condemned to perpetual laughter! Alas! It's a hard thing to have waited so long for the hour of retribution, and for it to be over in one thrust of the dagger! If only he'd known what hand was striking him down! But I was too eager to hear him breathe his last: I thrust the knife in too quickly; he died without recognizing me. My vengeance was cheated by my fury! This time, at least, it will be more complete. You see me all too well, do you not? True, you must find it hard to recognize me in this new light that reveals me to you! You only ever saw me looking happy, joyful; now that nothing prevents my soul from appearing in my eyes, I must no longer look like myself. You knew only my mask; here is my face!'

It was a horror.

'You monster!' I exclaimed, 'you're mistaken. The atrocity of your features and your heart still has something clownish about it.'

'Don't talk about atrocity!' Habibrah interrupted. 'Think about your uncle's cruelty …'

'Miserable creature!' I went on indignantly. 'If he was cruel, it was through you! You express pity for the fate of the poor slaves, but why then did you turn the influence that your master's indulgence granted you against your brothers? Why did you never try to use it in their favour?'

'That's the last thing I would have done. I, stop a white man from staining himself with an atrocity? No! No! On the contrary, I encouraged him to treat his slaves even more badly so as to hasten the hour of rebellion, so that the excess of oppression would finally bring about the time for vengeance! In appearing to injure my brothers, I was actually serving their interests!'

Such thoroughgoing scheming in the service of hatred left me dumbfounded.

'So!' the dwarf continued. 'When it comes to planning and execution I know a thing or two, wouldn't you say? What do you think of the jester Habibrah now? What do you think of your uncle's fool?'

'Finish what you have so well begun,' I answered him. 'Kill me, but be quick about it!'

He started to parade back and forth along the platform, rubbing his hands.

'But what if I don't want to be quick about it? What if I want to enjoy your distress ... at my leisure? You see, Biassou owed me my share of the booty from the last raid. When I saw you in the black camp, your life was the only thing I asked for. He willingly granted it to me, and now it's mine! Mine to play with. Don't worry, you'll be going down those falls into that chasm soon enough. But first I should tell you something: having learned where your wife has been hidden, I today prevailed upon Biassou to set the forest on fire; it must be starting right about now. Your uncle died by the sword, you will die by water, and your Marie by fire!'

'Wretch! Miserable wretch!' I exclaimed, and made a move to throw myself at him.

He turned toward the negroes.

'Come, tie him up! He is hastening his final hour.'

In silence, the negroes began to tie me up with some ropes they had brought along. All of a sudden, I thought I heard the distant barking of a dog; I took this sound for an illusion caused by the roaring of the falls. The negroes finished strapping me up and moved me closer to the chasm that was to engulf me. Folding his arms, the dwarf looked at me in triumphant joy. I raised my eyes toward the crevice so as to avoid the odious sight of him, and to take one last look at the sky. Just then, there was another bark, louder and more pronounced. The enormous head of Rask passed through the opening. I gave a start. The dwarf exclaimed: 'Get going!' The blacks, who had not noticed the barking, got ready to fling me into the midst of the abyss.

53

'COMRADES!' a thunderous voice cried out.

Everyone turned round. It was Bug-Jargal. He was standing on the edge of the crevice, a red feather fluttering over his head.

'Comrades,' he repeated. 'Stop!'

The blacks prostrated themselves. He continued:

'I am Bug-Jargal.'

The blacks struck their foreheads against the ground, letting out a series of shouts, the tenor of which was difficult to discern.

'Untie the prisoner,' their chief cried out.

Here the dwarf appeared to awaken from the state of shock into which he'd been thrown by this unexpected apparition. Brusquely, he stayed the arms of the blacks who were ready to cut the rope that bound me. 'What's going on here?' he exclaimed. '*Que quiere decir eso?*'

Then he raised his head in the direction of Bug-Jargal:

'Chief of Morne Rouge, why have you come here?'

Bug-Jargal answered:

'I have come to command my brothers!'

'In effect,' the dwarf said with intensified rage, 'these blacks are from Morne Rouge! But by what right,' he added, raising his voice, 'do you dispose of my prisoner?'

The chief answered:

'I am Bug-Jargal.'

The blacks struck their foreheads against the ground.

'Bug-Jargal,' Habibrah persisted, 'cannot undo what Biassou has done. This white man was given to me by Biassou. It is my wish that he die; he will die. *Vosotros,*' he said to the blacks, 'obey! Throw him into the chasm.'

At the obi's powerful voice, the blacks got back up and took a step toward me. I thought I was done for.

'Untie the prisoner!' Bug-Jargal cried out.

In the blink of an eye, I was free. My surprise was as great as the obi's rage. The blacks held him back. He wanted to throw himself at me. Then he let loose a flood of curses and threats.

'*Demonios! Rabia! Infierno de mi alma!* What is this! You miserable creatures! You refuse to obey me! You disregard *mi voz*! I ought to have had him thrown to the fish *del baratro* immediately! For having wanted my vengeance to be complete, I am losing it! *O rabia de Satan! Escuchate, vosotros!* If you don't obey me, if you don't hurl this loathsome white man into the torrent, I will put a curse on you! Your hair will become white; gnats and midges will eat you alive; your legs and your arms will bend like reeds; your breath will scorch your gullet like burning sand; you will die in short order, and after your death your spirits will be forever condemned to turn a millstone as big as a mountain, in the moon where it's very cold.'

This scene had a singular effect on me. Alone of my kind in this dank, dark cavern, surrounded by these demon-like negroes, tottering on the brink of this bottomless abyss, alternately threatened by the hideous dwarf—that misshapen sorcerer, whose gaudy outfit and pointed mitre could just barely be made out in the faint light—and protected by the huge black man looming above me at the only spot where you could see the sky, it seemed to me as if I were at the gates of hell awaiting the loss or salvation of my soul, bearing witness to a relentless struggle between my guardian angel and my evil genius.

The blacks seemed terrified by the obi's curse. He attempted to take advantage of their indecision and cried out:

'It is my wish that the white man die. You will obey; he will die.'

Bug-Jargal answered back solemnly:

'He will live! I am Bug-Jargal. My father was king in the land of Kakongo and dispensed justice at the threshold of his door.'

The blacks had prostrated themselves again.

Their chief continued speaking:

'Brothers! Go and tell Biassou that the black flag which is supposed to signal this captive's death to the whites is not to be displayed on the mountain. For this captive has saved Bug-Jargal's life, and it is Bug-Jargal's wish that he live!'

They got back up. Bug-Jargal threw his red feather into their midst. The leader of the detachment folded his arms on his chest and reverently picked up the plume; then they left without uttering a word. The obi disappeared along with them into the gloom of the subterranean passageway.

I will not try to depict for you, gentlemen, the situation in which I found myself. My eyes, moist with tears, fastened on Pierrot, who was gazing at me from his side with a singular expression of goodwill and pride.

'God be praised,' he said finally. 'All is saved. Brother, return the way you came. You will find me back in the valley.'

He made a sign to me with his hand and took his leave.

54

INTENT ON making the rendezvous and discovering what marvelous good fortune had led my saviour to me at such a timely moment, I made ready to leave that awful cavern. New dangers were in store for me, however. As I started off toward the subterranean gallery, its entrance was suddenly blocked off by an unforeseen obstacle. It was Habibrah again. Instead of following the negroes, which is what I thought he had done, the vindictive obi had hidden behind a pillar of rocks, awaiting a more auspicious moment for taking his vengeance. That moment had come. The dwarf leapt out and broke into a laugh. I was alone, unarmed. A dagger—the same one that he had used as a crucifix—gleamed in his hand. At the sight of him, I drew back involuntarily.

'Ha! Ha! *Maldicho!* So you thought you were going to escape me! But the fool is less of a fool than you. I've got you, and this time I won't make you wait. And your friend Bug-Jargal isn't going to wait in vain for you either. You will go to the rendezvous in the valley, yes, but it's the waters of this torrent that are going to take you to him.'

As he said this, he rushed at me with his dagger raised.

'You monster!' I shouted at him, drawing back onto the platform. 'A short while ago you were only an executioner, but now you're an assassin!'

'Vengeance is mine!' he answered, gnashing his teeth.

At that moment I was on the edge of the precipice; suddenly, he pounced on me, attempting to push me into the depths with a thrust of his dagger. I dodged the attack. He lost his footing on the slippery moss coating the damp rocks, which were worn smooth by the water's flow. Down the slope he rolled. 'A thousand demons!' he roared out … He had fallen into the abyss.

I mentioned to you that a root of the old tree was sticking out from clefts in the granite, a little below the edge. The dwarf crashed into it as he fell. His spangled skirt became tangled in the gnarled trunk; grabbing hold of this last resort, he clung to it with extraordinary energy. His peaked bonnet flew off his head; he had to let go of his dagger. The jester's murderous weapon and his jangling gorra disappeared together, banging against one another in the depths of the cataract.

Suspended over the horrifying chasm, Habibrah at first tried to climb back onto the platform, but his little arms couldn't reach all the way to the ridge of the escarpment. He wore his nails down in unavailing attempts to dig into the viscous surface of the rock that overhung the shadowy abyss. He howled with rage.

The slightest movement on my part would have been enough to send him crashing, but it would have been an act of cowardice to do so. I did not give it a moment's thought. This moderation made an impression on him. Thanking heaven for having rescued me in such an unexpected manner, I decided to abandon him to his fate and was on the point of leaving the underground chamber when, all of a sudden, I heard the dwarf's voice rise out of the abyss, imploring and sorrowful:

'Master!' he shouted. 'Master! Do not go away, for pity's sake! In the name of the *bon Giu*, do not let a human whom you could save die impenitent and guilty. Alas! My strength is failing, the branch is slipping and bending in my hands, the weight of my body is dragging me down. Either I will have to let go of it or it will break. Alas! Master! The horrendous chasm whirls below me! *Nombre santo de Dios!* Will you have no pity on your poor jester? His crimes are great, but will you not prove to him that whites are more worthy than mulattoes, masters more worthy than slaves?'

Almost moved, I had drawn near the precipice, and in the dim light that descended from the crevice I could see on the dwarf's repulsive face emotions I had yet to associate with him: entreaty and distress.

'*Señor* Leopold,' he continued, encouraged by the pitying reaction I'd let slip. 'Is it possible that a human being, seeing his fellow man in such a horrible predicament, could be in a position to help that man and yet not do so? Alas! Reach out your hand to me, master. It would take only a little help to save me. That which is everything for me is such a small matter for you! Pull me up, for pity's sake! My gratitude will be as great as my crimes.'

I interrupted him:

'You wretch! Do not remind me of them.'

'I do so only in order to execrate them, master!' he answered back. 'Ah! Be more generous than I! O heaven! O heaven! I'm getting weaker! I'm falling. *Ay desdichado!* A hand! Your hand! Reach out your hand to me! In the name of the mother who bore you!'

I can't begin to tell you just how plaintive this voice full of terror and suffering was! I let the past go. He was no longer an enemy, a traitor, an assassin: he was a poor wretch who could, with a slight effort on my part, be rescued from an awful death. He was imploring me so pitiably! Any word, any reproach, would have been useless and ridiculous; his need for help appeared urgent. I stooped down and—kneeling along the edge, with one of my hands braced against the trunk of the tree that was holding the unfortunate Habibrah up by its root—I reached out my other hand to him ... As soon as it was within his grasp, his two hands seized hold of mine with tremendous force and, far from acquiescing in my efforts to pull him up, I could feel they were trying to drag me down with him into the abyss. If the tree trunk had not afforded me such a solid support, I would without fail have been pulled over the edge by the unexpected, violent tug that the miserable creature gave me.

'Blackguard!' I exclaimed. 'What are you doing?'

'Vengeance is mine!' he answered with a shrill and diabolical laugh. 'Ah! I've got you at last! Imbecile! You have snared yourself. I've got you. You were saved, I was lost, and of your own free will you have returned into the jaws of the alligator, just because it groaned after it had roared! This is my consolation: my death is an act of vengeance! You are caught in the trap, *amigo*, and I will have a human companion amongst the fishes of the lake!'

'Ah! Traitor!' I cried, straining every muscle. 'So this is how you reward me for having tried to deliver you from danger!'

'Yes,' he answered back. 'I know I could have been safe with you, but I'd rather you perish alongside me. I prefer your death to my life! Come!'

At the same time, with an incredible effort his two bronze, calloused hands were clutching onto mine. His eyes were blazing. He was foaming at the mouth. His strength, the loss of which he had been so sorrowfully lamenting a moment before, had returned to him, stimulated by rage and the desire for vengeance. His feet were braced like two levers against the perpendicular walls of the rock and he was leaping like a tiger on the root. His clothes were entangled in the root, which held him up despite his efforts; what he wanted was to break it so that, having to bear his full weight, I could be dragged down more quickly. Every so often he bit into it in a frenzy, interrupting the dreadful laughter that was streaming out at me from his monstrous face. It was as if he were the horrifying demon spirit of this cavern, seeking to draw his prey down into a palace of the deep, the palace of darkness where he lived.

Fortunately, one of my knees had become stuck in a cavity of the rock, and my arm had gotten itself twisted round the tree that was supporting me; I struggled against the dwarf's efforts with all the energy that the instinct of self-preservation can produce at such moments. From time to time, and with a huge effort, I raised my chest up and called out with all my might: 'Bug-Jargal!' But the roar of the falls and the distance left me very little hope that he could hear my voice.

Meanwhile the dwarf, who had not expected so much resistance, redoubled his furious tugging. I was beginning to lose my strength, even though this struggle had been going on for much less time than it's taking me to tell you about it. My arm was almost paralysed with an unbearable, wrenching pain. My eyes were clouding over. Glimmers of light, livid and indistinct, flickered back and forth in front of me. My ears were ringing. I heard the root cracking; it was ready to break. I heard the monster laughing; he was ready to fall. It felt as if the howling chasm were rising up toward me.[101]

Before giving in completely to exhaustion and despair, I tried calling out one last time. I rallied my spent forces and once again shouted: 'Bug-Jargal!' A bark answered me. Recognizing it to be Rask's, I turned my head. Bug-Jargal and his dog were on the edge of the crevice. I don't know if he had heard my voice or if some misgiving had brought him back. He saw my danger.

'Hold tight!' he shouted.

Fearing my rescue, Habibrah was shouting at me in a frenzy, his mouth foaming:

'Come! Come!' And he gathered up what was left of his preternatural power for the final onslaught.

At that moment, my wearied arm came loose from the tree. I was done for! But then I felt myself being snagged from behind. It was Rask. At a sign from his master, he had leapt from the crevice onto the platform and his jaws were locked on to the skirts of my coat. This unexpected help was what saved me. Habibrah's latest effort had drained him of all his strength; I summoned up my own in order to snatch my hand from him. His fingers, numb and stiff, finally had to let go of me; the root, trampled on for such a long time, broke under his weight and, as Rask gave me a violent backward pull, the miserable dwarf was engulfed in the spume of the dark falls. As he fell, he hurled a curse at me which I did not hear; it sank back down with him into the abyss.

Such was the end of my uncle's jester.

55

THIS FRIGHTFUL scene, this frenzied struggle and its harrowing dénouement, had overwhelmed me. I was practically inanimate and unconscious. The voice of Bug-Jargal brought me round.

'Brother!' he shouted to me. 'Make haste and get out of here! The sun will have set in half an hour. I will go and wait for you down below. Follow Rask.'

These friendly words all at once restored in me hope, vigour, and courage. I got back up. The mastiff quickly disappeared into the subterranean passageway. I followed him; his yelping guided me in the darkness. After a short while, I once again saw light in front of me. We finally reached the exit, and I could breathe freely. As I went out from under the dank, black vault I recalled the dwarf's prediction when we entered it:

'Only one of us will return along this path.'

His expectation had been mistaken, but his prophecy had come true.

WHEN I got back to the valley, Bug-Jargal was there waiting for me. I threw myself into his arms, and there I remained, thoroughly overcome, with no end of questions to ask him and yet unable to speak.

'Listen,' he said to me, 'your wife, my sister, is safe. I have returned her to the white camp; she is in the hands of one of your relatives, who is in command of the outposts. I wanted to give myself up as a prisoner, fearing that the ten heads answering for mine would be sacrificed in my place. Your relative told me to go back and try to prevent your execution, since the ten black hostages were going to be put to death only if you were—which, if it happened, Biassou was supposed to announce by hoisting a black flag on the highest of our mountain tops. So I started running, Rask leading the way, and I arrived in time, thank heaven! You will live, and so will I.'

He reached out his hand to me:

'Brother, are you glad?'

I clasped him in my arms once more. I entreated him never to leave me again, to remain with me among the whites; I promised him a commission in the colonial army. He interrupted me with a brutal look.

'Brother, am I proposing that you should enlist among my own people?'

I kept silent, knowing I was at fault. He added cheerfully:

'Come, hurry, let us go see your wife and put her mind at rest!'

This proposal corresponded to my heart's urgent desire; I got up, in a rapture of happiness, and we set off. The black man knew the way. He was walking in front of me, Rask was following us ..."

Here d'Auverney broke off and cast a gloomy look around him. Great beads of sweat were streaming down his forehead. He covered his face with his hand. Rask looked at him anxiously.

"Yes, that is how you looked at me then!" he murmured.

Immediately after, he got up in a violent state of agitation and exited the tent. The sergeant and the mastiff went with him.

"I'D WAGER," Henry exclaimed, "that we're nearing the final act of the tragedy! I'd really be sorry if something were to happen to Bug-Jargal. He was a first-class fellow!"

Paschal, who had been taking a drink from his wicker-covered bottle, lifted it from his lips and said:

"I would have given twelve hampers of port to see that coconut shell he emptied at one go."

Alfred, who had been dreamily playing a tune on the guitar, broke off and inquired of Lieutenant Henry whether he'd be so good as to reattach his aiguillettes. He added:

"This negro interests me a great deal. Only I haven't yet dared ask d'Auverney if he also knew the tune for 'La hermosa Padilla.'"

"Biassou is much more remarkable," Paschal countered. "His pitch-wine can't be much good, but at least that fellow knew what a Frenchman's made of. If I'd been his prisoner, I would have let my moustache grow, so that he might lend me a few piastres on it, the way the city of Goa did for that Portuguese captain.[102] I tell you, my creditors are even more ruthless than Biassou."

"By the way, Captain, here's the four louis I owe you!" Henry exclaimed, tossing his purse to Paschal.

The captain looked in astonishment at his generous debtor, who could with more justice have called himself his creditor. Henry hastily started up again.

"So, gentlemen, what do you think up to now about the story the captain's been telling us?"

"Well," said Alfred, "I haven't been listening very attentively, but I must admit to you that I'd have hoped for something more interesting coming from the mouth of a dreamer like d'Auverney. Moreover, it's got a romance in prose, and I don't like romances in prose; what tune would you sing it to? In sum, the story of Bug-Jargal bores me; it's too long."

"You're right," agreed the aide-de-camp Paschal. "It's too long. If I hadn't had my pipe and my flask, I'd have had a sorry time of it. Besides, you can't have failed to notice all the absurdities. How believable is it, for example, that this little Barbary ape of a sorcerer ... What was his name again? *Habi-bit-the-dust?*[103] How believable is it that he'd be ready to drown himself just so that he could drown his enemy?"

Henry interrupted him, smiling:

"And in water, no less! Isn't that so, Captain Paschal? As for me, what amused me the most during d'Auverney's tale was seeing his lame dog raise its head every time he mentioned Bug-Jargal's name."

"And in that respect," Paschal interrupted, "he was doing exactly the opposite of what I've seen the old ladies of Celadas do when the preacher mentions the name of Jesus. I was entering the church with a dozen cuirassiers when ..."

The noise of the sentry's rifle alerted them that d'Auverney was returning. Everybody broke off talking. His arms folded, he silently paced back and forth for a while. Old Thaddeus, who had returned to his seat in the corner, was furtively watching him, trying hard to appear engrossed in the act of stroking Rask so as not to let the captain notice his anxiety.

At length, D'Auverney resumed his tale:

58

"RASK WAS following us. The sun was no longer to be seen on the highest crag of the valley. A gleam of light suddenly appeared on it and then vanished. The black man gave a start; he took my hand and squeezed it hard.

'Listen,' he said to me.

A muffled noise, like an artillery piece being discharged, could be heard in the valleys, followed by one echo after another.

'That is the signal!' said the negro in a grim voice. 'That was a cannon shot, was it not?' he then asked.

I nodded in agreement.

In two bounds he reached the top of a big rock; I followed him. He folded his arms, and began to smile sadly.

'Do you see?' he said to me.

I looked in the direction he was pointing to and saw the peak he had shown me after I was reunited with Marie. It was the only one still lit up by the sun. Rising above it was a large black flag."

At this point, d'Auverney paused.

"I have since found out that Biassou—eager to set off and believing me dead—had made them hoist the standard before the return of the detachment that was supposed to have executed me.

Bug-Jargal, still standing there with arms folded, gazed at the flag of ill omen. All of a sudden, he turned round and took a few steps as if to get down from the rock.

'God! Oh God! My poor companions!'

He returned toward me. 'Did you hear the cannon?' he asked. I did not answer.

'Well, brother! That was the signal. They are being led off now.'

His head sank. He drew even closer to me.

'Go and join your wife, brother; Rask will guide you.'

He whistled an African tune; the dog began to wag its tail, and seemed to want to head for a certain point in the valley.

Bug-Jargal took my hand and made an effort to smile, but it was little better than a convulsion.

'Farewell!' he cried out in a loud voice before vanishing into the clumps of trees that surrounded us.

I was petrified. The little I understood of what had just taken place made me expect the worst.

Seeing his master disappear, Rask moved up to the edge of the rock and started shaking his head, howling plaintively. He returned with tail lowered. His big eyes were moist; he gave me an anxious look, then went back to the spot where his master had last been and barked a number of times. I understood him; I felt the same fears as he did. I took a few steps in his direction and then he was off like a shot, following the tracks of Bug-Jargal. Even though I too was running as hard as I could, I would have lost sight of him in short order if from time to time he hadn't stopped, as though he were giving me the chance to catch up with him. We made our way through several valleys; we crossed over some hills thick with clusters of trees. Finally ..."

D'Auverney's voice died away. His every feature was marked by a gloomy despair. He could barely utter the words:

"Carry on, Thaddeus, for I have no more strength than an old woman."

The old sergeant was no less moved than the captain. Nevertheless, he set about obeying him.

"By your leave ... Since you desire it, my Captain ... I have to tell you, officers, that even though Bug-Jargal, otherwise called Pierrot, was a splendid negro, very gentle, very strong, very courageous, and the bravest warrior in the land—after you, my Captain, if I may be so bold— all that didn't keep me from being very much incensed with him, for which I will never forgive myself, even though the captain has pardoned me for it. So much so, my Captain, that after hearing you were to die on the evening of the second day I was overcome with a furious anger toward that poor man, and it was with a truly diabolical pleasure that I let him know it would be he—or, in his absence, ten of his men—who would be keeping you company and who would be shot by way of reprisal, as they say. He showed no reaction on hearing this news, except that an hour later he escaped by creating a big hole in ...''

D'Auverney gestured impatiently. Thaddeus proceeded:

"Right you are! When the large black flag appeared on the mountain, since he hadn't returned—which, by your leave, officers, in no way astonished us—a cannon shot was fired off as a signal, and I was put in charge of leading the ten negroes to the place of execution, which was called *Bouche-du-Grand-Diable*,[104] and was distant from the camp by about ... Anyway, what does that matter! When we got there, you can imagine, gentlemen, there was no question of setting them loose. I had them bound, as one does in those situations, and I drew up my firing squad. And just then I see the big negro coming out of the forest. I was stunned. He came up to me all out of breath.

'I have arrived in time!' he said. 'Hello, Thaddeus.'

Yes, gentlemen, that was all he said. He went over to untie his compatriots. Me, I just stood there, completely dumbfounded. Then, by your leave, my Captain, a big dispute broke out between himself and the blacks about who was going to be the more generous party; it really ought to have lasted just a little longer ... No matter! Yes, the blame is mine, I was the one who brought it to an end. He took the place of the blacks. At that moment his big dog ... Poor Rask! He arrived on the scene and leapt at my throat. He really ought to have kept hold of it, my Captain, a few moments longer! But Pierrot made a sign, and the poor mastiff let go of me. However, Bug-Jargal couldn't stop Rask from going over to lie down at his feet. And then, I thought you were dead, my Captain. I was in a rage ... I shouted 'open ...'''

The sergeant stretched out his hand, looked at the captain, but could not bring himself to utter the fateful word.

"Bug-Jargal fell ... A bullet had fractured his dog's paw ... Since that time, officers" (and the sergeant shook his head sadly), "since that time he's been lame. I heard groans in the near-by wood; I went over and there you were, my Captain. A bullet had hit you at the very moment you were rushing up to save that splendid negro ... Yes, my Captain, those groans were yours, but they were all for him! Bug-Jargal was dead!... As for you, my Captain, they brought you back to the camp. Your wound was less serious than his, for you healed—thanks to the good offices of Madame Marie."

The sergeant came to a stop. Solemnly, in a voice racked with pain, d'Auverney finished off the story:

"Bug-Jargal was dead!"

Thaddeus lowered his head.

"Yes," he said. "And he had spared my life. And I'm the one who killed him!"

NOTE

As readers are generally in the habit of insisting upon definitive clarifications regarding the fate of each of the characters in whom one has tried to interest them, investigations have been made, with the intention of gratifying this habit, into the subsequent destiny of Captain Leopold d'Auverney, his sergeant, and his dog. The reader perhaps recalls that the captain's dark melancholy arose from a double cause: the death of Bug-Jargal, otherwise known as Pierrot, and the loss of his dear Marie, who had been saved from the conflagration of Fort Galifet only to perish a short time later in the first conflagration of the Cape. As for the captain himself, here is what has come to light about him.

One day after a great battle won by the troops of the French republic against the army of Europe, Division-General M...,[105] serving as commander-in-chief, was alone in his tent writing up the report, based on his chief of staff's notes, that was to be sent to the National Convention[106] regarding the previous day's victory. An aide-de-camp came in to tell him that the people's representative assigned to him was asking to speak with him. The general abhorred these red-bonneted quasi-ambassadors that the Mountain[107] delegated to the camps in order to degrade and decimate them: accredited informers, entrusted by a bunch of executioners with the task of spying on glory. However, it would have been dangerous to deny one of them a visit, especially after a victory. Back then, the bloody idol of those times had a fondness for illustrious victims, and the sacrificing priests of the Place de la Révolution were overjoyed when with one and the same blow they could chop off a head and a crown—were it only one of thorns, like that of Louis XVI; of flowers, like that of the young ladies of Verdun;[108] or of laurels, like that of Custine and André Chénier.[109] The general thus directed that the representative be shown in.

After a few ambiguous and guarded words of congratulation on the recent triumph of the republican armies, the representative, drawing closer to the general, said to him in an undertone:

"That is not all, Citizen-General. It is not enough to vanquish the enemies from without, one must also exterminate the enemies from within."

"What do you mean, Citizen-Representative?" replied the astonished general.

"There is in your army," the commissioner of the Convention went on mysteriously, "a captain by the name of Leopold d'Auverney; he serves in the 32nd demi-brigade. General, do you know him?"

"Yes, indeed!" the general answered. "I was just now reading a report from the adjutant-general, chief of the 32nd demi-brigade, which concerns him. The 32nd had an excellent captain in him."

"What, Citizen-General!" the representative exclaimed haughtily. "You have not given him a promotion, have you?"

"I will not hide from you, Citizen-Representative, that such was indeed my intention ..."

Here the commissioner peremptorily interrupted the general.

"Victory is blinding you, General M...! Take care what you do and what you say. If you are nourishing vipers in your bosom, enemies of the people, tremble lest the people trample you down while trampling the vipers! This Leopold d'Auverney is an aristocrat, a counter-revolutionary, a royalist, a Feuillant, a Girondist.[110] Public justice lays claim to him. He must be handed over to me at once."

The general responded icily:

"I cannot."

"What! You cannot!" the commissioner went on, his fit of anger growing. "Are you unaware, General M..., that there is only one unlimited power here and that it belongs to me? The republic orders you, and you say you cannot! Listen to me. I would like, as a courtesy owed your successes, to read you the note that was given me regarding this d'Auverney and which I am to send along with his person to the public prosecutor. It is taken from a list of names that you will be so good as not to force me to conclude with your own. Listen: 'LEOPOLD AUVERNEY (ci-devant DE), captain in the 32nd demi-brigade: guilty, *primo*, of having recounted in a secret assembly of conspirators a would-be counter-revolutionary story tending to ridicule the principles of equality and liberty, and to exalt the old superstitions known under the names of *royalty* and *religion*; guilty, *secundo*, of having made use of expressions condemned by all good sansculottes when characterizing various memorable events, notably the enfranchisement of the ci-devant "blacks" of Saint Domingue; guilty, *tertio*, of having always made use of the word "monsieur" in his tale, and never of the word "citizen"; and finally, *quarto*, of having, through said tale, openly conspired to overthrow the republic in the interests of the Girondist and Brissotin factions.[111] He deserves death …' Well then, General! What do you say to that? Will you still protect this traitor? Will you waver in the matter of handing over this enemy of the fatherland for punishment?"

"This enemy of the fatherland," retorted the general with dignity, "has sacrificed himself for it. I will answer the extract from your report with an extract of my own. Now you listen in turn: 'LEOPOLD D'AUVERNEY, captain in the 32nd demi-brigade, played the decisive role in the latest victory that our arms have secured. A formidable redoubt had been established by the coalition forces: it was the key to the battle; it was imperative that it be taken. Certain death faced any man brave enough to be the first to attack it. Captain d'Auverney dedicated himself to the task. He took the redoubt, met his death there, and we were victorious. Sergeant Thaddeus of the 32nd and a dog were found dead next to him. We propose to the National Convention that it declare Captain Leopold d'Auverney to have deserved well of the fatherland.' You see, Representative," the general continued calmly, "the difference between our two missions: both of us are sending, each from his side, a list to the Convention. The same name is found in the two lists: you denounce it as the name of a traitor, I declare it to be that of a hero; you consign him to ignominy, I to glory; you erect a guillotine for him, and I a memorial. To each his role. It is a mercy, though, that this brave soldier was able to die in battle and escape being tortured by you. God be thanked! He whom you would put to death is already dead. He did not wait for you."

Furious at seeing his conspiracy vanish along with his conspirator, the commissioner muttered:

"He's dead! That's a pity!"

The general heard him, and exclaimed indignantly:

"There still remains one course of action open to you, Citizen-Representative of the people! Go find the body of Captain d'Auverney in the ruins of the redoubt. Who knows? Perhaps the enemy's cannon-balls may have spared the corpse's head for the national guillotine!"

Endnotes to *Bug-Jargal*

1 A playful allusion to the Danish linguist Erasmus Christian Rask (1787-1832), author of *Recherches sur l'origine de la langue islandaise* (1818), one of Hugo's sources for *Han of Iceland* (1823).

2 Thaddeus gets his declensions wrong (*cornus* is the genitive of *cornu*). This is not the only shaky Latin we will encounter in the novel (see Chapter 35).

3 Théophile-Malo Corret de La Tour d'Auvergne (1743-1800). This legendary soldier who refused to be promoted beyond the rank of captain was indeed named "First Grenadier of the Republic" by order of Napoleon, but only in 1800. Since the opening chapters take place in 1794, the reference is a minor anachronism.

4 In English in the original.

5 This notoriously ambiguous word is here being used in the one sense recognized by the *Dictionnaire de l'Académie française* at the time Hugo wrote his novel: as a noun, referring to "a person of European origin who is born in America" (1798 edition). Elsewhere in the novel it is used as an adjective modifying words like "negro" and "jargon," and means "born in or originating from America rather than Europe or Africa." As with "negro" and "black," it is a word that is capitalized in many of Hugo's sources, so the lack of capitalization on his part is a conscious decision that the translator needs to respect.

6 Probably an allusion to the Spanish saying, "Por un perro que maté, mata-perros me llamaron" (literally, "I killed a dog, so they called me dog-killer").

7 For dramatic purposes, Hugo has turned the big house of the Galifet (or, more correctly, Galliffet) plantation into a fort; the plantation was located a little to the south of Cap Français, in the district of Petite Anse. Most of the Saint Domingue place names referred to in this novel can be found on the map in Appendix G, and will thus not be noted.

8 Meaning "heretofore, formerly," the adjective "ci-devant" took on a new importance as of 1789 when the phrase "ci-devant noble" became the official term used for members of the French aristocracy. Hugo's deployment of this word throughout the novel is an ironic dig at the ways in which the French Revolution attempted to transform reality by transforming the French language (e.g., inventing new names for the months of the year).

9 Thomas Howard, Third Earl of Effingham (1746-91), Governor of Jamaica (March 1790-November 1791).

10 Hugo picked this word up from a glossary of "terms commonly used in Saint Domingue" that Lacroix included at the beginning of his *Mémoires* (v-viii). Hugo utilized 26 of the 42 terms in this glossary, incorporating a number of Lacroix's definitions verbatim.

11 Louis-Antoine Thomassin, Count de Peynier (d. 1790), Governor of Saint Domingue from August 1789 to October 1790. A partisan of the Ancien Régime, he opposed the autonomist tendencies of the St. Marc Assembly and succeeded in having it dissolved. (In colonial Saint Domingue, the Governor shared power with the Intendant: the former, always a noble, represented the person of the King and exercised military authority; the latter, often a bourgeois, managed the finances and oversaw application of the laws. "Together they represented the absolute authority of the king, against which there was no recourse, and thus created a constant source of bitterness for the colonists" [Fick 17].)

12 Philibert-François Rouxel de Blanchelande (1735-93), Governor of Saint Domingue from October 1790 to June 1792. Shortly after being relieved of his post, he was sent back to France, charged with having helped instigate the slave revolt in Saint Domingue for counter-revolutionary (royalist) purposes, and guillotined on 11 April 1793. Historical sources all seem to agree that his "weak and malleable personality in politics was among his most outstanding features as governor" (Fick 122).

13 Thomas-Antoine de Mauduit du Plessis (1753-91). Referred to by Garran as "one of the most fanatical partisans of the monarchy" (1.222), this Breton aristocrat led the royalist government troops that dispersed the independence-minded St. Marc Assembly, forcing many of its members to flee to France on 8 August 1790. Supporters of the Assembly, the so-called Patriots, had their revenge on 4 March 1791 in Port-au-Prince, when angry crowds and Mauduit's own soldiers turned on him as a counter-revolutionary; his mutilated body was dragged through the streets, his genitals being carried in triumph by a white woman (wrongly identified in Lacroix as a "woman of colour" [1.76]).

14 Saint Domingue was divided into three provinces: North (its capital, Cap Français), West (Port-au-Prince), South (Les Cayes). As of 1789, each province had its own assembly, with differing agendas and interests. The Assembly of the North—composed chiefly of lawyers and merchants at the Cape, "who represented the great financial and commercial interests of the maritime bourgeois" (James 53)—supported the bourgeois revolution in France but would contest the independentist inclinations of the anti-royalist Patriots, who dominated the Assembly of the West as well as the colony-wide Colonial Assembly.

15 The Colonial Assembly was formed by the three provincial assemblies in mid-April 1790, and met in the town of St. Marc, mid-way between the north and south coast of the colony. Preferring the title of General Assembly, it adopted increasingly inflammatory positions in support of the administrative, economic, and even political independence of the colony. The Assembly of the North soon distanced itself from the Colonial Assembly, and supported Governor de Peynier's suppression of it in August. A second Colonial Assembly would be convened in August 1791 (see notes to Chapter 16).

16 For details of this decree of the Constituent Assembly in France, which specified that *all* free persons meeting the requisite age, property, and residence qualifications were to be part of the new electoral process, see "1791, 1825: Haiti and Hugo—Historical and Biographical Contexts" in the Introduction.

17 D'Auverney and Marie could not have chosen a less auspicious date for their wedding (see "1791, 1825: Haiti and Hugo—Historical and Biographical Contexts" in the Introduction). For detailed descriptions of the early days of the insurrection, see the selections from Edwards (E.1) and Lacroix (E.2b-ii) in the Appendices.

18 "A Spanish measure of quantity, usually equal to a bushel or a bushel and a half" (*OED*).

19 Describing the language spoken by slaves (*and* masters) in the colony as "jargon" was a classic trope of French colonial discourse in the Caribbean. For instance, Moreau de Saint-Méry refers to Creole as "a corrupted French," "a way of talking that is really nothing more than jargon [*un langage, qui n'est qu'un vrai jargon*]" (1.80-81). See "Bug-Jargal, 1791: Language and History in Translation" in the Introduction for an account of the importance of jargon to an understanding of the novel's title.

20 The slave's outburst is unexpected not just because it re-cites the words of the Lord's Prayer in French ("*je viens de t'offenser*") but because he addresses his master as "*tu*"

rather than the more formal *"vous"* required of someone in his inferior position. Although the distinction between *"tu"* and *"vous"* adds an important dimension to a number of dialogues in the novel, it has not always been possible to preserve this nuance in translation.

21 "A device for raising water, used in Spain and in the East, consisting of a revolving chain of pots or buckets which are filled below and discharged when they come to the top" (*OED*). One of several geographical lapses in the novel (see Debien 309).

22 As Carolyn Fick notes, "by 1789, two-thirds of the roughly half a million slaves in Saint Domingue were African-born" (25). Hugo is here paraphrasing the definition of *Congos* in Lacroix's glossary as "negroes from a part of Africa; this general name is also applied to all blacks born in Africa. The creole blacks have contempt for them."

23 Hugo plucked this name out of Félix Carteaux's *Soirées bermudiennes* (1802). Recounting an episode from 1793 in which he witnessed a group of nine whites being herded along, "bound hand and foot, to the prisons of the Cape," Carteaux notes that he "will never forget that the negro Pierrot, chief of the Morne Rouge brigands, seeing them pass by strapped down on horses like this, forced those in charge to untie them" (6). Hugo would also have encountered the name Pierrot in Lacroix's *Mémoires*, which describe at some length the French siege of Crête-à-Pierrot in March 1802.

24 An episode in Colonel Malenfant's 1814 *Des colonies*, where he describes his conversation with a literate black slave (212-15), has been cited as the source of this episode (e.g., Cauna, "Sources" 29); however, the parallels appear far too general for this book to be treated with certainty as one of Hugo's sources.

25 Early nineteenth-century aria by the Spaniard Manuel Garcia (1775-1832); a minor anachronism.

26 "A rich outer petticoat worn by Basque and Spanish women" (*OED*).

27 Born in Dondon and raised in Bordeaux, Vincent Ogé (1768-91) was the wealthy son of a free woman of colour and a white butcher (this last detail being one that Hugo lingers over in Chapter 28). For details of the aborted revolt he led against the white colonists in October 1790, see "1791, 1825: Haiti and Hugo—Historical and Biographical Contexts" in the Introduction.

28 Hugo based this passage on a description in Carteaux's *Soirées bermudiennes* of the conflagration of the Northern Plain in the weeks following August 22 (e.g., "The most striking thing about this terrible spectacle was a *rain of fire*, composed of little bits of burning cane stalk that were flickering through the air. It was like a heavy snowfall, and depending on where the winds were blowing it would sweep over the harbour and the ships or over the city and the houses of the Cape" [see 87-88]).

29 Laurent François Lenoir, Marquis de Rouvray (1733-98). Along with de Touzard, he led the first military expeditions against the insurgent slaves after August 22. De Rouvray was a committed royalist (see Garran 2.104-05), and he is the one character to whom Hugo gives a certain degree of authorial sanction in this otherwise scathingly sarcastic chapter. "Respected by the mulattoes, whom he had commanded at the siege of Savannah, in the war of American independence," de Rouvray unsuccessfully urged the Provincial Assembly of the North to grant the *gens de couleur* their rights at this time. He proved more successful in pushing back the insurgent slaves in the months immediately following August 22 (see Dalmas 1.140-41).

30 Anne Louis, chevalier de Touzard (or more commonly Tousard) (1749-1817). Played a vital role in defending Cap Français from the rebel forces during the early months of

the revolt. Arrested in October 1792 as a counter-revolutionary, he was sent back to France for trial and acquitted.

31 C.L.R. James provides a memorable description of this "idiotic expedition." Upon first hearing news of the fall of the Bastille, nearly all the white Creoles were overcome with enthusiasm for the Revolution: "The militia was transformed into a National Guard in imitation of the National Guards of revolutionary France. The colonists gave themselves striking uniforms and military decorations, christened themselves captains, brigadiers and generals. They lynched the few who openly opposed them, and having no enemy to fight against they invented some. A detachment of the National Guard marched out of Le Cap against some rebel Negroes and after hours of weary tramping returned to the town with one of their number mortally wounded, not by the revolting Negroes (there were none) but by the bullets of his own companions. When, two years later, the insurrection broke out, the first chiefs were the blacks [notably Jeannot] who had served as guides in this idiotic expedition" (50). (See the excerpt from Lacroix, Appendix E.2b-i, which James is very closely paraphrasing here.)

32 "Absurd mouse," from Horace, *Ars Poetica*, l.139: "The mountains will go into labour; an absurd mouse will be born." (Hugo also uses this phrase in the 1824 preface to his *Nouvelles Odes*, Appendix C.2.)

33 "A man of colour, named *Lacombe*, was hanged at the Cape [in 1789] for having submitted a petition in which he laid claim to the rights of man. The so-called colonial Patriots treated this piece of writing as inflammatory and, by way of proving it, they claimed that it was not composed in the customary style of petitions, because it began with these words: 'In the name of the Father, the Son, and the Holy Ghost'" (Lacroix 1.19).

34 Literally meaning "hunchbacked" and "crooked," these two terms were used to describe the antagonistic parties in the 1791 Colonial Assembly. The *Bossus* were partisans of the Government, and the *Crochus* were for the most part composed of former members of, or sympathizers with, the independence-minded St. Marc Assembly which had been disbanded the previous year by Governor de Peynier.

35 Royalists wore a white pompom in their hats, and were for that reason known as *pompons blancs*. More ardent supporters of the French Revolution (who were also, somewhat paradoxically, very often in favour of independence) were variously known as *pompons rouges*, Patriots, or *indépendants*. The former tended to be *grands blancs*, members of the planter class or the maritime bourgeoisie, whereas the latter were predominantly *petits blancs*, from the middle or lower classes.

36 Commonly identified as a Jamaican slave (although the historian Pierre Pluchon asserts that "there is no evidence he was originally from an English colony" [461]), Boukmann was one of the early leaders of the 1791 slave revolt. A vodou high priest, he is said to have presided over the ceremony at Bois Caïman that preceded the revolt (see "(1791)/2002, 2004: Reading Hugo and the Haitian Revolution" in the Introduction for more details on this ceremony). His death (in mid-November 1791) will play an important role in chapter 31. In his 1820 short story, Hugo spells the name "Boukmant" (a spelling which he almost certainly got from Malo [184] rather than from Garran, as Debien claims [302]).

37 Hugo's definition of the "small whites" is taken directly from Lacroix's glossary. The *petits blancs* envied the wealth of the plantation-owning *grands blancs* and were bitter rivals of the mulatto class. As Fick puts it, "with the advancement and expansion of Saint Domingue's sugar economy, the *petits blancs* witnessed the progressive closing off of their chances for property ownership, the one criterion that would guarantee their

social integration and satisfy their frustrated aspirations. In addition, they suffered increasing competition from the *affranchis* and even the upper-strata slaves for jobs in the trades" (18).

38 Paul de Cadusch (d. 1795). President of the second Colonial Assembly and strong advocate of colonial independence, Cadusch was suspected of conspiring to hand the colony over to England. He died soon after in Jamaica.

39 French military honour, created by Louis XIV in 1693. In Chapter 28 both Biassou and Ogé will be seen wearing these Crosses, thereby providing ample evidence for Hugo's parodic identification of mulattoes as illegitimate *bricoleurs* (a point discussed at the beginning of "(1791)/ 2002, 2004: Reading Hugo and the Haitian Revolution" in the Introduction).

40 As Hugo knew from his sceptical reading of the abolitionist Abbé Grégoire, this word had already been found: *blancophage*. Describing "the merchants of human flesh," Grégoire states that they "get indignant when anyone troubles the enjoyment of tigers devouring their prey. They have even attempted to vilify the name of *philanthropist*, or friend of men—a name that anyone who has not renounced all affection for his fellow beings is proud to bear. They have created the epithets of *negrophile* and *blancophage* in the hope of sullying their opponents. Their assumption is that every Friend of the Blacks is an enemy of the whites and of France, and in the pay of England" (72-73).

41 Unquestionably refers to the Marquis de Caradeux (1742-1810), a wealthy planter associated with the Patriots of Port-au-Prince (see Appendix E.2b-ii). Described by the Haitian historian Madiou as "perhaps the cruellest white man who ever existed in Saint Domingue" (39-40), he fled to South Carolina in 1792.

42 As a footnote in the 1833 English translation of *Bug-Jargal, The Slave-King*, points out, Hugo's sense of Haitian geography lets him down here. Having chosen to translate the phrase as "from Fort Picolet to the Barrier Bouteille," the translator provides a footnote that reads: "In the original, 'from Fort Picolet to Cape Caracol;' but this would not form a line round the city, Cape Caracol being some miles down the coast, and on the wrong side for that purpose. Fort Picolet and the barrier Bouteille are the extreme north and south points of the city" (148).

43 Hugo got all these names from the introductory pages (v-x) of the Abbé Grégoire's *De la littérature des nègres* (1808), dedicated "to all the courageous men who have pleaded the cause of the unhappy Blacks and Sang-Mêlés." In his edition of *Bug-Jargal*, Toumson provides some useful details regarding these negrophiles, some of whom had been long dead by 1791 (418-19).

44 One of the novel's most obvious anachronisms (see Mouralis 57). The *Leopard* was the ship that rescued eighty-five members of the *first* Colonial Assembly in August of the previous year (1790), when that Assembly was forcibly disbanded by Mauduit. The *Leopard* took the eighty-five men to France, where they received the "risible ovation" referred to by the member of the Provincial Assembly earlier in this chapter.

45 Another anachronism. These five hundred rifles were sent to the white colonists of Saint Domingue in *response* to a request for help that the Assembly sent to the Governor of Jamaica, Lord Effingham, after the outbreak of the slave revolt.

46 Sébastien Le Prestre, Marquis de Vauban (1633-1707), engineer and soldier in the armies of Louis XIV, famous as a builder of fortifications; Jean-Charles de Folard (1669-1752), soldier and tactician, author of *Nouvelles Découvertes sur la guerre* (1724); Etienne Bezout (1730-83), mathematician and author of a number of military textbooks.

47 When specific, technical information of this sort about Saint Domingue is presented in the novel, it often comes more or less directly from one of Hugo's sources (in this case, Lacroix: see Appendix E.2b-ii); Hugo's not infrequent insertion of such passages into his novel creates an awkward tension between the informal, speaking voice of the character (here, de Rouvray) and the more formal tone of the published words that he is made to speak.

48 Georges Biassou (d. 1801), one of the first leaders of the slave revolt, "a fire-eater, always drunk, always ready for the fiercest and most dangerous exploits" (James 76). He plays a central role in *Bug-Jargal*, where Hugo misrepresents him as a mulatto rather than a black (see endnote 61). The importance Hugo places on Biassou can be directly traced to the latter's prominent role in Jean-Baptiste Picquenard's 1798 novel, *Adonis* (see Appendix F.1). Biassou, under whom Toussaint Louverture served during the early years of the revolt, would eventually become an auxiliary officer in the Spanish army; he died in Spanish Florida, where he received a full military funeral (see Geggus, *Haitian* 184-85).

49 Soon after the uprising in August 1791, this former slave emerged as the supreme leader of the insurgent blacks. He would remain so until the spring of 1794, when Toussaint Louverture went over from the Spanish to the French side. After 1795, when the Spanish ceded their part of Hispaniola to the French, Jean-François was sent to Spain where he lived until his death in 1805 (see Geggus, *Haitian* 197-200). He was notorious for his sense of pomp and circumstance, as Hugo notes in Chapter 42; in Garran's words, "this man, who had always been shut up in a plantation gang, knew how to gain people's high regard by adopting a sumptuous and splendid outward appearance. He wore a general's outfit, magnificently trimmed with galloons, and decorated with ribbons taken from whites during battle. He always travelled on a splendid charger or in a carriage drawn by six horses" (2.256-57).

50 Mayor of Port-de-Paix in 1791, and a friend of Félix Carteaux, who describes de Maigné and eight other whites being dragged by a group of mulattoes to Cap Français during the summer of 1793 (6); see endnote 23 for further details.

51 Hugo would have come across this name in Carteaux, where Poncignon is described as someone who, in the early days of the revolt, was put in command of some militias "even though the only fire he had ever seen was in his kitchen" (89). Vice-president of the second Colonial Assembly under Cadusch, Poncignon had acquired, we learn from a delightfully Flaubertian moment in the colonist Dalmas's account of the slave revolt, "a sort of reputation for his knowledge of the decrees of the Constituent Assembly, all of which he had classified in his head. One made use of him as of a table of contents; every man has his merit, and that was his" (1.192).

52 Literally, the "Mulatto-Tamer." Hugo read about this defile, which is actually located in the far south of Saint Domingue in the La Hotte mountains, in Lacroix's *Mémoires* (1.204). His willingness to recreate Haitian geography for his own symbolic purposes arguably says a great deal about the anti-mulatto bias that is so central to the novel's ideological project: the place name culled from Lacroix situates us in a world where mulattoes, and the hybrid threat they both pose and embody, can and must be subdued.

53 For the "Camp du Grand-Pré," see the excerpt from Grégoire (Appendix E.3). I have not been able to trace the reference to "Wa-Nassé."

54 The first martyr, Stephen, was stoned to death (Acts 7.56-60); the Moses-chasing Pharaoh suffered death by water (Exodus 14).

55 Literally, "Peacock Peak" (possibly a name of Hugo's own invention).

56 The next few sentences are taken almost verbatim from Abbé Grégoire's *De la littéra-ture des nègres* (see Appendix E.3); the griotes' cry of "Wanga" is taken from Lacroix's glossary.

57 Moreau de Saint-Méry's description of this "dance of African origin" draws out its "las-civious" dimensions: "The talent required of the female dancer is to move her hips and the lower part of her loins while keeping all the rest of her body in a state of perfect stillness, which is not broken even by the slight trembling of her arms as they balance the two ends of her skirt or handkerchief. A male dancer comes up to her, springs for-ward all of a sudden, and drops down in time to the music, almost touching her. He draws back, springs forward again, and incites her to engage in the most seductive of struggles. The dance quickens, and soon all the aspects of it that had at first appeared voluptuous turn lascivious. It would be impossible to paint the true character of the *Chica*, and I will limit myself to saying that the impression it causes is so powerful that any African or Creole, of whatever hue, who saw it being danced and felt nothing would be deemed to have lost every last spark of sensibility" (1.64).

58 "'The name applied to the highest court of justice and supreme council at Jerusalem, and in a wider sense also to lower courts of justice'... Also, the title given to the assembly of representative Jewish rabbis and laymen convened by Napoleon I in 1807 to report on certain points of Jewish law" (*OED*).

59 This definition of *ajoupa* is taken from Lacroix's glossary ("huts covered in palm or banana leaves, the conical form of which is similar to the tents that are known as bell-tents"); the gastronomic description in the following sentences is likewise taken from Lacroix's definition of *vivres* (provisions) as a "generic name which collectively desig-nates the country's raw produce used by the indigenous peoples, such as sweet pota-toes, taro or Caribbean cabbage, yams, bananas, peas, maize, coconut, and all fruits in general."

60 A Spanish cap.

61 As with griffe, Hugo gets this term from Moreau de Saint-Méry, via Lacroix. Moreau notes that "this class can barely be said to exist, and although it is looked upon as supe-rior to the negro, it differs from them only in an almost imperceptible manner, since it is only one full part white as against seven full parts black" (1.94). Hugo's identification of Biassou as a dark-skinned mulatto rather than a *nègre*, while practically inevitable given the novel's ideological biases, is among the novel's most glaring his-torical errors. In the 1820 short story, Hugo mistakenly identified Biassou as a mulatto; as one critic familiar with Hugo's sources puts it, in the story "one fact alone is dis-torted, perhaps due to a moment of inattentive reading—Hugo takes Biassou for a mulatto at the head of a band of mulattoes" (Debien 303). Rather than correct this mis-take in the novel, Hugo chose to build upon it, even though his main source, Lacroix's *Mémoires*, clearly identifies Biassou as a *nègre*.

62 Chavannes fought in the American War of Independence and was second-in-com-mand of Vincent Ogé's October 1790 revolt in support of full civil rights for free per-sons of colour. More radical than Ogé, he wanted to involve the slaves in this revolt. Although in theory sympathetic to the idea of freedom for all inhabitants of the island, Ogé declined to take this bold step. Chavannes nonetheless fought and died alongside his friend (not, as d'Auverney here states, in the "preceding year" [1790] but on 25 February 1791).

63 Here Hugo is basing himself on Lacroix's description of the trial of Ogé: "The court declared 'the said *Vincent Ogé* the younger duly accused and convicted of having, over an extended period of time, planned the project of inciting the people of colour (and

notably those from the districts of Grande Rivière) to revolt, by means of his speeches, false qualifications and external decorations.' (Knowing how much the people of colour are given to vanity, Ogé had—in order to gain credit among his people—bought from the Prince of Limburg the order of merit of the Lion, and had had himself painted in a colonel's uniform, decorated with the Saint-Louis Cross" (1.62). Garran also provides a vivid description of Ogé's accoutrements (2.67-69).

64 I have not found this name in any of Hugo's known sources.

65 "People of the king." (Believing that the kings of France and Spain were favourable to the idea of their liberty, in the months following the initial revolt the insurgent slaves positioned themselves as supporters of the monarchy, referring to themselves as the *gens du roi*.)

66 See Judges 6.19-24 and Joshua 8.30-31.

67 One of several examples in which Hugo takes an anecdote about Toussaint Louverture from Lacroix's *Mémoires* and credits it to Biassou. Only a few years later, in his *The French Revolution* (1837), Thomas Carlyle will take the same anecdote and ascribe it to Ogé: "What a change here [in Saint Domingue], in these two years [since 1789]; since that first 'Box of Tricolor Cockades' got through the Custom-house, and atrabiliar Creoles too rejoiced that there was a levelling of Bastilles! Levelling is comfortable, as we often say: levelling, yet only down to oneself. Your pale-white Creoles have their grievances:—and your yellow Quarteroons? And your dark-yellow Mulattoes? And your Slaves soot-black? Quarteroon Ogé, Friend of our Parisian-Brissotin *Friends of the Blacks*, felt for his share too, that Insurrection was the most sacred of duties. So the tricolor Cockades had fluttered and swashed only some three months on the Creole hat, when Ogé's signal-conflagrations went aloft; with the voice of rage and terror. Repressed, doomed to die, he took black powder or seedgrains in the hollow of his hand, this Ogé; sprinkled a film of white ones on the top, and said to his Judges, 'Behold they are white'; then *shook* his hand, and said 'Where are the Whites, *Où sont les Blancs?*'" Carlyle then famously concludes his description of the events of Autumn 1791: "Poor Ogé could be broken on the wheel; this fire-whirlwind too can be abated, driven up into the Mountains: but Saint-Domingo is *shaken*, as Ogé's seedgrains were; shaking, writhing in long horrid death-throes, it is Black without remedy; and remains, as African Haiti, a monition to the world" (2.29-30).

68 It is not clear exactly which of a half dozen lupine saints Biassou is thinking of here. Contenders include: Saint Lupus of Troyes (feast day 29 July); Saint Lupus of Lyons (feast day 25 September); Saint Lupus of Sens (feast day 1 September).

69 Along with Megaera and Tisiphone, one of the three Furies in Greek mythology.

70 André Rigaud (1761-1811). Born in Les Cayes (on the south coast of the colony), educated in France, a volunteer in the French army during the American War of Independence (where he fought at Savannah under the Marquis de Rouvray), Rigaud emerged as a prominent leader of the mulattoes in the West and South Provinces. (His presence at Biassou's side in the Northern mountains is an invention on Hugo's part.) He eventually became Toussaint Louverture's chief rival for power in the second half of the decade, and was exiled to France in 1800, after the great bloodbath of the "war of colour" between his forces and Toussaint's. He returned to the island in 1802 as part of the army organized by Napoleon to oust Toussaint from power but, once his usefulness was exhausted, he was deported to France. He escaped back to the island in 1810, succeeded in detaching the South Province from Pétion's Republic and became its president, only to die within a year of his return.

71 Metoposcopy is "the art of judging a person's character or of telling his fortune from his forehead or face" (*OED*).

72 Hugo culled this depreciatory word for "aged negro" from Lacroix's glossary. The word, as Hugo knew, was also associated with Toussaint Louverture, who as a youth was called "Fatras-Bâton" (Little Stick) because of his frail constitution (see James 74).

73 This is a very garbled reminiscence of a passage in Grégoire's *De la littérature des nègres*. At the beginning of Chapter 4, Grégoire notes that "for over a century, the negro maroons of Jacmel have been the terror of Saint Domingue. In 1785 Bellecombe, the most imperious of Governors, was forced to enter into negotiations with them" despite their small numbers (107-08). Hugo has thus transformed Jacmel (on the south coast of the colony) into Jamaica and transported Guillaume-Léonard de Bellecombe (1728-1792; Governor of Saint Domingue from 1782-1785) to that same English colony.

74 In his edition of *Bug-Jargal*, Toumson provides details on some of these individuals (422-23). Hugo's obi here indiscriminately mixes together Old Testament characters (Solomon, Zorobabel), medieval philosophers (Albertus Magnus, Averroës), Moorish sultans (Boabdil), Italian mathematicians (Girolamo Cardan), and obscure figures who may or may not have really existed (Rachel Flintz, Altornino).

75 Debien plausibly suggests (308) that the source for this *petit blanc* is to be found in Bryan Edwards, who mentions a colonist by the name of Blen and immediately after describes another colonist, a carpenter, being sawn in half. (See the excerpt from Edwards in Appendix E.1.)

76 Better known as Labatut; a Gascon plantation owner on the Ile de la Tortue (Tortuga).

77 Anne-Robert-Jacques Turgot (1727-81), author of *Réflexions sur la formation et la distribution de la richesse* (1766), and briefly minister of finance under Louis XVI; Guillaume-Thomas, abbé de Raynal (1713-96), author, with Diderot, of a multi-volume work on the European colonies, *Histoire philosophique et politique des établissements et du commerce des Européens dans les deux Indes* (1770), and derided by the proponents of slavery as "the first apostle of freedom for the negroes" (Clausson 43); Victor Riqueti, marquis de Mirabeau (1715-89), father of the French revolutionary leader, author of many works of political economy, and self-styled "friend of mankind."

78 "Farms" translates the word "hattes," which Hugo found in Lacroix's glossary. The various place names in the rest of the paragraph refer to a wide variety of locations on the Spanish side of the island, Santo Domingo (present-day Dominican Republic).

79 After this long list of trees, the 1833 translation supplies the following footnote: "The *tocuma*, a medlar-tree, and the cedar, are trees of St. Domingo; but the other names are unknown there. Why should not the reader be puzzled as well as Biassou?" (152).

80 On the death of this planter, see the excerpt from Edwards (Appendix E.1).

81 Literally, two hundred "carreaux." A *carreau*, according to Moreau de Saint-Méry, is "a square tract of land in Saint Domingue that takes up more than one and a quarter English acres" (1.14-15).

82 "When Israel went out of Egypt" (Psalms 114.1). For the genesis of this episode, see the excerpt from Lacroix about Toussaint's similar deployment of Latin (Appendix E.2d-i).

83 Protagonist of Molière's *Le Médecin malgré lui* (1667), known for his obfuscatory use of Latin (see Act 2, scene 4).

84 As a footnote in the 1833 translation puts it, "Some of these are real creole dishes; but the others to be rendered palatable to the critics, must be taken *cum grano salis*" (166). *Olla podrida* is a spiced stew of various meats and vegetables.

85 One of the early rebel leaders, best known for his role in helping burn down Cap Français in June 1793 at the instigation of the French Commissioners, who were in a desperate power struggle with the forces of the counter-revolution led by the new Governor-General Galbaud. Hugo incorporates a statement of Macaya's from 1793 that he found in Lacroix's *Mémoires* into the letter that Biassou asks d'Auverney to correct in Chapter 38 (see Appendix E.2c-ii).

86 The feast-day of Saint Sabas (439-532) is indeed December 5.

87 Presumably a distortion of *gabacho* ("Frenchie"). As Léon-François Hoffmann reminds us, "Hugo had nothing more than vague and approximate recollections of Spanish, and he never bothered to correct the numerous Spanish mistakes in the text" ("Victor Hugo" 71). In the last third of the novel (notably chapters 52 & 53), Hugo obviously tires of supplying a footnote translation for every Spanish word and phrase he uses, and I will follow his lead in this respect.

88 The preceding description is taken almost word for word from an anonymous 1819 *Histoire de l'île de Saint-Domingue* (142), which in turn is an unacknowledged translation of Edwards (see Introductory Note to Appendix E; the translation would later be claimed by Charles Malo and has been listed under his name in the Works Cited). Chevaux-de-frise are wooden or iron obstacles covered in spikes or spears and used for defensive purposes.

89 This decree of the Constituent Assembly ordered the departure of Commissioners for Saint Domingue bearing new instructions regarding the powers of the Colonial Assembly and who could participate in it. The decree of 15 May, which was to have enforced at least some participation of the free coloureds in the legislative process, had been rescinded on September 24, and the whites on the island were now reinvested with the power of deciding on their own whether the free coloureds could be part of the political process. The decree of 28 September also included a general amnesty for the free coloureds.

90 Authentic signatories of the 1791 letter. Toussaint Louverture here makes "his first appearance on the political scene" (Pluchon 117).

91 Leader of a band of mulattoes who later went over to the side of the French, Candy had the reputation of being "cruel to the point of ferocity." Carteaux, one of Hugo's sources, reminds his readers that Candy "is reputed to have pulled out the eyes of white men with a corkscrew" (101).

92 No doubt an allusion to the Disinherited Knight (*Desdichado*) in Walter Scott's *Ivanhoe* (1819), which Hugo reviewed in the *Conservateur littéraire (OC* 1.625-31).

93 Here Pierrot takes on the characteristics of Toussaint Louverture as conventionally portrayed in many a Victorian work of fiction, such as G.A. Henty's *A Roving Commission: or Through the Black Insurrection of Hayti* (1900), where a sympathetic young black man in the service of Toussaint remarks to Nat Glover, the novel's English hero, that "Biassou hates [Toussaint] because he does not like his cruel ways and speaks boldly against them, which no one else dare do.... There have been many quarrels, but Biassou knows well enough that if he were to hurt Toussaint there would be a general outcry, and that he and the men who carried out his orders would assuredly be killed. For all that no one doubts that he would get Toussaint removed quietly if there was a chance of doing so, but we do not mean to give him the chance" (308). Such

identifications of the "good" Pierrot with Toussaint have to be counter-balanced, however, with those established between the "bad" Biassou and Toussaint whenever Hugo attributes historical anecdotes about the latter to the former.

94 Unflatteringly characterized by C.L.R. James as "a cruel monster who used to drink the blood of his white victims and commit abominable cruelties" (76). Jean-François did indeed have this rebel leader put to death at the beginning of November for his violent excesses, as Hugo knew from Lacroix, whom he is closely paraphrasing here (see Appendix E.2b-iii).

95 Hugo learned about this intriguingly named rebel leader, who was active in the early months of 1792, from Lacroix: "A Spanish griffe named *Romaine-Rivière*, more popularly known as *Romaine the Prophetess*, had settled in Trou-Coffy [near Port-au-Prince] with a fanatical band of Blacks and men of colour. From the heart of his camp, where he profaned the sacred mysteries, he summoned the slave gangs of the hills and the Léogane plain to murder and carnage. He claimed to be inspired by the Virgin Mary, whom he consulted by placing his head in the tabernacle, and then passing along her answers, which always promised certain victories and easy pillaging. That was more than enough to seduce barbarians" (1.142).

96 Rigaud's line comes straight from Lacroix: "When [Rigaud] was told about cruelties committed by his men, rather than aggressively addressing them in the way that his all-powerful influence would have allowed, he limited his displeasure to exclaiming: 'Ah, dear God! How terrible the fury of a people can be!'" (1.195).

97 "One of the local coastal kingdoms comprising the Ancient Congo—an area figuring prominently in the latter eighteenth-century French slave trade" (Fick 180-81). In the short story, Bug-Jargal identifies his father as "king of the lands of Gamboa." The change to Kakongo was inspired by Hugo's reading of the following passage about African self-government from Abbé Grégoire's *De la littérature des nègres*: "No doubt civilization is practically non-existent in several of those negro States, where one is allowed to talk to the kinglet only through a blow-pipe, and where after he has finished dining a herald announces to the other little despots that they can now dine in turn. He is nothing more than a barbarian, that king of Kakongo who, combining all powers in his own person, judges each and every case, drinks down a cup of palm wine after every sentence that he passes (because otherwise it would be illegal), and sometimes finishes off fifty proceedings in one sitting. But the ancestors of the civilized Whites were barbarians as well; compare Russia in the fifteenth century with Russia in the nineteenth" (157-58).

98 Leader of what is generally identified as the first slave revolt against the French, which took place in Port-de-Paix in 1679. In the original, Hugo spells the name Padrejan, which almost certainly proves that he read about Padrejean in Malo (81-83), the only source I know of that uses this erroneous spelling.

99 Identified by some as from Genoa and by others as from Malta, Jacques Praloto was a key agitator in the independentist, anti-mulatto ranks of the *petits blancs* from 1791 to 1792, during which time he was in command of the artillery at Port-au-Prince. He was exiled and put to death in late 1792 (Lacroix 1.192). Port-au-Prince is far enough away from Biassou's camp that it seems unlikely any of his artillery would have found its way there; equally implausible is the reference to Cape Cabron (at the eastern tip of the Samaná peninsula in present-day Dominican Republic).

100 I have not come across this name in any of Hugo's known sources.

101 This struggle over the abyss clearly echoes a brief vignette by Hugo's brother Eugène, "Le duel au précipice" (*OC* 1.1197-99), lending some credence to the notion that Habibrah is in part an unconscious projection on Hugo's part of his insane brother (see the end of "1791, 1825: Haiti and Hugo—Historical and Biographical Contexts" in the Introduction).

102 A reference to João de Castro, Fourth Viceroy of the Portuguese Indies, who in 1547 did indeed raise a loan from the city of Goa on the security of his facial hair.

103 "*Habit-bas*" in the original French. "*Habit*" (costume) + "*bas*" (low) functions at one level as a jocular reference to the dwarf's size; the expression "mettre habit bas" would also have conveyed in Hugo's time the sense of "to take off one's coat" and "to die."

104 Literally, "Great-Devil's-Mouth" (almost certainly a name of Hugo's invention; "Great-Devil's-Pillar" in the short story).

105 Commonly identified as Jean-Victor Moreau (1763-1813), who was named Division-General on 14 April 1794. After initially supporting Napoleon's rise to power, he later became an opponent of the Emperor and was exiled from France in 1804; he died at the battle of Dresden in 1813, having returned from America to fight with the Allies against his rival. During Hugo's youth, his mother was deeply implicated in anti-Napoleonic cabals that centred around people like Moreau and her lover, Victor de Lahorie; as Robb puts it, "while Colonel Hugo [eventually made a General by Napoleon] was helping to spread the branches of the Empire, his wife was sawing at the base of the trunk" (29).

106 Legislative body elected to provide a new constitution for France after the overthrow of the monarchy on 10 August 1792. First met on 20 September 1792 and two days later declared France a Republic; last met on 26 October 1795, after which it was replaced by the Directory. Hugo associates the National Convention not only with disloyal republicanism but especially with the excesses of the Terror when it was under control of the Jacobins (June 1793-July 1794).

107 Left-wing of the National Convention, associated with the likes of Marat, Robespierre, and Danton. With the help of the Paris masses, the Jacobins took over power from the Girondins on 2 June 1793, and exercised dictatorial authority (the Terror) until the fall of Robespierre on 27 July 1794.

108 A reference to the so-called "virgins of Verdun," a dozen mostly young women who were executed on 26 April 1794 for having collaborated during the Prussians' brief occupation of the city in September 1792; they are the subject of one of Hugo's earliest published poems, "Les vièrges de Verdun" (1819). Louis XVI was executed on 21 January 1793, after being dethroned on August 10 of the previous year.

109 Armand-Louis-Philippe-François de Custine (1768-94), ex-noble who sided with the French Revolution but was put to death by the Jacobins for supposedly conspiring with the enemy; Marie-André de Chénier (1762-94), poet, executed on dubious grounds by the Jacobins. Hugo refers to Chénier dismissively in an early article for the *Conservateur littéraire* (see *OC* 1.467-73), but nonetheless cautions: "Who will dare reproach him for his imperfections, when the revolutionary axe still rests all bloody in the midst of his unfinished labours?" (468)

110 The Feuillants (so named because they met at the Feuillants convent in Paris) were constitutional royalists who defected from the increasingly radical Jacobin Club in July 1791. They exercised power during the first months of the Legislative Assembly, which met from 1 October 1791 to 21 September 1792 (after which France became a republic), but gradually lost ground to the Girondists. The Girondists (so-named because

their leaders were deputies from the *département* of Gironde) represented bourgeois republican interests and first came to power in March 1792; occupying the right-wing of the National Convention, they controlled it during the early months of the Republic but were eventually purged by the Jacobins in June 1793.

111 The Brissotins were followers of the leader of the Girondists, Jacques Pierre Brissot de Warville (1754-93). Brissot, who helped found the Société des Amis des Noirs in 1788, was executed by the Jacobins after they came to power.

Appendix A: "Bug-Jargal" (1820)

[Whether true or not, there exists a well-known story, circulated in his wife's *Victor Hugo raconté par un témoin de sa vie* (1863), that Victor was dining with his brothers and other friends toward the end of 1818 and the decision was made to write a "collective book." Each of the friends was to come up with a tale in which soldiers on the eve of battle would tell one another stories to kill the time; Victor insisted that these tales should be completed within fifteen days, and was the only one to produce the goods. (The manuscript of "Bug-Jargal" is, in fact, dated April 1819 and internal textual evidence suggests that the 1818 date is apocryphal.) Hugo gestures toward this possibly fictional origin at the end of his 1826 preface when he informs his readers "that the story of *Bug-Jargal* is only a fragment of a more extensive work, which was to have been entitled *Tales under the Tent*" (a title no doubt modelled on Scott's *Tales of my Landlord*; see Ntsobé 24-38). Although this collection of stories was never completed, "Bug-Jargal"—which a recent biographer has judged to be "assuredly the most controlled work of his early years" (Hovasse 187)—eventually found its way into print in the journal he and his brothers had begun publishing at the end of 1819, *Le Conservateur littéraire* (May-June 1820).

Can we understand the novel without having read the short story? I strongly believe that the two texts have to be read together, but it is a useful mental exercise to imagine reading the novel without knowledge of the story. Interestingly enough, the prestigious Ivy League press that initially agreed to publish this new translation of *Bug-Jargal* balked at including the story along with the novel (or, for that matter, any contextual material aside from an introduction and a brief set of footnotes). Inexplicable as I found their decision from the perspective of someone whose interpretation of the novel largely depends upon its differences from the story, they certainly had a point: after all, the idea of publishing the story and the novel together is the invention of twentieth-century French editors, and it might be argued that yoking the story to the novel only muddies the water as far as our understanding of the latter goes.

The novel certainly does seem a lot "muddier" when juxtaposed with the story. Hugo scholar Georges Piroué once went so far as to identify the two texts with two different "levels of thought" that progress in parallel from one end of Hugo's career to the other: the short story, Piroué argued, unfolds at "the level of clear consciousness, heroic moralism, associated with a classical or at least realist form, an objective approach, nourished by

Homeric reminiscences"—a level he associates with such later novels as *Ninety-Three* and *Toilers of the Sea*; the novel, by contrast, explores "the level of the unconscious, of a visionary adventuring into the realm of what appears rather than what is, the descent into the primordial, into the underbelly of the fantastic, which could only take the form of a baroque romanticism tinged with occultism and satanism"—a level that predominates in *Notre-Dame de Paris* and *The Man Who Laughs*. The parallel existence of these two universes, Piroué concluded, was necessary for the development of Hugo's work as a whole, and thus, "despite their dissimilarity the two *Bug-Jargals* are nonetheless one and inseparable because of what they foreshadow; it is impossible to eliminate either one at the expense of the other" (viii). A comment like this, to be sure, pushes us back into the claustrophobic world of Hugo studies and its incessant attempts to justify the parts—and especially the early parts—of Hugo's oeuvre in the name of the whole, but it is nonetheless of interest because it takes the short story seriously as a work unto itself (and one that, Piroué unconventionally argued, in certain respects may actually be more effective than the novel): it insists on reading the two texts together, and forces us—in different terms, to be sure—once again to contemplate that *differing relation* between the clear and the opaque, between 1791 (history) and Bug-Jargal (language), that I discussed in the opening section of the Introduction.

When one examines the actual texts together, it is not difficult to pick out the major differences between them. Most of these differences stem from Hugo's additions to the text. He retained roughly ninety per cent of the story in his novel, distributing bits and pieces of it into 38 of the novel's 58 chapters. He kept the basic narrative progression of the story, merely adding episodes to it (especially in the middle third of the novel), as well as compressing the distance between the frame narrative and the events of 1791 (in "Bug-Jargal," the tale is narrated during the Napoleonic Wars, sometime around 1806, whereas in the novel it is recounted at the height of the Terror in 1794). Roger Toumson has efficiently summed up Hugo's changes with four words: *eroticization, historicization, exoticization,* and *mythification* (14). Most obviously, the novel introduces a new erotic element by creating a sexual rivalry between Bug-Jargal and the twenty-year-old d'Auverney (who has been transformed from the seventeen-year-old Delmar of the story): what some might wish to interpret as the queer erotics of male bonding in the story are to an extent diluted by the introduction of d'Auverney's fiancée, Marie. Whether this turn toward heterosexual romance and the spectre of inter-racial coupling that it raises results in a psychologically more probing narrative or marks the melodramatic limits of the young Hugo's novelistic imagination will be up to readers to decide, but there is no denying its central importance to the novel, for all that one has to keep in mind what this centrality might be marginalizing or masking.

Predictably enough, Bug-Jargal's desire is emptied out by novel's end; the black man nobly renounces his erotic claims on the white woman, Marie. However, if the threat of Bug-Jargal's inter-racial desire for Marie is emphatically averted in the novel, the consummation of that desire has already been tacitly acknowledged by virtue of the ubiquitous presence of mulattoes in it, the most prominent of these being the other major new character introduced alongside Marie in the 1826 version, the dwarf Habibrah, who grotesquely embodies the fact that the erotic threat posed by Bug-Jargal's desire for Marie has, as it were, always-already been realized. Just as predictably as the noble black Bug-Jargal is made to renounce his desire for Marie, the villainous mulatto Habibrah will be turned into the novel's chief scapegoat, he and his mixed identity being spectacularly purged in the closing pages. This scapegoating of mulattoes, as I have argued at length in *Islands and Exiles* (231-61), provides the thematic and ideological glue holding the novel together: it is, to put it bluntly, the key to understanding Hugo's translation of "Bug-Jargal" into *Bug-Jargal*. Unlike the short story, the novel features a dense array of historical details about Saint Domingue, and a great many of these details are manipulated in such a way as to support the novel's anti-mulatto bias and its critique of revolutionary history. In the passage from short story to novel, Hugo settles upon the figure of the mulatto as the embodiment not merely of a desire, inter-racial or otherwise, with which he is profoundly uncomfortable, but of a revolutionary modernity that he would like to expunge from the historical record.

What *Bug-Jargal* ultimately bears witness to, however, is the failure of Hugo's desire to restore the longed-for clarity of a black and white world; indeed, despite itself, the novel reveals the entanglement of the author's anti-historical desire with the mixed-up world of modernity he is critiquing. The novel, which is so obviously anxious about cultural and racial hybridity (see, e.g., Gaitet, Rodriguez), is itself fully implicated in, and perhaps subconsciously drawn toward, the source of its anxiety: as Régis Antoine puts it, Hugo's "attraction for the rebel camp, the novelist's taste for profusion and confusion, even when he is denigrating the procession of hordes marching past Biassou, aesthetically contradicts the [novel's] conservative discourse" (185). The short story is an orderly text; the novel, by contrast, is a text that attempts to *restore* order, but that fails to do so because it has become immersed in, or contaminated by, the disorderly—one might even say carnivalesque—world that it is contesting. As Pierre Laforgue has argued, "in the *Bug-Jargal* of 1825 carnival is what allows for the transformation of an elegant tragedy in five instalments into a polyphonic and proliferating novel" (31). The tightly constructed short story gives way to a novel bursting to the seams with material brought forward as a case for the Restorationist prosecution but that—in its sprawling heterogeneity, so at odds with the homogeneous order the young *ultra* was bent on (re)consecrating—might actually be of more use to the defence of a modernity which, to recall his disapproving description of the French Revolution in the 1824 Preface to the *Nouvelles Odes* (Appendix C.2), disunites everything and mixes it all together.

In order to facilitate comparison of the two texts, material from the story that was included in the novel (though often with minor and occasionally significant revisions) will be preceded by a number in square brackets, signalling the chapter from the novel in which it appears: [1], [2], etc. Passages of any significant length that were left out of the novel are preceded by an asterisk in square brackets: [*].]

[1] When Captain Delmar's turn came up, he looked surprised and admitted to the assembled gentlemen that he really knew of no deed in his life which would merit their attention.

"And yet, Captain," Lieutenant Henry said to him, "you've seen your fair share of the world: the Colonies, Egypt, Germany, Italy, Spain … Captain, look, it's your lame dog!"

Startled, Delmar dropped his cigar and turned abruptly toward the entrance of the tent where an enormous dog was limping toward him as quickly as it could.

On its way over, the dog trampled on the cigar, not that the captain took any notice of this.

Licking the captain's feet and rubbing against him with its tail, the dog gambolled about to the best of its ability, then came and settled down in front of him. Overcome with emotion, the captain mechanically stroked it with his left hand, while with his other he undid the strap of his helmet, repeating from time to time "It's you, Rask! You're here!" At length, he exclaimed: "But who was it that brought you back?"

"By your leave, my Captain …" It had been several minutes now since Sergeant Thaddeus had lifted up the flap of the tent. He had been standing there all that time—his right arm wrapped in his overcoat, tears in his eyes, gazing in silence at the concluding act of this Odyssey. Finally, he ventured those words: "By your leave, my Captain ..." Delmar looked up.

"Thad, it's you. How the devil were you able to...? Poor dog! I thought he was in the English camp. Where did you end up finding him?"

"God be thanked! As you can see, my Captain, I'm as overjoyed by it all as your son gets when you make him do his declensions: *cornu*, the horn ..."

"But where did you end up finding him?"

"I did not find him, my Captain. I went out in search of him."

The captain stood up and held out his hand to the sergeant. Although the captain failed to notice it, the sergeant's hand stayed wrapped in his overcoat.

"You see, my Captain, ever since this poor Rask got lost, it was very clear to me—by your leave, Sir—that you were missing something. Truth to tell, the evening when he didn't show up as usual to share my ration of bread, I believe it wouldn't have taken much ... But no, God be thanked, I've only cried twice in my life. The first time, when ... The day that ..." And the sergeant gave his master an anxious look. "The second time, when that scatterbrain Balthazar got it into his head that he'd make me peel a bunch of onions."

Henry burst out laughing. "It seems to me, Thaddeus, that you haven't told us what made you cry for the first time."

"No doubt, old friend, it was when you received that cross?" the captain asked affectionately, while continuing to stroke the dog.

"Oh, my Captain! If Sergeant Thaddeus cried, it could only have been, you will have to admit, Sir, on the day when he gave the order to open fire on Bug-Jargal, otherwise known as Pierrot."

Delmar's entire face clouded over. He rushed over to the sergeant and made to squeeze his hand, but despite such an excess of honour old Thaddeus kept it hidden under his greatcoat.

"Yes, my Captain," Thaddeus continued, stepping back a few paces, while Delmar's distraught eyes tracked his every move. "Yes, that time I cried ... He was quite the man, that's for certain! So strong, so robust. And such a handsome appearance for a negro! And Sir, remember when he got there all out of breath, at the very same time as his ten comrades? There was no getting around it, we'd had to tie them up. I was the one giving the orders. And then when he himself went and untied them and took their place even though they didn't want him to? But there was no stopping him ... Oh, he was a man, he was! A real rock of Gibraltar. And then, my Captain, when he was standing there, as stiff-backed as Antoine when he takes his turn at a dance, and his dog, the very same Rask who's here, who understood what they were going to do to him, and who leapt at my throat ..."

"As a rule, Thad," interrupted the captain, "you wouldn't let this part of your tale go by without giving Rask a stroke or two. See the way he's looking at you."

"Ah! The fact is ... You see, my Captain, old Malagrida once told me that if you stroke anything with the left hand it brings misfortune."

"And why not the right hand?" Delmar asked with surprise, noticing for the first time that the sergeant's hand was wrapped in the overcoat and that his face was all pale.

"By your leave, my Captain, the fact is ... You already have a lame dog. I fear you will end up with a one-armed sergeant as well."

The captain sprang out of his seat.

"What? How in the...? Thad, old man, what are you saying? One-armed? Let's see your arm ... One-armed, good God!"

Delmar was trembling. The sergeant slowly peeled off his coat, revealing to his master an arm wrapped in a bloodied handkerchief.

"What the deuce...!" the captain murmured, as he cautiously lifted up the cloth. "But, my friend, what's the meaning of this...?"

"Oh, Sir, it is a simple enough matter. I told you I had seen how distressed you were since those confounded Englishmen robbed us of that fine dog of yours, poor Rask, the mastiff of Bug ... Well, in short, today I resolved to get him back, whatever the cost, so that at least I could eat with a hearty appetite this evening. That's why, after giving your full-dress uniform a good brushing for tomorrow's battle, I slipped away from the camp, without a peep, armed with only my sabre. I cut through the hedges so as to get to the English camp sooner. I hadn't even reached the first line of trenches when, by your leave, Sir, in a little wood to the left I saw a great mob of redcoats. I edged forward to see what was going on. They didn't notice me, and that gave me a chance to locate Rask. There he was, in their midst, leashed to a tree, while two fine gentlemen, naked as heathens down to here, were going at one another with their fists, cracking blows that made as much noise, Sir, as the big drum of the 37th. It was two English chaps, if you will, who were fighting a duel for your dog. But now Rask sees me, and he gives such a tug on the rope that it breaks, and in the blink of an eye the rascal's at my heels. As you can imagine, the rest of the pack aren't slow to follow. I shoot into the woods. Rask follows me. Several bullets go whistling by my ears. Rask was barking, but luckily they couldn't hear him because they kept shouting 'French dog! French dog!'—as if your dog weren't a Saint Domingue dog bred and born. No matter. I'm making my way through the thicket, and I was almost clear of it when two redcoats pop up in front of me. My sabre got rid of one of them, and it would have rid me of the other, no doubt, if the bullet from his pistol hadn't ... You see my right arm? But no matter! 'French dog' grabbed hold of his neck, and I can assure you that he wasn't sparing with his attentions. That devil of a fellow, why did he have to go chasing after me, like some pauper dogging a seminarian? In any case, here I am, and Rask as well. My only regret is that the good Lord did not choose to send this my way at tomorrow's battle instead."

The old sergeant's features turned gloomy at this thought.

"Thaddeus!..." the captain burst out in an irritated tone. Then he added, more gently: "How could you have done it, old friend, for a dog...?"

"It was not for a dog, my Captain, it was for Rask."

Delmar's expression softened entirely. The sergeant continued: "For Rask, the mastiff of Bug ..."

"Enough, Thad! Enough of that, my friend," the captain appealed, placing his hand over his eyes. "Let's go," he added after a brief silence. "Lean on me, and come along to the ambulance wagon."

After putting up a respectful resistance, Thaddeus obeyed. The dog, who during this scene had joyfully gnawed its way through a good half of the captain's fine bearskin, got up and followed the two of them out.

[2] This episode had caught the attention of the high-spirited story-tellers, keenly arousing their curiosity.

[3] "I'd wager," Lieutenant Henry exclaimed, as he wiped away a large patch of mud that the dog, on its way over, had deposited on his red boot, "I'd wager that the captain wouldn't exchange his dog's broken paw for those twelve hampers of Madeira we laid eyes on the other day in the wagon of Brigadier ..."

"Hush, now! That would be a bad transaction," Philibert said merrily. "The hampers are empty at present, and I should know. Moreover," he added with a serious look, "you have to admit, Lieutenant, that thirty opened bottles are most certainly not worth that poor dog's paw. After all, that paw has its uses: you could turn it into a bell-handle."

At the solemn tone with which the captain uttered these last words, the assembled company broke out in laughter. Alfred, the only one not to have laughed, had a peeved look on his face.

"I fail to see, gentlemen, any reason for mockery with regard to what has just taken place. If anything, this dog and this sergeant, whom I have always seen by Delmar's side for as long as I have known him, seem to me capable of eliciting a certain interest. This scene, when all is said and done ..."

Philibert, nettled both by Alfred's peevishness and the other soldiers' mirthful spirits, interrupted him:

"This scene is very sentimental. Come now! A rescued dog and a broken arm!"

"Captain, you're mistaken," said Henry, throwing the bottle that he had just emptied out of the tent. "This Bug-Jargal, otherwise known as Pierrot, piques my curiosity tremendously ..."

Philibert, on the point of getting angry, calmed down when he saw that his glass, rather than being empty as he had imagined, was full. Delmar returned. He went back to his place and sat down without uttering a word, lost in thought but with a calmer look on his face. So preoccupied did he appear that he heard nothing of what was being said around him. Rask, who had followed him, lay down at his feet and watched him anxiously.

"Your glass, Captain Delmar. Have a try of this ..."

"How is Thaddeus, you ask?" said the captain, thinking that he was answering Philibert's question. "Oh, thank God! The wound isn't dangerous, the arm isn't broken."

The involuntary respect that the captain inspired in all his comrades-in-arms was the only thing that kept Henry from bursting out in laughter.

"Since you're no longer as worried about Thaddeus," he said, "I hope, my dear Delmar, that you'll be so good as to fulfil your part of the bargain by recounting to us the story of your lame dog and of Bug-Jargal, otherwise known as Pierrot, that real rock of Gibraltar!"

To this question, offered in a tone that was half-serious and half-joking, Delmar would have made no reply had everybody else present not joined in with the same request as the lieutenant.

"I'll grant your wish, gentlemen, but don't expect anything more than the recital of an extremely simple anecdote, in which I play only a very secondary role. If the affection that exists between Thaddeus, Rask, and myself has made you hope for something extraordinary, I warn you that you'll be disappointed. So, to begin."

Everyone fell silent. Philibert emptied his brandy flask with one swig, and Henry wrapped himself in the half-gnawed bearskin to keep away the chill of the night, while Alfred left off humming the tune "*Mataperros.*"

Delmar remained lost in thought for a moment, as if conjuring up in his memory events long since gone by. At length, he began to speak.

[4] "Although born in France, I was sent at an early age to Saint Domingue to stay with one of my uncles, a very rich colonist whose daughter I was intended to marry.

My uncle's settlements were near Fort Galifet, and his plantations occupied the greater part of the Acul plains. This ill-fated location, the details of which will no doubt seem of little interest to you, was one of the primary causes of the disasters and total ruin that befell my family.

Eight hundred negroes worked the immense domains of my uncle. I will admit to you that the wretched condition of these slaves was made even worse by the insensitiveness of their master, whose heart had been hardened by a longstanding habit of absolute despotism. Accustomed to seeing himself obeyed at the first blink of an eye, he would punish the slightest hesitation on a slave's part with the greatest severity, and often the intercession of his children served only to heighten his anger. So we could do no more than relieve in secret the ill-usage we could not prevent ..."

"What? There's some high-sounding talk, Captain! Keep going! It wouldn't do to let the misfortune of the *ci-devant* "blacks" pass by without contributing some nice little commonplaces about humanity."

"I thank you, Henry, for saving me from ridicule," said Delmar icily.

He continued:

[*] "Among this crowd of unhappy souls, in whose midst I would often spend the entire day, I had noticed a [11] young negro who appeared to command the deepest respect of his companions. A mere sign from him was enough for them to obey him, even though he was a slave like them. This young man was of [9] an almost gigantic height. His face, where the characteristic signs of the black race were less apparent than on that of the other negroes, exhibited a mixture of ruggedness and majesty that you would be hard pressed to imagine. His strongly pronounced muscles, the width of his shoulders, and the animation of his movements indicated an [11] extraordinary strength combined with the greatest suppleness. It often happened that he would end up doing in one day the work of eight or ten of his comrades so as to shield them from the punishment specified for negligence or fatigue. He was adored by the slaves, yes, but their respect for him—I would even go so far as to say their worship of him—appeared to stem from another cause. What astonished me above all was to see him being as gentle and as humble toward those who considered it an honour to obey him, as he was proud and haughty in his relations with our drivers. It is fair to say that these privileged slaves, whose lowly condition was coupled to the insolence of their authority, took a malignant pleasure in overburdening him with work and badgering him in all sorts of ways. However, not a one of them dared inflict any humiliating punishments on him. If it so happened that any were imposed on him, twenty negroes would offer to undergo them in his place, and he,

standing still as could be, would coolly watch the punishments being carried out as if these men were doing nothing more than their duty. This remarkable man was known in the slave huts by the name of Pierrot.

[*] You can well imagine, gentlemen, that it was a long time before I understood this individual, a few of whose traits I've just recalled for you. Today, even though fifteen years' worth of memories ought to have erased the memory of that negro, I must admit I have yet to encounter in the world of men anyone as noble and as original as he.

I had been forbidden any and all communication with Pierrot. I was seventeen years old when I spoke with him for the first time. Here's how it happened. [End of first instalment.]

I was walking one day with my uncle on his vast estates. The slaves, [10] trembling in his presence, doubled their efforts and their activity. Irascible by force of habit, my uncle was on the point of getting angry at not having anything to get angry about when he suddenly noticed a black man who had fallen asleep under a clump of date-palms, overcome with weariness. He rushes over to this poor wretch, wakes him up with a push, and orders him back to work. In a fright, the negro gets up and, as he does so, reveals the presence of a fledgling *randia* he had lain down on by accident. The shrub, which my uncle took particular pleasure in growing, was ruined. At this sight the master, already irate at what he called the slave's laziness, becomes furious. Beside himself with rage, he dashes over to pick up the axe which the negro had left on the ground and raises his arm to use it against him. The axe didn't come down. I'll never forget that moment. A powerful hand stayed the hand of the colonist. A black man, [8] of colossal stature, [10] cried out to him in French: 'Kill me, for I have just trespassed against thee, but spare the life of my brother, who has only laid hands on your *randia*.' These words, far from shaming my uncle, merely increased his rage. I don't know what he might have been capable of doing, had I not immediately thrown the axe into the bushes. I pleaded with him, but to no avail. The negligent black man was punished with a flogging and his defender was thrown into the dungeons of Fort Galifet for having raised his hand against a white man.

This negro was Pierrot. The scene that I had just witnessed stimulated [11] my curiosity and my interest so much that [12] I resolved to visit him and be of what service I could. I mulled over the best means of approaching him.

Although very young, as the nephew of one of the richest colonists in the Cape I was captain of the Acul parish militias. Fort Galifet was entrusted to their care, as well as to that of a detachment of yellow dragoons whose leader—normally a non-commissioned officer in that company—had command of the fort. It so happened that at precisely this time the officer in command was the son of a poor colonist for whom I had been lucky enough to perform some by no means negligible services; he was entirely devoted to me ..."

"And whose name was Thaddeus?"

"Exactly the case, my dear Lieutenant. You can easily imagine that I had no difficulty in getting him to admit me into the negro's cell. As captain of the militias, I had every right to visit the fort. However, in order not to arouse any suspicions in my uncle, I took care to go there only when he was taking his siesta.

All the soldiers, except those on guard, were asleep. Guided by Thaddeus, I arrived at the cell door; Thaddeus opened it and withdrew. I entered. The black man was sitting down, for his great height prevented him from standing. He was not alone: an enormous mastiff reared up, growling, and came toward me. 'Rask,' the black man called out. The young mastiff fell silent and returned to lie down at its master's feet, where it finished off devouring some miserable scraps of food.

I was in uniform; what little light there was coming through the vent-hole in this narrow cell was so dim that Pierrot didn't recognize me.

'I am ready,' he said to me calmly.

As he spoke these words, he got up in a crouch. 'I am ready,' he repeated.

'I thought,' I said to him, surprised by the freedom of his movements, 'that you were in chains.'

With his foot he pushed bits and pieces of something that made a clinking noise.

'I have broken them.'

There was something about the way in which he uttered these last words that seemed to say: 'I am not made to bear chains.' I proceeded:

'They did not tell me they had let you keep a dog.'

'I am the one who let him in.'

I was ever more astonished. The cell door was shut from outside with a triple bolt. The vent-hole was scarcely six inches wide and had two imposing iron bars across it. He seemed to understand where my thoughts were tending. He stood up and effortlessly detached an enormous stone from beneath the vent-hole; taking away the two bars fastened above this stone, he thereby made an aperture through which two men could easily have passed. This aperture opened out on a level with the stand of date and coconut trees that covers the morne directly behind the fort.

The dog, seeing the breach opened, thought its master wanted it to go out. It sat up, ready to leave; the black man motioned it back to its place.

Surprise rendered me speechless. The black man recognized me in the broad light of day but showed no reaction.

'I can live two more days without eating …' he said.

I made a horrified gesture. It was then I noticed how thin the poor prisoner was. He added:

'My dog will only eat from out of my hand. Had I not been able to enlarge this hole, poor Rask would have died of hunger. Better it be me than him, since I have to die anyway.'

'No,' I exclaimed. 'No, you will not die of hunger!' He misunderstood me.

'No doubt,' he responded, smiling bitterly, 'I could have gone two more days without eating, but … I am ready, officer. Better today than tomorrow. Do no harm to Rask.'

I realized then what his 'I am ready' meant. Accused of a capital crime, he thought I had come to lead him to his death. Just think, a colossal man, with all means of escape available to him, gently and calmly repeating to a child, 'I am ready.'"

[*] Henry could not stop himself from murmuring: "More high-sounding talk."

Delmar, who had paused to recover his breath, did not hear this interjection. He continued his tale:

[12] "'Do no harm to Rask,' he repeated yet again.

I could not contain myself. 'What!' I protested. 'Not only do you take me for your executioner, but you even have doubts regarding my humanity toward a poor animal who has done me no wrong!'

He was moved; his voice faltered.

'White man,' he said, holding his hand out to me, 'white man, pardon me. I love my dog. And,' he added after a brief silence, 'your people have done me much harm.'

I embraced him, squeezed his hand, set him straight.

'Don't you recognize me?' I asked him.

'I knew you were a white man, and as far as the whites are concerned, no matter how good they might be, a black man counts for so very little! Even so, I am not of a rank inferior to yours!' he added.

My curiosity was keenly stimulated: I urged him to tell me who he was and what he had suffered. He maintained a gloomy silence.

My conduct had touched him; my offers of assistance, my appeals, overcame his indifference to life. He went out and brought back some dates and an enormous coconut. Then he closed up the aperture and set about eating. Conversing with him, I noticed that he spoke French and Spanish fluently, and that he did not appear devoid of learning. This man was so astonishing in so many other respects that up until then the purity of his speech had not struck me. I tried yet again to find out the cause of this, but he remained silent. At length, I took my leave, ordering my faithful Thaddeus to show him every possible attention.

[13] I saw him every day at the same hour. His case worried me: despite my appeals, my uncle insisted on prosecuting him. I did not hide my fears from Pierrot. He listened to me with indifference.

Often while we were together Rask would show up carrying a large palm leaf around his neck. The black man would untie it, read the unknown characters which were traced on it, and then rip it up. I made it a point not to ask him any questions about this.

One day I entered without his seeming to take any notice of me. He had his back turned to the door of his cell and was singing in a melancholy tone the Spanish tune 'Yo que soy contrabandista.' When he had finished, he turned abruptly toward me and exclaimed:

'Brother, promise, if ever you find yourself doubting me, put aside all your suspicions when you hear me singing that tune.'

He cut an imposing figure. I promised what he asked. He took the deep shell of the coconut that he had culled on the day of my first visit, and which he had kept ever since; filling it with palm wine, he bade me put it to my lips, and then emptied it at one go. From that day on, he only ever referred to me as his brother.

Meanwhile I began to have some reason for hope. My uncle's anger had started to abate. Every day I pointed out to him that Pierrot was the most vigorous of his slaves; that, single-handedly, he did the work of ten men; and that, after all, he had simply wanted to prevent his master from committing a crime. He listened, and gave me to understand that he would not be following up on the charge. I said nothing to the black man about my uncle's change in attitude, wishing to have the pleasure of announcing his outright liberty to him, if I obtained it. What astonished me was that, believing himself condemned to die, he did not take advantage of any of the means of escape that were in his power. I asked him about this. 'I must stay,' he answered icily. 'They would think I was afraid.'

[14] My uncle withdrew his complaint. I ran to the fort to give Pierrot word of this. Knowing that he was free, Thaddeus entered the prison cell along with me. He had vanished. Rask, who was there alone, came up to me wagging his tail. A palm leaf was attached to his neck. I removed it and

read these words: 'Thank you, you have saved my life. Do not forget your promise.'

Thaddeus, unaware of the secret of the vent-hole, was even more astonished than I; he imagined that the negro had changed into a dog. I let him believe what he wanted, merely insisting that he keep silent about what he had seen.

I wanted to take Rask along with me, but no sooner were we out of the fort than he dashed into the near-by hedges and disappeared.

[15] My uncle was incensed at the slave's escape and ordered that he be tracked down. [*] This order, however, was rendered irrelevant by the events that I'm about to recount to you.

It was three days after Pierrot's puzzling flight, the famous night of 21–22 August 1791. Having just visited the post at Acul, [15] I was taking a turn near the batteries on the bay when I noticed a reddish light on the horizon flaring up and spreading out from the direction of the Limbé plains. The soldiers and I at first attributed it to some accidental fire, but a moment later the flames became so conspicuous and the smoke, driven by the wind, began to mass and thicken to such an extent that I promptly set off back to the fort to sound the alarm and have a relief force sent out. Passing by the huts of our blacks, I was surprised by the extraordinary commotion that was going on there; most of them were still up, and they were talking in an extremely animated manner. I crossed a thicket of mangroves where we came upon a pile of axes and picks. I overheard a few words, the gist of which seemed to me to be that the slaves of Limbé were in full revolt and were setting fire to the settlements and the plantations situated on the other side of the Cape. Justifiably worried, I there and then put the Acul militias on armed alert and ordered that an eye be kept on the slaves. Calm was restored.

Meanwhile, with every passing minute the havoc appeared to be growing in Limbé. You could even, it seemed, make out the distant sound of artillery and rifle fire. Around two in the morning, unable to contain myself, I left a portion of the militias in Acul under the lieutenant's orders and, despite the injunctions of my uncle and the pleas of my family, set off with the rest of the soldiers on the road to the Cape.

I shall never forget the sight of that city as I approached. The flames, devouring the plantations of Limbé, were casting over it a sombre light darkened by the torrents of smoke that were being driven through the streets by the wind. Like a thick snowfall, a whirlwind of sparks formed by little bits of blazing sugar cane was furiously piling onto the roofs of the houses and the rigging of the ships anchored in the harbour. Any minute now it was threatening the city of the Cape with a conflagration no less heart-rending than the one that was devouring the surrounding areas. It was an awful, imposing spectacle to behold: on land, pale settlers still risking their lives in order to save their houses, all that remained to them of so many riches, from the terrible scourge; in the harbour, ships—fearing the same fate, but at least favoured by the wind that was proving so deadly to the luckless colonists—bearing off under full sail on a sea coloured with the blood-red fires of the conflagration. [16] Deafened by the gunfire coming from the forts, the panic-stricken cries of those fleeing, and the crash of buildings caving in, I was at a loss where to take my soldiers. On the parade ground, though, I ran across the captain of the yellow dragoons, and he served as our guide. I will not linger, gentlemen, over descriptions of the fire-ravaged plain we saw before us; many another person has depicted those disasters that befell the Cape, and Henry's smile warns me not to follow in their footsteps. I will simply tell you that we found the rebels already masters of Dondon, the town of Ouanaminthe, and the ill-fated plantations of Limbé. [*] Aided by the militias from Quartier-Dauphin and by companies of yellow and red dragoons, we could do no more than drive them out of Petite Anse, where they were beginning to establish a foothold. During their withdrawal, they left many a trace of their cruelty: all the whites were massacred or mutilated in the most barbarous manner. We hurriedly stationed a sizable garrison in the Petite Anse fort, and around six o'clock in the morning—blackened by the smoke, overwhelmed by heat and weariness—we returned to the Cape. Hoping to get a little rest, I had stretched out on my coat in the middle of the parade ground, [17] when I saw a yellow dragoon covered with sweat and dust riding toward me at full speed. I got up right away, and from the few broken words that escaped his lips, I learned with renewed dismay that the revolt had reached the Acul plains and the blacks were laying siege to Fort Galifet, where the militias and the colonists were holed up. There wasn't a minute to lose. Those of my soldiers willing to follow me were given horses and, guided by the dragoon, I arrived in sight of the fort around seven o'clock. My uncle's domains were laid waste by the flames, just like those at Limbé. The white flag was still fluttering over the fort's central tower. A moment later, the entire building was enveloped in a whirlwind of smoke. When it eventually cleared away, we could see the red flag flying atop it. The game was up. [18] Redoubling our speed, we soon reached the slaughter-field. The blacks fled at our approach, but we had a clear view of them—to our right and our left, in front of us and behind us—massacring whites and burning down the settlements. Thaddeus came up to me, all covered in wounds; he recognized me in the midst of the fray. 'My Captain,' he said, 'your Pierrot is a sorcerer, or at the very least a devil. He found his way into the fort, I don't know how, and look...! As for your uncle and his family ...' Just then, a huge black man emerged from behind a burning sugar refinery; he was carrying off an old man who was screaming and struggling in his arms. The old man was my uncle; the black man was Pierrot. 'Traitor...!' I screamed back at him. I levelled a pistol at him. A slave threw himself in the bullet's path and fell dead. Pierrot turned round, and seemed to shout out some words to me; then he vanished into the blazing canebrakes. Seconds later, an enormous dog followed in his wake, its jaws holding a cradle I recognized as being that of my uncle's youngest son. The dog was Rask. Beside myself with rage, I fired my second pistol at him but missed. [End of second instalment.]

[*] In the meantime, the conflagration continued to wreak havoc. The blacks, whose exact number we couldn't make out because of the smoke, appeared to have withdrawn. We were obliged to return to the Cape.

There, I was pleasantly surprised to find my uncle's family; they owed their safety to a young negro who had escorted them through the midst of the slaughter. Only my uncle and his youngest son were missing. I hadn't a doubt that Pierrot had sacrificed them to his vengeance. I recalled any number of mysterious incidents that now seemed to me to have a clear explanation, and I completely forgot my promise to him.

[20] The Cape had been hurriedly fortified. The insurrection was making alarming progress: the negroes of Port-au-Prince were beginning to stir; Biassou was in command of those from Limbé, Dondon, and Acul; Jean-François had had himself proclaimed generalissimo of the insurgents from the Maribarou plain; Boukmant, since made famous by his tragic end, was patrolling the banks of the Limonade with his brigands; and, lastly, the bands of Morne Rouge had recognized as their leader a negro named Bug-Jargal.

The latter's character, if one were to believe the reports about him, was in singular contrast with the ferocity of the others. While Boukmant and Biassou devised any number of ways to kill the prisoners who fell into their hands, Bug-Jargal made every effort to furnish them with the means to get off the island. Those two leaders negotiated with the Spanish vessels that cruised around the coasts, enriching themselves on whatever they had managed to plunder from the poor souls they were forcing to flee; Bug-Jargal scuttled several of these corsairs. Monsieur Colas de Maigné and eight other prominent colonists were, by his orders, released from the wheel on which Boukmant had them bound. Countless other acts of generosity were reported of him—too many to tell you about here.

I heard nothing more about Pierrot. The rebels, commanded by Biassou, continued to harass the Cape; the Governor resolved to drive them back into the interior of the island. Our army in the field was made up of the militias of Acul, Limbé, Ouanaminthe, and Maribarou, along with the Cape regiment and the redoubtable yellow and red companies. The militias of Dondon and Quartier-Dauphin, reinforced by a volunteer corps under the command of the merchant Poncignon, formed the city's garrison. The general wanted first to eliminate Bug-Jargal, whose diversionary tactics alarmed him. He sent out the Ouanaminthe militia and a battalion from the Cape against him. The detachment returned two days later, utterly defeated. Intent on trying to subdue Bug-Jargal, the general had the same detachment set out again, this time with a reinforcement of fifty yellow dragoons and four hundred militiamen from Maribarou. The second army fared even worse than the first. Thaddeus, who took part in that expedition, came back from it bearing a real grudge; he swore to me in turn that he'd have his revenge on Bug-Jargal."

There was a tear in Delmar's eyes. He folded his arms on his chest and for several minutes seemed immersed in a painful reverie. At length, he resumed his tale:

[21] "News arrived that Bug-Jargal had left Morne Rouge and was leading his troop through the mountains to join up with Biassou. The general could not have been more elated: 'We've got him!' he said, rubbing his hands. The next day, the colonial army was a league's distance from the Cape. At our approach, the rebels hastily abandoned Port Margot and Fort Galifet. All the bands fell back toward the mountains. The general was triumphant. We kept moving forward. As we passed through those barren and devastated plains, each of us sadly cast a look around for the place where his fields, his settlements, and his riches had been; often you couldn't even tell where they were any more. I will spare you my reflections ... [22] On the evening of the third day, we entered the gorges of the Grande Rivière. It was estimated that the blacks were some twenty leagues away in the mountains. We pitched our camp on a small morne, which—to judge by the way it was stripped bare—seemed to have served the same purpose for the blacks. This position was by no means ideal, but it was certainly peaceful enough. Sheer cliffs, covered with dense forests, towered over the morne on all sides. Behind the camp flowed the Grande Rivière. Boxed in by the cliffs, it was narrow and deep in this spot. Sloping down abruptly, its banks were blanketed with clumps of bushes

that were impenetrable to the eye. Even the flow of the river was often hidden by garlands of lianas. Clinging to the branches of red-flowering maples scattered amongst the bushes, these vines worked their way across the river, joining their shoots with those on the other side; criss-crossing one another in a myriad of ways, they formed large tents of foliage over the water. Anyone contemplating them from the top of the neighbouring rocks would think he was looking at meadows still wet with dew. A muffled noise or the occasional wild teal suddenly piercing through this flowery curtain provided the only evidence of the water's presence. The sun's golden hues soon disappeared from the jagged peak of the distant mountains of La Treille. Little by little darkness spread over the camp and silence fell, broken only by the cries of a crane and the measured steps of the sentinels. Then all at once, directly above our heads, was heard the fearsome strain of 'Wa-Nassé.' The palm trees and cedars atop the rocks blazed up, and the livid glow of the conflagration revealed to us numerous bands of mulattoes on the neighbouring summits, their copper complexion appearing red in the gleam of the flames. These were Biassou's men. Danger was imminent. Startled out of their sleep, the commanding officers hurriedly rounded up their soldiers. The trumpet sounded the alarm. In a jumble, our lines were formed. The blacks, instead of taking advantage of our disorderly state, just stood there watching us and singing 'Wa-Nassé.' A gigantic black man appeared, alone, on the highest peak above the Grande Rivière. A feather the colour of fire fluttered over his brow; an axe was in his right hand, and a red flag in his left. I recognized Pierrot. If there had been a carbine within my reach, sheer rage might perhaps have made me commit a cowardly act. The black man repeated the chorus of 'Wa-Nassé,' planted his flag on the peak, threw his axe into our midst, and was then swallowed up by the current. A sense of regret came over me at the thought that now he would no longer die by my hand. The blacks then began rolling enormous blocks of stone onto our columns; bullets and arrows showered down on the morne. Furious at not being able to get at their attackers, our soldiers were drawing their last desperate breath: they were being crushed by the boulders, riddled with bullets, pierced by arrows. A horrible confusion held sway over the army. All of a sudden, a frightful noise seemed to issue from the middle of the Grande Rivière. An extraordinary scene was taking place there. The yellow dragoons, faring very poorly against the mass of stones that the mulattoes were launching from the mountain tops, had hit upon an idea for how to avoid them: by taking refuge under the pliant liana arches covering the river. Thaddeus was the first to suggest this plan of action—which was, by the way, an ingenious one ..."

[23] "You are too kind, my Captain ..."

More than a quarter of an hour had passed since Sergeant Thaddeus, his right arm in a sling, had slipped back unnoticed into a corner of the tent. Until that moment, only his bodily gestures testified to his involvement in the captain's tales but now, believing it would be disrespectful to let such direct praise go by without thanking the captain for it, he stammered confusedly: "You are too kind, my Captain."

A general outbreak of laughter ensued. Delmar turned round and burst out at him in a stern tone:

"What! *Vous!* Thaddeus, you're here...! And your arm...?"

Hearing himself addressed in this unaccustomed way, the old soldier staggered, his features darkening; he tilted his head back, as if to stop the tears that were welling up in his eyes.

"I did not believe," he said finally, in a whisper, "I would never have believed, that my captain would be so discourteous to his old sergeant as to address him as '*vous*.'"

Delmar hastily rose to his feet.

"Forgive me, my old friend," he exclaimed. "I didn't realize what I was saying. Thad, come now, won't you forgive me?"

Tears gushed from the sergeant's eyes, despite himself.

"So this is the third time," he stammered. "But this time it is for joy."

Peace was made. A short silence followed.

"But, tell me, Thaddeus," the captain asked gently, "why did you leave the ambulance wagon to come back here?"

"It's that, by your leave, Sir ... I had come to ask you, my Captain, if the horse-cloth, with galloons, should be placed on your charger tomorrow."

Henry started laughing. "You'd have done better, Thaddeus, to ask the army surgeon if two ounces of lint, in shreds, should be put on your game arm tomorrow."

"Or," Philibert followed up, "to inquire if you could drink a little wine to refresh yourself. Until you find that out, here's some brandy, which can only do you good. Have a try, my brave sergeant."

Thaddeus came forward, made a deferential bow, excused himself for taking the glass with his left hand, and emptied it after toasting their health. He grew animated.

"You had arrived at the moment, my Captain, at the moment when ... Well then, yes, I was the one who suggested going under the lianas so that we good Christians wouldn't be crushed to death by the stones. Our officer, he didn't know how to swim and so he was afraid of drowning—a natural enough reaction. He fought the idea as hard as he could until—by your leave, Sir—he saw a huge slab of rock, which just missed smashing into him, get stopped by the vines as it hurtled toward the river. So my suggestion was accepted, on condition that I be the first to try it out. I'm on my way. I go down the bank. I leap under the trellis, holding on to the branches above, and then, my Captain? Well, I feel my leg being grabbed. I fight back. I shout for help. A sabre cuts into me several times. And now here come the dragoons, real devils they were, hurling themselves under the lianas, one on top of the other. The blacks of Morne Rouge had been lying in wait there, without anyone suspecting it, probably in order to fall upon us, like a sack full to bursting, when they had a chance. It certainly wouldn't have been a good time to go fishing! There was fighting, swearing, shouting. Since they were completely naked, they moved around more easily than we did, but our blows hit home more than theirs. We were swimming with one arm and fighting with the other, as one does in those cases. And those who didn't know how to swim, my Captain? Well, they were hanging from the lianas with one arm, and the blacks were grabbing them by the legs. Right in the thick of the fray, I saw a big negro defending himself against eight or ten of my comrades, like Beelzebub himself he was. I swam over and recognized Pierrot, otherwise called Bug ... But we don't find that out yet, right, Sir? I recognized Pierrot. Ever since the capture of the fort, we hadn't been on the best of terms. I seized him by the throat. He was about to dispose of me with one thrust of his dagger when he saw who I was and, instead of killing me, surrendered. Which was a great misfortune, my Captain, for had he not surrendered ... Well, in short, as soon as the negroes saw he was captured, they leapt on us and tried to free him. So much so that the militias were also going to jump in the water when Pierrot, no doubt seeing that the negroes were all going to be slaughtered, said a few words of real hocus pocus since it put them all to flight. They dived down and disappeared in the blink of an eye. This underwater battle would have been really quite agreeable, it would have amused me no end, had I not lost a finger in it and drenched ten cartridges, and if ... poor man! But the writing was on the wall, my Captain." After respectfully placing the back of his left hand over the ornament on his forage cap, the sergeant raised it upward with an inspired look.

Delmar seemed violently agitated.

"Yes," he said. "Yes, you're right, my old Thaddeus, that night was a fateful night indeed."

He would have fallen into that state of deep reflection to which he was prone had not his listeners eagerly urged him to continue. He took up his tale again:

[24] "While the scene Thaddeus has just described ..."

Thaddeus went and sat down in triumph behind the captain.

"...While the scene Thaddeus has just described was taking place behind the morne, I had managed, with a few of my men, to scramble up from one bush to another onto a peak called the *Pic du Paon*, which was on a level with the positions held by the blacks. Now that a path had been cleared, the summit was soon rife with militia, and we opened fire with a vengeance. The negroes, less well armed than we, couldn't return our fire as briskly. They started to lose heart; we responded even more fiercely. Soon the nearest rocks were evacuated by the rebels. They nonetheless made sure before leaving to roll the bodies of their dead comrades down onto the rest of our army, which was still marshalled on the morne. With the help of several palm trunks that we felled and tied together, we crossed over onto the abandoned peaks, and a part of our army thus found itself in an advantageous position. The sight of this unnerved the insurgents. We kept up our fire. Plaintive howls, mixed in with the name of Bug-Jargal, suddenly rang through Biassou's army. They sounded terror-stricken. A number of the Morne Rouge blacks appeared on the rock where the scarlet flag was flying; they prostrated themselves, removed the standard, and hurled themselves along with it into the chasms of the Grande Rivière. This clearly signified that their leader was dead or captured. We grew so bold on seeing this that I resolved to attack the rebels at close quarters and drive them from the cliff-tops they still controlled. I had my men fell some trees to form a bridge between our peak and the nearest rock. I was the first to dash across it into the negroes' midst. My men were about to follow when one of the rebels, with the stroke of an axe, smashed the bridge to pieces. The debris fell into the abyss, striking against the rocks with a dreadful noise. I turned my head. At that moment I was grabbed hold of by six or seven blacks, who disarmed me. I fought back like a lion. They tied me up with strips of bark, heedless of the bullets raining down on them from my side. Only one thing alleviated my despair: the shouts of victory that I heard all around me an instant later. It wasn't long before I saw the blacks and mulattoes scrambling pell-mell up the steepest summits, letting out howls of distress as they went. Those guarding me imitated them. The most vigorous one among them loaded me onto his shoulders and carried me off toward the forests, leaping from rock to rock with the agility of a chamois. The gleam of the flames soon ceased to guide him; the faint light of the moon was all he needed. He kept on walking, but at a slower pace. [End of third instalment.]

[25] After travelling through various thickets and crossing over a number of torrents, we reached a valley situated in the heart of the mountains; it was a place absolutely unknown to me. [*] A great many of the rebels, whose camp this was, had already assembled there. The black man who had been carrying me untied my feet and handed me over to several of his comrades. They encircled me. Soon, day began to break. The black man returned, accompanied by some passably well-armed negro soldiers, who grabbed hold of me. I thought they were leading me to my death, and I steeled myself to undergo it with courage. They led me to a grotto which was lit up by the first rays of the rising sun. We entered. [28] Between two lines of mulatto soldiers, I caught sight of a black man seated on a baobab trunk, which was covered by a carpet of parrot feathers. His outfit was bizarre. A magnificent belt, from which dangled a Saint-Louis Cross, was helping keep up a pair of striped breeches made out of coarse fabric. He had no other costume. He was wearing grey boots, a round hat, and a pair of epaulettes, one of which was made of gold and the other of blue wool. A sabre and several impressive pistols were next to him. This man was of middling height; his ignoble features presented a peculiar mixture of shrewdness and cruelty. He bade me approach and studied me for some time in silence. At length, he began sniggering.

'I am Biassou,' he said to me.

At the sound of this name I shuddered inwardly, but retained a calm, proud demeanour. I made no reply; the look on his own face turned mocking.

'You seem to me to be a man of great heart,' he said in bad French. 'Well then, listen to what I'm going to tell you. Are you creole?'

'No, I am French.'

My self-assurance made him frown. Sniggering, he went on:

'All the better! I see from your uniform that you're an officer. How old are you?'

'Seventeen.'

'When did you turn seventeen?'

'On the day your companion Leogri was hanged.'

His features contorted with anger, but he kept control of himself.

'It's been twenty days since Leogri was hanged,' he said to me. 'Frenchman, this evening you'll have a chance to tell him from me that you outlived him by twenty-one days. [*] Until then, you've got a choice: either you're kept in custody, or you give me your word that you'll be back here this evening, two hours before sunset, to carry my message to Leogri. [43] You're a Frenchman, right?'

[*] I was almost grateful for those few extra hours of liberty—even if it was only out of a refinement of cruelty that he granted them to me, simply a way of making me regret all the more the life I was losing. I gave him my word that I would do what he asked. He ordered that I be untied and that I be left entirely at liberty.

I wandered around in the camp first. Although my thoughts were by no means cheerful, I could not [27] help laughing at the silly vanity of the blacks, almost all of whom were wearing some form or other of military or ecclesiastical clothing, which they had stripped from their victims. It wasn't rare to see a gorget underneath a priest's collar, or an epaulette on top of a chasuble. They were in a state of inactivity that you do not find among our soldiers, even when they are back under their tents: most of them were sleeping out in the sun, their heads next to a scorching fire; others, their heads still brimming with their [30] old superstitions, were applying fetish stones wrapped in compresses to their most recent wounds. [27] Their ox-carts, loaded with booty and munitions, were their only line of defence in case of attack. Every last one of them cast a menacing look my way.

[*] Consigned to a certain death, I had the idea of climbing up onto a big rock to see if I could catch one more glimpse of the blue-tinged summits of the mornes near which I'd spent my childhood. I left the small valley and clambered up the first mountain I came across; soon the camp was totally hidden from view by clumps of greenery. I sat down, and one after another a thousand painful thoughts rushed through my mind. I was like the traveller who, hurtling down an inexorable slope toward the precipice that is going to swallow him up, casts one last look at the fields he's journeyed through and at those through which he hoped to journey."

Henry smiled, but did not dare interrupt Delmar with one of his usual commentaries.

"Death, no doubt a cruel one, awaited me. I no longer had any hope; this life's horizon, which in my dreams I had been so fond of extending, now took up no more than a few hours. Neither present nor future existed for me any longer. Casting about for some diversion, I turned to memories of a happier time. I conjured up Pierrot, and those days of youth and innocence when my heart opened to the sweet warmth of friendship, but the thought of the slave's treachery made my withered heart bleed. Embittered by misfortune, I blamed it all on that ingrate, and I cursed him. Even the certainty that he was dead offered me no solace.

At that moment, a familiar tune reached my ears; I was startled to hear [40] a manly voice singing '*Yo que soy contrabandista.*' This voice was none other than Pierrot's. A mastiff bounded up to me, joyously rolling about at my feet. It was Rask. I thought I was dreaming. The craving for vengeance overwhelmed me; surprise left me frozen to the spot. Out of an opening in a dense thicket, Pierrot appeared: with an overjoyed expression on his face, he reached out his arms to me. I turned away in horror. At the sight of this, his head sank to his chest.

'Brother,' he complained in a whisper, 'you promised you would never doubt me if you heard me singing that tune. Brother, have you forgotten your promise?'

Anger restored my voice.

'You monster!' I exclaimed. 'So I finally meet up with you again! Butcher! You murder my uncle, and you dare to call me your brother? Don't you come any closer!'

Almost involuntarily I reached down at my side for my sword. This action of mine struck him. An emotional, but gentle, look came over him.

'No,' he said. 'No, I will not come any closer. You are unhappy, and I have pity for you. You, you do not have pity for me, even though I am worse off than you.'

Motioning with my hand, I pointed out to him the place where our incinerated properties and plantations had been. He understood this silent reproach. He gave me a faraway look.

'Yes, you have lost a lot. But, believe me, I have lost more than you.'

Indignantly, I replied:

'Yes, I've lost a lot. But, tell me, who caused me to lose it? Who ransacked our houses, who burned down our crops, who massacred our friends, our compatriots...?'

[41] 'It is not I, it is my people, who did it. Look, one day I told you that your people had done me great harm, and you answered me that it was not you who had done it. So what is it that I have done?'

His countenance brightened; he expected to see me fall into his arms. I said nothing. 'May I call you "brother?"' he asked, full of emotion.

My anger flared back in all its violence.

'You ingrate!' I exclaimed. 'You dare to remind me of that time...?'

His eyes were swollen with tears. He interrupted me:

'It is not I who am the ungrateful one!'

'Well then, speak!' I answered back in a fury. 'What have you done with [*] my uncle? Where is his son?'

He kept silent for a moment.

'Yes, you doubt me,' he said at length, shaking his head. 'I could scarcely believe it. You take me for a brigand, a murderer, an ingrate. Your uncle is alive, his child as well. You have no idea why I came.

Farewell. Come along Rask.'

Rask got up. Before taking his leave, the black man stopped and looked at me, sorrow and regret in his eyes. With these last words, that extraordinary man had just brought about a revolution in me: I feared I might have judged him too rashly. I did not yet understand him; everything about him astonished me. I had thought he was dead, and there he was in front of me, strong and glowing with health. If my uncle and his son were alive, then those words of his—'it is not I who am the ungrateful one'—certainly came home to me. I raised my eyes. He was still there. His dog was looking anxiously at both of us. Pierrot heaved a long sigh, and finally took a few steps toward the thicket.

'Stay.' I shouted at him haltingly. 'Stay.'

Looking at me with an air of indecision, he stopped.

'Will I see my uncle again?' I asked him in a faint voice.

He had a grim look on his face.

'You doubt me,' he said, making a move to withdraw.

'No,' I exclaimed, in thrall to the ascendancy of this bizarre man. 'No, you are still my brother, my friend. Young man, I do not doubt you. I thank you for having kept my uncle alive.'

[45] The look on his face remained surprisingly forbidding. He appeared to be undergoing a violent struggle within himself: he moved toward me and then drew back; he opened his mouth but then shut it again. This moment of hesitation did not last long. He threw himself into my arms.

'Brother, I have trust in you.'

After a slight pause, he added:

'You are a good man, but your unhappiness made you unjust.'

'I have regained my friend,' I said to him. 'I am no longer unhappy.'

'Brother, you are unhappy still. Soon, perhaps, you will no longer be so; I owe you my life. As for me, I will always be so!'

[46] The first transports of friendship had made his face sparkle with a joy that soon vanished. His features took on an odd, intensely sad expression.

'Listen,' he said to me in an icy tone of voice. 'My father was king in the land of Gamboa. The Europeans came and gave me all that useless knowledge you were so struck by. Their leader was a Spanish captain; he promised my father lands more vast than his own and white women. My father followed him with his family. Brother, they sold us!'

The black man's chest heaved; his eyes sparkled with anger. Heedlessly, he snapped in two a young papaya tree that happened to be next to him. Then he proceeded, seemingly oblivious to me:

'The master of the land of Gamboa had acquired a master, and his son became a slave stooped low over the fields of Santo Domingo. The young lion was separated from his old father so that the two of them might be more easily tamed; the young wife was taken from her husband with an eye to the profit that would come from coupling them with others; the little children looked for the mother who had nourished them, for the father who used to bathe them in the torrents, but they found only barbarous tyrants and were made to sleep with the dogs!'

He fell silent. Even though he was no longer speaking, his lips kept moving. His expression was blank, his eyes wild. At length, he grabbed me roughly by the arm.

'Brother, do you understand? I was sold to different masters as one sells a head of cattle. You remember when Ogé was tortured to death? On that day I saw my father again. I saw him broken on the wheel! Do you hear me?'

I shuddered. He added:

'My wife was prostituted to the whites. Do you hear me, brother: she died, begging that I avenge her.

All my people were urging me to free them and take my revenge. Rask would bring me their messages. I was unable to do what they wanted. I myself was in your uncle's prisons. The day when you obtained my pardon, I left to rescue my children from the hands of a ferocious creature. I arrived at the place ... Brother, the last of the king of Gamboa's grandsons had just expired under the blows of a white man. The others had preceded him.'

He broke off and asked me icily: 'Brother, what would you have done?'

This heart-rending account had left me frozen with horror: I answered his question with a menacing gesture. He understood me, and started smiling sadly. He continued his account:

'The slaves rose up against their master and punished him for the murder of my children. They elected me their leader. You know the calamities that came about as a result of this rebellion. I learned that your uncle's slaves were preparing to follow the same example. I arrived in Acul the very night of the insurrection. You were away. The blacks were already setting fire to the plantations. I was unable to calm their fury, for they believed that by burning down your uncle's properties they were avenging me. I had to save your family. I found my way into the fort through the breach I had created there during my imprisonment, and I entrusted your relatives to several faithful blacks, who were charged with escorting them to the Cape. Your uncle could not follow them; he had run toward the burning house to rescue the youngest of his sons. Some blacks had him encircled; they were going to kill him. I stepped forward and ordered them to let me take my own revenge; they withdrew. I took your uncle in my arms, I entrusted the child to Rask, and I lodged them both in a secluded cavern known to me alone. So there you have my crime, brother.'

Overwhelmed by remorse and gratitude, I would have thrown myself at Pierrot's feet but, with an offended look, he stopped me.

'Come, let us go,' he urged a moment later, taking me by the hand.

Surprised, I asked him where he wanted to take us.

'To the camp of the whites,' he answered me. 'We do not have a moment to lose: ten heads are answering for mine. We can hurry, because you are free; we must hurry, because I am not.'

These words increased my astonishment; I asked him to explain what he meant.

'Have you not heard that Bug-Jargal was being held prisoner?' he asked impatiently.

'Yes, but what does Bug-Jargal have to do with you?'

He seemed astonished in turn:

'I am Bug-Jargal,' he said solemnly.

[47] You might say that when it came to this man I was accustomed to being surprised. Not without astonishment had I seen the slave Pierrot transformed just moments earlier into the son of the king of Gamboa; I was all the more struck with admiration now that I recognized in him the redoubtable and generous Bug-Jargal, leader of the insurgents from Morne Rouge.

He did not appear to notice the impression made on me by these last words of his.

'I had been told,' he carried on, 'that you were yourself a prisoner in Biassou's camp. I came to deliver you.'

'Why then did you say to me just now that you were not free?'

He looked at me as if trying to guess what had brought about this entirely natural question.

'Look,' he said to me. 'This morning I was a prisoner amongst your people. I heard it announced in the camp that Biassou had declared his intention to have a young captive by the name of Delmar killed before sunset. They put more guards around me. I found out that my execution would follow yours, and that were I to escape ten of my comrades would answer for me. You see that I am pressed for time.'

Still I kept at him. 'So you escaped?' I asked him.

'And how else would I be here? Did I not have to save you? Do I not owe you my life?'

[*] 'Did you speak to Biassou?' I inquired.

He pointed down to the dog lying at his feet.

'No. Rask led me here. To my joy, I saw that you were not a prisoner. Now, follow me. Biassou is treacherous; if I had spoken to him, he would have had you seized and would have forced me to stay. [48] He is not a black man, he is a mulatto. Brother, time is short.'

'Bug-Jargal,' I said, reaching out my hand to him, 'return to the camp alone, for I am unable to follow you.'

He drew up, a look of pained astonishment on his face.

'Brother, what are you saying?'

'I am a captive. I swore to Biassou that I would not run away. I have promised to die.'

'You have promised,' he said to me grimly. 'You have promised,' he repeated, shaking his head in a doubtful manner.

Again, I assured him it was so. Lost in thought, he scarcely seemed to hear me; he pointed out a peak to me, the summit of which towered over the surrounding countryside.

'Brother, do you see that crag? When the sign of your death appears there, it will not be long before people hear word of my own. Farewell.'

[*] He plunged into the thicket and disappeared along with his dog, leaving me there by myself. The meaning of those last words seemed inexplicable to me. Our encounter had left me deeply moved. My feelings were as much of a puzzle as the man who had just taken his leave of me forever. Life mattered to me at present as little as it did to him, and the thought that my death would somehow bring about his was unbearable to me. I now had further cause for despair and yet I felt in a way consoled. I remained seated in the same place for a good length of time, immersed in thought and confounded by the slave's unprecedented generosity. [End of fourth instalment.]

In the meantime, the sun was slowly sinking in the west; the elongated shadow of the palm trees informed me that it was time to get back to Biassou. [50] I entered his grotto; he was surrounded by various instruments of torture and was busy testing out their springs. At the sound of his guards ushering me in, he turned. My presence did not appear to astonish him.

'Do you see?' he said, displaying the horrible apparatus around him.

I remained calm; I was familiar with the cruelty of this chief, and I was determined to endure everything without blanching.

'Is it not the case,' he sniggered, 'that Leogri was very lucky to have suffered nothing more than a hanging?'

Without answering, I looked at him with cold disdain.

'Ah! Ah!' he said, nudging the instruments of torture with his foot. 'It seems to me that you're starting to feel quite at home with these. It annoys me no end, but I'm afraid I don't have the time to try them out on you. This position is a dangerous one; I have to abandon it.'

He began sniggering again, and pointed to a large black flag situated in a corner of the grotto.

'This is what will let your people know when it's time to give your epaulette over to your lieutenant. By then, you understand, I'll already be on the move. What did you think of the surroundings?'

'It struck me,' I answered icily, 'that there were enough trees around to hang you and your entire troop.'

'Well now,' he retorted with a forced snigger, 'there is one place that you have doubtless not seen, and with which I'd like to make you acquainted. Farewell, young captain. Give my regards to Leogri.'

He gesticulated and then turned his back to me. His guards dragged me away.

[51] I was walking in their midst without putting up any resistance; true, to have done so would have been useless. We climbed to the brow of a mountain that was situated to the west of the valley and there we stopped to rest for a while. I cast one last look at the sea, which was visible in the distance and already red with the light of the setting sun—a sun that I would never see again. My guides got up; I followed them. We descended into a small valley, the appearance of which would have enchanted me at any other time: a torrent ran through it from one end to the other, imparting a fertile moistness to the soil. It was dominated by mighty sycamore maples of an extraordinary height. You could see the blue-azure haloes found on that species of wild honeysuckle the negroes call *coali* mixed in with the pale yellow flowers of the Canadian osier. Green expanses of liana vines hid from sight the brownish slopes of the neighbouring crags. We were walking on a trail that ran along the edge of the torrent; to my surprise, the trail ended abruptly at the foot of a sheer rock face, at the bottom of which I noticed an opening in the form of an

arch from which the torrent streamed forth. A muffled noise and a raging wind rose up from this opening. The negroes bore left, and we scaled the rock face, following a winding and uneven path which seemed to have been hollowed out of the rock by the waters of a torrent that had long since dried up. Then a vault appeared, half blocked by the brambles and lianas that grew there. From under this vault you could hear a noise similar to the one heard earlier. The blacks hauled me into it. We advanced further into the darkness. The noise was getting louder and louder; we could no longer hear our own footsteps. I concluded that it had to be coming from a waterfall and I was not mistaken. After ten minutes of walking in the gloom, we arrived at a platform of sorts formed by nature in the very heart of the mountain; most of this semicircular platform was covered by the torrent, which made a dreadful noise as it gushed out of the mountain's veins. Over this subterranean chamber, the vault formed a sort of dome clad with yellowish ivy. In the middle of the dome, you could make out a crevice through which daylight penetrated; its edge was crowned with green shrubs, which at that moment were tinged gold by the rays of the sun. At the north end of the platform, the torrent disappeared with a roar into a chasm; the shadowy glimmer of light descending from the crevice seemed to be floating at the bottom of the chasm without being able to penetrate it. The only discernible object in the abyss was an old tree, rooted in the rock one or two feet below the edge and so stripped of foliage that its species was unrecognizable. This plant was an altogether singular phenomenon: the moisture soaking its roots was all that kept it from dying, while the violence of the cataract kept stripping off its new limbs, forcing it to retain the same branches for all eternity. [52] Here, in this awe-inspiring place, the blacks came to a halt, and I saw that the time had come for me to die. In silence, they had begun to tie me up with some ropes they had brought along, when I thought I heard the distant barking of a dog; I took this sound for an illusion caused by the roaring of the falls. The negroes finished strapping me up and moved me closer to the chasm that was to engulf me. I raised my eyes toward the crevice so as to take one last look at the sky. Just then, there was another bark, louder and more pronounced, and the enormous head of Rask passed through the opening. I gave a start. The barking had made no impression on the blacks, who got ready to fling me into the midst of the abyss …

[53] 'Comrades!' a thunderous voice cried out.

Everyone turned round. It was Bug-Jargal. He was standing on the edge of the crevice, a red feather fluttering over his head.

'Comrades,' he repeated. 'Stop!'

The blacks prostrated themselves. He continued:

'I am Bug-Jargal.'

The blacks struck their foreheads against the ground, letting out a series of shouts, the tenor of which was difficult to discern.

'Untie the prisoner,' their chief cried out.

In the blink of an eye I was free. The negro kept speaking:

'Brothers! Go and tell Biassou not to display the black flag on this captive's behalf. For he has saved Bug-Jargal's life, and it is Bug-Jargal's wish that he live!'

He threw his red feather into their midst. The leader of the detachment laid hold of it, and they left without uttering a word.

I will not try describing for you, gentlemen, the situation in which I found myself. My eyes, moist with tears, fastened on Pierrot, who was gazing at me from his side with a singular expression of goodwill and pride. [*] He made a sign, and Rask jumped down next to me.

'Follow him,' he cried out to me. He disappeared.

The mastiff was walking in front of me, and his yelping guided me through the gloom. We made our way out of the mountain. Once we got to the valley, Bug-Jargal came up to me, a calm look on his face. I threw my arms around him. We remained silent for a while, quite overwhelmed; at length, he began speaking again.

'Listen, brother: my execution or that of my ten comrades was to have followed yours. But I have sent word to Biassou telling him not to display the black flag. [56] You will live, and so will I.'

Surprise and joy prevented me from answering him. He reached out his hand to me.

'Brother, are you glad?'

I regained my power of speech. I embraced him. I entreated him to live by my side from that moment on; I promised to secure a commission in the colonial army for him. He interrupted me with a brutal look.

'Brother, do you hear me proposing that you should enlist among my own people.'

He added cheerfully:

'Come; do you want to see your uncle?'

I made it clear to him how badly I wanted to go and console that poor old man; he took me by the hand and guided me. Rask was following us ..."

Here Delmar broke off and cast a gloomy look around him. Great beads of sweat were streaming down his forehead; he covered his face with his hand. Rask looked at him anxiously. "Yes, that is how you looked at me then!" he murmured. Immediately after, he got up in a violent state of agitation and exited the tent. The sergeant and the mastiff followed him.

[57] "I'd wager," Germon exclaimed, "that we're nearing the final act of the tragedy!"

Philibert, who had been taking a drink from his bottle, lifted it from his lips.

"I'd really be sorry if something were to happen to Bug-Jargal. He was a first-class fellow. I would have given twelve hampers of port to see that coconut shell he emptied at one go."

Alfred, who had been dreamily playing a tune on the guitar, broke off and inquired of Major Berval whether he'd be so good as to join him in a toast. He added:

"This negro interests me a great deal. Only I haven't yet dared ask Delmar if he also knew the tune for 'La hermosa Padilla.'"

"Biassou is much more remarkable," the major countered. "Good for him, that fellow knew what a Frenchman's made of. If I'd been his prisoner, I would have let my moustache grow, so that he might lend me a few piastres on it, the way the city of Goa did for that Portuguese captain. I declare, my creditors are even more ruthless than Biassou."

"Major, here's the four Louis I owe you!" Henry exclaimed, tossing his purse to Berval.

The major looked fondly at his generous debtor, who could with more justice have called himself his creditor. Henry hastily started up again:

"As for me, what amused me the most during Delmar's tale was ... seeing his lame dog raise its head every time he mentioned Bug-Jargal's name." "And in that respect," Philibert interrupted, "he was doing exactly the opposite of what I've seen the old church-going ladies of Celadas do when the preacher mentions the name of Jesus. I was entering the church with a dozen cuirassiers when ..."

The noise of the sentry's rifle alerted them that Delmar was returning. Everybody broke off talking. His arms folded, he silently paced back and forth for a while. Old Thaddeus, who had returned to his seat in the corner, was furtively watching him, trying hard to appear engrossed in the act of stroking Rask so as not to let the captain notice his anxiety.

At length, Delmar resumed his tale:

[58] "Rask was following us. The sun was no longer to be seen on the highest crag of the valley. A gleam of light suddenly appeared on it and

then vanished. The black man gave a start; he took my hand and squeezed it hard.

'Listen,' he said to me.

A muffled noise, like an artillery piece being discharged, could be heard in the valleys, followed by one echo after another.

'That is the signal!' said the negro in a grim voice. 'That was a cannon shot, was it not?' he then asked.

I nodded in agreement.

In two leaps he reached the top of a big rock. I followed him. He folded his arms, and began to smile sadly.

'Do you see?' he said to me.

I looked in the direction he was pointing to and saw the peak he had shown me that morning. It was the only one still lit up by the sun. Rising above it was a large black flag."

At this point, Delmar paused.

"I have since found out that Biassou—eager to set off and believing me dead—had made them hoist the standard before the return of the detachment that was supposed to have executed me.

Bug-Jargal, still standing there with arms folded, gazed at the banner of ill omen. All of a sudden, he turned round and took a few steps, as if to get down from the rock. 'God! Oh God! My poor companions!' He returned toward me. 'Did you hear the cannon?' he asked. I did not answer.

'Well, brother! That was the signal: they are being led off now.'

His head sank. He took a few steps and drew closer to me.

'Go and see your uncle, brother; Rask will guide you.' He whistled an Indian tune; the dog began to wag its tail, and seemed to want to head for a certain point in the valley.

Bug-Jargal took my hand and made an effort to smile, but it was little better than a convulsion.

'Farewell!' he cried out to me in a loud voice before vanishing into the clumps of trees that surrounded us.

I was petrified. The little I understood of what had just taken place made me expect the worst.

Seeing his master disappear, Rask moved up to the edge of the rock and started shaking his head, howling plaintively. He returned, with tail lowered. His big eyes were moist; he gave me an anxious look, then went back to the spot where his master had last been and barked a number of times. I understood him; I felt the same fears as he did. I took a few steps in his direction and then he was off like a shot, following the tracks of Bug-Jargal. Even though I too was running as hard as I could, I would have lost sight of him in short order if from time to time he hadn't stopped, as though he were giving me the chance to catch up with him. We made our way through several valleys, we crossed over hills and mountains thick with forests. Finally ..."

The captain's voice died away; his every feature was marked by a gloomy despair. He could barely utter the words:

"Carry on, Thad, for I have no more strength than an old woman."

The old sergeant was no less moved than the captain. Nevertheless, he set about obeying him.

"By your leave ... Since you desire it, my Captain. I have to tell you, gentlemen, that even though Bug-Jargal, otherwise called Pierrot, was a splendid negro, very gentle, very strong, very courageous, and the bravest warrior in the land—after you, my Captain, if I may be so bold—all that didn't keep me from being very much incensed with him, for which I will never forgive myself, even though my captain has pardoned me for it. So much so, Sir, that when I heard in the morning you were to die that evening I was overcome with a furious anger toward that poor man. It was with a truly diabolical pleasure, my Captain, that I let him know it would be he—or ten of his men—who would be keeping you company. To which he showed no reaction, except that an hour later he escaped by making a big hole in ..."

Delmar gestured impatiently. Thaddeus proceeded:

"Right you are! When the large black flag appeared, since he hadn't returned—which, by your leave, Sir, in no way astonished us—a cannon shot was fired off as a signal, and I was put in charge of leading the ten negroes to the foot of the *Pilier du Grand-Diable*, which was distant from the camp by about ... Anyway, in short, when we got there, you can imagine, gentlemen, there was no question of setting them loose. I had them bound, as one does in those situations, and I drew up my firing squad. And just then I see the big negro coming out of the forest; I was stunned. He came up to me all out of breath.

'I have arrived in time,' he said. 'Hello, Thaddeus.'

No, gentleman, that was all he said. He went over to untie his compatriots. Me, I just stood there, completely dumbfounded, as they say. Then, by your leave, my Captain, a big dispute took place between himself and the blacks about who was going to be the more generous party, which really ought to have lasted just a little longer. No matter! Yes, the blame is mine, I was the one who brought it to an end. He took the place of the blacks. At that moment his big dog, poor old Rask, arrived on the scene and leapt at my throat. He really ought to have kept hold of it, my

Captain, a little longer, but Pierrot made a sign, and the poor mastiff let go of me. However, he couldn't stop Rask from going over to lie down at his feet. And then, I thought you were dead, my Captain ... I was in a rage ... I shouted 'open ...'"

The sergeant stretched out his hand, looked at the captain, but could not bring himself to utter the fateful word.

"... Bug-Jargal fell. A bullet had fractured his dog's paw ... Since that time, gentlemen"—and the sergeant shook his head sadly—"since that time he's been lame. I heard groans in the near-by wood; I went over and there you were, my Captain. A bullet had hit you at the very moment you were rushing up to save that splendid negro. Yes, my Captain, those groans were yours, but they were all for him. However, gentlemen, Bug-Jargal wasn't dead. They brought him back to the camp. His wound was more serious than yours, my Captain, for you healed, and he, he lived ..."

The sergeant came to a stop. In a slow, muffled voice, Delmar finished off the story:

"He lived until the next day."

Thaddeus lowered his head.

"Yes. And he had spared my life. And I'm the one who killed him!"

The sergeant fell silent.

Appendix B: "The Saint Domingue Revolt" (1845)

[After 1826, revolutionary Saint Domingue and post-revolutionary Haiti figure barely at all in Hugo's writings. One finds in *Les Châtiments* a few disdainful references to Haiti's President-turned-Emperor Faustin Soulouque (1847-59)—New World double of Hugo's *bête noire*, Napoleon III—and in 1859-60, after the fall of Soulouque, Hugo wrote a couple of glowing letters to Haitian intellectuals that Léon-François Hoffmann, in his exhaustive study of Hugo's representations of blacks and slavery, has referred to as "the only texts in which Hugo ever had a kind word to say about Haiti and Haitians" ("Victor Hugo" 83). The only text of any substance in which Hugo returns to the Caribbean territory he explored with such ambivalence in *Bug-Jargal* is a dream sequence entitled "The Saint Domingue Revolt," which he apparently dictated in 1845 and which was included in the posthumous *Choses vues* (OC 7.952-54). Hoffmann cites this extremely vivid and disturbing document from the 1840s as evidence that the "regrettable Manicheism" of *Bug-Jargal* is not simply due to "the intransigence that comes with youth" but "becomes even more marked once he has reached the age of reason" ("Victor Hugo" 73). Is the carnivalesque nightmare that Hugo assiduously records simply (in Hoffmann's words) a "racist" document, or is it a prime example of cathartic "dream work" in which personal and cultural anxieties about racial difference have risen so blatantly to the surface of Hugo's consciousness that they can henceforth be questioned and dissolved, allowing him to move on to the more generous—or at the very least more rhetorically effective!—sentiments that one finds in his later favourable pronouncements about blacks and in his strong indictments of slavery (notably, in his 1859 defence of the U.S. abolitionist John Brown)? However one answers this question, the sheer intensity of "The Saint Domingue Revolt" confirms that *Bug-Jargal* is something more than a youthful exercise in literary exoticism; it is Hugo's therapeutic attempt at giving novelistic form to a shapeless nightmare that would haunt him for decades to come.]

Dictated by me on the 25th September 1845. (The Saint Domingue Revolt)

It seemed to me as if I was taking part in a dream. Without having seen this spectacle, you would have no way of imagining it. Nevertheless, I am going to try to paint a picture of it for you. I will simply tell you what was right there before my very eyes; scrupulously reproducing this minute portion of a large-scale scene will give you an idea of the general appearance of the city during the three days of pillaging. Multiply these details to infinity and you will have the overall picture.

I had taken refuge near the city gate—a flimsy lattice barrier made of long strips of yellow-painted wood, joined by cross-pieces and tapered at their upper end. Next to me, there was a sort of shed under which a group of those poor dispossessed colonists had taken shelter. They were silent as could be and seemed frozen in all the poses of despair. Just outside the shed, one of them, an old man, had sat down on the trunk of a mahogany tree that was lying on the ground like the shaft of a column, and he was weeping. Another man was trying in vain to hold back a white woman: wild with fright, she wanted to bolt off with her child, without knowing where, through that crowd of furious, bellowing negroes in their rags and tatters.

Yet the negroes—free, victorious, drunk, crazed—were paying no attention to this wretched and disconsolate group. Only a few steps away from us, two of them, knives between their teeth, were kneeling on an ox and slitting its throat. A little further off, their feet planted in the blood of the ox, two negresses dressed as marchionesses—a hideous sight, all covered in ribbons and pompoms, their bosoms bared, their heads littered with feathers and lace—were squabbling over a magnificent dress made out of Chinese satin, which one of them had clawed into with her nails and the other with her teeth. At their feet, a few pickaninnies were foraging the smashed-open trunk from which this dress had been snatched.

The rest was incredible to see and impossible to relate. It was a crowd, a mob, a masquerade, a witches' sabbath, a carnival, a veritable hell, a thing both farcical and terrible. Negroes, negresses, mulattoes, assuming every posture, every disguise, flaunting every sort of outfit and, what's worse, every form of nudity.

Over there, a big-bellied mulatto with a ghastly countenance, dressed like the planters with a jacket and pants of white dimity, wearing a bishop's mitre, the crook in his hand and a furious look about him. Elsewhere, three or four negroes—naked as could be, sporting three-cornered hats and dressed in red or blue soldier's uniforms, white leather trappings strapped over their black skin—were badgering a hapless militiaman who had been taken prisoner and whom they were dragging through the city with his hands tied behind his back. They smacked his powdered hair with the flat of their hand and pulled its long queue to the accompaniment of great bursts of laughter. From time to time, they stopped and made him get down on his knees, signalling to him that this was the place where he was going to be shot. Then, with a whack of the crook, they forced him back on his feet, and after going a little way they started harrying him all over again.

A troop of old mulatresses gambolled about in the middle of the crowd. They had rigged themselves out in the freshest dresses of the youngest and prettiest of our white women, and they were lifting up their skirts while they danced in such a way as to show off their wizened legs and their yellow thighs. And nothing could be stranger than all those charming fashions from the frivolous age of Louis XV, those large baskets, those rustic outfits, those flounces, those velvet caraco jackets, those silk skirts, the lace, the plumes—all that coquettish, whimsical luxury mixed together with those misshapen, black, flat-nosed, crinkly, horrendous faces. Decked out in this manner, they were no longer even negroes and negresses: they were she-monkeys and apes. Add to all that the deafening uproar. Every mouth that was not locked in some sort of contortion was letting off a howl.

I haven't finished: it is necessary that you take in the whole of this picture, right up to the smallest of details.

At twenty paces from me, there was a tavern; on its sign-board was a crown of straw run through by a pickaxe. A ghastly hovel. Nothing but a garret window and three-legged tables. Hobbling tables for a one-eyed tavern. Some negroes and mulattoes were drinking there; they were getting drunk, stupefying themselves, fraternizing. You have to have seen these things in order to depict them. In front of the tables, some drunkards were strutting about with a rather young negress who was dressed in a man's jacket that was unbuttoned and a woman's skirt that was barely attached. She was wearing a massive judge's wig; she had a parasol on her shoulder and a bayonet rifle on the other, no shirt and a naked belly to boot.

I've already told you: nudity of all sorts, everywhere. A few whites, naked as the day they were born, were running forlornly through this pandemonium. The corpse of a stout man, entirely naked, was being carried on a stretcher; a dagger protruded from his chest like a cross stuck in the ground.

From every direction, all you could see were gnomes—copper-coloured, bronzed, red, black, kneeling, seated, squatting, huddled together, opening trunks, forcing locks, trying on bracelets, fastening necklaces, slipping on jackets or dresses, breaking, destroying, snatching. Two black men were simultaneously trying on the two sleeves of the same outfit while going at one another with their two remaining fists.

Theft: the second phase of a city being sacked. Joy after rage. Yes, here and about, a number of them were still killing off people, but most of them were pillaging.

They were all carrying their booty away—piled up in their arms, in baskets on their back, in wheelbarrows.

Strangest of all, in the midst of this ghastly crowd, marching and parading about in orderly fashion with all the solemnity of a procession, was an interminable file of pillagers who were rich enough or lucky enough to have a horse and carriage. Yet another motley crew!

Imagine wagons of all types dragging along every sort of load. A four-horse carriage full of broken plates and kitchen utensils, and on each of those horses two or three negroes harnessed up and bedecked with plumes. A large ox-wagon laden with packages that were carefully tied up and stacked; damask armchairs on each of its sides; pans for frying; pitchforks for the manure heap; and on the very top, at the tip of the pyramid, a negress with her bosom hanging out, a necklace round her neck, a feather on her head. An old cabriolet from the countryside, pulled by a solitary mule and bearing ten trunks and ten negroes, three of whom were astride the beast. Mix in with that vinaigrettes, hand-barrows, sedan chairs—with every imaginable thing heaped on top of them, as I told you. The most precious furniture with the most sordid of objects. The tumble-down shack and the salon, their contents emptied out pell-mell into a cart. Imagine a massive exodus of crazy people trooping across a city.

What was incomprehensible was the tranquillity with which the little thieves were looking at the big ones. The pillagers on foot would step aside to let those on wheels pass by.

There were, to be sure, some patrols. If you can call a patrol a squad of five or six apes disguised as soldiers, every last one of them banging randomly on a drum.

There was a massive file of vehicles exiting through the city gates, near which a mulatto on horseback was capering about—a big rogue of a fellow, wizened, yellow, thin, decked out in a white rebato and a judge's robe with its sleeves rolled up. He had a sword in his hand, his legs were bare, and he was digging his heels into a paunchy horse that was prancing through the crowd. He was the magistrate assigned the task of maintaining order as they exited the city.

A little further on, another group was riding along. A negro in a red outfit with a big blue ribbon and a general's epaulettes, as well as a massive hat loaded down with tricolour feathers, was making his way through all this riff-raff. He was preceded by a horrid little pickaninny, wearing a helmet and banging a drum, and he was followed by two mulattoes—one in a colonel's uniform, the other dressed like a Turk with a *mardi gras* turban on his ghastly Chinaman's head.

Far off in the distance, I could make out battalions of soldiers in rags and tatters on the plain; they were marshalled around a great big house that had a tricolour flag and a balcony full of people. It gave every appearance of being a balcony from which one might deliver a harangue.

Even further off—beyond those battalions, that balcony, that flag, and that harangue—I saw nothing except nature in all its magnificence, full to bursting with a massive calm, delightful trees in full leaf, splendidly formed mountains, a sky without a cloud, an ocean without a ripple.

Such a strange and sad thing, to see the grimace of man show itself with such effrontery in the presence of the face of God!

Appendix C: Politics and Poetics

[By the time he came out with *Bug-Jargal* in January 1826, the twenty-three-year-old Hugo had already published an impressive array of critical writing, much of it in the *Conservateur littéraire* (1819-21) and the *Muse française* (1823-24). In order to give readers some sense of both the politics and poetics of the self-styled "young Jacobite" who wrote *Bug-Jargal*, I have provided translations of what are probably the two most important literary essays he wrote in the years immediately preceding that novel's publication: a review of Walter Scott's *Quentin Durward* (1823) and the Preface to his *Nouvelles Odes* (1824). In both of these essays, one finds Hugo attempting to balance politically conservative views with arguments for poetic renovation. This unlikely combination of reactionary politics and innovatory poetics would soon give way—in the Preface to *Cromwell* (December 1827), that massively influential literary manifesto which established Hugo as the spokesperson of Romanticism in France—to a "revolutionary" argument against classicism and for such things as genius, originality, Shakespeare, and the grotesque. With the Preface to *Cromwell*, Hugo succeeded in detaching his poetics, superficially at least, from an explicit political agenda, freeing himself up to promote increasingly avant-gardist claims about literature as an autonomous cultural practice.]

1. Review of Sir Walter Scott's *Quentin Durward; or, A Scot at the Court of Louis XI* (1823)

[Hugo had already published brief reviews of two other Scott novels (*The Bride of Lammermoor, Ivanhoe*) in the *Conservateur littéraire*, and he returned to the topic of Scott in 1823, fresh from the experience of having published his first novel, *Han of Iceland*. This review of *Quentin Durward*, Scott's novel about fifteenth-century France, was originally published in the July issue of the *Muse française* (*OC* 2.432-38), and constitutes what one critic has referred to as "for all intents and purposes the only theoretical reflection that he would ever devote to the novelistic genre, his one and only manifesto for a new type of novel" (Roman 127). Hugo here argues that Scott's novels anticipate a new, "dramatic" form of the novel that would synthesize the inadequate approach to storytelling adopted in the "narrative" and "epistolary" novels of the past. (Hugo later reprinted this article in *Littérature et philosophie mêlées* (1834), with a few significant revisions that have been included in the footnotes.)]

QUENTIN DURWARD; or, A SCOT AT THE COURT OF
LOUIS XI
By Sir Walter Scott
Translated from the English by the translator of the historical novels
of Sir Walter Scott, with the following epigraph:

La guerre est ma patrie, / Mon harnois ma maison, / Et en toute saison
/ Combattre c'est ma vie. (*Old French Ballad*)[1]

There is most assuredly something bizarre and marvellous about the talent
of this man who has his way with the reader as the wind has its way with
a leaf—this man who escorts the reader on a journey to whatever time and
place his fancy chooses; who, without even trying, unveils for his reader
the most secret recesses of the human heart, the most mysterious phenomena of nature, the most obscure pages of history; whose imagination
dominates and flatters everything it imagines, investing the rags of the
beggar and the robes of the king with the same astonishing truth, assuming all guises, donning all modes of attire, speaking all languages; who lets
the physiognomy of each age reveal its true features, those that bear the
mark of everything immutable and eternal placed there by the wisdom of
God and those that bear the mark of everything variable and transitory
deposited there by the folly of men; who, unlike certain ignorant novelists, does not force characters from times gone by to apply the same
powder and paint, the same varnish, as we would use today, but who
instead, like a wise and adroit counsellor encouraging ungrateful sons to
return to their fathers, obliges contemporary readers through his magical
power to reinvest themselves, at least for a few hours, with the spirit of
olden times (which is such an object of disdain these days). What the
artful magician wants above all, though, is to be exact: there is no truth to
which he denies his pen access, not even the truth that comes from the
depiction of error, that daughter of men whom one might believe immortal were it not that her capricious and changing temperament quells any
doubts regarding her eternal nature. Few historians are as faithful as this
novelist. One gets the feeling that he wanted his portraits to be tableaux
and his tableaux portraits; he paints our forefathers with all their passions,
their vices, and their crimes, but in such a way that the fleetingness of
superstitions and the impiety of fanaticism only serve all the better to
accentuate the perennial nature of religion and the sanctity of beliefs. And
in any case, we take as great a pleasure in re-encountering our ancestors
and their prejudices, which were often so noble and so salutary, as we do

their comely plumes and their fine armour. That man who tried to rejuvenate the Louvre and to plaster over the monarchy of Charlemagne was very much out of touch with the spirit of the people.[2] Walter Scott has a better understanding of his mission as poet than that blind giant did the mission of founder. Let us lose no more time over this casual comparison between two men whose spheres of celebrity are so different from one another; let us, rather, limit ourselves to considering the case of Walter Scott, this singular man who succeeded in drawing a hitherto unknown genre from the fountain-head of nature and truth—a genre that is new because it makes itself as old as it wishes, and that is composed of works in which the scrupulous exactness of the chronicles is conjoined with the majestic grandeur of history and the compelling interest of the novel. Walter Scott: this powerful and inquisitive genius divining the past; this candid paintbrush sketching a faithful portrait from an indistinct shadow, forcing us to recognize even that which we have never seen; this adaptable and sturdy mind taking, like soft wax, the imprint of each century and each country's particular style, and conserving, like indelible bronze, this imprint for posterity.

We could perhaps be mistaken, but it seems to us that few writers have so effectively discharged the duties of the novelist with respect to his art and his century as has Walter Scott: for it would be an almost unpardonable error in a man of letters were he to believe himself above the common good and the nation's needs; were he to exempt his mind from exercising any influence over his contemporaries and egotistically isolate his life from the greater life of the social body. Who, after all, will devote himself to these things if not the poet? What voice will rise up in the storm if not that of the lyre which can calm it? And who will brave the hatred bred of anarchy and the contempt born of despotism if not he to whom the wisdom of the ancients ascribed the power of reconciling the people and the king, and to whom the wisdom of the moderns has allotted that of dividing them from one another.

It is thus not to mawkish gallantries, shabby intrigues, and filthy liaisons that Walter Scott dedicates his talent. Forewarned by the instinct of his glory, he sensed that something more than that was needed for a generation which had just written with its blood and its tears the most extraordinary page in all of human history. The years that immediately preceded and followed upon our convulsive revolution were like those spells of extreme debility that a person suffering from fever experiences before and after his attacks. They were times when the most unimaginatively atrocious, the most stupidly impious, the most monstrously obscene books were avidly devoured by a sick society whose depraved tastes and benumbed faculties would have rejected any and all savoury or salutary nourishment. This is what explains the scandalously triumphant fanfare with which, back in those days, the plebians of the salons and the patricians of the street stalls greeted inept or smutty writers whom we will not deign to name here and who today are reduced to begging for the applause of lackeys and the laughter of prostitutes. Now, by contrast, popularity is no longer bestowed by the populace: it comes, rather, from the only source that can impress upon it a character of immortality as well as universality—namely, the approbation of that small number of delicate minds, exalted souls, and serious individuals who represent morally civilized peoples. That is the sort of popularity Scott has obtained by borrowing from the annals of particular nations to compose works that will appeal to all nations, and by drawing on the records of times past to write books that will live for all time. No novelist has hidden more instruction beneath more charm, more truth inside fiction. His muse is visibly allied to all the muses; one could look upon the epic novels of Scott as marking a transition from the literature of today to the grand epics that this poetic age of ours promises us and with which it will provide us.*

After having shown how he seeks to better the age in which he lives, let us now try and see how he works toward bringing his art to perfection by drawing it closer to nature. What, in effect, ought to be the novelist's intention? To express a useful truth in an interesting tale. Now, once that fundamental idea has been identified, that illustrative action dreamed up, should he not by way of developing it look for a means of realizing it that will make the novel similar to life, the imitation alike to the model? And is not life a bizarre drama in which the good and the bad, the beautiful and the ugly, the high and the low are all mixed together—according to a law that only ceases to hold sway beyond the bounds of creation? Why then should one limit oneself to painting, like the Flemish, works of total gloom or, like the Chinese, works of sheer luminosity, when nature everywhere reveals a struggle between shadow and light? Before Walter Scott, novelists had generally adopted two contending methods of composition, each defective precisely because it contended with the other. Some novelists would give their work the form of a narration, arbitrarily

---

* This age of ours has, indeed, already given us [Chateaubriand's] *Martyrs* [1809], for despite the fact that the author of this admirable poem has not subjected it to the metrical yoke, the only people who will refuse him the epic palm are those who would like to bestow it upon their arid *Henriade*, that news-sheet in verse, in which Voltaire has carefully avoided poetry the way one stays clear of a friend with whom one wants to start up a quarrel.

divided into chapters without it being particularly clear why or even simply in order to give the reader a moment's respite—as was acknowledged by a Spanish author of old, rather ingenuously, when he placed the title of *Descanso* (rest) at the head of his chapters.* Others would spin out their tale in a series of letters, which one was to assume were written by the various actors in the novel. With narration, the characters disappear and you only ever find yourself in the presence of the author; with the letters, the author vanishes and all you ever see are his characters. The novelist who narrates cannot make room for natural dialogue, for real action: in place of these, he has to substitute a monotonous forward progression, which is like a stylistic mould in which the most diverse events take on the same form and which obliterates the loftiest and most inventive creations in the same way that the bumpy parts of a field are flattened under a roller. In the epistolary novel, this same monotony stems from another cause: each character arrives in turn with his letter, like those fairground actors who—being allowed to appear only in succession and being forbidden to speak on stage—show up one after the other, carrying above their head a great big placard which identifies for the public what their role is. One can further compare epistolary productions to those laborious conversations between deaf-mutes who have to write down what they want to say to one another, so that the expression of their anger or their joy always requires them to have pen in hand and writing-box in pocket. Now, I ask you, how timely can a tender reproach be when it has to be carried to the post? And the fiery explosion of the passions, is it not somewhat impeded by the obligatory preamble and the polite endings that are the advance- and rear-guard of every letter penned by a well-born man? Do you think that the procession of compliments, the impedimenta of civilities, are any help in getting the reader more quickly involved in the novel and speeding up the course of the action? Should one not, in brief, assume that there is some radical and insurmountable flaw in a genre of composition that could occasionally cool off even the burning eloquence of Rousseau?

---

* [Vincent Epinel's] *Marcos Obregón* [1618], to which [Alain-René] Lesage is rather greatly obliged, although he is far from being indebted to it, as Voltaire claims, for his ingenious *Gil Blas* [1715-35]. In our days, these claims [about Lesage's plagiarisms] have been repeated by the learned Llorente, and countered successfully and with talent by Count François de Neufchâteau. Lesage borrowed from *Obregón* a few ideas that were if not comic then at least diverting, but in polishing the old Castilian storyteller's rough edges, he often deprived the latter of his biting candour and his singular originality. [Editor's note: For the young Hugo's central role in this simmering polemic about the originality of Lesage's novel, see Hovasse 164-67.]

Let us, thus, imagine a creative mind replacing the *narrative* novel (where the absurd practice of having each chapter preceded by an often very detailed summary, which is like the story of the story, makes it seem as if everything has been accounted for—everything, that is, except keeping the reader's interest) and the *epistolary* novel (the very form of which precludes all vehement emotion and rapid response) with the *dramatic* novel: a novel in which the imaginary action unfolds in truthful, varied tableaux, just as real events do in life; a novel which would make use of no divisions except those that the various scenes required for their elaboration; a novel which would, in a word, be a long dramatic play, where descriptions supplemented the sets and costumes, where the characters could be entrusted with portraying themselves and representing, through their various and sundry confrontations, all the forms that the idea underpinning the work might take. In this new genre, you will find the advantages of the two old genres combined, without any of their drawbacks. Having at your disposal the picturesque, and in a certain respect magical, resources of the dramatic play, you will be able to keep off the stage those innumerable pointless and evanescent details that, when left to himself, the narrator—obliged to follow his actors step by step, as if they were children still learning to walk—has to go into at great length if he wants to be clear. Moreover, the dynamism that is inherent in a dramatic scene forces to the surface something that the rapidity of narrative positively excludes, something that you can use to advantage: those bold, quick strokes that give you as much to muse over as any number of pages might do.

This, then, is the genre for which Sir Walter Scott has already provided us so many excellent models. One could argue that he has not yet unreservedly accepted all the conditions that this creation of his entails, but if, to date, he has often fallen short of his goal, he has at the very least opened up the path that leads to it. Thus it is that during his career he has been assailed by unrelenting criticisms. He who reclaims a swamp must resign himself to hearing the frogs croak around him.[3]

As a Frenchman, we are hardly grateful to Sir Walter Scott for the incursion he has just made into our history: rather, we would be tempted to take this Scotsman to task for it. Most assuredly, it is only a foreigner who—given the choice of all our kings: our Charlemagne, our Philippe-Auguste, our Saint Louis, our Louis the Twelfth, our Francis the First, our Henry the Fourth, and our Louis the Fourteenth—could select Louis the Eleventh as his hero. This is truly an inspiration of the English muse.

However, we are not going to let such a grievance unfairly affect us, and conscience demands that we place *Quentin Durward* among the better productions of the worthy baronet. It is difficult to imagine a more tightly woven plot and a more successful linkage of moral and dramatic effects.

The author's intention, it seems to us, was to show that loyalty—even in someone of humble origins, young and poor—arrives more surely at its goal than does treachery—even when it is helped along by all the resources of power, wealth, and experience. He has entrusted with the first of these roles his Scotsman Quentin Durward, an orphan who finds himself confronted with one danger after another, a prey to the best laid traps, without anything to guide him except a love that borders on madness—but it is often when one loves to distraction that this love becomes a virtue. The second role is confided to Louis XI, a king more adroit than the most adroit courtier, an old fox armed with the claws of a lion, powerful and shrewd, someone served by night as by day, unceasingly protected by his guards as by a shield and accompanied by his executioners as by a sword. These two very different characters play off against one another in such a way as to make manifest, with an unusually striking degree of truth, the author's fundamental point: it is in faithfully obeying the king that the loyal Durward serves, without knowing it, his own interests, while the projects of Louis XI, of which Durward was to have been both the instrument and the victim, result at one and the same time in the humiliation of the crafty old king and in the advancement of the plain-dealing young man.

A superficial examination might at first lead one to believe that the primary intention of the poet resides in the historical contrast, depicted with so much talent, between the king of France, Louis de Valois, and the duke of Burgundy, Charles the Bold. This fine episode is perhaps, when all is said and done, a weakness in the overall conception of the work inasmuch as it vies in interest with the main theme itself. But this fault, if you can call it that, takes away nothing from the simultaneously imposing and comic aspects of this opposition between the two princes—the first of whom, a supple and ambitious despot, is contemptuous of the other, a hard and bellicose tyrant who would scorn the former if he dared. Both men hate each other, but Louis braves the hatred of Charles because it is uncouth and wild; Charles fears the hatred of Louis because it comes in the form of a caress. Like a bloodhound in the vicinity of a cat, the duke of Burgundy, even though he is encamped in the heart of his dominions, gets nervous in the presence of the defenceless king of France. The duke's cruelty is born of his passions; the king's comes from his character. The Burgundian is loyal, because he is violent: he has never dreamt of hiding his bad deeds; he has no remorse, for he has forgotten his crimes just as he has forgotten his fits of anger. Louis is superstitious, perhaps because he is hypocritical: religion is not enough for the man tormented by his conscience and who has no desire to repent. But believe as he might in vain acts of expiation, the memory of the evil he has done always stays with him; it lingers there, next to the thought of the evil that he is about to do—because one always remembers what one has for a long time contemplated doing, and it cannot but be the case that one's crime, when it has been a desire and a hope, also becomes a memory. The two princes are devout, but Charles swears by his sword before swearing by God, while Louis attempts to win the saints over through pecuniary gifts or court expenses, mixes diplomacy in with his prayers, and involves even heaven in his intrigues. Should a war break out, Louis will still be mulling over its potential dangers when Charles is already enjoying the fruits of victory; the latter's politics reside entirely in his recourse to arms, but the king's eye sees farther than the duke's arms. What Walter Scott ends up demonstrating, by pitting these two rivals against one another, is just how much stronger prudence is than daring and how the man who appears to fear nothing is actually afraid of the man who seems in dread of everything.

With what skill does the illustrious writer portray the king of France for us when, through a refinement of deceit, he turns up at the palace of his "fair cousin" from Burgundy and asks for his hospitality—at the very moment when that haughty vassal is on the point of declaring war on him! And what could be more dramatic than having the news of a revolt, fomented in the duke's domains by the agents of the king, fall on the two princes like a bolt from the blue at the very moment when they are seated at the same table! Thus, one act of fraud is thwarted by another, and the prudent Louis finds that he has handed himself over, defenceless, to the vengeance of a legitimately irate enemy! History certainly gives some account of all this, but here I would rather believe in the novel than in history, because I prefer moral truth to historical truth. Perhaps an even more remarkable scene is the one in which the two princes, between whom even the wisest of counsels have not yet succeeded in bringing about a rapprochement, are reconciled through an act of cruelty that the one imagines and the other carries out.[4] For the first time, they share a hearty laugh born of pleasure, and this laughter, provoked by an act of torture, momentarily dissolves the bad blood between them; this is a terrifying idea, which makes one shiver with admiration.

We have heard criticisms directed at the depiction of the Orgy: that it is hideous and revolting.[5] As far as we are concerned, it constitutes one of the finest chapters in this book. Walter Scott, having taken it upon himself to portray that famous brigand called "the Wild Boar of the Ardennes," would have failed in his enterprise if the scene had not provoked horror. A writer must always engage unreservedly with the dramatic elements facing him and look for the heart of the matter in all things. There, and there alone, are emotion and interest to be found. It is only timid minds who capitulate in the face of an intense conception and beat a retreat from the path that they have chosen for themselves.

We will justify, in the light of this same principle, two other passages that appear to us no less worthy of being meditated upon and commended. The first is the execution of Hayraddin, that singular character, whom the author could perhaps have put to even greater use.[6] The second is the chapter where King Louis XI, arrested by order of the duke of Burgundy, arranges in his prison through Tristan l'Hermite for the punishment of the astrologer who deceived him.[7] It is a strangely beautiful idea to have displayed this cruel king in such a light for us—this king who even in a prison cell finds enough room for his vengeance; who demands that his remaining servants become executioners; and who exercises the last vestiges of his authority by ordering that a man be tortured to death.

We could make many more such observations, and go on to try and demonstrate the ways in which Sir Walter Scott's new drama seems faulty to us, particularly in its concluding act; but the estimable novelist would no doubt have much better grounds for justifying himself than we would have for attacking him, and it is not against such a formidable champion that our feeble weapons would be tried out to best advantage. We will limit ourselves to pointing out to him that the bit of repartee he places in the mouth of the duke of Burgundy's fool upon King Louis XI's arrival at Peronne actually belongs to Francis the First's fool, who uttered it at the time of Charles Quint's passage through France in 1535. This poor fool owes his immortality to that one bit of repartee, so he should be allowed to keep it.[8] We likewise believe that the ingenious expedient used by the astrologer Galeotti to escape from Louis XI had already been imagined a few thousand years before by a philosopher whom Dionysius of Syracuse wanted to put to death.[9] We do not attach to these remarks any more importance than they merit: a novelist is not a writer of chronicles. We are merely astonished that, in the council of Burgundy, the king should find himself addressing "the Knights of the Holy Spirit"—that order having been founded only a century later by Henry III. Indeed, we believe that the order of Saint Michael, with which the worthy author decorates his brave Lord Crawford, was only instituted by Louis XI after his captivity [in Burgundy]. May Sir Walter Scott permit us these little chronological

quibbles: in gaining a tiny pedantic victory over such a learned and illustrious archeologist, we cannot deny ourselves that innocent joy which
overcame young Quentin Durward after he had unhorsed the Duke of
Orleans and held his own against Dunois, and we would be tempted to
beg his pardon for our victory with the same words Charles Quint
addressed to the Pope [after the sack of Rome in 1527]: "*Sanctissime pater,
indulge victori.*"

Since we have taken Sir Walter Scott to task for his choice of royal
protagonist, we will not draw this article to a close before thanking him
for his touching and clever preface.[10] His old marquis never fails to elicit
smiles and tears. It is by no means our intention here to stir up the slightest partisan reaction! If there are, as one hears tell, Frenchmen out there
who dare to laugh at a few old men, Frenchmen like themselves, who
have lived in exile and who are dying in poverty—let them read the preface to *Quentin Durward* and they will surely make their peace with those
whose misfortunes come from acting honourably. We only regret that
this service has been rendered them by a foreigner. As for us, it has always
been our belief that there could well be things in the world that are more
worthy of ridicule than old age and adversity.

2. Preface to *Nouvelles Odes* (1824)

[Hugo's Preface to his *Nouvelles Odes*, dated February 1824 and published
in March of that year (*OC* 2.469-76), makes particularly manifest the tension between political conservatism and artistic innovation that is a hall-
mark of the early Hugo, up to and including *Bug-Jargal*. Here, he is
building on the much shorter prefaces to the first two editions of his *Odes*,
published in June 1822 and 1823 (*OC* 2.5, 2.27-28), where he argued
that, throughout history, poetry has always been "judged from the exalted
perspective of monarchical ideas and religious beliefs," and explained that
his decision to write odes was motivated by the fact that their "austere,
consoling, and religious language is the very thing required by an old
society in the process of leaving behind the saturnalia of atheism and anarchy that have left it staggering" (2.28). As one critic puts it, "the principal themes developed by Hugo [in the 1824 preface] show no rupture in
relation to his previous theses, but they are deployed with a new assurance" (Degout 408). These conservative theses are maintained in the next
version of this essay, which serves as the preface for his *Odes et Ballades*,
published in August 1826 (*OC* 2.709-13), but that later version already
shows a growing sensitivity to the values of liberty and originality, and

offers a stronger and more overtly Romantic critique than does the 1824 preface of classical authors who "confuse routine with art" (2.712). (Several minor footnotes of Hugo's have been left out or incorporated into the text.)]

Here are new proofs for or against the system of lyric composition sketched out elsewhere [in the 1823 preface] by the author of these Odes. It is not without an extreme reluctance that he offers them up for the consideration of people of taste: for, if he believes in theories that have been generated by conscientious study and diligent meditation, by contrast he believes very little in his own talent. For this reason, he begs those insightful men who, no doubt with justification, will pass negative judgment upon his poetical efforts to be so good as not to extend that judgment to his literary principles. One can, after all, hardly blame Aristotle for the Abbé d'Aubignac's tragedies![11]

However, despite the author's lack of renown, he has already had the sorrow of seeing his literary principles, which he thought irreproachable, slandered or at least poorly interpreted. This is what has now decided him to fortify this new publication with a simple and forthright declaration which should safeguard him from any suspicion of heresy in the quarrel that is currently setting members of the reading public against one another. There are now two parties in literature as in government, and the poetic war does not appear as if it is going to be any less cut-throat than the social war is violently impassioned. The two camps seem more eager to fight than to negotiate. They steadfastly refuse to speak the same language. They only know one way of talking: watchwords for those who are of their party and battle cries for those who are not. That is no way to come to an understanding with other people.

Still, some important voices have for some time now made themselves heard above the clamouring of the two armies. Peacemakers, offering words of wisdom, have taken up a position between the two attacking fronts. Perhaps they will be the first to be immolated, but what does that matter! It is among their ranks that the author of this book wishes to be placed, even at the risk of being confounded with them. He will discuss matters, if not with the same authority, then at least with the same good faith. He does not expect to be spared the strangest imputations, the most peculiar accusations. Given people's current state of agitation, the danger of speaking is even greater than that of remaining silent, but when what is at stake is providing and gaining insight you have to look to where duty lies and not to where the peril is. The author thus resigns himself to the task: he will, without wavering, air the most delicate questions and, like the little Theban child, he will dare to give the lion's mane a tug.

And, for a start, so as to bestow some dignity on this impartial discussion, in which it is much less a question of the author casting light upon the matter than of his seeking it, he repudiates all those conventional terms that the contending parties are throwing at one another like deflated balloons— signs that signify nothing, expressions that express nothing, vague words that each person defines according to the requirements of his hatreds and his prejudices and that only serve as justifications for those who do not have any. As for him, he really does not have a glimmer of an idea as to what is meant by the "classical genre" and the "romantic genre." According to a woman of genius, who was the first person to utter the words "romantic literature" in France, "this division refers to the world's two great epochs, that which preceded the establishment of Christianity and that which followed it."[12] According to the literal meaning of this explanation, it would appear that *Paradise Lost* is a *classical* poem and *La Henriade* a *romantic* work.[13] Rigorous proof that the two words imported by Madame de Staël are understood in this way today is, it would appear, lacking.

In literature, as in all things, there is only the good and the bad, the beautiful and the misshapen, the true and the false. Now, without drawing parallels that would require provisos and qualifications, the *beautiful* in Shakespeare is just as classical (if *classical* signifies worthy of being studied) as the *beautiful* in Racine, and the *false* in Voltaire is just as romantic (if *romantic* means bad) as the *false* in Calderón.[14] These are the sort of simple truths that seem more like pleonasms than axioms, but is there any depth to which one does not have to stoop when trying to prevail upon obstinacy and to unsettle bad faith?

It will perhaps be objected here that for some time now the acceptation of the two slogans has changed, and that certain critics have come to an agreement that they will henceforth honour with the name *classical* all mental productions dating from before our own age, while the label *romantic* would be limited in particular to that literature which has arisen and developed in the nineteenth century. Before examining what it is about this literature that is particular to our own century, one has to wonder what there is about it that could have merited, or incurred, a special designation. It has been acknowledged that each literature bears the imprint, be it more or less deeply, of the climes, the customs, and the history of the people of whom it is the expression. Thus it is that there are as many diverse literatures as there are different societies. David, Homer, Virgil, Tasso, Milton, and Corneille: these men, each of whom represents a form of poetry and a nation, have among them nothing in common except genius. Each of them expressed and fecundated public thought in his country and in his time. Each of them created for his social sphere a world of ideas and feelings appropriate to the orientation and the size of that sphere. Why, then, group their creations under a vague collective rubric? For despite their all being animated by the same spirit, the spirit of truth, these creations are nonetheless dissimilar and often anti-thetical in form, content, and nature. And why this bizarre contradiction of conferring on another literature—which is the as yet imperfect expres-sion of an as yet incomplete era—the honour, or the insult, of an equally vague but exclusive label which separates it from the literatures that pre-ceded it? As if it could only be weighed in the other tray of the scales! As if it could only be entered at the back of the book in which literary records are kept! Where did it get this name *romantic*? Have you per-chance detected some glaring and deep-rooted connection with the *Romanic* or *Romance* languages? If so, explain yourselves: let us examine the worth of this allegation. First of all, prove that it is founded; even then, you will still have to show that it is not a trivial one.

But these days people take good care not to broach a discussion along such lines, which might only engender the *ridiculus mus*.[15] People want this word *romantic* to retain a certain fantastic, indefinable vagueness that redoubles the horror it provokes. And so it is that all the anathemas cast against illustrious contemporary writers and poets can be reduced to this mode of argument: "We condemn the literature of the nineteenth cen-tury, because it is *romantic* ..." "And why is it *romantic*?" "Because it is the literature of the nineteenth century." After close examination, one dares to affirm here that the evidence on which such reasoning is based does not appear totally incontestable.

But let us leave this question of words behind; it can only satisfy those superficial minds whose risible purview it is. Let us leave them in peace, that procession of rhetors and pedagogues, as they solemnly bear fresh water to the empty tub. Let us wish them much wind, all those poor out-of-breath Sisyphuses, as they roll their stone and roll it again, endlessly, to the top of a little hill:

Palus inamabilis undâ;
Alligat, et novies Styx interfusa coercet.[16]

Let us move on, and take up the question of the things themselves, for the futile quarrel of the *romantics* and the *classics* is simply the parodic echo of an important discussion that is currently occupying those with discerning minds and meditative souls. Let us then leave behind the *Batrachomyomachia* for *The Iliad*.[17] Here, at least, adversaries can hope to come to an understanding, because they are worthy of it. When it comes to the rats and the frogs, the discordance is absolute, whereas with Achilles and Hector there exists a deep-rooted connection, one of nobility and grandeur.

It has to be admitted that a transformation, broad-ranging and deep, is being brought to bear from within on the literature of this century. A few distinguished men find this astonishing; as it so happens, their surprise is the only astonishing thing about what is happening. Indeed, if—after a political revolution which affected all levels of society from top to bottom, which touched on every glory and every infamy, which disunited everything and mixed it all together, to the point of erecting scaffolds in the military camps and placing the executioner's axe under the protection of the soldier's blade; after a dreadful upheaval that has stirred up every recess of the human heart, displaced every aspect of the order of things—if, we say, after such a tremendous event no change in the spirit and character of a people were discerned, would that not be a proper cause for astonishment, indeed for an astonishment without bounds? Here, one could raise a specious objection that has already been put forward with a conviction worthy of respect by men of talent and authority. It is, they say, precisely because this *literary revolution* is the result of our *political revolution* that we deplore its triumph and condemn its works. But this inference seems incorrect. Literature of the present day can be in part the *result* of the revolution without being the *expression* of it. The society fashioned by the revolution had its literature, and like that society it was hideous and fatuous. That literature and that society died together, and they will not be revived. Wherever you look, order is returning to institutions as it is to the world of letters. Religion consecrates liberty: now we have citizens. Faith purifies the imagination: now we have poets. The truth is returning, everywhere: in customs, laws, the arts. The new literature is true. What does it matter if this literature is the result of the revolution? Is the harvest any less lovely because it has ripened on the volcano? What connection do you see between the lava that destroyed your house and the ear of corn that nourishes you?

The world's greatest poets came on the scene after great public calamities. Leaving aside the holy bards, who were always inspired by past or future misfortunes, we behold Homer appearing after the fall of Troy and the catastrophes of the Argolid, and Virgil after the triumvirate. Caught up in the midst of the conflict between Guelphs and Ghibellines, Dante was a proscript before being a poet. Milton was conceiving Satan while serving Cromwell. The murder of Henry IV preceded Corneille. Racine, Molière, and Boileau all lived through the stormy days of the Fronde. After the French revolution, Chateaubriand comes to the fore, and the balance is maintained.

Let us not, moreover, be astonished by this remarkable link between the eras of great political upheaval and those of literary grandeur. The grim, imposing course of events through which the power from above makes its presence felt to the powers here below; the eternal unity of their cause; the solemn harmony of what results from them: there is something about all this that affects the mind deeply. What is sublime and immortal in mankind awakens, as if started out of its sleep, at the sound of all those marvellous voices that tell of God. In a religious silence, from catastrophe to catastrophe, a people's spirit hears the long reverberations of the mysterious word that bears witness in the darkness:

Admonet, et magna testatur voce per umbras.[18]

Some chosen souls harvest this word and become the stronger for it; when it has ceased thundering in the realm of events, this word is heard a second time, exploding in their works of inspiration, and thus it is that heavenly teachings are perpetuated in poetry. Such is the mission of genius: its elect are "those watchmen set by the Lord upon the walls of Jerusalem, which shall never hold their peace day nor night."[19]

Literature of the present day, as it has been created by the likes of Chateaubriand, Staël, and Lamennais thus in no way belongs to the revolution. Just as sophistical and disorderly writings by the likes of Voltaire, Diderot, and Helvétius were expressions, before the fact, of the social innovations hatched in the waning days of the last century, contemporary literature—which is attacked so instinctively on one side [by the liberals], and so unwisely on the other [by the royalists]—is the anticipatory expression of the religious and monarchical society that will no doubt emerge from out of the midst of so much old rubble, so many fresh ruins. It must be said, and said again: it is not a need for novelty that drives people on, but a need for truth, and this need is immense.

Most of the superior writers of the age tend to satisfy this need for truth. Taste, which is nothing other than *authority* in literature, has taught them that their works, true as far as the content goes, must be equally true in the form they adopt; in this respect, these writers have helped poetry take a step forward. Writers hailing from other places and other times, even the admirable poets of the seventeenth century, too often forgot in the execution of their works the principle of truth with which they were infusing them. In their loveliest passages, one frequently comes across details borrowed from customs, religions, or epochs that are too divorced from the subject matter. Thus, the *clock* which, to Voltaire's great amusement, alerts Shakespeare's Brutus to the hour when he must strike Caesar, this same *clock*—which existed, as one can see, long before there were any clockmakers—crops up in the middle of a splendid description of the mythological gods by Boileau,[20] who places it "in the hand of Time." In "Ode on Namur," the *cannon*—with which Calderón arms the soldiers of Heraclius, as Milton does his rebel angels—is fired by "ten thousand valiant Alcides" who make "the ramparts crackle" with them. Now, most assuredly, if the legislator of Parnassus has his Alcides fire off a cannon, then Milton's *Satan* can look upon this anachronism as a fair enough way of staging war. If, in a still barbarous literary epoch, Father Lemoyne,[21] author of a poem on *Saint Louis*, has "the horns of the black Eumenides ... sound the Sicilian Vespers," an enlightened age shows us J.-B. Rousseau sending (in his "Ode to the Comte de Luc," whose lyrical effects are altogether remarkable) a "faithful prophet all the way to the gods to interrogate his Fate."[22] And while agreeing that the *Nereids* with which Camoëns importunes Gama's companions are altogether ridiculous,[23] one would hope, in Boileau's celebrated "Passage of the Rhine,"* to see something other than "fearful naiads" fleeing before Louis, king of France and Navarre by the grace of God, accompanied by his brigadier-generals.

Quotations of this sort could be drawn out to infinity, but there is no point in piling up more of them. If such faults with regard to truth show up frequently in our best authors, one should guard against putting them on trial for it. No doubt they could have confined themselves to studying the pure forms of the Greek divinities without borrowing their pagan attributes. When at Rome they wanted to convert an *Olympian Jupiter* into *Saint Peter*, they at least began by removing from the master of thunder the eagle that he was trampling underfoot. But when one considers the immense services rendered to the language and to the world of letters

---

* People with open minds will have no trouble understanding why we are frequently citing the name of Boileau here. Faults in taste, in a man of such pure taste, have something striking about them that makes them a useful example. That the absence of truth runs very much counter to poetry must be the case, since it spoils even Boileau's verse. As for the malicious critics who would like to interpret these quotations as evidencing a lack of respect for a great name, let them be informed that no one has a greater esteem for this excellent mind than the author of this book. Boileau shares with our Racine *sole* credit for having fixed the French language, which is proof enough that he also possessed a *creative genius*.

by our first great poets, one stands humbled before their genius and does not feel it in one to reproach them with a defective taste. Certainly this defect was extremely regrettable, since it introduced into France what you might call a false genre, which has been very aptly named the *scholastic genre*—one that is to the *classical* what superstition and fanaticism are to religion—and which today only stands as a counterbalance to the triumph of true poetry because of the respectable authority of the illustrious masters whose works, unfortunately, serve as models for it. In the above paragraph, we gathered together a few interchangeable examples of this false taste, culled from writers who could not be more different from one another: on the one hand, those whom the scholastics call *classics* and, on the other, those whom they label *romantics*. The purpose of this little exercise was to show that if Calderón could sin through a surfeit of ignorance, Boileau could err through a surfeit of knowledge, and to show, moreover, that while it is true, when studying the latter's writings, that one must religiously follow the rules the critic imposed on the language,* one must at the same time scrupulously guard against adopting the false turns of speech the poet sometimes employed.

Let us further note in passing that if the literature of that grand age when Louis the Great reigned [1643-1715] had invoked Christianity instead of worshipping pagan gods, if its poets had been what those of primitive times had been—namely, priests singing the great deeds of their religion and their fatherland—then the triumph of the *sophistic* doctrines of the last century would have been much more difficult, perhaps even impossible. No sooner had the innovators begun their attacks than religion and morals would have taken refuge in the sanctuary of the world of

---

* Let us insist on this point in order to deprive those of malevolent intent with the slightest pretext. If it is useful and sometimes necessary to inject new life into a few worn-out turns of phrase, to reinvigorate a few old expressions, and perhaps to persevere in the attempt at embellishing our versification by means of the plenitude of metre and the purity of rhyme, it cannot be repeated often enough that this is as far as the improving impulse should go. All innovation contrary to the nature of our prosody and the genius of our language must be exposed as an assault on the first principles of taste.

After such a frank declaration, it will no doubt be permitted to point out to the *hypercritics* that true talent rightly looks upon the rules as the boundary that one must never cross, and not as the path that one must always follow. The rules continually draw our thinking back to a single centre—the *beautiful*—but they do not circumscribe our thinking. The rules are to literature what laws are to morals: they cannot foresee everything. A man will never gain a reputation for being virtuous simply for having restricted his conduct to the observance of the Code. A poet will never gain a reputation for being great simply for having contented himself with writing according to the rules. Morality is not the result of laws, but of religion and virtue. Literature does not live by taste alone; it must be infused with poetry and fecundated by genius.

letters, under the protection of so many great men. National taste, accustomed to not separating the notions of religion and of poetry, would have repudiated every attempt at irreligious poetry and stigmatized that monstrosity as being no less a literary than a social sacrilege. Who can reckon what would have happened to *philosophy*, if the cause of God, defended in vain by virtue, had also been pleaded by genius. But France did not have this good fortune: its national poets were almost all pagan poets, and our literature was rather the expression of an idolatrous and democratic society than of a monarchical and Christian one. Thus it was that the philosophers managed, in less than a century, to drive out of people's hearts a religion that held no place in their minds.

It is above all to repair the damage done by the sophists that the poet of today must apply himself. He must march ahead of the people and, like a light, show them the way. He must lead them back to all the great principles of order, morals, and honour; furthermore, that his power be agreeable to them, all the strings of the human heart must vibrate under his fingers like the strings of a lyre. He will never be the echo of any word, unless it be the word of God. He will always remember what his predecessors have too often lost sight of: that he also has a religion and a fatherland. His poems will ceaselessly sing the glories and misfortunes of his country, the austerities and the raptures of his creed; they will do so in order that his forbears and his contemporaries may harvest something of his genius and of his soul, and so that, in days to come, other peoples do not say of him: "That man sang in a barbarous land."

In quâ scribebat, barbara terra fuit![24]

Endnotes to Appendix C

1 In French in Scott's original. ("War is my country, / My harness is my home, / And wheresoe'er I roam / Battling's the life for me.")

2 This and the next two sentences refer to Napoleon; Hugo excised them from the 1834 version of the article.

3 In the 1834 version, this paragraph is replaced by the following key statement: "After the picturesque, but prosaic, novel of Walter Scott, there remains yet another novel to create, one that will be, as far as we are concerned, more beautiful and even more comprehensive: namely, the novel—at once drama and epic, picturesque yet poetic, real yet ideal, true yet noble—that will embed Walter Scott in Homer." The subsequent paragraph disparaging Scott's choice of Louis XI is dropped—understandably, given that in 1831 Hugo had chosen the same historical backdrop for his *Notre-Dame de Paris*!

4 Hugo is referring here to the end of Chapter 33, "The Herald," when Charles decides to treat the false herald Rouge Sanglier as a beast of chase and set boar-hounds on him. "Not even Charles himself," we are told, "was so delighted with the sport as King Louis, who, partly from political considerations, and partly as being naturally pleased with the sight of human suffering when ludicrously exhibited, laughed till the tears ran from his eyes, and in his ecstasies of rapture, caught hold of the Duke's ermine cloak, as if to support himself; whilst the Duke, no less delighted, flung his arm around the King's shoulder, making thus an exhibition of confidential sympathy and familiarity very much at variance with the terms on which they had so lately stood together" (420-21).

5 See Chapter 22, "The Revellers," where William De la Marck has the Bishop of Liege brutally murdered at a banquet.

6 See Chapter 34, "The Execution." (Hayraddin Maugrabin, or Hayraddin the African Moor, is the gypsy who had been masquerading as the herald Rouge Sanglier.)

7 See Chapter 28, "Uncertainty," where Louis makes plans for killing his astrologer Martius Galeotti, who maliciously encouraged the king's calculated decision to place himself in the power of his rival, the duke of Burgundy.

8 See the end of Chapter 25, "The Unbidden Guest."

9 See Chapter 29, "Recrimination," where Galeotti succeeds in circumventing Louis's murderous intentions by predicting that his own death "shall take place exactly twenty-four hours before that of your Majesty" (371).

10 In the 1834 version, Hugo suppresses this final paragraph—one that is clearly generated by the anti-revolutionary, pro-monarchical views that were so dear to him in 1823. (Scott's gently ironic portrait of the Marquis de Hautlieu identifies him as "one of the few fine old specimens of nobility who are still be found in France"; Scott's narrator visits with the Marquis in his family's dilapidated chateau, which had been looted by a "revolutionary mob" in 1790 [33].)

11 Author of the *Pratique du Théâtre* (1657), a commentary on Aristotle's *Poetics*, as well as of a number of wretched tragedies written to confirm the rules laid down in the *Pratique*. As the young Hugo stated elsewhere, "the Abbé d'Aubignac confined himself to *following* the rules, Racine to *not breaking them*" (OC 2.535-36).

12 From Madame de Staël's *De l'Allemagne* (1810), Book 2, Chapter 11 ("De la poésie classique et de la poésie romantique").

13 A derisory contrast between Milton's great epic poem (1667) and Voltaire's failed epic tribute to Henry IV (1723/28). Voltaire was a favourite target of the young Hugo, who referred to him as "that ingrate who profaned the chastity of the muse and the holiness of the fatherland" (*OC* 2.449), and imputed to him a good many of the "monstrous" aspects of the "deplorable" French Revolution (2.451).

14 Pedro Calderón de la Barca (1600-81), Spanish playwright who, like Shakespeare, was looked down upon at the time by the more fastidious advocates of classicism, for whom the tightly-knit tragedies of Racine (1639-99) were the model that dramatists should seek to imitate.

15 "Absurd mouse," from Horace, *Ars Poetica*, l.139: "The mountains will go into labour; an absurb mouse will be born." (Hugo also uses this phrase in Chapter 16 of *Bug-Jargal*.)

16 Virgil, *Aeneid*, Book 4, 438-39 ("The drear hateful swamp / Has pinned them down here, and the Styx that winds / Nine times around exerts imprisoning power" [175]). (Also in *Georgics*, Book 4, 479-80.)

17 Commonly attributed to Homer, the *Combat of the Rats and Frogs* is a parody of the epic battles in *The Iliad*.

18 Virgil, *Aeneid*, Book 6, 619 ("Phlegyas in his misery teaches all souls / His lesson, thundering out amid the gloom" [181]).

19 Isaiah 62.6.

20 Nicolas Boileau-Despréaux (1636-1711), author of the influential *Art poétique* (1674), a treatise in verse that laid out the aesthetic rules that Classicism would follow and Romanticism contest. Hugo also refers here to Boileau's little-prized "Ode sur la prise de Namur" (1693).

21 Pierre Lemoyne (1602-72), a Jesuit priest who wrote the epic poem *Saint Louis, ou la Couronne reconquise sur les infidèles* (1653).

22 Jean-Baptiste Rousseau (1671-1741), French lyric poet, known as the "Pindar of the Regency"; still respected by some anti-Romantic critics in the 1820s, but on the point of having his reputation definitively demolished by Hugo's friend Sainte-Beuve in a scathing 1829 article.

23 Luis de Camões recounts the adventures of the Portuguese explorer Vasco da Gama in his epic poem *Os Lusíades* (1572).

24 Ovid, *Tristia*, Book 3, l.18.

Appendix D: Contemporary Reviews

[As Max Bach put it in an article devoted to reviews of Hugo's early novels, "Hugo's ambiguous attitude on the colonial question and on the emancipation of slaves [in *Bug-Jargal*] left everyone dissatisfied" (143). Of the following five reviews, virtually all of them, while focusing on the novel's literary merits or lack thereof, also find time to discuss its historical accuracy and its political ramifications, often from highly partisan perspectives that range from the extremely conservative (e.g., *Le Drapeau blanc*) to the solidly liberal (e.g., *Le Globe*). A significant exception to this is the last review, written by the famous critic Charles-Augustin Sainte-Beuve in 1832 as part of an overview of Hugo's first four novels. Sainte-Beuve's evolutionary thesis—that Hugo's first novels lack the "maturity" one finds in *Notre-Dame de Paris*—establishes one of the main tropes of Hugo criticism: *Bug-Jargal*, along with his other "immature" novel, *Han of Iceland*, is already being shunted to the margins of Hugo's oeuvre. Significantly enough, perhaps, Sainte-Beuve's review—full of biographical and thematic insights into the novel—makes no mention of the slave revolt, which still features prominently in the other four reviews. It is not just *Bug-Jargal* that is being shunted to the margins in Sainte-Beuve's review, the first serious piece of Hugo criticism; revolutionary transatlantic history is being exiled as well in an act of critical omission that has had far-reaching effects on mainstream Hugo criticism up to and including the present.]

1. From *Le Globe* (*Journal littéraire*) (2 March 1826)

There is nothing more awkward than discussing a novel. To do so is to take away the great source of interest that for many readers, and especially for women, resides in curiosity and surprise. So let us be careful not to summarize the contents of *Bug-Jargal*, and merely urge each of you to read it.

It will suffice simply to provide an idea of the setting and the subject matter. During one of the revolutionary wars, some officers have agreed to fill the long nights spent bivouacking by telling, each in turn, the tale of one of their adventures; when Captain Leopold d'Auverney's turn comes up, he tells the story of Bug-Jargal. This choice of structure is perhaps not a happy one—not because, as one could very well object, nights out on a bivouac are spent sleeping rather than telling stories, but because placing a tale in the mouth of a fictional character precludes the sort of reflections, descriptions, and limitless details that a writer speaking in his own name can permit himself. Now, as it happens, the author has not spared us any of those sorts of things. This narration features speeches, dialogues, artistically composed descriptive passages, all of which deprive the young officer's tale of any appearance of free and natural improvisation. This lack of verisimilitude is glaring because gratuitous. To be sure, the same rules do not apply to writing as they do to talking, and a certain amount of artfulness is to be expected; nevertheless, one needs to keep a certain sense of proportion and not forget that a "tale under the tent" ought to avoid giving the appearance of a book. The short stories of Monsieur Xavier de Maistre [in *Voyage autour de ma chambre* (1794)], for example, could very well be taken as tales that were actually told, heard straight from the mouth of those who play a role in them. When reading *Bug-Jargal*, it is impossible to accept that premise.

Another weak point stemming from the same cause is that the author is obliged to bestow an important role upon the narrator, even though he is not the tale's hero. Born in France, d'Auverney crossed over to Saint Domingue where he fell in love with Marie, the daughter of his uncle, a rich planter in the colony. The very day he marries her, the insurrection at the Cape breaks out and his happiness is forever blighted. The heroic conduct of a Negro who endeavours to save him and Marie, and who manages to combine a generous attitude toward whites with a passion for the liberty of blacks, is the true subject-matter of the novel and its principal source of interest. But since d'Auverney is the one speaking, we inevitably hear him talk about his personal feelings, his love, his unhappiness; the author has thereby limited himself, of his own accord, to making the entire Saint Domingue revolution pivot around a sentimental episode that inspires only the vaguest of interest. Again, he has only himself to blame for this drawback. The young Frenchman, melancholy lover and impassioned dreamer like all heroes in the poems and novels of today, does not have an individual character that in any way connects up with the time and place of the action.

A great deal more could be said about the way that events are presented: relegated to the background, the historical tableaux always give the impression of being parasitical ornamentation, even though they are, without a doubt, the most novel and remarkable aspect of the work. This stems from the general flaw in the way the author has gone about composing it: too often the author manages to tie his novelistic intrigue to real events only at the expense of verisimilitude and, especially, of clarity—a far more precious quality than verisimilitude. He finds himself obliged to resort to mysterious goings-on, to disguises and surprises. It is all too evident that the tale has been put together in a slap-dash manner.

Bug-Jargal is himself the biggest source of improbability, and the one most open to reproach. He is, as it happens, [to cite the title of Joseph Lavallée's novel *Le nègre comme il y a peu de blancs* (1789)] "a negro as there are few" and even "as there are few white men." He is a model of magnanimity, unselfishness, courage, abnegation, gentleness, delicacy, and good taste. He knows two or three languages; he writes romances; he plays the guitar; he is the son of an African king; he has been taught by Europeans; he reasons like [the Enlightenment philosopher] Raynal, loves like [Goethe's proto-Romantic hero] Werther, and has the size and strength of Hercules. To be sure, I am not of the opinion that there is any fine quality which is inaccessible to the African race, and our author has every right to make a hero out of his negro. But what I would have liked was a hero characterized by the contrast between an uncultivated and a generous attitude, between a ferocious and a merciful disposition, between ignorance and genius. I would have liked to see how a good, energetic nature overcame in him the flaws arising from his servile upbringing and the habits acquired as a result of this. Alongside his virtues and his noble instincts— the blatant signs of his distinction among men—I would have liked to have witnessed him struggling with the unbridled needs and brutal passions that reveal a man who is still a slave and half wild, and which would stand as the proof of his origin and the mark of his chains. A great negro man must be, as has been said of a Shakespearean tragedy, a mixture of the sublime and the uncouth. I can certainly see why it would, in this respect, be terribly difficult to get it right and strike a perfect balance; one would always reach a point at which one was obliged to represent this reality solely by means of the ideal. But if the ideal is almost always the impossible, it is neither the false, nor the factitious, nor even the improbable: it must call to mind that reality of which it is not the exact copy but the pure conception. This is one of the prime resources and one of the first rules of the fine arts. I regret that the author of *Bug-Jargal* paid it no heed. Had he done so, he would have avoided a real flaw in the book without sacrificing a single one of its charms.

Nevertheless, one cannot help taking an interest in this black man of his, and the tale has a kind of intensity and forward momentum that scarcely allows one to put the book down. Moreover, the subject-matter is new, the events treated are momentous, and the author has talent. Especially notable is the singular and striking depiction of the black chief Biassou in the midst of his army. It has pleased the author to bestow upon him some of the traits of the celebrated Toussaint, and to combine the deep, abiding shrewdness that distinguished the latter with a ferocity that the historical Biassou indeed displayed but that Toussaint never possessed. This entire episode gives evidence of a lively wit; unfortunately, one is too aware of the effort and calculation that went into it. Strongly conceived is the character of a certain Habibrah—a *griffe* slave, a monster of sorts, and a jester, who cold-bloodedly cuts the throat of a master whom he has spent twenty years entertaining and who with unbending cruelty hunts down the whites whose abject servant he has been. The author has given him a speech of some eloquence, which runs the risk of being persuasive, where he talks about his condition, his sufferings, his humiliations, and his hatreds. But, once again, the laboured nature of this character makes itself felt. He is not a living man but, rather, the product of a convention, the means to an effect. What strikes me as a fine scene is the one where Biassou forces a mulatto—who under the whites had made a point of being a cruel enemy of the blacks, so as to make people forget his origins, and who, taken prisoner by the blacks, now lays claim to his colour as if it were a lifeline—to kill in cold blood a white man, his fellow captive, so as to legitimate his claim and prove his mixed blood. This manner of judging questions regarding a man's status is in character and true to the spirit of Biassou; the struggle between pity and love of life that goes on inside this wretched mulatto—the mixture of cowardice, remorse, shame, and egotism when he throws himself onto his victim, drags him down, and tears him up, guided by no other passion than fear—is an energetically conceived tableau that strikes one as both terrible and true.

Bug-Jargal is far from being a work without merit. But with his subject-matter and his talent the author could have done much better. Above all, he should have refrained from straining after so many different and conflicting stylistic effects, from imitating one literary school or author after another, depending on circumstances. Thus it is that when he has Captain d'Auverney and his sergeant converse he imitates [Laurence] Sterne, instead of undertaking to depict our camps the way they are. If he wants to represent a location in the New World, he copies the descriptive style of Monsieur de Chateaubriand, sketching brilliant but unimaginable pictures and inventing impossible landscapes. Should he wish to initiate us into the thoughts of his narrator, he turns meditative in the manner of Lord Byron. When it is his intention to guide us through the deliberations of the government on the island, or the ranks of the blacks, he gives his dramatic talents a run and tries to capture the tone of Walter Scott. Very rarely is he ever himself; in the midst of so many imitations, one never catches sight of him. One has difficulty imagining what his style would be like if those four authors I have just named had never put pen to paper.

The author of *Bug-Jargal* is not a liberal, as can be seen from certain provisos and certain epigrams. Obliged to interest himself in the blacks, and to interest readers in their favour, he has taken the greatest pains to distinguish himself from writers who have previously pleaded their cause. Without justifying the colonial regime, he seems to assume that the tyranny of the masters was an exception when it was actually the rule. To hear him tell it, one would almost believe that only blacks had the right to find that regime deleterious, and that a white man should hesitate to find fault with it and, even more so, to reform it, for fear of being mistaken for a revolutionary. This fear somewhat gets in the way of his talent, restricting his mind's freedom of movement to some extent. Nevertheless, it is certain that his general intention with regard to black people is benevolent and that, notwithstanding all the difficulties in which the double necessity of interesting in favour of their liberty and condemning all insurrection places him, whosoever reads his book will have experienced new grounds for thanking heaven for the existence and liberty of Haiti.

2. From *Le Drapeau blanc* (20 March 1826)

[In the first part of this article (15 March), signed B. d'E., the author provides a negative account of Walter Scott, which concludes with the claim that "the school that in France bears the title 'romantic' has adopted in him a dangerous model: difficult to emulate when it comes to what he excels in, too easy to imitate in his numerous faults. It is most assuredly not by following the footsteps of the illustrious Scotsman that one will succeed in producing a work of art such as every poetic composition must be, whatever name one gives to it. In my opinion, this is the only rock upon which the nascent, but already vigorous, genius of Monsieur Victor Hugo might founder. That will be the guiding assumption according to which, in an upcoming article, we will examine the latest, and be it said altogether remarkable, production of this young author."]

[...] The characters of Han of Iceland, in the novel by that name, and of Habibrah in *Bug-Jargal* are fantastic monstrosities, cast in the same mould as those one finds in the novels of Walter Scott. Monsieur Victor Hugo, like the man he has modelled himself after, has gotten his proportions all wrong. Even when it comes to grotesque figures, exaggeration is not what is called for if one wants to captivate people's imaginations, either by making them laugh or by inspiring terror in them. The author has no familiarity with such figures, as one can see from the painstaking way in which he portrays them for us, supplying even the most minor details, which at times makes them come across in a heavy-handed, monotonous way. However, in this regard, there is an essential distinction to be made between Monsieur Victor Hugo and the Scottish writer.

Indisputably, Walter Scott has a far greater mastery of his talent and his language than does his young rival, who is scarcely launched upon his career. Scott's imagination is also richer, more fertile, and more original; yet, offsetting this, it is far more shallow. Perhaps this stems from the Protestantism that can be detected in every one of Walter Scott's works, and which brings with it an array of prejudices that are often of the most vulgar kind. Monsieur Hugo is Catholic, a belief that runs deep with him, and this is warrant enough to ensure that his mind can reach the loftiest heights. He is thus very much more capable of embracing the poetic assumptions of the sort of works which feature supernatural and extraordinary beings, characters who are sublime and imposing, bizarre and fantastic. If he feels a decided vocation for reading the heavens or conjuring up infernos, let him study and he will succeed.

When I address myself to a young writer with the talent of Monsieur Hugo and suggest that he apply himself seriously to the study of poetic matters, I am by no means saying that he needs to read a lot of books or peruse a great many sources. You cannot make poetry out of erudition, and if Walter Scott has succeeded in giving us such a good sense of Scotland, that is because, acquainted with it from a very young age, he has the image of his country perpetually in his sight. By contrast, in his first novel Monsieur Victor Hugo endeavoured to depict Norway and Iceland and in *Bug-Jargal* he has done likewise with negroes and Saint Domingue; from two such visions—part erudition, part fantasy—a truly Scandinavian or a genuinely African tableau could never result. It is evident that the author has done his reading, that he has studied and learned; it is equally evident in what he has composed that none of this has yet blended together to form a fully harmonious whole.

For a poet, the veritable object of study is God, man, nature—poetry, in brief, regardless of the costume or the circumstances in which it is cloaked. The imagination of Shakespeare had certainly taken many a voyage in many a country and had absorbed a great deal; however, that poet knew one can only be at home in one's home country. Although he faithfully depicted the Romans after studying them in Plutarch's *Lives*, he has reproduced them as men, attending to their core and not, like an antiquary, to the details of their costumes and accessories, which for those who know nothing about the places in question can never convey the truth and which give the appearance of being something learnt rather than poetically apprehended. Thus, when Raphael composed works dealing with subjects that were either not Italian or were from another epoch he was content to show as much of them as the general truth required, and took good care not to abandon the Italian character and laboriously attempt to convey a sense of foreign localities with which he was not familiar. [...]

We have just examined the terrain on which the author of *Han of Iceland* and *Bug-Jargal* has constructed his stories. Now all that remains for us is to praise him in a great many respects, while nonetheless reproaching him for an overall flaw in the book's construction, a lack of harmony and wholeness in its stylistic forms, as well as for its incongruities; these incongruities serve as evidence of what must have been a strenuous effort on his part at conveying to us some sense of a world that he has never observed, and which forces him to resort to botanical nomenclature in order to give us some image of that world. We make allowances to the author for the difficulties attached to his undertaking; his attempt at making the bizarre nature of foreign men and peoples known to us has often obliged him to consult the accounts of travellers, and his compositions as a whole visibly bear the imprint of this erudition. But aside from this, we can only admire the gifted heart and mind, the strong and powerful imagination, the mighty creativity of thought which distinguish this young disciple of the muses. At times he is truly inspired, and at those moments he creates extraordinary, dramatic scenes; the way he puts things is stirring, the way he feels them is intense. One should not be astonished if, alongside so many outstanding qualities, there is lacking that maturity of mind and judgment which is only acquired with age.

The scene where the negro Biassou reviews his troops goes on too long and is too loaded down with details. It is evident that the author has consulted materials that he has not sufficiently hidden from view. Moreover, he has weighed his narrative down with reflections which give proof that he has not always mastered his subject. This scene nevertheless reveals a writer gifted with great creative powers, whose mind has a firm grasp on the character of things. Whatever its imperfections might be, this scene by itself is as good as the rest of the work put together and is worthy of holding readers' attention.

The main character, Bug-Jargal, is perhaps fantastical in certain respects, but he does move and interest the reader. The contrast between this negro and those monsters of cruelty and debauchery who go by the names of Biassou and Rigaud sets the imagination at rest and reconciles it with human nature. And yet one can scarcely accustom oneself to a Congo negro who is represented as a model of greatness, heroism, and sensibility, and who is draped in a character that is, as it were, positively chivalrous. Representing him in this way is to grant the African race a capacity for advanced civilization that it in no way possesses. But, this incidental remark aside, we do not blame Monsieur Victor Hugo for having painted his hero in the most glittering colours, thereby placing him beyond the jurisdiction of too commonplace and trivial a truth.

Perhaps it would have been preferable had the author not presented his novel in the form of a story told by one of the characters in the action, Captain d'Auverney. The result of this choice is that he himself does not come out strongly enough. His misfortunes and those of his beloved to some extent pale when compared to the other events that this officer recounts. But Monsieur Victor Hugo has taken care to inform us that *Bug-Jargal* is only a piece extracted from a series of stories that he considered publishing. Given this fact, it could be that the flaw we have just mentioned would not have been apparent in the completed version of the work.

3. From *Le Mercure du dix-neuvième siècle* 12 (1826) [Signed H. (Henri de Latouche)]

This one novel belongs to two genres: Horror and Borer. But the Borer has the upper hand. It is a long account of a paltry tale, which would scarcely have furnished enough material for a short story had the author not time and again interrupted his narrative so as to tack on to it a few commonplaces and some high-sounding tittle-tattle regarding past crimes that two peoples, who are today reunited, have a common interest in forgetting. He might well be accused of wanting to bully the future and punish the present. The book is styled an episode from the revolt of the Saint Domingue slaves in 1791. Perhaps you have some expectation that you'll find someone in whom to take an interest here? You hope that one of your options would be to feel that generous pity which Colonists full of humanity—planters who have not abused the rights of *masters*—naturally inspire when they become victims of the dreadful reaction of Blacks against tyranny. You fondly delude yourself that among these Blacks, condemned for too long a time to slavery, there will be some who will break their chains with nobility, who will show some sense of virtue amidst the horrors of a legitimate revolt. Don't you believe it. There is no one to like, there are no sentiments worthy of esteem. There is no one to like, for the Colonists are herein represented as egotists or imbeciles, who answer to the name of "colonials" and "provincials"; the negroes are stupid and barbarous, like their generalissimo Biassou. No sentiment seems generous, because those defending themselves offer only armed egotism, and liberty such as it is practised by Rigaud, Jean-François, and even Bug-Jargal, fosters no grandeur of the soul. Masters, slaves, France, the Constituent Assembly, the great name of the foremost of our orators [Mirabeau]: everything is belittled or misconstrued.

It must be granted that Bug-Jargal, called *Pierrot*, the great man of this little plot, has a few spurious qualifications for being a novelistic hero: he prides himself on obeying a point of honour, a sentiment with which savages are hardly familiar, but just when you're starting to take a liking to him, he goes and compares his submissive attitude toward a white man to that of a dog. You hear him say: "See Rask (that's the dog), I would have no problem slitting his throat, he would offer no resistance. But I could never force him to fight against me. He would not understand me. I do not understand you. I am Rask for you."

To top it all off, this slave is a King, and while he busies himself performing a few sentimental absurdities for the love of a white woman who loves another white man, this King in slave's breeches—alternating between the role of lover and leader of men—loses his own wife and allows his children to be slaughtered.

Maria is the book's heroine and the object of her love is Captain d'Auverney, who narrates the anecdote. The author presents you with the spectacle of his death four times, and four times he defers it, for the sole pleasure of describing various forms of torture. Were it not for that perverse little satisfaction, it would be impossible to explain this succession of death-rattles, for they are clumsily incorporated into the novel. The only variety in this monotonous situation is supplied by the different methods of cutting people up and killing them. The first time, it's a question of "saws, the points of sabre blades, long sail-needles, and the jaws of pairs of pincers heated in the fire." The second time, he's going to be killed with a rope like the one that hanged the negro *Leogri*. The third time, it's a dagger in the hands of an executioner that's going to do him in ... And, finally, the fourth time, there's an abyss into which he's going to be pushed—that same abyss drawn and engraved in such a burlesque fashion on the volume's frontispiece.

You are not spared the torturing of twenty other characters, nor the recitals of cannibals who come forward to crow about their heinous crimes: this little book would be an excellent manual for the use of future officers of the Inquisition. The author seems to be inviting you to a picnic—a picnic where the main fare consists of the gallows, the wooden horse, the wheel, and the knife, all of them drenched in blood. The disastrous memories of France in 1791 are often invoked here, and the looming presence of the guillotine—the "national" guillotine, as it is charitably referred to!—prominently backgrounds, as it were, this graceful tableau.

Either the author or we ourselves are strangely mistaken about the influence that literature should always strive to exercise. We had believed that its mission was one of drawing parties closer, not increasing the hatred between them. The poet's vocation, it seemed to us, was one of love and forgiveness. The pardoning of wrongs and resignation at the human condition: we thought those to be talent's due admonition. A book's principal success, so we thought, lay in bettering those who read it, in tightening the knots of fraternity, in encouraging a belief in the blessings of a world to come while mitigating the hatreds of this one.

The author of *Bug-Jargal* (the same one who gave us *Han of Iceland*) would appear not to understand this ministry, which was so evangelically filled by Fénelon and Jean-Jacques Rousseau. At least he has shown no trace of such sentiments except in an "Ode" published some time ago about the young Duke of Bordeaux ["La naissance du duc de Bordeaux" (1820)], and in some graceful stanzas addressed to a child in the latest volume of the *Romantic Annals*. Elsewhere, he seems intent on aggravating wounds, not healing them. If he comes across an open wound, be it moral or political, he gives every impression of trying to deepen it. Callow young men, who have seen nothing and suffered nothing, yours is a laughable yet also wretched undertaking: the disparaging of an entire century, of republican ideas which you understand hardly at all, and of the dead whom you have not fought against.

As a writer, the author of *Bug* lacks all modesty. At one point we find him using his own verse for the epigraph to his prose, affecting anonymity in a most jesuitical fashion; at another point, we are told that "his book has not accommodated itself to events, but the events to his book." Further on, we are informed that "the work of which this episode was to have been a part is not finished, will never be finished, is not worth the trouble of finishing"! He shows little resourcefulness when it comes to the imagination: if the monstrosities of *Han of Iceland* were what attracted attention to it, at the foreground of the new tableau there are once again monsters to catch the audience's eye. [Samuel] Richardson may have deviated from nature, but he created Grandison [in *The History of Sir*

Charles Grandison (1753-54)]. The author of *Bug* and *Han* paints a man drinking other men's blood or salt water; he paints "a hideous dwarf, moving about with exceptional rapidity on two thin, spindly legs which, when he sits down, fold up under him like the limbs of a spider. His head, awkwardly squashed between his shoulders, is accompanied by two ears so large that his fellow slaves say he uses them to dry his eyes whenever he cries."

It must surely be agreed that if it was in order to produce such winsome delicacies that the government handed out pensions to writers, then one might feel, and quite naturally so, the stirrings of a certain pity for those impoverished families in our little villages who have been expropriated in order that they might pay their "fair" share to the agents of the Crown.

To sum up, there were a great many horrors and some talent to be found in the novel *Han of Iceland*; in the novel *Bug-Jargal*, one finds the same horrors and little talent. Our "fair-minded" enemies will not be slow to associate it with our own literary doctrines and label it "romantic."

4. From C.A. Chauvet, "Des romans de M. Victor Hugo," *Revue encyclopédique* 50 (April-June 1831)

[Chauvet's lengthy retrospective of Hugo's first four novels (including the 3rd edition of *Bug-Jargal*) has as its overarching thesis the claim that "there can be no real glory in the arts without a lasting influence, and no lasting influence without a moral direction" (83). For Chauvet, himself well versed in the subject, Hugo's vague grasp on the *history* of the Saint Domingue insurrection was the primary evidence that no such "moral direction" was to be found in *Bug-Jargal*.]

[...] In *Bug-Jargal* the author has come closer [than in *Han of Iceland*] to taking the ordinary route, by placing the focus of interest on virtuous characters [instead of on monsters such as Han]. Unfortunately the assumption on which the novel is based is one that is scarcely to be found in nature: a black man head over heels in love with a white woman, and who manages to be both gallantly respectful and ardently passionate. There is, indeed, even something jarring about Bug-Jargal's chivalrous magnanimity in a book where his race is represented as being so worthy of contempt, and Marie's nullity as a character weakens the effect even more. The merit of this book lies in its fine-spun details. It abounds, especially in the opening chapters, with lively descriptions and gripping situations; in the dénouement, the scene between Duverney [*sic*] and the dwarf Habibrah on the edge of the chasm is full of dramatic intensity and provokes real terror. But, over and above this, it is as historical portraiture that *Bug-Jargal* is a defective work. It is evident from a certain vague pallor which colours over his descriptions that the author has not seen the country he is describing, nor any country that resembles it. He gives a thoroughly incomplete and inexact idea of the revolution of Saint Domingue. A peculiar state of affairs! On this canvas the details are generally true, but the overall picture is false. Monsieur Hugo has neither got to the core of his subject-matter nor embraced it. He has listened to the tales of some colonist and has not pursued the question any further, sticking to this suspect testimony, haphazardly throwing odium and ridicule on various classes of inhabitants without instructing us, as he should have, as to the deep-seated causes of the mass conflagration which devoured that fine colony. The colonist, the negrophile, the man of colour, the negro: they are all, by his account, cruel—especially the last three. But what combination of events could have led to such a depravation of human nature? Nowhere does the author provide an explanation for this, and yet such an explanation was required, both to hold the reader's interest in the subject and to ensure his comprehension of it. In Saint Domingue, there was a root cause for people's cruelty: slavery, such as it had been shaped by our colonial system. Slavery is always equally iniquitous, but it is not always equally catastrophic. In a community that is only just establishing itself, where there is little in the way of education and few means of accumulating riches or taking pleasure to extremes, the slave's situation is tolerable: between himself and his master there is no strongly drawn line of demarcation; he lives with him as with a member of his own family, and is not subjected to excessive labours. But as education and riches increase, so too, and just as rapidly, do arrogance and greed: soon, the slave becomes in the eyes of the master nothing more than an animal like any other, which he exploits according to his interests and his passions. This unfortunate wretch's life becomes so dismal that he refuses to pass it on. So it was that the Roman world eventually came to be depopulated; and so it is that the black population in our colonies, which is ever on the decrease, would end up withering away were it not continually being regenerated by the slave trade. We should add that in those colonies the aristocracy of the skin is yet another cause for the rigours of slavery—a cause that has indelible effects. It is easy to conceive that these various corrupting elements, left to ferment in the scorching climate of Saint Domingue, must have profoundly affected the natural disposition of masters and slaves. If we now take that same colony and try to imagine a white society so blinded as to fly in the face of the home country's authority by asserting democratic principles that were even more high-minded than those stirring up France at the time, and if we imagine the members of that society dedicating themselves to putting those principles into practice, but without giving any thought to the fact that they were living alongside men of colour who were half free and negroes who were slaves—any more than the demagogues in France would have worried about their beasts of burden rising up against them—then we should have no difficulty in understanding how, little by little, these two classes of oppressed people were won over by the idea of insurrection; how the authorities in the colony were forced, in order to combat the ever growing anarchy, to seek out in turn the support of one class and then the other; and how, in the end, the anarchy was only brought to a close when political power had shifted from top to bottom and been united with material force in the person of a black man of genius, Toussaint Louverture. As for the cruelty of the slaves, it can be sufficiently accounted for by the sort of education they had received: after being treated like animals, it is not the ferocity with which they reacted that should astonish one but, rather, the genius that assured their triumph. It seems to me that these are ideas that an historical novel about Saint Domingue should put into play: developing them could be very productive from a moral point of view. Why is it that the author of *Bug-Jargal* did not produce a picture of this sort? And why is it that he nowhere acknowledges Spain's role in inciting the negro insurrection and assisting it? No doubt the Spanish titles that the leaders of the revolt assumed were extremely ridiculous, but their relations with Spain are nonetheless an established fact, one which can no longer be omitted from the historical record. Whatever *Bug-Jargal*'s merits, such an incomplete picture of the Saint Domingue revolution can satisfy neither those who are familiar with it nor those who know nothing about it. [...]

5. From Charles-Augustin Sainte-Beuve, "Les Romans de Victor Hugo," *Journal des débats* (24 July 1832)

[In this 1832 article Sainte-Beuve, who that very year had become Hugo's wife Adèle's lover, provides an overview of the four novels that his friend had produced up to that point (including the 5th edition of *Bug-Jargal*). The main thesis of this article, which is notable for offering "the first comparative study of the two versions" of *Bug-Jargal* (Hovasse 545-46), is that novels, unlike poetry or drama, must be informed by a certain maturity of outlook and hence should be written only by those who have gained an extensive experience of life and the world: the novel, according to Sainte-Beuve, is "not the sort of work suited to the first flush of youth." He thus privileges Hugo's most recent novel, *Notre-Dame de Paris*, over his more "youthful" efforts, adopting an evolutionary perspective that would set the tone for much future Hugo criticism, as would his claim that Hugo's third novel, *Last Day of a Condemned Man*, marked an important step forward for him as a novelist. With that novel, Sainte-Beuve asserts, "maturity graced his genius and his temperament, at least a relative maturity; from that point on, the novel as a genre truly opened up to him. Not, to be sure, the novel steeped in the milieu of ordinary experience, caught up in the steady current of manners, passions, and human frailties—not the novel as most people know it, but his own type of novel, still a little fantastical, angular, imperious, *vertical*, so to speak: picturesque on all fronts, and simultaneously insightful, mocking, disabused. He could now give birth to *Notre-Dame de Paris*."]

[...] In a short preface added to this fifth edition of *Bug-Jargal*, Monsieur Hugo informs us that in 1818, at sixteen years of age, he wagered that he would write a novel in fifteen days and that *Bug-Jargal* was the result of this wager. And, indeed, the first edition of this short story can be found in the second volume of the *Conservateur littéraire*—a journal that the young writer, helped by his brothers and a few friends, began editing in 1819—where it was said to be part of an unpublished work entitled *Tales under the Tent*. Reshaped and rewritten almost in its entirety, it would be published by the author only in 1825 [*sic*]. Drawing these two works into relation with one another is a stimulating and useful exercise: their content and form are essentially the same, but the novel has been subject to a good many insertions and modifications over that six-year span—over a time in one's life when for a poet each passing year amounts to a revolution, a moulting of plumage and voice. This exercise, which has moreover been useful in verifying our aforestated views about the novel, is an invaluable one for tracking and laying bare the inner workings of the poet's mind over this period of time.

The first tale is a simple enough affair: it is a short story of sorts narrated by Captain Delmar during a bivouac. The more or less felicitous commentaries with which his comrades interrupt his story, the interventions of Sergeant Thaddeus (who could very well be a nephew of Corporal Trim [from Sterne's *Tristram Shandy*], a long way from home), and the role played by the lame dog Rask: these all read naturally, seeming apt and in proportion. As for the sentiments of the tale, they will assuredly seem exaggerated. The captain's impassioned friendship for Bug; the violent despair he feels while reliving the fatal events; the lasting, mysterious sorrow which has enveloped his life since that time: there is not sufficient justification for any of these in the eyes of a mature reader, in the eyes of someone who knows how affections adjust themselves, how sorrows heal over. Delmar has lost his friend, his pledged brother the negro Bug, who has saved his life and whose death he has unintentionally caused. That is the source of his eternal mourning and his stifled sobs. When the author wrote this short story friendship, solemn and magnanimous friendship, was still at the forefront of his soul—Lacedaemonian friendship such as one idealizes it at fifteen years of age. Within a few months, though, love had already supplanted this ideal, leaving the statue of [Orestes's devoted friend] Pylades to gather dust: the sentiment that had inspired the poet to write this short story must have seemed too antiquated to him and too adolescent by far. He deemed it best not to have this piece published under separate cover. His attentions and preferences would go to *Han of Iceland*.

Then, later on, no doubt having realized that when it comes to illusions there is something to be said for those one can call one's first, he returned to *Bug*, reworked it, kept the frame, but redecorated it in any number of ways: enriching his descriptions of the landscape with those hues that the Muse had recently taught him how to employ, complicating the plot, and opening his characters up to the only sentiment that has a sovereign attraction for youth, and from which arise acts of treachery and of sacrifice, rivalries and incurable wounds—namely, love. He would unveil the sweet Marie. From that moment on, beneath Bug's royal ebony beauty something radiant began to stir; d'Auverney's melancholy took on a delicately tinged blush; the gardens flowered; the verdant mornes were covered in fragrance; everything came alive. There was still that matter of a certain pledge, a word of honour given by the captain to the ferocious Biassou, whose prisoner he was; but it hardly seems natural to make him keep it when doing so can cost the life of his friend, his young wife, and himself. This word of honour given to Biassou, which was present in the first version, rang truer there than in the second, where it is accompanied by an obstinate refusal to correct the faulty French of [Biassou's] proclamation. Without belonging to the [morally lax] school of [the Jesuit Antonio] Escobar or of Machiavelli, one could, I think, characterize these scruples as inopportune vainglories and finical prejudices—as a naive quirk of the categorical and puritan good faith that comes with youth. The considerable developments that *Bug-Jargal* underwent in its second version have led to some flaws in proportion, which clash with the tale's original framework: it is a tale, one must not forget, that is delivered orally to a circle of people during a bivouac. The descriptions, the soul-searchings, the reported conversations, the diplomatic documents that are quoted at length: such things sometimes cause us to lose sight of the audience, and when the dog Rask wags his tail or Sergeant Thaddeus bursts out with an exclamation, it takes a bit of effort to remind oneself of the place and the circumstances of the tale's telling.

But the most distinctive aspect of the additions, which signals an important shift on the author's part, is that alongside Marie—which is to say grace, virginal beauty, and the blissful virtues of existence—we are now confronted, in almost parallel fashion, with the hateful, deformed, cruel aspect of human nature, a swelling evil that is personified in the dwarf Habibrah, Han of Iceland's African brother, in the same way that Marie is the sister of Ethel [in *Han of Iceland*], of Pepita the Spaniard [in *Last Day of a Condemned Man*], and the high-spirited Esmeralda [in *Notre-Dame de Paris*]. Marie and Habibrah are two warring principles: a dove's egg, a serpent's egg, each hatched by the bright heat of this rising star. This perception of the grotesque and of evil signals a true progress, a first step beyond the simple ideals of a fifteen-year-old and toward reality and its disappointments. Initially, however, this perception has an air of falsity about it, cloaking itself in the exceptional, the misshapen, the monstrous, and the imaginary, be it in the fires of the tropic's scorching clime or in Iceland's rigid grottos. In the same way that Jupiter is represented to us drawing from two urns [in Book 24 of Homer's *Iliad*], the poet possesses two types: pure good and pure evil. But Jupiter mixes the doses, whereas the poet does not. He remains caught in the realm of abstraction—especially when it comes to the perception of evil and ugliness—by dint of wanting to individualize them as one, relentlessly infernal type. It is quite evident that he has not yet lived, not yet felt the infinite measure that tempers life; he has not experienced the simultaneous taste of honey and of wormwood mixed together in the same drink. All sweet and all sour, nectar here and venom there: that is how he orders the world. "Sing, Poet, sing! Give vent to joy or to despair. Exhaust your lordly pride, *fight your fight*. Or fly away higher, to the regions of enchantment. The many strings of the lyre belong to you: sing! But you have not yet found your way down into the life that everyone leads, this human life. You have not yet arrived at the novel…!" […]

Appendix E: Historical and Cultural Sources

[A good deal of work has been done on Hugo's sources (see, notably, Debien, Etienne), not all of it as reliable as one might wish. A single example should give readers a sense of the wariness with which one needs to approach these earlier studies: in an important article published in 1952, Gabriel Debien—one of the preeminent historians of colonial Saint Domingue—stated that Hugo had three basic guides when writing his short story (301): either the 1802 or the 1812 translation of Bryan Edwards's *Historical Survey of the French Colony in the Island of St. Domingo* (1797); an anonymous pamphlet entitled *Saint-Domingue ou Histoire de ses révolutions* (1804); and Jean-Philippe Garran's multi-volume *Rapport sur les troubles de Saint-Domingue* (1797-99). This apparently authoritative claim, which gets repeated in subsequent studies (e.g., Cauna, "Sources"), proves—upon close consideration—rather misleading. First, while it is conceivable that Hugo read one of the translations of Edwards, the only direct textual evidence linking Hugo and Edwards is to be found in an anonymous 1819 *Histoire d'Haiti* (subsequently credited to Charles Malo), one section of which is an unacknowledged translation of Edwards that Hugo appropriates almost verbatim in Chapter 38 (see *Bug-Jargal* endnote 88). Second, as a comparative analysis of the two texts shows, there is not a shred of evidence that Hugo consulted the extremely rare pamphlet *Saint-Domingue*. And finally, Debien's claim that "Hugo read Garran-Coulon closely" (302) is entirely reliant on the fact that in the short story Hugo spells the name of the revolutionary leader Boukmann "Boukmant," as does Garran. Contrary to what Debien states, however, Garran was not the only writer before 1820 to use this spelling: one finds it as well in an undeniable source such as Malo—and nothing else in Garran's massive four-volume account of the events in Saint Domingue can be cited *with certainty* as having found its way directly into *Bug-Jargal*.

That said, however, existing source studies have correctly identified much of the material that Hugo appropriated in his readings about Saint Domingue. Although Hugo almost certainly made use of other, as yet unidentified sources (some of them, doubtless, oral), those assembled here and in the footnotes ought to provide readers with more than enough material to get a sense of how Hugo went about constructing his own portrait of revolutionary Saint Domingue out of the words and experiences of other writers.]

1. From Bryan Edwards, *An Historical Survey of the French Colony in the Island of St. Domingo* (1797)

[Edwards (1743-1800), member of the Jamaica parliament and zealous defender of the plantation-owning class, arrived in Saint Domingue very soon after the outbreak of the slave revolt aboard one of the three English frigates that brought, in response to pleas from the Saint Domingue Assembly, an insignificant number of rifles and ammunition to aid the besieged city of the Cape. Sympathetic to the plight of the white colonists, he made unavailing efforts at getting Jamaica to provide them with more aid. Britain was not interested in helping the French colonists, although two years later it would embark on a costly and futile invasion of the island which lasted five years and cost the lives of some fifteen thousand soldiers (Geggus, *Haitian* 20).

Debien states that Edwards was "the essential source for the young Victor Hugo," adding that "perhaps he even found the idea for his novel in it" (301), but as we have just seen Hugo's access to Edwards was most probably more indirect than Debien claims. Be that as it may, the famous description in Chapter 6 of Edwards's *Historical Survey* of the events leading up to and following upon August 22 certainly fed into Hugo's representation of the Saint Domingue revolt—if not in the English original, or the at times periphrastic 1802 and 1812 translations, then at the very least in the anonymous 1819 *Histoire de l'île de Saint-Domingue*, republished in a new edition in 1825 as *Histoire d'Haiti* by Charles Malo.]

I am now to enter on the retrospect of scenes, the horrors of which imagination cannot adequately conceive nor pen describe. The disputes and contests between different classes of French citizens, and the violences of malignant factions towards each other, no longer claim attention. Such a picture of human misery;—such a scene of woe, presents itself, as no other country, no former age has exhibited. Upwards of one hundred thousand savage people, habituated to the barbarities of Africa, avail themselves of the silence and obscurity of the night, and fall on the peaceful and unsuspicious planters, like so many famished tygers thirsting for human blood. Revolt, conflagration and massacre, every where mark their progress; and death, in all its horrors, or cruelties and outrages, compared to which immediate death is mercy, await alike the old and the young, the matron, the virgin, and the helpless infant. No condition, age, or sex is spared. All the shocking and shameful enormities, with which the fierce and unbridled passions of savage man have ever conducted a war, prevail uncontrouled. The rage of fire consumes what the sword is unable to destroy, and, in a few dismal hours, the most fertile and beautiful plains in the world are converted into one vast field of carnage;—a wilderness of desolation!

There is indeed too much reason to believe, that these miseries would have occurred in St. Domingo, in a great degree, even if the proceedings of the National Assembly, as related in the latter part of the preceding chapter, had been more temperate, and if the decree of the 15th of May had never passed into a law. The declarations of the dying Ogé sufficiently point out the mischief that was meditated, long before that obnoxious decree was promulgated. But it may be affirmed, with truth and certainty, that this fatal measure gave life and activity to the poison. It was the brand by which the flames were lighted, and the combustibles that were prepared set into action. Intelligence having been received of it at Cape François on the 30th of June, no words can describe the rage and indignation which immediately spread throughout the colony; and in no place did the inhabitants breathe greater resentment than in the town of the Cape, which had hitherto been foremost in professions of attachment to the mother country, and in promoting the spirit of disunion and opposition in the colonial assembly. They now unanimously determined to reject the civick oath, although great preparations had been made for a general federation on the 14th of July. The news of this decree seemed to unite the most discordant interests. In the first transports of indignation it was proposed to seize all the ships, and confiscate the effects of the French merchants then in the harbour. An embargo was actually laid, and a motion was even made in the provincial assembly to pull down the national colours, and hoist the British standard in their room. The national cockade was every where trodden under foot, and the governor-general [Blanchelande], who continued a sorrowful and silent spectator of these excesses, found his authority, as representative of the parent country, together with every idea of colonial subordination in the people, annihilated in a moment.

The fears and apprehensions which the governor felt on this occasion have been well described by that officer himself, in a memorial which he afterwards published concerning his administration. "Acquainted (he observes) with the genius and temper of the white colonists, by a residence of seven years in the Windward Islands, and well informed of the grounds and motives of their prejudices and opinions concerning the people of colour, I immediately foresaw the disturbances and dangers which the news of this ill-advised measure would inevitably produce; and not having it in my power to suppress the communication of it, I lost no time in apprizing the king's ministers of the general discontent and violent fermentation which it excited in the colony. To my own observations, I added those of many respectable, sober, and dispassionate men, whom I thought it my duty to consult in so critical a conjuncture; and I concluded my letter by expressing my fears that this decree would prove the death-warrant of many thousands of the inhabitants. The event has mournfully verified my predictions!"

On the recommendation of the provincial assembly of the Northern department, the several parishes throughout the colony now proceeded, without further hesitation, to the election of deputies for a new general colonial assembly. These deputies, to the number of one hundred and seventy-six, met at Leogane, and on the 9th of August declared themselves *the general assembly of the French part of St. Domingo.* They transacted however but little business, but manifested great unanimity and temper in their proceedings, and resolved to hold their meetings at Cape François, whither they adjourned for that purpose, appointing the 25th of the same month for opening the session.

In the mean-while, so great was the agitation of the publick mind, M. Blanchelande found it necessary not only to transmit to the provincial assembly of the North, a copy of the letter which he mentions to have written to the king's ministers, but also to accompany it with a solemn assurance, pledging himself *to suspend the execution of the obnoxious decree, whenever it should come out to him properly authenticated*; a measure which too plainly demonstrated that his authority in the colony was at an end.

Justly alarmed at all these proceedings, so hostile towards them, and probably apprehensive of a general proscription, the mulattoes throughout the colony began to collect in different places in armed bodies; and the whites, by a mournful fatality, suffered them to assemble without molestation. In truth, every man's thoughts were directed towards the meeting of the new colonial assembly, from whose deliberations and proceedings the extinction of party, and the full and immediate redress of all existing grievances, were confidently expected. M. Blanchelande himself declares, that he cherished the same flattering and fallacious hopes. "After a long succession of violent storms, I fondly expected (he writes) the return of a calm and serene morning. The temperate and conciliating conduct of the new assembly, during their short sitting at Leogane, the characters of most of the individual members, and the necessity, so apparent to all, of mutual concession and unanimity on this great occasion, led me to think that the colony would at length see the termination of its miseries; when, alas, the storm was ready to burst, which has since involved us in one common destruction!"

It was on the morning of the 23rd of August, just before day, that a general alarm and consternation spread throughout the town of the Cape, from a report that all the negro slaves in the several neighbouring parishes had revolted, and were at that moment carrying death and desolation over the adjoining large and beautiful plain to the North-east. The governor, and most of the military officers on duty, assembled together; but the reports were so confused and contradictory, as to gain but little credit; when, as day-light began to break, the sudden and successive arrival, with ghastly countenances, of persons who had with difficulty escaped the massacre, and flown to the town for protection, brought a dreadful confirmation of the fatal tidings.

The rebellion first broke out on a plantation called *Noé*, in the parish of *Acul*, nine miles only from the city. Twelve or fourteen of the ringleaders, about the middle of the night, proceeded to the refinery, or sugar-house, and seized on a young man, the refiner's apprentice, dragged him to the front of the dwelling-house, and there hewed him into pieces with their cutlasses: his screams brought out the overseer, whom they instantly shot. The rebels now found their way to the apartment of the refiner, and massacred him in his bed. A young man lying sick in a neighbouring chamber, was left apparently dead of the wounds inflicted by their cutlasses: he had strength enough however to crawl to the next plantation, and relate the horrors he had witnessed. He reported, that all the whites of the estate which he had left were murdered, except only the surgeon, whom the rebels had compelled to accompany them, on the idea that they might stand in need of his professional assistance. Alarmed by this intelligence, the persons to whom it was communicated immediately sought their safety in flight. What became of the poor youth I have never been informed.

The revolters (consisting now of all the slaves belonging to that plantation) proceeded to the house of a Mr. Clement, by whose negroes also they were immediately joined, and both he and his refiner were massacred. The murderer of Mr. Clement was his own postillion, a man to whom he had always shewn great kindness. The other white people on this estate contrived to make their escape.

At this juncture, the negroes on the plantation of M. Flaville, a few miles distant, likewise rose and murdered five white persons, one of whom (the *procureur* or attorney for the estate) had a wife and three daughters. These unfortunate women, while imploring for mercy of the savages on their knees, beheld their husband and father murdered before their faces. For themselves, they were devoted to a more horrid fate, and were carried away captives by the assassins.

The approach of day-light served only to discover sights of horror. It was now apparent that the negroes on all the estates in the plain acted in concert, and a general massacre of the whites took place in every quarter. On some few estates indeed the lives of the women were spared, but they were reserved only to gratify the brutal appetites of the ruffians; and it is shocking to relate, that many of them suffered violation on the dead bodies of their husbands and fathers!

In the town itself, the general belief for some time was, that the revolt was by no means an extensive, but a sudden and partial insurrection only. The largest sugar plantation on the plain was that of Mons. Gallifet, situated about eight miles from the town, the negroes belonging to which had always been treated with such kindness and liberality, and possessed so many advantages, that it became a proverbial expression among the lower white people, in speaking of any man's good fortune, to say *il est heureux comme un nègre de Gallifet* (he is as happy as one of Gallifet's negroes). M. Odeluc, the attorney, or agent, for this plantation, was a member of the general assembly, and being fully persuaded that the negroes belonging to it would remain firm in their obedience, determined to repair thither to encourage them in opposing the insurgents; to which end, he desired the assistance of a few soldiers from the town-guard, which was granted him. He proceeded accordingly, but on approaching the estate, to his surprise and grief he found all the negroes in arms on the side of the rebels, and (horrid to tell!) *their standard was the body of a white infant, which they had recently impaled on a stake!* M. Odeluc had advanced too far to retreat undiscovered, and both he, and a friend that accompanied him, with most of the soldiers, were killed without mercy. Two or three only of the patrole, escaped by flight; and conveyed the dreadful tidings to the inhabitants of the town.

By this time, all or most of the white persons that had been found on the several plantations, being massacred or forced to seek their safety in flight, the ruffians exchanged the sword for the torch. The buildings and cane-fields were every where set on fire; and the conflagrations, which were visible from the town, in a thousand different quarters, furnished a prospect more shocking, and reflections more dismal, than fancy can paint, or the powers of man describe.

Consternation and terror now took possession of every mind; and the screams of the women and children, running from door to door, heightened the horrors of the scene. All the citizens took up arms, and the general assembly vested the governor with the command of the national guards, requesting him to give such orders as the urgency of the case seemed to demand.

One of the first measures was to send the white women and children on board the ships in the harbour; and very serious apprehensions being entertained concerning the domestick negroes within the town, a great proportion of the ablest men among them were likewise sent on shipboard and closely guarded.

There still remained in the city a considerable body of free mulattoes, who had not taken, or affected not to take, any part in the disputes between their brethren of colour and the white inhabitants. Their situation was extremely critical; for the lower class of whites, considering the mulattoes as the immediate authors of the rebellion, marked them for destruction; and the whole number in the town would undoubtedly have been murdered without scruple, if the governor and the colonial assembly had not vigorously interposed, and taken them under their immediate protection. Grateful for this interposition in their favour (perhaps not thinking their lives otherwise secure) all the able men among them offered to march immediately against the rebels, and to leave their wives and children as hostages for their fidelity. Their offer was accepted, and they were enrolled in different companies of the militia.

The assembly continued their deliberations throughout the night, amidst the glare of the surrounding conflagrations; and the inhabitants, being strengthened by a number of seamen from the ships, and brought into some degree of order and military subordination, were now desirous that a detachment should be sent to attack the strongest body of the revolters. Orders were given accordingly; and M. de Touzard, an officer who had distinguished himself in the service of the North Americans, took the command of a party of militia and troops of the line. With these, he marched to the plantation of a M. Latour, and attacked a body of about four thousand of the rebel negroes. Many were destroyed, but to little purpose; for Touzard, finding the number of revolters to encrease in more than a centuple proportion to their losses, was at length obliged to retreat; and it cannot be doubted, that if the rebels had forthwith proceeded to the town, defenceless as it then was towards the plain, they might have fired it without difficulty, and destroyed all its inhabitants, or compelled them to fly to the shipping for refuge.

Sensible of this, the governor, by the advice of the assembly, determined to act for some time solely on the defensive; and as it was every moment to be apprehended that the revolters would pour down upon the town, the first measure resorted to was to fortify the roads and passes leading into it. At the eastern extremity, the main road from the plain is intersected by a river, which luckily had no bridge over it, and was crossed in ferry boats, For the defence of this passage, a battery of cannon was raised on boats lashed together; while two small camps were formed at proper distances on the banks. The other principal entrance into the town, and contiguous to it towards the south, was through a mountainous district, called *le Haut du Cap*. Possession was immediately taken of these heights, and considerable bodies of troops, with such artillery as could be spared, were stationed thereon. But these precautions not being thought sufficient, it was also determined to surround the whole of the town, except the side next the sea, with a strong palisade and *chevaux de frize*; in the erecting and completing of which, all the inhabitants laboured without distinction or intermission. At the same time, an embargo was laid on all the shipping in the harbour; a measure of indispensible necessity, calculated as well to obtain the assistance of the seamen, as to secure a retreat for the inhabitants in the last extremity.

To such of the distant parishes as were open to communication either by land or by sea, notice of the revolt had been transmitted within a few hours after advice of it was received at the Cape; and the white inhabitants of many of those parishes had therefore found time to establish camps, and form a chain of posts, which for a short time seemed to prevent the rebellion spreading beyond the Northern province.[*] Two of those camps however, one at *Grande Riviere*, the other at *Dondon*, were attacked by the negroes (who were here openly joined by the mulattoes) and forced with great slaughter. At Dondon, the whites maintained the contest for seven hours; but were overpowered by the infinite disparity of numbers, and compelled to give way, with the loss of upwards of one hundred of their body. The survivors took refuge in the Spanish territory.

These two districts therefore; the whole of the rich and extensive plain of the Cape, together with the contiguous mountains, were now wholly abandoned to the ravages of the enemy, and the cruelties which they exercised, uncontrouled, on such of the miserable whites as fell into their hands, cannot be remembered without horror, nor reported in terms strong enough to convey a proper idea of their atrocity.

They seized Mr. Blen, an officer of the police, and having nailed him alive to one of the gates of his plantation, chopped off his limbs, one by one, with an axe.

A poor man named *Robert*, a carpenter by trade, endeavouring to conceal himself from the notice of the rebels, was discovered in his hiding-

---

[*] It is believed that a general insurrection was to have taken place throughout the colony on the 25th of August (St. Louis's day); but that the impatience and impetuosity of some negroes on the plain, induced them to commence their operations two days before the time.

place; and the savages declared *that he should die in the way of his occupation*: accordingly they bound him between two boards, and deliberately sawed him asunder.

* M. Cardineau, a planter of *Grande Riviere*, had two natural sons by a black woman. He had manumitted them in their infancy, and bred them up with great tenderness. They both joined in the revolt; and when their father endeavoured to divert them from their purpose, by soothing language and pecuniary offers, they took his money, and then stabbed him to the heart.

All the white, and even the mulatto children whose fathers had not joined in the revolt, were murdered without exception, frequently before the eyes, or clinging to the bosoms, of their mothers. Young women of all ranks were first violated by a whole troop of barbarians, and then generally put to death. Some of them were indeed reserved for the further gratification of the lust of the savages, and others had their eyes scooped out with a knife.

In the parish of *Limbé*, at a place called the Great Ravine, a venerable planter, the father of two beautiful young ladies, was tied down by a savage ringleader of a band, who ravished the eldest daughter in his presence, and delivered over the youngest to one of his followers: their passion being satisfied, they slaughtered both the father and the daughters.

Amidst these scenes of horror, one instance however occurs of such fidelity and attachment in a negro, as is equally unexpected and affecting. Mons. and Madame Baillon, their daughter and son-in-law, and two white servants, residing on a mountain plantation about thirty miles from Cape François, were apprized of the revolt by one of their own slaves, who was himself in the conspiracy, but promised, if possible, to save the lives of his master and his family. Having no immediate means of providing for their escape, he conducted them into an adjacent wood; after which he went and joined the revolters. The following night, he found an opportunity of bringing them provisions from the rebel camp. The second night he returned again, with a further supply of provisions; but declared that it would be out of his power to give them any further assistance. After this, they saw nothing of the negro for three days; but at the end of that time he came again; and directed the family how to make their way to a river which led to Port Margot, assuring them they would find a canoe on a part of the river which he described. They followed his directions; found the canoe, and got safely into it; but were overset by the rapidity of the current, and after a narrow escape, thought it best to return to their retreat in the mountains. The negro, anxious for their safety, again found them out, and directed them to a broader part of the river, where he assured them he had provided a boat; but said it was the last effort he could make to save them. They went accordingly, but not finding the boat, gave themselves up for lost, when the faithful negro again appeared like their guardian angel. He brought with him pigeons, poultry, and bread; and conducted the family, by slow marches in the night, along the banks of the river, until they were within sight of the wharf at Port Margot; when telling them they were entirely out of danger, he took his leave for ever, and went to join the rebels. The family were in the woods nineteen nights.

Let us now turn our attention back to the town of the Cape; where, the inhabitants being at length placed, or supposed to be placed, in some sort of security, it was thought necessary by the governor and assembly, that offensive operations against the rebels should be renewed, and a small army, under the command of M. Rouvray, marched to the eastern part of the plain, and encamped at a place called *Roucrou*. A very considerable body of the rebel negroes took possession, about the same time, of the large buildings on the plantation of M. Gallifet, and mounted some heavy pieces of artillery on the walls. They had procured the cannon at different shipping places and harbours along the coast, where it had been placed in time of war by the government, and imprudently left unprotected; but it was a matter of great surprize by what means they obtained ammunition.*
From this plantation they sent out foraging parties, with which the whites had frequent skirmishes. In these engagements, the negroes seldom stood their ground longer than to receive and return a single volley, but they appeared again the next day; and though they were at length driven out of their entrenchments with infinite slaughter, yet their numbers seemed not to diminish:—as soon as one body was cut off, another appeared, and thus they succeeded in the object of harassing and destroying the whites by perpetual fatigue, and reducing the country to a desert.

To detail the various conflicts, skirmishes, massacres, and scenes of slaughter, which this exterminating war produced, were to offer a disgusting and frightful picture;—a combination of horrors;—wherein we should behold cruelties unexampled in the annals of mankind; human blood poured forth in torrents; the earth blackened with ashes, and the air

---

* It was discovered afterwards, that great quantities of powder and ball were stolen by the negroes in the town of Cape François from the king's arsenal, and secretly conveyed to the rebels. Most of the fire-arms at first in their possession were supposed to have been part of *Ogé's* importation. But it grieves me to add, that the rebels were afterwards abundantly supplied, by small vessels from North America; the masters of which felt no scruple to receive in payment sugar and rum, from estates of which the owners had been murdered by the men with whom they trafficked.

tainted with pestilence. It was computed that, within two months after the revolt first began, upwards of two thousand white persons, of all conditions and ages, had been massacred;—that one hundred and eighty sugar plantations, and about nine hundred coffee, cotton, and indigo settlements had been destroyed (the buildings thereon being consumed by fire), and one thousand two hundred christian families reduced from opulence, to such a state of misery as to depend altogether for their clothing and sustenance on publick and private charity. Of the insurgents, it was reckoned that upwards of ten thousand had perished by the sword or by famine; and some hundreds by the hands of the executioner;—many of them, I grieve to say, under the torture of the wheel;—a system of revenge and retaliation, which no enormities of savage life could justify or excuse.[*]

2. From Pamphile de Lacroix, *Mémoires pour servir à l'histoire de la Révolution de Saint-Domingue* (1819)

[Having risen through the ranks during the 1790s, Joseph-François-Pamphile Lacroix (1774-1841) took part in Leclerc's expedition to reclaim Saint Domingue from Toussaint Louverture; he fought there from February 1802 to March 1803, participating in some key events such as the siege of Crête-à-Pierrot and being promoted to the rank of general. His highly readable book, written in the years following Waterloo, has been referred to by C.L.R. James as "indispensable and fully deserv[ing] its reputation" despite its French bias (329); indeed, *The Black Jacobins* owes a large debt to Lacroix, whom James often paraphrases at length. Hugo's debt to Lacroix's *Mémoires*, if not to the pragmatically

---

[*] Two of these unhappy men suffered in this manner under the window of the author's lodgings, and in his presence, at Cape François, on Thursday the 28th of September 1791. They were broken on two pieces of timber placed crosswise. One of them expired on receiving the third stroke on his stomach, each of his legs and arms having been first broken in two places; the first three blows he bore without a groan. The other had a harder fate. When the executioner, after breaking his legs and arms, lifted up the instrument to give the finishing stroke on the breast, and which (by putting the criminal out of his pain) is called *le coup de grace*, the mob, with the ferociousness of cannibals, called out *arretez!* (stop) and compelled him to leave his work unfinished. In that condition, the miserable wretch, with his broken limbs doubled up, was put on a cart-wheel, which was placed horizontally, one end of the axle-tree being driven into the earth. He seemed perfectly sensible, but uttered not a groan. At the end of forty minutes, some English seamen, who were spectators of the tragedy, strangled him in mercy. As to all the French spectators (many of them persons of fashion, who beheld the scene from the windows of their upper apartments), it grieves me to say, that they looked on with the most perfect composure and *sang froid*. Some of the ladies, as I was told, even ridiculed, with a great deal of unseemly mirth, the sympathy manifested by the English at the sufferings of the wretched criminals.

liberal outlook that characterizes it, is equally great: in Debien's words, the book served as his "colonial encyclopedia" (309). First read in 1819, and then re-read in 1825, Lacroix was Hugo's single most important source of information about Saint Domingue (see Etienne 120-40 for an exhaustive list of Hugo's borrowings from, and occasional plagiarisms of, Lacroix); indeed, the material from Lacroix of direct relevance to *Bug-Jargal* is so extensive that I have divided this section into four thematically organized sub-sections, each with its own headnote. (Lacroix's highly readable *Mémoires* have, happily, been recently republished with extensive annotations by Pierre Pluchon under the title *La Révolution de Haïti* [see Works Cited].)]

a. Racial Taxonomies

[Lacroix prefaces his book with an explanation of the differences between the various "generic types" that make up the island's intermediary coloured population. He bases his discussion of the diverse types of "coloured people" on Moreau de Saint-Méry's influential account in *Description ... de l'isle Saint Domingue* (1797) of the nine different shades separating "pure" black from "pure" white. As Joan Dayan aptly puts it, "stranger than any supernatural fiction, the radical irrationality of Moreau's method demonstrates to what lengths the imagination can go if driven by racial prejudice" (232)—a prejudice that, in Moreau's case, is interestingly complicated by the likelihood that he was one of those "supposedly 'white' *créoles* [who] were really of mixed blood, but had secured acceptance as whites" (Nicholls 73). (For more on Moreau, see Editor's notes, p. 67, and *Bug-Jargal* endnotes 19, 57 & 61.) While Lacroix makes use of Moreau's taxonomy, he does not blindly buy into it, as the end of his discussion makes clear when he refuses to draw a firm line between "pure" whites and "coloured" peoples. Tellingly, when Hugo incorporates this passage from Lacroix in his footnote glossing the word "griffe" (Chapter 4), he stops plagiarizing his source at precisely the point where Lacroix emphasizes that there is no absolute distinction between "black" and "white," and reverts instead to the line-in-the-sand logic of Moreau (see Bongie, *Islands and Exiles* 472).]

Note Relative to the Coloured Population:
   "Coloured population" sometimes signifies the collective mass of blacks and men of colour, but most often what is understood by the words *coloured population, coloured caste, people of colour, men of colour* are those who

are neither black nor white; they are also known under the general name of *sang-mêlé* [mixed bloods].

Whether it is a question of the collective or particular usage of "coloured population" depends on the sense of the phrase in which it is employed.

To distinguish the colour of the individuals [discussed in this book], and to make it immediately visible, the names of blacks have been printed in SMALL CAPITALS, those of mulattoes in *italics*, and those of whites in normal text.

Monsieur Moreau de Saint-Méry, building on Franklin's system, has classified into generic types the different hues displayed by the mixtures of the coloured population.

He posits that men are made up of a total of one hundred and twenty-eight parts, the parts being white in the case of the whites and black in the case of the blacks.

Starting from this principle, he establishes that how close to or far away from one or the other colour you are depends on your proximity to or distance from the sixty-fourth term, which serves as their proportional mean.

According to this system, any man not in possession of eight full parts white is said to be black.

Moving from this colour toward the white, nine principal stocks can be identified, which have even more varieties between them according to how many or how few parts they retain of one or the other colour.

The sacatra is the nearest to the negro; he is produced in three ways, and can have between eight to sixteen parts white and one hundred and twelve to one hundred and twenty parts black.

	white parts	black parts
Born of the sacatra and the negress, he has	8	120
Born of a male and female sacatra	16	112
Born of a griffe and a negress	16	112

The griffe is the result of five combinations, and can have between twenty-four to thirty-two parts white and ninety-six or one hundred and four parts black.

	white parts	black parts
Born of the marabou and the sacatra, he has	32	96
Born of the griffe and the griffone	32	96
Born of the negro and the mulatress	32	96
Born of the negro and the female marabou	24	104
Born of the griffe and the female sacatra	24	104

[Similar tables follow for the marabou, mulatto, quadroon, metiff, mameluco, and quarteronné.]

The *sang-mêlé* is formed in four ways; he goes from being one hundred and twenty-five to one hundred and twenty-seven parts white, and from one to three parts black.

	white parts	black parts
Born of a white man and a sang-mêlée, he has	127	1
Born of a white man and a quarteronnée	126	2
Born of a sang-mêlé and a sang-mêlée	125	3
Born of a sang-mêlé and a quarteronnée	124	4

The sang-mêlé, if he keeps on uniting with the white, ends up becoming confused with this colour.

According to the above system, the person who arrives at the eighth remove has one hundred twenty-seven and sixty-three sixty-fourths white parts against one sixty-fourth of one black part, or eight thousand one hundred and ninety-one parts white against one part black, which no longer constitutes a difference, since a great many individuals from the south of Europe—in Spain, Provence, Italy, Turkey, and Hungary—have in their blood more than one sixty-fourth of one black part.

Doctor Franklin was the first to think up this system, which brings into relief the power and the infinite goodness of the Creator: thus it is that the species, always restructuring itself through a series of variations, renews itself at the end of twenty or so generations without retaining anything of the organic blemishes that could have impaired it.

Philosophy has made use of this observation in order to underscore the nullity of hereditary pride. This pride makes us believe, in spite of nature, that we retain the pure blood of our ancestors from sixteen generations back, whereas we only possess a very small part of it. It has, for better and for worse, been infinitely divided up between the existing community of our species.

b. White Mimeticism, Black Fury

[Hugo's grasp on the events in Saint Domingue owes a lot to Lacroix's vivid account of the early years of the insurrection, as the excerpts in this sub-section attest. The first selection describes the rabid enthusiasm with which whites in Saint Domingue initially greeted the outbreak of the French Revolution in 1789, while the second provides an account of the weeks immediately preceding and succeeding upon August 22: an impressive number of details from both these selections find their way into Chapter 16. The third selection is a description of the rebel leader Jeannot's misdeeds and execution, which Hugo repackages in Chapter 42.]

i.

One exaggerates what one imitates, and so it was that the phases of the [French] revolution were reflected in Saint Domingue with the intensity of a burning mirror.

The national colours, which had not been adopted with any particular enthusiasm in France, were ecstatically displayed under the Antillean sky. A settler from Les Cayes, having responded with some abusive comments about the revolution when he was criticized for showing himself in a public place without the new cockade, was forthwith shot dead with a pistol and his head was carried about on the top of a pike without the authorities wishing or being able to prevent it.

A resolution having been adopted to put the local militias in the same category as the national guards in France, service in the militia, which up to that point had been considered the equivalent of forced labour, turned into a mania. Everyone rushed to sign up. People were coming from all over to be enlisted. The rivalry of different uniforms, the conceit of preferential treatment, the hope of promotions, the desire for military decorations—they all fired up everyone's ambitions. It was no longer enough to be an officer, a colonel, a general: everywhere you went, people were aspiring to the highest rank they knew of in the colony. Every commander of the national guard in the cities wanted to be a captain-general and took that title for himself.

The military craze became even more of an epidemic when it was learned that serving as a private counted among the qualifications for the Saint-Louis Cross; everywhere you went service records were being drawn up, and soon the colony was inundated with an irruption of these Crosses—without it being of any benefit to the government, which with more shrewdness could have turned creole vanity to good account by this means.

By way of enhancing this new military veneer, expeditions were dreamt up. A rumour was spread that a despicable plot, hatched by the authorities, was going to annihilate the colony. It was announced at the Cape that three thousand insurgent Blacks were getting ready to lay waste the city and were assembled on the morne overlooking it.

No sooner had this been announced than a substantial detachment of the national guard set off there; after a hard march, this detachment returned to the city with one volunteer mortally wounded—not by the revolters (none existed as yet), but by his own side.

However barbarous the multitude might be, it puts two and two together and starts drawing conclusions. In this respect, it was as dangerous as it was impolitic to put such ruinous schemes into the slaves' heads. The upshot of this became only too apparent later when, during the insurrection of the Blacks, those who had served as guides in this mad undertaking ended up becoming the first leaders of the revolt.

ii.

As early as June and July, several slave gangs in the West formed themselves into insurrectionary units; these isolated mobs were easily dispersed by the marshalcy in concert with a few settlers. There had previously been a rise in the number of harsh punishments; now it was the number of executions that likewise increased. The executioners were not equal to their grisly task, as can be seen in this extract from a letter dated July 18: addressed to the President of the Massiac Club by the author of a work intended to prove the necessity of maintaining slavery in the colony in perpetuity, this letter—the original of which was presented to the National Convention at the time—notes that "if there is any problem cutting off heads, one need only call on General Caradeux (commander of the districts of Port-au-Prince), who had fifty or so of them lopped off on the Aubry plantation during the time when he was farming it, and who, so that there could be no doubt about it in anybody's mind, stuck them on pikes and planted them along the hedgerows of his plantation as if they were palm trees."

The revolt in the West was stamped out and seemed dormant. The Creoles, to cite Mirabeau's phrase, were sleeping on the edge of Vesuvius. The first blasts of the volcano did not awaken them. In their spellbound eyes, the Blacks were simply not creatures of any consequence.

In mid-August, a conflagration broke out in the north on the Chabaud plantation; simultaneously, in a neighbouring quarter, the gang of the La Gossette plantation made an attempt on the life of its manager. The explosion of the great disaster had already begun; the premature nature of these incidents was due to a misunderstanding about the day it was to take place. Creole justice devoured whatever guilty parties it could lay hands on, without taking pains to unravel the plot of which it held the thread.

On August 22 the insurrection broke out in full force.

The slaves of the Turpin plantation, under the command of an English Negro named Boukmann, set off at ten in the evening, and convinced the gangs of the Flaville, Clément, Trémès, and Noé plantations to go in with them; scenes of horror quickly followed that make human nature shudder.

They are no longer human beings, they are tigers seeking to quench their rage; they take the most beautiful country in the world and cover it in fire and ruins. Without distinction of age or sex, they strike down every White they can lay hands on and slit their throats; with a ferocious joy, they watch the agonies, the death-rattles, of those toward whom in the past they dared not even raise their furtive glances.

The city of the Cape only learns of the disaster through the flames that light up the horizon and through the cries of the people who have taken flight and are hurrying toward its gates.

The inhabitants of this city, at first in a state of shock, hastily shut themselves up in their houses so as to keep their slaves under lock and key; only the troops are still out on the streets, heading off to their various posts. The alarm-gun soon calls the entire population to arms. The inhabitants go back out, accost and question one another, and immediately their courage flares up at the thought of vengeance. Fury drives the *petits Blancs* wild, and they launch one long cry of indignation against the sang-mêlés, accusing them of the scenes of horror taking place outside the city. In the delirium of a first impulsive reaction, several men of colour are treated in the same manner as the revolters have treated the Whites who were taken unawares on the plantations. To put a stop to the excesses of this rage, the Provincial Assembly of the North had, on the spot, to identify places of refuge for the coloured population, who quickly made their way there to put themselves under the protection of the military. All of them, but especially those among that population who were landowners, asked for arms to go and fight the common enemy. Such was the blindness and the strength of biases that there was an initial hesitation in accepting their offer.

The insurrection spread like electric fluid: in four days a third of the Northern province had been reduced to a heap of ashes.

Several members of the Colonial Assembly, which had adjourned to the Cape for the end of August, were ambushed on their way there by the revolters and fell under their attack; a substantial detachment had to be sent out to help ensure the arrival of the President, the secretaries, and the archives.

Bodies of troops of the line and national guards were sent into the plain, while the lieutenant-colonel of the Cape regiment, Monsieur de Touzard—with the grenadiers and the chasseurs of his regiment, supported by several cannons—made for Limbé, where the bulk of the revolters were gathered. That his troop maintained its composure and strength of purpose was due to nothing less than this leader's valorous comportment. The soldiers were clearing a path through the swarm of revolters, brushing aside their resistance, when an order from the Governor, who had yielded to the anxieties of the settlers, recalled him to the Cape, which was in a state of general consternation; this ill-starred city was, in effect, encircled by the revolt. A military post stationed on the Bongars plantation had let itself be scared off, and its hasty retreat had delivered over to the torches of the slaves the two finest quarters of the colony, those of Morin and Limonade.

The incendiaries had then advanced toward the Haut du Cap. The city's cannons were blasting away at them with redoubled force, but stopping their forward march proved difficult. The return of Monsieur de Touzard had broken up their attack, but this return—by leaving the revolters absolute masters of the countryside—had made them all the bolder and given them free run of the country. Their depredations spread from the plain to the hills; as they got further away, their fury seemed to abate, but what they were actually doing was organizing themselves more systematically. The colonists took advantage of this pause and finally put up some resistance.

The parishes to the east of the Cape set up camps at Trou and Vallière; the plains of Fort Dauphin were skilfully and methodically protected by Monsieur de Rouvray, brigadier-general and landowner at Saint Domingue. These plains, encircled by the sea and the Spanish frontiers, have the shape of a peninsula, and it is this same configuration that kept the Môle peninsula out of harm's way for such a long time.

The systematic approach that the revolters were following proved that their undertaking was being directed by people of an intelligence superior to theirs. They did not expose themselves in a body, like madmen or fanatics; they kept themselves spread out and dispersed, positioning themselves by platoons in thickly wooded places that were particularly suited for circling round and crushing the enemy by force of numbers.

While the preparations for battle were being carried out in the greatest silence, their obis would perform wangas and inflame the imaginations of the women and children, who would sing and dance as if possessed by demons. Then, with dreadful cries and howls, the attack would begin.

If they encountered resistance, they did not waste their energy, but if they saw the defence in any way hesitate then they became extremely daring, and would settle for nothing less than stifling the enemy's cannons with their arms and bodies and thereby completing the rout.

Contorting their bodies and howling to the wind were not the only way they had of sowing fear ahead of them. There was also fire. They set the sugar canes on fire, all the buildings, their own huts, their ajoupas; during the day it covered the sky with whirlwinds of smoke and during the night it lit up the horizon, an aurora borealis that cast its volcano-like reflection over a great distance and tinged everything with the livid colour of blood.

The most absolute silence was followed by a dreadful uproar, which would then be succeeded by the plaintive cries of dying prisoners, as the barbarians made sport of slaughtering them in their outposts.

These transitions from silence to a dreadful clamour, and from that clamour to the piercing cries of distress, were the coiled springs unleashed by the instigators of this awful catastrophe.

It was at this time, in the midst of these horrifying events, that the sessions of the new assembly—still calling itself the *general* instead of the *colonial* assembly—opened. Led astray by prejudices and distress, its first hopes did not turn toward the fatherland, which it blamed for its disasters; it did not deign to send word of these disasters to France, and in order to prevent the Governor from fulfilling his duty in this regard it put a strict embargo on all ships in the colony. When leading merchants offered to send a dispatch-boat to France, at their own expense, the assembly responded that there was no reason to deliberate over the offer. Believing itself to be up to the task of controlling the situation on its own, the assembly decreed that three regiments of paid guardsmen be formed, that provostal commissions be set up, that city levies be increased, and that, contrary to its own statutes, the term of the presidency of Monsieur de Cadusch be extended in order to give him time to pursue the negotiations that the assembly had entered into with the Governor of Jamaica, to whom it had sent two of its members in the capacity of commissioners. [...]

The aid that people were so confidently expecting amounted to nothing more than a weak show of force and empty vows. Lord Effingham, Governor of Jamaica, limited himself to having a fifty-gun vessel cruise up and down the coast of the Western province, and sending three corvettes to the Cape bearing five hundred rifles along with some ammunition and food—"being unable to take upon himself," so he said, "the diverting of any troops from his garrison, given the critical circumstances in which all of the Antilles found itself."

iii.

Jeannot, who had served as guide in the first, and extremely injudicious, attempt at flushing negroes out of the mornes of the Cape, had emerged as one of the most savage leaders of the revolt. Suspecting the fidelity of one of his men, by the name of Paul Blin, because he had saved his masters when he first joined the uprising, Jeannot had him cut into pieces and thrown into the fire under the specious pretext that he had contributed to a defeat his band had suffered by removing the bullets from their cartridges.

Other cruelties are attributed to this Jeannot that are only too well documented.

Monsieur Paradole had been captured by him on his plantation in Grande Rivière. Together, four of his children, who during the first wave of terror had thought only of their own safety, made their way back to him in order to beg for their father's life. This filial devotion only irritated Jeannot: it struck his fancy to murder the wretched Paradole five times over by striking him down only after having drawn the last breath from his four sons, whom he slaughtered one after the other in front of their father. The atrocity of this deed roused the indignation of Jean-François, who so envied Jeannot's ostentatious trappings that he had taken to driving to the curé of Grande Rivière's mass in nothing less than a six-horse carriage. Jean-François attacked him, captured him, and had him brought before the firing squad. Cruelty is often nothing more than the energy of cowardice. Jeannot supplies the proof of that; he did everything he could to avoid being put to death. When he saw that his pardon had not been granted to the curé of Marmelade, who had been assigned the task of exhorting him, Jeannot clung to him with so much energy that he had to be violently pried off him. Jean-François did not resort to torturing Jeannot for the tortures he had inflicted on others: he had him put before the firing squad at the foot of a tree that was lined with iron hooks from which this monster used to fasten his victims by their midriffs.

Around this same time, nature was also purged of Boukmann, the first leader of the insurrection; this Black, just as cruel as Jeannot, was killed in combat. His head was displayed on the parade ground of the Cape; the torso and the atrocious soul to which it had once belonged were gone, but the horror of them remained, preserved in that head.

c. *Bricolage* with a Vengeance

[The two passages in this sub-section include, first, a letter from Biassou and Jean-François dating from late 1791 and, second, a brief letter from them dating from the summer of 1793 as well as an oral statement by another rebel leader, Macaya. Separated by more than one hundred pages in Lacroix, these historical documents are appropriated by Hugo in order to create the "ridiculous" fictional letter from Biassou and Jean-François that provides the centrepiece of Chapter 38. See "(1791)/2002, 2004: Reading Hugo and the Hatian Revolution in a Post/Colonial Age" of the Introduction for a discussion of this parodic act of *bricolage* on Hugo's part.]

i.

The leaders of the revolt—fearful of the future, weary of the present on account of the scenes of carnage and horror with which they had soiled themselves, and still too barbarous to conceive the idea of liberty for all those of their colour—appeared open to mending their ways. Father Sulpice, curé of Trou parish, took it upon himself to nurture these good intentions and to explain to them the sentiments of benevolence contained in the amnesty of 28 September. Having so greatly transgressed divine and human laws, and these same laws having been so greatly violated at their expense, their remorse and terror was such that it took them a long time to find one of their own who was willing to take it upon himself to present their grievances to the colonial assembly and the civil commissioners.

Two men of colour named *Raynal* and *Duplessis* dared to accept this hazardous mission; they reported to the outposts in the capacity of negotiators, and were led blindfolded to Governor de Blanchelande's residence, from there to that of the civil commissioners, and finally to the bar of the colonial assembly.

Their charge was to ask that the past be forgotten and that the four hundred principal leaders of the revolt be manumitted; these leaders committed themselves, if that condition were met, to bringing the revolt to an end, and offered as a guarantee of their good faith to hand over any white prisoners who were in their hands.

Here is the letter that these deputies presented to the colonial assembly on the part of their leaders:

"The king's proclamation of 28 September marks a formal acceptance of the French constitution. In this proclamation, one sees his paternal solicitude: he ardently desires that the laws be brought fully into force, and that all citizens contribute collectively toward reestablishing the just equilibrium which has for such a long time now been unsettled by the repeated upheavals of a tremendous revolution; his spirit of justice and moderation is therein clearly and precisely manifested. These two laws are for the *mère-patrie*, which requires a system of government absolutely distinct from that of the colonies, but the sentiments of clemency and kindness, which are not laws but affections of the heart, will surely cross oceans, and we ought to be included in the general amnesty that he has declared for one and all.

We now pass to the law of 28 September 1791 relative to the colonies. We see by this law that the National Assembly and the king authorize you to formulate your requests with regard to certain points of legislation, and grant you the power to rule definitively on certain others; among these latter are the status of those persons who are not free and the political status of the men of colour. We most surely respect the decrees of the National Assembly sanctioned by the king. Indeed, we go further than this: we will defend those decrees to the last drop of our blood as we will defend yours, presuming they bear the requisite formalities. We will allow ourselves, hereinafter, to lay out for you our reflections, entirely persuaded as we are that you will treat them with all possible indulgence.

Lastly, the letter of the Minister of the Marine gives formal expression to the king's firm intention to uphold the decreed articles by all the means that are in his royal power. This then, gentlemen, is our reading of the documents under consideration. We are now going to make our profession of faith to you regarding all the current troubles, and we are convinced in advance that you will have every indulgence for us—the same indulgence that is shown toward us by the legislative and sovereign body.

Great misfortunes have afflicted this rich and important colony; we have been caught up in them, and that is all that can be said by way of our justification. The address that we have taken the liberty to send you leaves nothing to be desired in this regard; but at the moment when we composed it, we had no knowledge of those various proclamations. Today, now that we are informed of the new laws, today, now that we cannot doubt the *mère-patrie*'s approval of all the legislative acts that you will decree concerning the internal running of the colonies and the legal status of persons, we will not prove refractory. Rather, we will show ourselves to be full of the keenest gratitude and, in turn, reiterate our assurances to you confirming our desire that peace be restored to you. You will find our requests formulated in the address that we have had the honour of transmitting to you; we believed them to be acceptable on every possible grounds, including the love of doing good. We believed it our duty, in the name of the imperilled colony, to request that you pursue the one and only means of promptly and without detriment reestablishing order in such an important colony; you have by now surely weighed the request and the motives that dictated it. The first proposed article is of absolute expediency: your wisdom will dictate to you the part you will need to play in this respect. A substantial population that trustingly submits itself to the orders of the monarch and the legislative body, which it invests with its power, assuredly merits consideration at a time when all parties in the colony should—following the example of the metropolis—through their union and through their respect for the laws and for the king be working toward providing this country with the level of growth that the National Assembly has the right to expect from it. The laws that will be in force regarding the status of free and non-free peoples must be the same throughout the entire colony; it would indeed be a point of interest were you to *declare*, by way of a decree ratified by the Governor-General, that you intend to turn your attention to the condition of the slaves. Knowing that they are the object of your solicitude, and knowing it by way of their leaders, to whom you will send this decree, they would be satisfied, and that will facilitate reestablishing the broken equilibrium without detriment and in short order. We take the liberty of making these observations to you, persuaded that, once it is in the general interest, you will receive them kindly. Finally, gentlemen, our peaceful dispositions are not equivocal, and they never have been. Unfortunate circumstances seem to make them appear doubtful, but one day you will do us all the justice that our position merits, and will be convinced of our submission to the laws, as of our respectful devotion to the king. We await impatiently the conditions that you may think fit to place on this extremely desirable peace. We will only point out to you that, from the moment you shall have spoken, our adherence will be uniform, but that we believe the first article of our address to be indispensable, and that this belief of ours is informed by the experience that a knowledge of the local conditions necessarily gives us."

Signed JEAN-FRANÇOIS, General; BIASSOU, Brigadier-General; *Desprez*, *Manzeau*, TOUSSAINT and AUBERT, *Ad hoc* Commissioners

The wording of this letter alone ought to have made the colonists understand that it was time to settle up with these men, behind whom controlling forces of a political and fanatical sort were beginning to stir.

The colonial assembly seemed unconcerned by such considerations.

ii.

The inflexible commissioners [Sonthonax and Polvérel], surrounded by their roving auxiliaries [the insurgent slaves, who by burning down the Cape had enabled the commissioners to maintain power in the face of a royalist coup, and to whom the latter had just (on 29 August 1793) given freedom and equal citizenship], had no idea how to go about putting a stop to the excesses and the chaos nor how to organize the dangerous support to which, in their desperation, they had resorted.

They had it announced that "the new free men could not be good citizens if, irrespective of the advantage that had accrued to them [i.e., emancipation], they were not more closely bound yet to the fatherland by the touching ties that come with being husbands and fathers; that, as a consequence, the new citizens henceforth had the right to pass their liberty on to the wives they possessed and the children who were born from those unions."

The commissioners deluded themselves into thinking that these new concessions made to emancipation would be keenly appreciated by the new free men. The Blacks were still too barbarous to appreciate these advantages. Hardly eager for the title of free men, and insensible to the spousal and paternal duties by which discipline and regular habits, it was thought, might be instilled in them, they for the most part showed themselves inclined to listen to the voice of the leaders who were summoning them to the wandering life and the licentious brigandage to which they had become accustomed. Disinclination and desertion combined forces and, when there was nothing more to pillage, the commissioners even had difficulty keeping Pierrot, whom they had named to the rank of general, on their side. They failed completely in their attempts at seducing the other leaders, to whom Spain—by giving them promotions and decorations and letting them gorge themselves with looting and pillaging—granted favours that proved to have far greater allure than natural and political rights.

Pierrot's lieutenant, whose name was Macaya, had taken it upon himself to bring to Jean-François and Biassou the proposals that the Abbé de la Haye had made on the part of the commissioners. He had promised that in case of refusal he would bring these two chiefs back dead or alive; on that condition, he had obtained permission to leave the Cape with his band, who were loaded down with booty.

On July 6, Jean-François and Biassou answered the proposals made to them with the following declaration:

"We cannot conform to the will of the nation, in view of the fact that ever since the world began we have only carried out the will of a king. We have lost that of France, but we are held dear by that of Spain, who gives proof of his rewards to us and is constantly coming to our aid; for this reason, we can only recognize you as commissioners when you shall have throned a king."

Macaya did not come back; the Spanish, to retain him, had named him to the rank of brigadier-general. The Abbé de la Haye, who held a great deal of sway over him, tried to arrange another meeting between him and the commissioners; Macaya consented to this after having taking the necessary precautions for his safety.

Commissioner Polvérel found out on this occasion that one does not win over an obstinate barbarian by means of cosy fraternal decorum. Try as he might to lavish upon Macaya the title of citizen-general, he could only reduce him to silence and never convert him. Macaya, whom the Spanish addressed as His Excellency, made it clear through his responses that he was attached to them as much out of personal interest as out of religious fanaticism. His obstinacy took refuge in a single phrase that seemed to have been taught to him, since it was his response to every proposal that commissioner Polvérel made to him: "I am the subject of three kings: the king of Congo, master of all the Blacks; the king of France, who represents my father; and the king of Spain, who represents my mother. These three kings are the descendants of those who, guided by a star, went to worship the Man-God. If I were to pass into the service of the Republic, I would perhaps be led into making war on my brothers, the subjects of these three kings to whom I have promised fidelity."

Jean-François and Biassou rejected, in a public proclamation, the commissioners' secret proposals, seized hold of the camp at La Tannerie, broke through the cordon of troops to the West, and pledged that they would avenge the victims of the conflagration of the Cape.

d. The Shadow of Toussaint and Dessalines

[Hugo's reading of Lacroix's *Mémoires* was not limited to its opening chapters, which deal with the early years of the revolt. He appropriates a good many details from later on in the book and transposes them back onto 1791. Most often, these transpositions involve attributing episodes in the life of Toussaint Louverture to Biassou, as in the first four selections here, which all come from the years 1800-1802, when Toussaint reigned supreme over the colony; the final selection is taken from Lacroix's account of independent Haiti during the time of Dessalines's short-lived empire. Key details from these five selections find their way, respectively, into Chapters 35, 29, 36, 50, and 34 of *Bug-Jargal*.]

i.

No one who had been invited to a reception at Toussaint Louverture's dared not to attend. During these receptions, which were of two types, the manner in which he conducted himself had something truly admirable about it.

One got asked to the grand receptions. At these, Toussaint Louverture would wear the undress uniform of a general officer. In the midst of such finery, his simple mode of dress contrasted with the dignified tone he was so adept at maintaining.

When he made his entrance into the great hall where the guests had been assembled in advance, everyone, without distinction of sex, had to stand up. He required that one keep a very respectful bearing, and liked to be approached, especially by Whites, with due regard to the formalities. The epitome of tact when it came to judging just how well those formalities had been met, he would exclaim, when he was particularly impressed: "Well done! That is how one should introduce oneself." Then, turning toward the black officers who were standing around him, he would say to them: "See, you Negroes, work at picking up those manners, and learn how to introduce yourselves the way it is meant to be done. This is what comes from having been raised in France; my children will be like that."

He desired that the women, and especially the white women, be dressed as if they were going to church and that their bosom be entirely covered. More than once he was seen sending one of them away while averting his gaze and exclaiming that "he had not thought it possible that decent women could be so lacking in a sense of propriety." Another time he was seen throwing his handkerchief over a girl's breasts while saying in a severe tone to her mother "that modesty ought to be the prerogative of her sex."

At these receptions, he affected only to talk to the wives of the old colonists as well as to those of the foreigners who frequented Saint Domingue; he always addressed them as "Madame." If he was talking to women of colour, or by some unlikely chance to Black women, he called them "citizens." Every white woman was received as of right. As for the others, he only admitted those whose husbands held high office. After he had spoken to everyone, done the rounds of the room, and returned to the door through which he had entered, he would make a dignified bow, turn his head to the right and the left, wave with both hands, and slowly withdraw along with his officers.

The lesser receptions consisted of public audiences that took place every evening. Toussaint Louverture appeared at these dressed like the landowners of old on their plantations, that is to say in trousers and a white jacket of fine linen, with a Madras handkerchief around his head. All the citizens entered the great hall, and he spoke to everyone.

He had a penchant for embarrassing the Blacks who came to these audiences. He affected kindness for those whose awkwardness stemmed from the respect and admiration he inspired in them, but when a Black man answered him with some degree of self-assurance he made a point of posing, in a harsh tone, some question on the catechism or on agriculture which the disconcerted Black had no idea how to answer—after which he made sure to add to this man's confusion by reproaching him in severe terms for his ignorance and his incompetence. So it was that he was seen saying to Blacks and men of colour who were requesting they be made judges: "It would please me greatly to do so, because I presume that you know Latin." "No, my General." "What, you want to be judges and you don't know Latin?" Then he showered them with a flood of Latin words that he had learned by heart from the Psalter or elsewhere and that bore no relation to the present circumstances. The Whites kept their laughter in check, because one did not laugh in front of Toussaint Louverture, and the Blacks withdrew, entirely resigned to not being judges and truly convinced that their general-in-chief knew Latin.

After having made a round of the great hall during these lesser receptions, Toussaint Louverture would have the people with whom he wanted to pass the evening brought into a room that was outside his bedroom and which served as a study. The majority of these people were always made up of the principal Whites of the country. There, he would have everyone sit down and then he himself would sit down and speak about France, his children, religion, his former masters, the blessing that God had bestowed on him by making him a free man and granting him the necessary tools to fill the post in which France had placed him. He would also talk about advances in agriculture and commerce, though never about political tidings. He would question each person about his particular affairs, about his family, and looked as if he were taking an interest in it all; with mothers, he would discuss the rearing of their children and would inquire if they had made sure to have them take their first communion. If there happened to be some youngsters present, he enjoyed asking them questions about the Catechism and the Gospel.

When he wanted to draw the reception to a close, he would get up and take a deep bow. That was the signal for people to withdraw; he would accompany his guests to the door, arranging individual meetings with those who asked it of him. Then he would shut himself away with his secretaries, usually working well into the night with them.

ii.

For the soldiers, he was a being who verged on the extraordinary; those who worked the land prostrated themselves before him as if he were a god. Every one of his generals trembled at his sight (Dessalines did not dare to look him in the face), and everyone else trembled in the presence of his generals.

No European army has ever been more strictly disciplined than were the troops of Toussaint Louverture. Every commanding officer worked with pistol in hand and had the right of life and death over his subalterns.

The system of forced labour on the plantations had ensured the well-being of the general and senior officers. It was with words that the subaltern officers and the soldiers were kept in a state of obedience differing little from that of slavery. They were told that they were free, and they believed it because a series of adroit insinuations put them above those who worked the land; whenever a soldier brought a complaint against a Black who was not a soldier it was always the former who was in the right. This supremacy of the enlisted Black man resulted in his always being feared and obeyed.

After Toussaint Louverture had established and consolidated this military supremacy, he had no qualms about arming those who worked the land.

The amount of money he spent on obtaining weapons and ammunition adds up to unbelievable sums. It was both with and without the knowledge of his own administrators that he made these purchases. Nobody but he knew exactly where it was all stored or how it was divided up on the principal plantations.

He never stopped repeating to those who worked the land that the freedom of the Blacks consisted in taking good care of the weapons and ammunition; that they were maintained in good condition was something he himself made sure of through frequent inspections.

It was during these inspections that he took on the appearance of a visionary and became the fetish of the Blacks who listened to him.

He would talk to them in parables so as to make himself better understood. One he often made use of goes as follows. In a glass vase full of grains of black maize, he would mix in some grains of white maize and say to those who were standing around him: "You are the black maize, the Whites who would like to enslave you are the white maize." He would shake the vase and, presenting it to their fascinated eyes, he would exclaim like a visionary: "*Guetté blanc ci la la*," which is to say, "see what the White man is in proportion to you."

iii.

[In 1801] several gangs in the Limbé plains, out of the blue, slit the throats of their managers and those Whites they could lay hands on. This unexpected uprising reached the gates of the Cape and cost the lives of three hundred Whites; however, as the revolt had not been long in hatching and since it was due more to their being tired of having to work the land than their being worried about the rumours of an upcoming peace [between France and its enemies, which might facilitate the restoration of slavery], the new revolters were easily contained by the ascendancy and the authority of Toussaint Louverture. On seeing him approach and hearing his voice, they fearfully returned to work. They declared that they had been pushed into revolting by people who said that they were once again going to be made slaves of the Whites and who assured them that Generals Dessalines and Christophe had agreed to the reimposition of slavery, but that [Toussaint's nephew] General Moïse had refused to agree to it.

Toussaint Louverture, who had no part in this event, understood the justified suspicions that it could arouse against people of his colour at a moment when peace was going to present the metropolis with new resources of strength and power. He did not hesitate to entertain the accusations identifying his nephew as chief of a movement that, given his hatred for the Whites, Moïse was very much capable of fomenting but that was at bottom due simply to a spirit of revolt against having to work.

General Moïse was handed over to a military commission, found guilty of negligence in the carrying out of his duties, and put before the firing squad.

Toussaint Louverture, by sacrificing one of his close relations, wanted to prove to France just how inflexible he could be; in order to show at the same time just how great a hold he had over them, how resigned they were to his will, he purposely carried out a number of solemn tests on that score, so as to have the results proclaimed far and wide.

On the parade grounds of the Cape, Fort Dauphin, and Limbé, he assembled the entire population and the troops that were garrisoned there. At any equivocal facial expression or responses to his questions, he would individually order Blacks to go and take a gun to their head. Not a murmur would pass from the victims he selected; they clasped their hands together, lowered their heads, humbly bowed down to him and, submissive and respectful, contritely went to blow their brains out.

iv.

Liberty   Equality
From the Governor-General to General Dessalines, commander-in-chief of the army of the West.
Written at Gonaïves, headquarters, the 15th of Pluviôse, Year 10 [1802]

The cause is not lost, Citizen-General, if you can succeed in denying the landing forces the resources that Port-Républicain offers them [the French]. Endeavour, by every means available to you, be it force or wile, to burn the place down; it is constructed entirely out of wood. If a few faithful emissaries were to gain entry, that is all it would take. Surely you must have some men under your command devoted enough to render this service? Ah, my dear General, what bad luck that there was a traitor in this city and that your orders and mine were not executed.

Await the moment when expeditions into the plains shall have weakened the garrison, and then endeavour to capture the city through a surprise attack from the rear.

Do not forget that while waiting for the rainy season, which should rid us of our enemies, we have no other resource than destruction and fire. Remember that the land bathed in our sweat must not furnish our enemies with the slightest nourishment. Block the roads, let corpses and horses be thrown in every well. Annihilate everything, burn it all down, so that those who come to make us slaves again will always have before their eyes the image of the hell that they deserve. Fare thee well my friend.

     Signed Toussaint Louverture

v.

Several months after the evacuation of our army from the Cape, Dessalines, whose misleading declarations had urged the Whites to remain on the island under his protection, turned his attention to inflaming the people's feelings of resentment; his aim was to cement with human blood that grand deed, the liberation of Haiti.

His secret orders of 28 February 1805 called for limited arrests and massacres; finally, on April 28, the massacre of the Whites—with the exception of the priests, medical officers, and some skilled workmen—was ordered in a public proclamation. This most frightful of precautionary measures was eagerly carried out: it was only a question of who would strike first, the Blacks or the men of colour. Generally, it was the men of colour who proved the most amenable as a group, and the most ruthless, because they had to defuse the jealous suspicions of the Blacks, who required from them the bloody guarantee that comes with having a personal stake in the defence of the rights of all should those rights ever come under threat.

Under the watchful gaze of Dessalines, the Haitian leaders proved inhuman, every last one of them; and if, during the butcheries exacted by this brutal politics, a few wretched Whites were saved from the disaster, they owed it only to the subaltern officers, generous and terrified souls who even today do not dare to admit the protection they covertly afforded at that time.

One still comes across traces of this distressing state of affairs: the bloodthirsty proclamations that paved the way for the general massacre of the Whites are included in the *Republican Almanach* of 1818. Serving in one of the Republic's high posts is a leader who resigned himself, at that deplorable juncture, to proving that he was coloured by stabbing to death, with a steady hand, several Whites who were brought before him. He struck in cold blood and was proclaimed Haitian. During the former regime, he had crossed swords with a man who accused him of being a sang-mêlé. It was memories of that duel which forced this horrible test upon him. The incident must cause him great grief because he is an educated man, and it is only barbarians who do not feel remorse. Through a clash between the prejudices of the time, the part of his being that had once been the source of his pride has become the object of his hatred and contempt, and that part through which he was affiliated to slaves today forms the source of his vanity and his power.

3. From Henri Grégoire, *De la littérature des nègres, ou Recherches sur leurs facultés intellectuelles, leurs qualités morales et leur littérature* (1808)

[The Abbé Grégoire (1750-1831) was to abolitionism in France what Clarkson and Wilberforce were to it in England. Grégoire spent a lifetime arguing for coloured and black rights: as he put it in *De la littérature des nègres*, "Negroes, being of the same nature as whites, have the same rights to exercise as do they, and the same duties to fulfil" (34). He was, not surprisingly, reviled by the proponents of slavery. The young Hugo, likewise, had a great deal of contempt for Grégoire, who embodied for him everything that he hated about the French Revolution. As Roger Toumson has usefully pointed out (19-20), Hugo had already taken direct aim at Grégoire in his 1819 poem "Le Télégraphe," where he makes reference to the Abbé's prominent role in the abolition of the monarchy and the execution of Louis XVI: "Quand Grégoire au Sénat vient remplir un banc vide, / Je le hais libéral, je le plains régicide, / Et s'il pleurait son crime, au lieu de s'estimer, / S'il s'exécrait lui-même, oui, je pourrais l'aimer." ["When Grégoire takes up an empty seat in the Senate / I hate him for being a liberal, I pity him for being a regicide; / And if he wept for his crime, instead of holding himself in such esteem, / If he loathed himself, yes, then I could hold him dear."]

Hugo takes a number of minor details from Grégoire's book (see *Bug-Jargal* endnotes 40, 43, 53, 56, 73, 97), turning them more or less on their head, transforming the latter's negrophilic argument into something resembling, albeit not identical to, the negrophobic rhetoric of Grégoire's detractors—as a comparison between the following selection on the musical "achievements of Negroes" and its parodic appropriation at the beginning of Chapter 26 should make clear.

This book was translated in 1810 as *An Enquiry concerning the Intellectual and Moral Faculties, and Literature of Negroes*, and again in 1996 as *On the Cultural Achievements of Negroes*.]

On music

[John Gabriel] Stedman, who thinks the Negroes capable of great improvement, and who in particular grants them poetical and musical genius, numbers their string and wind instruments at eighteen; and, even then, this list of his makes no mention of their famous *balafou*,* formed of twenty pipes of hard wood, of diminishing size, which resonate like a small organ.

[James] Grainger [in *The Sugar-Cane* (1764)] describes a kind of guitar invented by the Negroes, on which they play tunes that exude a sweet and sentimental melancholy; it is the music of afflicted hearts. The passion of Negroes for singing does not prove that they are happy, as has been pointed out by Benjamin Rush, who identifies the illnesses resulting from their distressed and wretched state.

Doctor Gall assured me that Negroes lack the two organs of music and mathematics. When, addressing the first point, I objected to him that one of the most distinguishing characteristics of the Negroes is their unconquerable taste for music, he acknowledged the fact but countered by citing their inability to perfect this fine art. But is not the energy of this inclination an incontestable sign of talent? It is through the acquisition of experience that men succeed in undertakings to which they are drawn by a decided propensity and a strong determination. Who can predict how far the Negroes will excel in this field when the knowledge of Europe comes within their reach? Perhaps they will have their Glucks and Piccinis. Even now, Gossec has not disdained to import the "*Camp de Grand-Pré*," a tune of the Negroes of Saint Domingue, into one of his occasional pieces.

France had formerly its *Trouvères* and Troubadours, as Germany its *Minne-singers* and Scotland its *Minstrels*. The Negroes have theirs, named *Griots*, who also attend kings and do what is done in all courts: praise and lie with wit. Their women, the *Griotes*, perform almost the same trade as the *Almahs* in Egypt, the *Bayadères* in India. This constitutes yet another trait of resemblance with the travelling women of the Troubadours. But these *Trouvères*, these *Minne-singers*, these *Minstrels*, were the forerunners of Malherbe, Corneille, Racine, Shakespeare, Pope, Gesner, Klopstock, &c. In all countries, genius is the spark concealed in the heart of a stone; once it has been struck by steel, the sparks come flying.

---

* Others say *balafat* or *balafo*, and compare it to the spinet.

Appendix F: Literary Sources

[The question of which literary texts might have influenced Hugo when he wrote *Bug-Jargal* opens up a large, indeed unwieldy, field of enquiry. To cite only four of the most obvious points of reference: first, Hugo's historical novel (as we saw in Appendix C.1) would have been unthinkable without the precedent supplied by Walter Scott, and a number of incidental details in the text can be traced to specific novels by Scott such as *Ivanhoe* (1820; for Scott's influence on *Bug-Jargal*, see Ntsobé 24-38); second, the exotic dimension of *Bug-Jargal* owes a tremendous debt to Bernardin de Saint Pierre's *Paul et Virginie* (1788) and the New World narratives of Chateaubriand, such as *Atala* (1801); third, in his portrayal of the noble black man, Bug-Jargal, Hugo draws on a long tradition of negrophilic literature, from Aphra Behn's *Oroonoko* (1688; translated into French 1745) to Joseph Lavallée's *Le Nègre comme il y a peu de blancs* (1789), although it is difficult to move beyond arguments about family resemblances between *Bug-Jargal* and any of these texts to evidence of specific instances of influence and appropriation; and, finally, as with his earlier *Han of Iceland*, the Gothic and frenetic novels in vogue at the time certainly had an impact on the more melodramatic elements of Hugo's plot. This already broad-ranging list of literary influences could be greatly expanded, and one might even wish to make a place here for texts that Hugo could not possibly have read but that are of unquestionable relevance to his novel, such as that other great Romantic encounter with the Haitian Revolution, Heinrich von Kleist's "The Betrothal in St. Domingo" (1811; see Bongie, *Islands and Exiles* 226-31).

Given the wealth of possible materials to choose from, but also the hard-to-pin-down or simply incidental nature of the influence exercised by the above-mentioned sources, I have decided to limit myself here to the one novelistic source that critics all agree played a vital formative role in the genesis of *Bug-Jargal*: the writings of Jean-Baptiste Picquenard. A little-known disciple of Bernardin de Saint-Pierre, Picquenard wrote two novels about Saint Domingue (where he had lived for several years) at the very end of the eighteenth century: *Adonis* (1798) and *Zoflora* (1800), the first of which almost certainly introduced Hugo to the historical figure of Biassou, who plays a central role in it. (It should be noted that at least one source critic has argued—unconvincingly, to my mind—that Hugo did not read *Adonis* itself but, rather, a 1798 melodrama of the same name by Beraud de la Rochelle and Joseph Rosny, which was loosely based on the novel [Etienne 74-78].) While by no means literary masterpieces, Picquenard's historical novels fascinatingly negotiate the transition between negrophilic eighteenth-century representations of the noble savage and of a still unsullied exotic nature, on the one hand, and the denunciatory, racist representations of blackness that would become so prominent after the Haitian Revolution. As Régis Antoine notes, *Adonis* was written at a time that saw "an undeniable erosion of the negrophilic sensibility," which was greatly exacerbated by events in the colonies (174), and Picquenard's portrait of the "loathsome" Biassou amply testifies to this erosion, even as it valiantly attempts to retain an Enlightenment belief in certain "universal" values—notably, "the precious seed of sensibility that nature has placed in all hearts," a common humanity shared by whites and blacks alike. Hugo's representation of Biassou deviates even further, if not completely, from those eighteenth-century values, and juxtaposing the two writers' portrayals of Biassou (F.1) or of cruel white slaveowners (F.2) should give readers a good sense of just how far Hugo has departed from the negrophilic tradition to which his novel nonetheless remains so obviously indebted (see Mouralis 49-53).]

1. From Jean-Baptiste Picquenard, *Adonis, ou Le bon nègre. Anecdote coloniale* (1798)

[The title of Picquenard's novel, as Régis Antoine has noted, "mixes together the theme of black beauty [*Adonis*] with that of the generous negro [*le bon nègre*]" (172), a clear sign of its continued affiliation with the ahistorical eighteenth-century negrophilic tradition; but the novel, he adds, also features "an increased role for historical truth which the title gives one no reason to suspect" (173), although it must be said that its subtitle, "Colonial Anecdote," certainly points in that new historical direction. *Adonis* tells the story of the owner of a small coffee plantation near Cap Français, D'Hérouville; freshly arrived from France with his wife, D'Hérouville is a good master who lives amongst his forty slaves "like a father in the bosom of his family" (23) and who develops a special friendship with his twenty-eight-year-old *commandeur*, the noble Adonis. When the slave revolt breaks out (Picquenard erroneously gives the date of this as January 1791—one of many such errors and anachronisms in his novels), D'Hérouville is taken prisoner by Biassou and, having gained the ruthless chief's confidence, reluctantly serves as one of his advisors. D'Hérouville spends much of the novel trying to escape Biassou's camp, and eventually succeeds: he and his wife, along with Adonis and Zerbine (a former member of Biassou's seraglio who has fallen in love with the noble negro), find their way to the coast and eventually to Virginia, where the white and black families live together happily ever after, far from war-ravaged Saint Domingue.

The two excerpts from *Adonis* I have selected both deal with Biassou. The first is a brief passage from early on in the novel in which he is introduced to the reader and the second is a lengthier account of his cruelties—a violent account that is nonetheless supplemented by the optimistic Enlightenment message, absent from Hugo's portrait of Biassou (see Bongie, *Islands and Exiles* 245), that "even in the heart of the most brutal of men nature preserves a place that is accessible to pity, tears, and decency."]

a.

It was the month of January 1791 when, in the north of the island, that terrible insurrection broke out which has had such disastrous consequences, costing the lives of more than two hundred thousand people of all colours.

And yet it was in the midst of so many horrors, crimes, and murders that I was privy to an anecdote, the touching details of which are all the more worthy of being passed on to posterity because they prove, in a truly consoling manner, that even in the heart of the most brutal of men nature preserves a place that is accessible to pity, tears, and decency.

All the white landowners were fleeing their peaceful plantations and seeking shelter in the towns or cities near them. While making their escape, a number of them fell into the hands of their cruel enemies and paid with their life for this ghastly misfortune.

Biassou, the most fearsome and the most ferocious of all the Africans, was proclaimed supreme leader of the insurrection by the revolted negroes. He soon found himself at the head of sixty thousand blacks whom he had assembled in the Northern Plain and distributed over a surface of nine leagues square in platoons of about a thousand men.

This ignorant and superstitious negro had succeeded in winning the trust of his brothers-in-arms through a cruelty of character so strongly pronounced that it inspired terror even in the most bloodthirsty among them. Lacking any knowledge of how to run an army, he was incapable of thinking ahead: when obtaining provisions for his still very inexperienced army he simply laid waste to everything; all the exertions of his evil genius resulted in nothing more than putting the torch to every place he passed through.

For an entire month, this plain—once so rich, so flourishing, so lovely on account of its plantations, its sugar mills (those artistic masterpieces), its long avenues, its cane fields, its magazines, and its country houses—was lit up only by the flames that were devouring those magnificent properties, those precious fruits of a slow and painful labour. *Biassou* soon reigned, but over a heap of ashes and the whitened remains of his luckless victims....

b.

Since the departure of Adonis [to retrieve D'Hérouville's wife from the Cape] everything had changed in the camp of Biassou. The army of this improvident chief had been hit by famine. The discontent of his soldiers had made itself felt in several abortive insurrections. His *Ibo* and *Mozambique* negroes had hatched the scheme of naming another chief, and Biassou had only managed to nip this revolt in the bud through an imposing display of the most frightful forms of torture. He had already detached the negresses from the camp, sending them off in little bands to the foot of the mountains, where they were to grow sweet potatoes, yams, and cassava (indigenous roots, standard fare for the inhabitants of the country and all the more effective in providing for the revolters because they produce their fruit in only six weeks). The blacks assigned the task of keeping an eye on them had orders to shoot down any of them who voiced the slightest complaint or got out of line in any way. He lorded over the entire black army with a rod of iron; under various pretexts, he had any number of old men and women put to death along with the disabled and the wounded. Terror ran through every soul; blood streamed from all sides; and the host of victims that he sacrificed each day so as to maintain his hold on power only seemed to make him grow even more ferocious. Thus it was that you saw, and perhaps for the first time ever, slaves regretting the heavy, shameful chains with which the whites had for such a long time oppressed them.

For their part the white settlers, having got over their initial state of fright, had formed themselves into a number of separate military units. The richest ones made up the cavalry and the *petits blancs* the infantry. The fact of being equally under threat had somewhat lessened the arrogance of the former toward their brothers. In the frequent sorties they had made into the plain it had dawned on them that the man with an income of two hundred thousand pounds was, under combat, just a man like any other, and that the enemy's bullets did not spare him any more than they did the poorest of foot-soldiers. Thus, for a time, there prevailed a sort of union and equality between the different classes of whites which often allowed them to triumph over their implacable enemies. It was a war to the death: no prisoners were taken on either side. Woe to anyone who fell into the hands of the enemy! He was certain to perish, and often in the cruellest manner possible.

Here is an account of the various forms of torture that the blacks inflicted on the whites when they had taken a sizable enough number of prisoners to satisfy their vengeance by sacrificing them. This is the most painful task that remains for me to discharge. I could have passed over it in silence but have chosen not to: men must be taught, through the most terrible lessons, what crimes our species is capable of when education has not developed the precious seed of sensibility that nature has placed in all hearts.

On the days reserved for this horrible butchery, Biassou would have his entire army assemble in one spot, which was situated just a short way from headquarters. It was a little savannah, or prairie, bordered on all sides by a sort of natural terrace forming an amphitheatre. All the negroes would get up on this mound of earth, leaving the centre clear with ample room for the executions. Naked, hands tied behind their backs, the hapless whites were brought forward pell-mell, without distinction of age or sex.

The cruellest forms of torture were reserved for the old people; by way of justifying this signal barbarity, the negroes argued that those whites, having been in the colony the longest, had tormented the negroes longer than any one else. Accordingly, these hapless wretches were hooked up by the chin on sharp bits of iron that had been bent back and which jutted out some twenty inches from the eight-foot-high posts into which they had been nailed. There, those miserable souls sometimes had to wait more than twelve hours running for death to come and put an end to their indescribable suffering because the executioners, through a refinement of cruelty, would from time to time unhook their victims and then hook them back up so that the agony which comes with the most painful of deaths would be all the more bitter to them.

The whites who had lived on the island only for ten years or so were placed, two by two, between planks their height which were firmly bound together and then placed on a scaffold, as if they were parts of a building frame; after that they were passed on to the sawyers, who cut them in half.

Those who had been on the island only for two or three years first had their eyes torn out with corkscrews, and after that they were dispatched with a sabre.

As for the poor women, the executioners varied their method of torture depending on the ghastly whims of their great leader. Often they were seen throwing themselves onto expectant mothers, tearing out of their quivering wombs the tender fruit of marital unions; they chopped this up into bits, forcing the wretched victim of their cruelty to eat that revolting flesh which they violently rammed down into the pit of her stomach. The young girls were made to suffer in another, no less cruel manner: for these brigands never abandoned their prey until the very moment when it became clear to them that what they were holding in their arms was now nothing more than an insensate corpse.

As for the children, they were plunged into huge sugar boilers filled with scalding hot water, or laid upon gridirons specially placed over a burning fire.

It is time to let the thick veil of silence fall over this appalling tableau. Yes, I will spare the reader a host of details no less horrendous than what has preceded but which would only serve to inspire in him a hatred of men and a deep contempt for humanity. It is not my goal here to devastate his heart by revolting his imagination, and the episode I am about to recount, by offering delectable nourishment for his sensibility, will prove to him that even the most brutal of men, the man most thirsty for the blood of his fellow man, is now and then capable of letting himself be moved simply by the voice of innocence, weakness, and ingenuousness.

On the day in question, Biassou had ordered the noble negro Adonis to follow him around, so that the latter might be witness to his cruelties and provide his masters with an account of the fate that awaited them if they ventured to betray him. He saw two little white boys, about five or six years old; they were completely naked and were being led forward to undergo the torture intended for them. These tender victims were holding their executioner by the hand and he was striding along, forcing them to run across the area separating them from the fateful fire that was going to devour them. They were about to reach the very end of their brief existence when two pickaninnies of the same age were seen coming down from the mound and running, with all their might, headlong into the arms of the little white boys. Both of them exclaimed: "Ah, *Joseph*, you is here! Ah, *Paulin*, you is here!" The little white boys in turn exclaimed, and in the same language: "Ah, *Zephyr*, you is here! Ah, *Zozo*, you is here!" And there and then they fall into their friends' arms, snuggle up to one another, hugging and stroking one another, leaping about and making the air resound with their cries of joy. Biassou was present at this spectacle; indeed, he was watching it with a sort of astonishment mingled with interest when the pickaninny *Zozo* gave the final tug on his heartstrings by breaking away from his little friends and throwing himself at the chief's feet, after which he cried out with all his might in a pleading voice: "Grand papa-we, grand mister negro, grand general, no kill *Zoseph*, no kill *Paulin*. They good whites, they never kill negroes. My mama, she their nurse. Beg you, grand master all d'world, grand friend of d'good Lord, pardon for them, if you please, for love of d'good Virgin." Biassou—who had resisted the tears of so many thousands of families, who had harshly rejected the touching appeals of any number of young women, tender-hearted mothers, and worthy old people—could not resist this maiden cry of nature, of innocence, and of humanity. His heart was moved, perhaps for the first time in his life; he was choked with sobs, and plentiful tears streamed down his face. The more difficult it was for sensibility to make itself felt in his heart, the stronger and more expansive its explosion .... Ah, if at this precious moment an eloquent and courageous philosopher could have shown him how to hear the sublime accents of humanity, the touching voice of nature, then there would have been an end to the scourge afflicting Saint Domingue, and that island would have been born anew for happiness, justice, and peace! But, aside from Adonis, who was kept in check by a deep-seated feeling of terror, Biassou was surrounded only by negroes bent on doing their utmost to surpass him in ferocity. Nevertheless, yielding to the power of the feeling that was touching him to the quick, he went up to these children, took hold of them with his mighty arms and, raising this captivating group to the level of his chest, squeezed them to his heart. Then, after having hugged them, he turned round toward those of his underlings who were nearest him and said to them, as he set the children down in their arms: "They shall be brought into my palace, they shall be cared for, and they shall be respected as if they were my own flesh and blood."

Joseph and *Paulin*, *Zephyr* and *Zozo* had drunk at the same teat. These poor children had all been raised together. The first two belonged to a white carpenter, who had been captured on the mountains near Vallière while trying to escape. Providence so willed it that the two pickaninnies, who had been in Biassou's camp for fifteen days with their mother, recognized their little friends at the very moment they were being led to their deaths.

Oh childhood! Your charms are thus very powerful indeed, since they disarmed and moved even that man—a man possessed of a brutality the likes of which had hitherto never been seen! And, indeed, who could find it in themselves to resist being interested by this touching mixture of weakness, candour, and lack of guile, which render a young person as lovable as he is interesting? Oh Frenchman! If ever there arises in your bosom a new Nero, take as the emblem of his country a tender child and show it to him: no matter how ferocious he might be, he will never have the courage to thrust a knife into it!

Such was the situation of the black army since Adonis's departure. You can imagine, then, to what point terror and servitude had anchored themselves in the souls of the revolters after such terrible and frequently repeated lessons in cruelty! So it was that there never lived a despot better obeyed than the loathsome Biassou, and all that one hears tell about the tyrants of Asia does not even come close to the power this negro had acquired over his unfortunate brothers.

2. From Jean-Baptiste Picquenard, *Zoflora; or, The Generous Negro Girl. A Colonial Story* (1804) [Translation of *Zoflora, ou La bonne négresse. Anecdote coloniale* (1800)]

[Although it is by no means certain that Hugo read the follow-up to *Adonis*, Picquenard's second novel about revolutionary Saint Domingue—translated into English in 1804—is so of a piece with the first as to be worth including here. It tells the tale of a noble-minded young man, Justin, nephew of one of the richest planters on the island, who arrives from France shortly before the outbreak of the slave revolt only to find that his uncle has died without arranging for his inheritance. Justin becomes a pedlar, selling merchandise from plantation to plantation, and on his travels gains the affection both of Amicia, daughter of the libertine slaveowner Valbona, and of Zoflora, the "generous negro girl" who manages to bury her desire for Justin while fending off the increasingly violent advances of Valbona. Valbona is eventually forced to flee to the Spanish side of the island, and when war is declared between Spain and France he turns traitor and joins the Spanish army; this dastardly villain is eventually put to death by Biassou, who plays a much more peripheral role than in *Adonis* and a rather more sympathetic one (he is, surprisingly, represented as "a man of daring and intrepid courage" [2.215]). As in *Adonis*, the novel ends with all the good characters united and re-located in a utopian space: in this case, Justin returns with Amicia and Zoflora to France where they all live happily together, "far from intrigue and noise [and] tasting the delicious sweets of an honorable ease, which they also share with the poor and the unfortunate" (2.233-34). (For a close reading of this novel, see Bongie, "'Of Whatever Color.'")

The following brief excerpts from the 1804 translation make manifest an important opposition between (ahistorical) exotic and (historicized) gothic representations of nature that is of no small importance to Hugo's novel. (Compare, for instance, the double portrait of the natural landscape in Chapter 51, alternating between what we might call a solar exoticism and a lunar gothicism.) The first excerpt, which explicitly invokes the author of *Paul et Virginie*, provides an effusive description of the Spanish part of the island, as yet untouched by the revolutionary turmoil affecting Saint Domingue. The pastoral exoticism of this first passage, its glowing portrayal of a beautiful American nature, is in stark contrast with the sublime landscape of "immense subterranean caverns" described in the second excerpt, which provides such a fitting backdrop for the white slaveowner Valbona's horrendous, almost Sadean, crimes— crimes that in *Bug-Jargal* are more or less entirely off-loaded onto the novel's mulatto protagonists.]

a.

Frolic youth! who wantonest through the mazes of pleasure, impelled by the instinct of nature alone; who feeling with extacy, stoppest not to analyze thy enjoyments! to Santo-Domingo wing thy flight; it is there that thou wilt prolong the sweet, but too short-lived illusions of thy gay and blooming season. In that charming city, beneath its genial climate, love seems to pervade all hearts, to preside in each society within its spacious bounds. In vain would the austere religion of Christ curb the impetuosity of that intoxicating passion; the little pagan deity triumphs, and the priests of Jesus themselves are the first officiators in the temple of voluptuousness. Monks, laity officers, nuns, all seem to hold intelligence[,] all agree in celebrating the festivals of pleasure. In the mansion of the archbishop is her altar placed: from thence each day issues the soft signal of the sacrifices to be offered her. The draperies of religion add a new charm to the enthusiastic fervor, and the happy maniacs of those beauteous regions seem to enjoy by anticipation the delights of that ideal paradise[*] which is so incessantly held out to them.

---

[*] After, having with reluctance, rendered this and some of the foregoing passages, with a few others of the same nature, which appear in different parts of this work, with that precision which truth demands; the translator has only to lament that the ingenious author, who shews himself a strenuous advocate for the purest system of morality, has, in point of religion, unfortunately imbibed those principles but too prevalent in the present day. [Translator's note.]

Let not the reader, however, who may be possessed of too ardent an imagination, be led astray as to the true picture of the manners of the country; or endeavour to develope through the play of its lights and shades, scenes which I have never had an idea of painting. In spite of the apparent licentiousness, which reigns in the societies of these happy colonists, I am thoroughly convinced of their wisdom and their virtues. But as the terrors of the inquisition have never frowned over them, the inhabitants are neither impostors nor hypocrites; and I may venture to assert, that the Spanish women of Santo-Domingo, whilst with graceful ease, and impelled by love, they commit a thousand little levities, have in reality a purity of mind and conduct, of which perhaps in any other part of the world the example is much more rare.

Happy genius, who hast immortalized Paul and Virginia! genuine painter of nature, Bernardin de Saint Pierre! Oh my master! why hast thou not with me trod the enchanting shores of the Spanish part of Saint Domingo, in the environs of its capital! With what charms of language hadst thou described the glittering bosom of that immense bay, indenting the surrounding banks, and opening its capacious basin to receive the chased waves of ocean, as if to restore their calm and limpid beauty. With what light and graceful touches wouldst thou have painted the smiling verdure of the gently rising hills by which it is encompassed! what stronger and more decided tints given to those venerable and majestic woods, whose never-fading foliage dispenses a refreshing coolness to passing lovers who wander beneath their shades. How again contrasted with both, those odoriferous groves of native American trees, whose thickly enwoven branches conceal from the eye of the delighted stranger who lands upon the coast, that humble chapel situated in the recesses of the enclosure! yet wouldst thou have thrown a mild and pleasing light upon that distant but interesting object, just enough to discover kneeling at the foot of its altar, yon devout and enamored pilgrim, holding in his hand a rosary, and invoking all the saints to soften the heart of his obdurate mistress. Then, how wouldst thou have enlivened thy enchanting and variegated picture, with the movements of those light gondolas passing successively over the liquid expanse elegantly decorated, their oars keeping time to the hoarse song of the Spanish rowers, and wafting to that flower enamelled green, monks, lovers, military heroes, musicians, and ladies; who all meet to enjoy a delicate collation on that point of the island, where Americus Vespacius made his descent. Thou wouldst also place to advantage, that solitary colonist whom I behold beneath, seated upon the level part of a rock, which projects over the sea; holding the rod to which his line is suspended between his crossed knees, a guitar in his hand, and absorbed in forgetfulness whilst he sings the tedious sufferings of his love, nor even perceiving the young and imprudent *dorado** who struggles with the guileful hook which had been hid beneath the specious bait. Further on, quite down upon the sand beach, thou wouldst also groupe that interesting family of young and naked negroes, exerting themselves to launch upon the tranquil bosom of the deep a light canoe, which their little hands had hollowed, and recalling by their innocent pastimes, the astonishing attempts of the first navigators!

Lastly, thou wouldst have made thy readers inhale the air of that burning atmosphere, impregnated with oxigen, which by infusing vigor into the impoverished blood, astonished old age, realizes to it the ingenious allegory of the fountain of youth.

But I must leave to the great masters, those bold and vigorous strokes with which they enrich their chef-d'oeuvres of genius, and content myself with putting the finishing hand to the humble sketch of the adventures of my heroine, the amiable Zoflora....

b.

The ferocious Boukmant, from the heights of his concealment, had heard the sound of cannon, and the noise of battle. His emissaries had informed him, that war had been declared between France and Spain, that the armies of the two contending nations had come to an engagement, and that from all appearances, the French had been successful. True to his horrid system of rapine, revenge, and murder, he had put himself at the head of his troop, and ran in pursuit of the vanquished, in the hope of finding them an easy prey, and of enriching himself by pillaging them. He knew also, that if he had the misfortune to fall into the hands of the French, he could make a merit with them of having come to the assistance of their army; and he was not without hopes of obtaining a free pardon from their generosity; as had been the case in many instances during former wars.

Upon the approach of the Spanish army, all the negroes of Corail had taken refuge in the woods, and Valbona on his arrival had found his plantation quite deserted. After having welcomed the Spanish generals to his house, he complained to them in the bitterest terms of his misfortune, in having become the victim of a ferocious negro, named Boukmant, who

---

* Dorado, a fish which by mariners is said to be the female dolphin.

had despoiled his house of every thing valuable, pillaged his plantation; assassinated his slaves, his steward, and even a number of white women, who he said, were living there in peace, at the time of his incursion. As Valbona was about to introduce the Spanish officers into the principal theatre of his crimes, he felt the necessity of charging Boukmant as the author of all the horror with which they must be inspired by the odious spectacle which must be presented to their view.

It is at length time that the reader should be informed of the origin and purposes of those immense subterranean caverns, the principal entrances to which were known only to Valbona, and some of his cruel and profligate companions.

When the Spaniards discovered Saint Domingo, they found that island inhabited by a people ignorant, it is true, but mild, hospitable, and governed by chiefs, to whom certain authors have given the title of caciques. This people from their color, customs, manners and religion appeared to be an emigration of Peruvians, to whom navigation was already known; and every circumstance gave room to imagine that in ancient times this colony had been formed of emigrants from Peru, by degrees as the inhabitants of that country advanced from island to island. Those principal chiefs had caused vast subterranean vaults to be formed, in which they were deposited after their deaths, upon a kind of bed, lined with pales of rough gold.*

Valbona having given orders that a kiln should be constructed for the burning of lime; his workmen in digging, accidentally discovered one of those caverns upon his plantation at Corail; he descended into it along with them, and by the assistance of torches, explored all the windings of this antique and curious monument. He succeeded in discovering all the principal passages which led to it, one of which terminated near the great house, but as it had been filled up by time, he had caused a covered way to be formed, which communicated directly with it, but of which he alone possessed the secret and the keys. This was the place which this abandoned and cruel man chose to hide from the eye of human justice, those unheard of crimes, with which he was each day defiled. It was thither that he dragged the unfortunate victims of his luxury and his barbarity.

Although he committed daily acts of outrage, by carrying off, and secreting the daughters of his most intimate friends, relations, or nearest neighbours, yet I dare scarcely believe that he would have carried his wickedness so far as thus to make away with them, but from the fear that there should be so many living witnesses of his atrocities, who by divulging

---

* There are many mines of gold and silver in Saint Domingo.

them, might expose him to punishment; but the sang-froid with which he condemned to death those unfortunate victims, proves into what a depth of brutal depravity that man may sink, who has committed a first crime of this nature, without expiring beneath the weight of his remorse.*

In these vast subterranean cavities were many spacious and lofty vaults, divided into seperate apartments by partitions in some parts cut in the rock, in others formed of the earth, composed of a rich red clay. Valbona had each of these recesses furnished in a stile suited to the gloom of the place, yet these notwithstanding were consecrated to purposes of conviviality. One was a banquetting room, another a dormitory, a third served as cellar, a fourth contained instruments of torture, which he called his *mechanics*. A fifth division was formed into an immense hall in the middle of which hung a lustre, which contained an infinite number of lights; round this were closets filled with obscene books, licentious engravings, and indecent groupes in sculpture. In short all there which met the eye, presented the hideous portrait of libertinism, cruelty, depravity and crime.

Ten negroes deaf and dumb from their birth, whom he had purchased for that purpose, were condemned to a living death in this abode of horror, and had charge of keeping all there clean and in order.

Towards the middle of the principal outlet, which communicated with the lime kiln, which he had caused to be sunk Valbona had a ditch dug entirely across it, more than sixty feet in depth, into which he had thrown a large quantity of quick lime: this ditch was covered over by an immense trap door, suspended in the middle to two pivots, which the least weight made incline to one side or other; two square stones marked the entrance to this fatal bridge. Woe to whoever attempted to cross the

---

* The imagination of the reader will find it difficult to conceive, or his mind to give credit to so many enormities; but those who are acquainted with the corruption and barbarity of the creolian character, when given up to its native unrestrained violence, will be astonished at nothing they hear on that subject.

All the inhabitants of the western part of the colony have seen or heard of that female creole of Leogane, so notorious for her crimes, and whose name, from respect to her family, shall be here suppressed. She carried her inhuman cruelty so far as to cause both blacks and whites whom she chose to say had been guilty of offences towards her, to be buried alive in the earth up to the chin, and in that position forced them to swallow boiling syrups, loading them all the time with the bitterest invectives. There were many attempts made to seize and bring her to justice, but with her own hand she blew out the brains of many troopers, who were sent in pursuit of her. Volumes might be filled were an account given of all the chastisements, tortures, and murders, of which this monster was guilty. She was made a horrible example of justice by the negroes during the time of one of their insurrections. She was impaled, and in that state led about for four-and-twenty hours to all the different plantations in the neighbourhood, from whence she had used to select her victims. At length wearied with seeing her survive such a punishment so long, she was flung alive into the flames.

hideous space! they were immediately engulphed, and quickly burned to cinders. It was here that this barbarian caused to be hid from sight the dead bodies of his victims.

Having preceded the advanced guard of the army some hours, he had already reached his plantation at Corail, and was busy in assisting his mutes to prepare for the reception of the Spaniards, by conveying away, hiding, and carefully locking up in his private vaults whatever could exhibit any proofs of his atrocities, when Boukmant at the head of a troop of chosen horsemen, poured down unawares upon the plantation, surrounded the great house belonging to Valbona, made him prisoner with his daughter, and whatever slaves remained there, and fled to the mountain, overjoyed at thus having it in his power to dispose at pleasure of the life of a man who had universally the character of being the most cruel and profligate white of all the colony.

Appendix G: Map of Saint Domingue

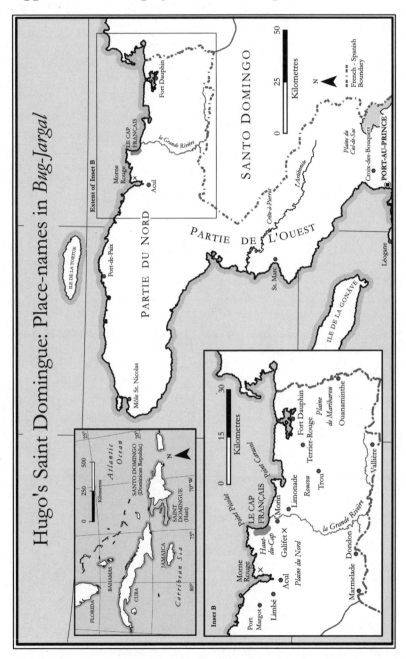

Hugo's Saint Domingue: Place-names in *Bug-Jargal*

Works Cited

Ahmad, Aijaz. *In Theory: Classes, Nations, Literatures*. London: Verso, 1992.

Antoine, Régis. *Les écrivains français et les Antilles: Des premiers Pères blancs aux surréalistes noirs*. Paris: Maisonneuve et Larose, 1978.

Bach, Max. "The Reception of V. Hugo's First Novels." *Symposium* 18.2 (1964): 142–55.

Bongie, Chris. "'Of Whatever Color': (Dis)locating a Place for the Creole in Nineteenth-Century French Literature." *Francophone Postcolonial Studies*. Ed. Charles Forsdick and David Murphy. London: Arnold, 2003. 35–45.

——. *Islands and Exiles: The Creole Identities of Post/Colonial Literature*. Stanford: Stanford UP, 1998.

Carlyle, Thomas. *The French Revolution: A History*. Ed. K.J. Fielding and David Sorensen. Oxford: Oxford UP, 1989.

Carteaux, Félix. *Soirées bermudiennes, ou Entretiens sur les événemens qui ont opéré la ruine de la partie française de l'isle Saint-Domingue*. Bordeaux: Pellier-Lawalle, 1802.

Cauna, Jacques. *Haïti: L'éternelle révolution*. Port-au-Prince: Henri Deschamps, 1997.

——. "Les sources historiques de *Bug-Jargal*: Hugo et la révolution haitienne." *Conjonction* 166 (1985): 21–36.

Clausson, L.J. *Précis historique de la révolution de Saint-Domingue*. Paris: Pillet Ainé, 1819.

Dalmas, [Antoine]. *Histoire de la Révolution de Saint-Domingue depuis le commencement des troubles, jusqu'à la prise de Jérémie et du Môle S. Nicolas par les Anglais*. 2 vols. Paris: Mame Frères, 1814.

Dayan, Joan. *Haiti, History, and the Gods*. Berkeley: U of California P, 1995.

Debien, Gabriel. "Un roman colonial de Victor Hugo: *Bug-Jargal*, ses sources et ses intentions historiques." *Revue d'histoire littéraire de la France* 52.3 (1952): 298–313.

Degout, Bernard. *Le sablier retourné: Victor Hugo (1816-1824) et le débat sur le 'Romantisme.'* Paris: Honoré Champion, 1998.

Edwards, Bryan. *An Historical Survey of the French Colony in the Island of St. Domingo.* London: John Stockdale, 1797.

Etienne, Servais. *Les Sources de 'Bug-Jargal,' avec en appendice quelques sources de 'Han d'Islande.'* Brussels: Académie royale de langue et de littérature françaises, 1923.

Farred, Grant. "First Stop, Port-au-Prince: Mapping Postcolonial Africa through Toussaint L'Ouverture and His Black Jacobins." *The Politics of Culture in the Shadow of Capital.* Ed. Lisa Lowe and David Lloyd. Durham, NC: Duke UP, 1997. 227-47.

Fick, Carolyn E. *The Making of Haiti: The Saint Domingue Revolution from Below.* Knoxville: U of Tennessee P, 1990.

Gaitet, Pascale. "Hybrid Creatures, Hybrid Politics, in Hugo's *Bug-Jargal* and *Le Dernier Jour d'un condamné.*" *Nineteenth-Century French Studies* 25.3-4 (1997): 251-65.

Garran, Jean-Philippe. *Rapport sur les troubles de Saint-Domingue.* 4 vols. Paris: Imprimerie Nationale, 1797-99.

Geggus, David Patrick. "The Bois Caïman Ceremony." *Journal of Caribbean History* 25 (1991): 41-57.

——. *Haitian Revolutionary Studies.* Bloomington: Indiana UP, 2002.

Gewecke, Frauke. "Victor Hugo et la Révolution haïtienne: Jacobins et jacobites, ou Les ambiguïtés du discours négrophobe dans la perspective du roman historique." *Lectures de Victor Hugo.* Ed. Mireille Calle-Gruber and Arnold Rothe. Paris: A.-G. Nizet, 1986. 53-65.

Grégoire, Henri. *De la littérature des nègres.* Paris: Maradan, 1808.

Gros. *Récit historique, sur les événemens qui se sont succédés dans les camps de la Grande-Rivière, du Dondon, de Saint-Suzanne & autres.* Paris: Potier de Lille, 1793.

Grossman, Kathryn M. *The Early Novels of Victor Hugo: Towards a Poetics of Harmony.* Geneva: Droz, 1986.

Henty, G.A. *A Roving Commission: or Through the Black Insurrection of Hayti.* Glasgow: Blackie and Son, 1900.

Hoffmann, Léon-François. "Histoire, mythe et idéologie: le serment du Bois-Caïman." *Haïti: Lettres et l'être*. Toronto: Ed. du GREF, 1992. 267-301.

———. "Victor Hugo, les noirs et l'esclavage." *Francofonia* 31 (1996): 47-90.

Hovasse, Jean-Marc. *Victor Hugo I. Avant l'exil, 1802-1851*. Paris: Fayard, 2001.

Hugo, Victor. *Oeuvres complètes* [cited as *OC*]. 18 vols. Ed. Jean Massin. Paris: Le Club français du livre, 1967-71.

———. *The Slave King, from the Bug-Jargal of Victor Hugo*. [Trans. Leitch Ritchie.] London: Smith, Elder and Co., 1833.

James, C.L.R. *The Black Jacobins: Toussaint L'Ouverture and the San Domingo Revolution*. 1938. Harmondsworth: Penguin Books, 2001.

Juin, Hubert. *Victor Hugo: 1802-1843*. Paris: Flammarion, 1980.

Lacroix, Pamphile de. *Mémoires pour servir à l'histoire de la Révolution de Saint-Domingue*. 2 vols. Paris: Pillet Ainé, 1819.

Laforgue, Pierre. "*Bug-Jargal*, ou de la difficulté d'écrire en *style blanc*." *Romantisme* 69 (1990): 29-42.

Madiou, Thomas. *Histoire d'Haïti. Tome I (de 1492 à 1799)*. 1847. Port-au-Prince: Ed. Henri Deschamps, 1989.

Malenfant, Colonel. *Des colonies et particulièrement de celle de Saint-Domingue*. Paris: Audibert, 1814.

[Malo, Charles]. *Histoire de l'île de Saint-Domingue, depuis l'époque de sa découverte par Christophe Colomb jusqu'à l'année 1818*. Paris: Impr. P.-F. Dupont, 1819.

Meschonnic, Henri. "Vers le roman poème: Les romans de Hugo avant *Les Misérables*." Victor Hugo, *OC*, vol. 7. Paris: Le Club français du livre, 1968. [i-xx].

Moreau de Saint-Méry, Médéric-Louis-Elie. *Description topographique, physique, civile, politique et historique de la partie française de l'isle Saint-Domingue*. 1797. 3 vols. Ed. Blanche Maurel and Etienne Taillemite. Paris: Société de l'histoire des colonies françaises, 1958.

Mouralis, Bernard. "Histoire et culture dans *Bug-Jargal*." *Revue des Sciences Humaines* 149 (1973): 47-68.

Nicholls, David. *From Dessalines to Duvalier: Race, Colour and National Independence in Haiti.* 3rd ed. London: Macmillan, 1996.

Ntsobé, André Marie. *'Bug-Jargal' de Victor Hugo: Etude historique et critique.* Paris: Ed. ABC, 1993.

Picquenard, Jean-Baptiste. *Adonis, ou Le bon nègre. Anecdote coloniale.* Paris: Impr. de Didot Jeune, 1798.

———. *Zoflora; or, The Generous Negro Girl. A Colonial Story.* 1800. 2 vols. London: Lackington, Allen, and Co., 1804.

Piroué, Georges. "Les deux Bug-Jargal." Victor Hugo, *OC,* vol 1. Paris: Le Club français du livre, 1967. [i-viii].

Pluchon, Pierre, ed. *La Révolution de Haïti.* Paris: Karthala, 1995.

Porter, Laurence M. *Victor Hugo.* New York: Twayne Publishers, 1999.

Renda, Mary A. *Taking Haiti: Military Occupation and the Culture of US Imperialism.* Chapel Hill: U of North Carolina P, 2001.

Robb, Graham. *Victor Hugo.* London: Picador, 1997.

Rodriguez, Ileana. "El impacto de la Revolucíon Haitiana en la literatura europea: El caso de *Bug-Jargal.*" *Sin Nombre* 10.2 (1979): 62-83.

Roman, Myriam. *Victor Hugo et le roman philosophique: Du 'drame dans les faits' au 'drame dans les idées.'* Paris: Honoré Champion, 1999.

Scott, Walter. *Quentin Durward.* London: J.M. Dent & Sons, 1960.

Seebacher, Jacques. *Victor Hugo, ou Le calcul des profondeurs.* Paris: Presses Universitaires de France, 1993.

Tarbé, Charles. *Rapport sur les troubles de Saint-Domingue, fait à l'Assemblée Nationale. Troisième partie.* Paris: Imprimerie nationale, 1792 (29 February).

Toumson, Roger. "Présentation." *Bug-Jargal, ou La révolution haïtienne vue par Victor Hugo.* Fort-de-France: Ed. Désormeaux, 1979. 7-85.

Vastey, Pompée Valentin de. *An Essay on the Causes of the Revolution and Civil Wars of Hayti.* 1819. Exeter: n.p., 1823.

Virgil. *The Aeneid.* Trans. Robert Fitzgerald. New York: Random House, 1983.